AMERICAN ODYSSEY

MICHAEL DE STEFANO

Night to Dawn Magazine & Books LLC
P. O. Box 643
Abington, PA 19001

www.bloodredshadow.com

Copyright © 2025 by Michael De Stefano
Paperback ISBN: 978-1-937769-89-5
Ebook ISBN: 978-1-937769-88-8

Cover Artist: Aniszewski/Dreamstime.com

Editor: Barbara Custer
Published in the United States of America

All rights reserved. No portion of this book may be reproduced or transmitted in any form or by any electronic or mechanical means, including photocopying, recording or by any information retrieval and storage system without permission of the publisher.

Ebooks are not transferrable, either in whole or in part. As the purchaser or otherwise lawful recipient of this ebook, you have the right to enjoy the novel on your own computer or other device. Further distribution, copying, sharing, gifting or uploading is illegal and violates United States Copyright laws.

Pirating of ebooks is illegal. Criminal Copyright Infringement, including infringement without monetary gain, may be investigated by the Federal Bureau of Investigation and is punishable by up to five years in federal prison and a fine of up to $250,000.

Names, characters and incidents depicted in this book are products of the author's imagination, or are used in a fictitious situation. Any resemblances to actual events, locations, organizations, incidents or persons – living or dead – are coincidental and beyond the intent of the author.

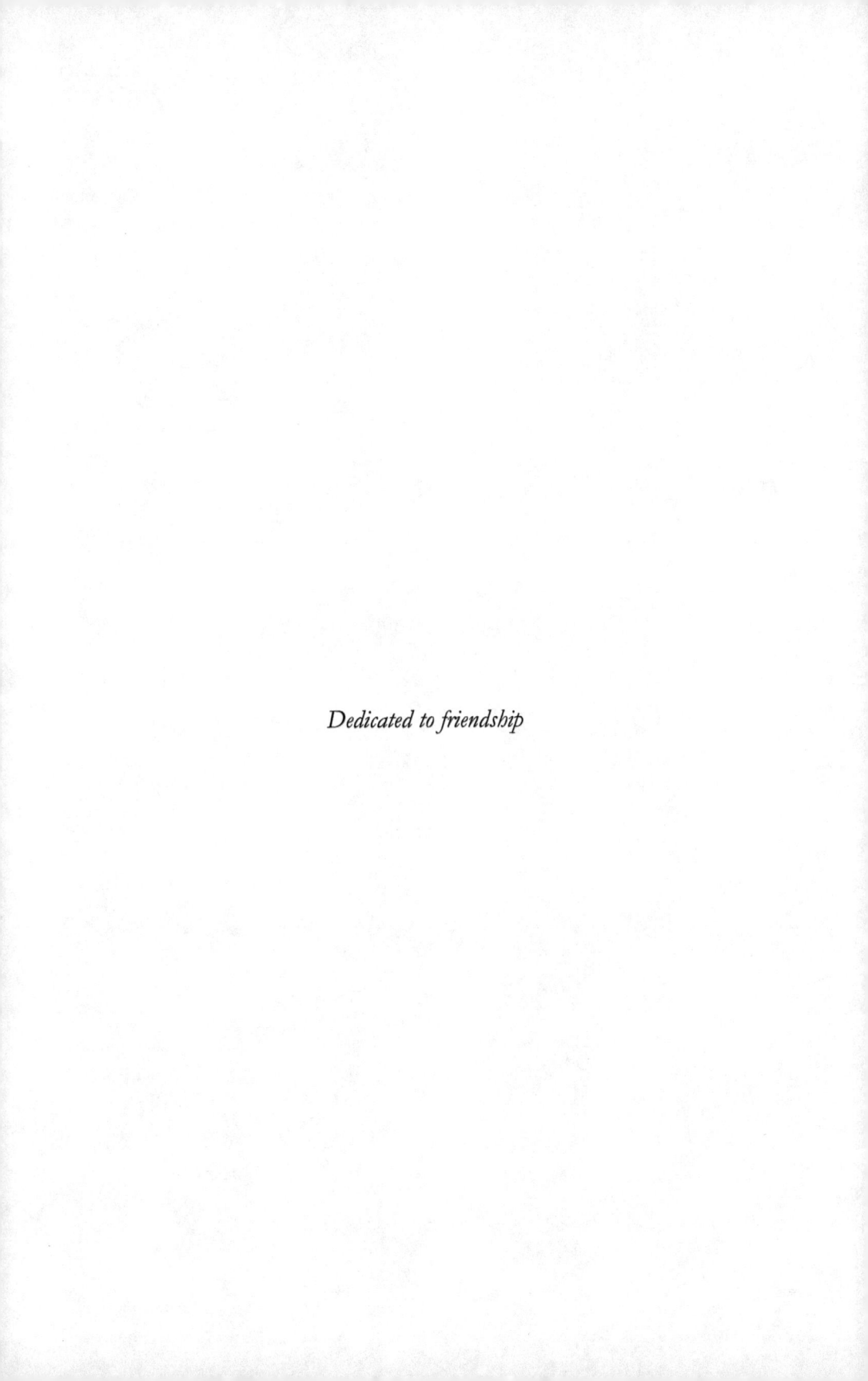

Dedicated to friendship

TABLE OF CONTENTS

CHAPTER ONE
THE FIRE

My name is Addison Caldwell, and I am an insufferable smartass. My best friend is Cillian James, known in most teen circles as CJ; they say we are two peas in a pod, though I prefer the expression *kindred spirits*. My other best friend is Joey Brosco. Somehow, Joey managed to get Cillian and me through school without expulsion. Trust me, it was no simple task; Cillian and I were a handful. Though, when those inclined asked Joey, "How'd you pull it off," he would offer a cavalier shrug, implying it was a task one could complete with one hand tied behind their back, and tell them, "It was nothing." Anyway, I would like to tell you a story—assuming you can spare a few hours—of an unlikely journey that began on the streets of Philadelphia and ended several hundred miles away on a farm in Western Pennsylvania. It was the summer of '77 when the unthinkable assailed three city rats. Rest assured, it is not my fondness for teenage hyperbole talking; the unthinkable *did* occur; the summer of '77 ended up a season for the ages. But a story must have a beginning. So, first things first:

I was three-quarters of the way through my thirteenth year, and by most accounts, "a real piece of work" when someone enlightened me that I, with no compunction, was heading straight for the abode of the damned. Yessiree, I was blazing a path to *you know where*. And why was this, might you ask? And who was the "someone?" My next-door neighbor, the inexhaustibly snooty Maryellen McNamara, represented the "someone." As for the why? Maryellen had just turned fourteen and developed yet another among her array of exasperating habits. The most current one? Advocating the theory that her three-month head start in life—despite the inculcation of Catholic School bullshit—endowed her with wisdom far superior to mine, and in weaponizing that wisdom, she informed me with delight bordering on antagonism—the evidence was her snarky puss—that masturbation ranked as a sin. You should have seen that smirk of hers; I'm telling you, you would have required a hand large enough to palm a basketball or beat off a rhinoceros to slap it off. And based on the satisfaction it provided her, you would have thought she had a crystal ball or peephole to spy into my bedroom, and because we were next-door neighbors living in adjoining city rowhomes, the latter seemed possible. My paranoia beset me so palpably I could have choked on it, and not because a staunch Catholic accused me of reckless self-indulgence; it was over the possibility that I was spied on and had a routine to which I was unwitting. Christ, I was traumatized! And the more I allowed Maryellen to engage me on the subject, the more under my skin she burrowed. Finally, our encounter reached an unfortunate pinnacle: I was beginning to accept the theory that her fourteen years to my measly thirteen-and-three-quarters was no narrow passageway but a chasm where amassed was all the world's wisdom, which she devoured like a ravenous wolverine, leaving me the bare bones of useless trivia.

"But wait, you haven't heard the worst part, Addison." Maryellen frothed with the satisfaction one derives when keeping meticulous records tantamount to empirical evidence, yielding supreme confidence. "It's a known fact that when you reach the five-hundredth time, you go blind! And not little by little, but all at once!"

Maryellen snapped her creamy white fingers to indicate how quickly the lights would go out on ol' Addison Caldwell. The snap would not have been so impressive if Maryellen had short, stubby digits. Instead, she was blessed with long, slender, and graceful fingers; the sort a guy, unless he is an idiot, would want to see navigating their way through his chest hair, assuming he had any, on the way down to where he imagines Maryellen touching him when busy contributing to his blindness.

Giddiness over informing a boy coming-of-age that he would go blind from too much onanism must be considered cherry-picking, even for a Catholic Schoolgirl in the 1970s. What made Maryellen truly euphoric was watching me zip through calculations in my head while pretending not to fret over a matter anyone would deem a cause for concern: For example, the consequences hastened by an alleged milestone. My effort was not only a failure but a colossal one! (I'm not typically this gullible.) Unfortunately, what happens to most guys also happens to yours truly when in the presence of a girl with whom my penis would appreciate achieving a certain level of familiarity; my bullshit detector, which in the past has proved reliable, goes haywire. Thus far, according to my rough calculations (my attention span did not permit a deep dive), I was in the clear but would have to taper my current trajectory if I planned to *watch* the Phillies in the playoffs and not have my baseball fandom relegated to my transistor radio.

The year was 1976; the Phillies had Mike Schmidt and Steve Carlton and were a lock to win the National League's Eastern Division. They also had a puncher's chance to make it to the Series, providing The Big Red Machine from Cincinnati conveniently underperformed while en route to a second straight pennant. I shall save you the suspense: The Reds did not underperform; they swept our upstart Phils in three straight. Easy come, easy go. Still, if you lived in Philly in 1976, it would have been an inconvenient time to go blind, and, at that moment, with snarky Maryellen McNamara standing before me wearing a celebratory smirk, I was far more fearful of blindness than I was of the hellfire she had me condemned to for obliterating a doctrinal no-no. After all, hellfire would not likely occur until shortly after my death. But who knows, maybe I'll spend a century or two in purgatory; guys like me tend to present a dilemma. Blindness, on the other hand, should I maintain my present trajectory, would strike sometime in mid-October. It was already the ides of May!

Had Maryellen enlightened me about the unfortunate consequences of masturbation a year ago, it would not have carried a note of relevance. You see, last year, the Philadelphia public school system decided to add sex education to its seventh-grade curriculum. Mr. Hubert, our vice-principal, taught sex-ed to the boys. He was a real piece of work, Mr. Hubert, and a big, fat bastard, too. In other words, he did not appear capable of practicing even the least ambitious aspects of what he was assigned to teach.

Meanwhile, Mrs. Lincoln—she styled her snow white hair in short sculpted curls that she accented with a blue rinse, wore a pearl necklace ala Pat Nixon, a dress that would have well-suited Lady Bird Johnson, and smelled like patchouli oil—was assigned the task of enlightening adolescent girls to the pitfalls of womanhood, most notably the dreaded sperm cell and how failing to adhere to measures of extreme caution, with abstinence heading the list, could flush all their lofty ambitions down the proverbial crapper. It was weeks before the girls would even walk near us boys, much less act friendly, and all because the school entrusted sex education to a penile antagonist. "And this is a *public* school," Cillian James cried despondently. "I don't even want to imagine what they're teaching up the street!" Up the street was where the virtuous Maryellen McNamara, five days a week, transports her unsullied vagina. "It wouldn't surprise me in the least if they warn the girls that sperm is an airborne virus," Cillian added.

Also, there raged a debate over what could more effectively wilt an erection: spotting a topless Mrs. Lincoln or a bottomless Mr. Hubert? We kept no official tally; it marked but one of those juvenile debates that provide idiotic young men the opportunity to summon their comedic genius: *Hey Addison, my prick was so hard, I could have used it to chisel my grave, but then I caught a glimpse of Mrs. Lincoln...* I'm sure you get the picture.

As for Mr. Hubert? A man of his imposing size deserves props for keeping his necktie straight and his shirt tucked in. Big, fat guys often have a helluva time keeping their clothes neat; I'm sure you've noticed. For example, by the third period, Mr. Hoffhauser— a fifth-grade history teacher and big, fat man in his own right— looked like a pile of laundry, like when your mother dumps your clothes on your bed before ordering them folded and promptly put away, or worse, how your unwashed clothes look when spilling over the hamper and stinking-up the room. Mr. Hoffhauser, in my experience, was the rule. Mr. Hubert was the exception, always neat as a pin.

Mr. Hubert was also a conservative who preached to the point ad nauseam the importance of hard work, conscientiousness, and preparation. I was uncertain what these three worthy virtues had to do with sex. Perhaps I was a bit too dismissive concerning preparation. Still, Mr. Hubert advocated for these qualities because he believed a person stood a chance to succeed if armed with them, no matter where they came from or how disadvantaged their origins. Half the black students aligned themselves with Mr. Hubert, the school's first black administrator; the other half dismissed him as "a coon." I went home and asked my dad, "What's a coon?" and he readily chirped, "One of those marmots that play dead, I believe." It ranked as one of those conversations that never had a chance. So I brought the question to my hippie mother, who informed me, "A coon is an Uncle Tom." Now we were getting somewhere; I was somewhat familiar with the abolitionist and author Harriet Beecher Stowe. I returned to school, having aligned myself (only in theory) with the students who had aligned themselves with Mr. Hubert. Meanwhile, hard work, conscientiousness, and preparation were nowhere on the horizon.

As we embarked upon our journey into the world of sex education, we did a fair amount of snickering at the beginning, which Mr. Hubert expected, though he issued the stern warning: "This is a serious class about a serious subject; there'll be no letter grades issued; it's strictly a pass or fail proposition." He leaned on his clenched fists—those meaty balled-up hands of his were flush to his desk—lurched forward and narrowed his eyes before adding, "And trust me; this is not a class you will want to fail."

Mr. Hubert was right; it would require someone of exceptional stupidity to want a failed sex-ed class on his resume. The stigma could prove unbearable, levying the sort of disgrace sure to follow a fellow around, perhaps even travel with him to high school graduation and beyond. And what girl would want to lose her virginity to a guy who failed a subject when the subject was *how* and *why* to use his penis? *Hey, there goes Addison Caldwell, the dumb bastard who flunked sex.* We were warned! Not only did the snickering stop, but we also came to understand just how serious the subject of sex education was, especially when Mr. Hubert enlightened us about a phenomenon known as nocturnal emissions. Holy shit! Everyone's smirky demeanor vanished faster than it would take Maryellen McNamara to snap her lovely fingers; a collective sense of foreboding burgeoned throughout the classroom. Nocturnal emissions? We thought the girls were screwed having to cope with bleeding once a month into sanitary napkins; just what in the hell was a nocturnal emission? Nothing before in our young lives sounded so daunting: not chickenpox, the removal of tonsils, not even the forceful extraction of wisdom teeth! The term "nocturnal emission" sounded technical and complicated, like alien abduction or photosynthesis. Suddenly, adding hard work, conscientiousness, and preparation to our lives seemed a friendlier proposition. But then Mr. Hubert explained to us stricken adolescents the whiteish and sticky substance that would come spouting from our penises sometime during the night. He made it seem like this mysterious substance would appear unannounced and unprovoked, less was it a byproduct of inspiration. In other words, he had us convinced its randomness was equal to getting shit on by a bird.

Nevertheless, I turned to Cillian James and said, "We sure dodged a bullet there." Cillian and I figured we would take whiteish, sticky ooze over a bloody crotch any day. Semen versus blood, are you kidding me? It pays to be born male! Okay, maybe men suffer more from alcoholism and drug addiction and have higher suicide and incarceration rates; the ratio of the latter is ten to one; it's not all peaches and cream, you understand. But, putting the extremes aside—when comparing shaving and nocturnal emissions to bleeding once a month from an organ, only to reach adulthood vulnerable to uterine, ovarian, and breast cancer, and other potential stressors aided by trait neuroticism and hyperactive amygdalae—if not for experiencing the utter dominion the vagina has over the male species, who in their right mind would want to be a woman?

****

The next day, every boy came to school droopy-eyed from a condition commonly known as sleep deprivation. The reason? All night we laid awake, confident our juvenile penises would send forth a mysterious and undesirable substance. I am confident there is nothing more mindless than waiting for your eyes to adjust to the dark so that you can spend the night gazing at your prick, all because you managed to convince yourself it owns the capacity to function independently. But I was young. Concerning stupidity, there would be numerous opportunities to ascend to greater heights.

Poor Joey Brosco, the little bastard—Joey was the smallest kid in our grade—he looked like he spent the night locked in a junkyard with a starving Rottweiler or some other food-deprived canine suited to tear an intruder to pieces. He was a wreck! Joey was one of those needless worriers; in that respect, he was more annoying than fourteen grandmothers, and all this business of nocturnal emissions caused him to suffer a bout of delirium. Anyway, before long, some of us, Cillian and me in particular, figured out it would require more than imagining Theresa Delvecchio's breasts to bring forth the whiteish, sticky ooze we were warned would appear sometime after our heads hit the pillow and before the ringing of our alarm clocks—that Mr. Hubert's fabled substance would require additional encouragement in the form of manual labor. Nature has a way; its coalescence with our progressions is seamless and flawless. And we were proud of our discovery, Cillian and I; it was like we started a movement! Okay, maybe it failed to reach the heights to which the hula-hoop had ascended, this masturbation craze we instigated, but it was a movement nonetheless.

It was only a week since my initial enlightenment, and I was already burning a path qualifying me as a chronic self-indulger trending toward psychosis; otherwise, behavior that led Maryellen McNamara to warn me of blindness and hellfire. I could well imagine several decades from now Maryellen, all in white, sitting on a white, puffy cloud in Heaven—her flowing red hair contrasting magnificently amid all the whiteness—surrounded by wreathed angels tooting horns and plucking harps to the music of her favorite group, the Bee Gees, while I'm down in hell choking, spitting, wheezing, coughing, vomiting, suffocating, while having a helluva time dodging rape, torture, fire, brimstone, poisonous snakes, and other hellish creatures deprived of food—the latter grouping would not persist as a source of menace because I was evil, or a malefactor, but undisciplined and went blind!

And speaking of hell and its cozy aspects, I began, while still in the presence of Maryellen's affecting smirk, to wonder whether the fires of hell resembled anything like Mr. Stroud's patio furniture the night it went up in flames.

Mr. Stroud could be a real sonofabitch, the sort who relished the role of a curmudgeon. As for his face? It had arranged itself into a scowl many assumed was permanent, and this enduring feature bore a resemblance to a surly old Bulldog owning the disposition of someone who had gone days deprived of a meaningful bowel movement. To suggest the oldster never was seen with his mouth creased into a smile was no inflation of the truth; not even the Broad Street Bullies winning a second straight Stanley Cup gave him a spark. "Hockey," he grumbled. "It's Un-American."

Meanwhile, Mrs. Stroud flitted about like a goddamn sparrow. Her disposition seemed anomalous for someone handcuffed to a gruff old Bulldog. Although you know what they say about opposites? And you would think the Stroud's daughter, Emily, bringing their two-year-old granddaughter, Patrice, over for Saturday afternoon visits would shine light into the life of one who flourished in the role of a storm cloud hovering over a parade. Not a chance! Mr. Stroud would stand in his backyard, arms folded, posed like a vigilant crocodile, and watch his granddaughter pedal her Big Wheel tricycle, his demeanor never approaching joy. Sometimes, I would cough up a few minutes of my Saturday to observe Mr. Stroud partaking in what, for him, passed for interacting with a granddaughter; it was especially amusing on the Saturdays of summertime when overseeing his tomato garden ranked as the prevailing initiative. This heightened level of supervision turned a man who would otherwise fall asleep holding the newspaper into a hawk-eyed gorgon. And poor Patrice, all she seemed interested in was getting her two-year-old hands wrapped around a plump, shiny beefsteak. So Mr. Stroud spent his summer Saturdays ambling about like a Border Collie, contorting himself in every which way to steer Patrice away from those meticulously staked red orbs. I am confident that grandfather and granddaughter triggered nightmares for one another.

In his gruff way—for he was miserable, not evil—Mr. Stroud adored Patrice. Still, the raising of homegrown tomatoes in a city garden marked the true joy of his life; if anyone dared to get too close to the fruits of his labor, his reaction would lead one to suspect they had committed an act parallel to breaching national security. And forget us boys having the audacity to assemble in the driveway for a game of stickball: Mr. Stroud would work himself into convulsions over the potential harm that might befall his red orbs, he would bang on his kitchen window to shoo us away, and when we met his banging with a disinclination to skedaddle, he would shake his fist, and when doing so his face would twist into that fierce Bulldog look for which he had become so infamous. Before long, he would dash to the phone and ring the police. Never too soon for Mr. Stroud, they would appear—and it was always the same two: Officers Genco and Morrison—and they would shake their heads apologetically for having to chase us from the driveway. "Sorry, fellas, we're just doing our job. We don't like it any better than you do." And they *did not* like it; men and women aspire to law enforcement to apprehend criminals, not chase juveniles from city driveways. Then Richie Costigan would always ask Genco and Morrison if they knew his father, "*Detective* Costigan," thinking it might sway the officers to ignore Mr. Stroud and allow us to continue our game. It never worked; Genco and Morrison always responded to Richie Costigan with the line: "Yeah, yeah, kid, we know who your old man is, but we still have a job to do."

On Friday night, we went creeping into Richie Costigan's garage. His old man, "the detective," had mounted shelving wrapping around the garage walls, and atop all that shelving sat no fewer than fifty gas cans! "What gives?" I asked. Richie told me, "Remember the gas crisis a little while back? That goddamn *A*-rab embargo?"

"Sure, I remember," I said. "Who doesn't? Everyone's old man was grumbling like a sonofabitch."

"Yeah, but my old man did something about it: he went around the neighborhood siphoning gasoline from all these poor suckers." Richie beamed with pride, though I cannot imagine why anybody would, over what even a morally bankrupt person would view as a shameful deed. But that was Richie, always bragging about his old man, "the detective," the sonofabitch could do no wrong. To hear Richie drone on about his old man, you would think he was a combination of Mean Joe Green and Captain America, if not eleven of the dirty dozen. "And whenever some shmuck dared to say anything to my old man about siphoning gasoline, he would threaten to have 'em locked up for looking cross-eyed or spitting on the sidewalk. And he could do it, too, because he's a detective."

See what I mean? When it came to his old man, it was blind admiration for Richie Costigan.

We grabbed one of the fifty gas cans from the Costigan's garage and headed straightaway to Mr. Stroud's backyard. His patio furniture was solid redwood, and we could tell he had just refinished it; the smell of an oil-based stain was still redolent. We doused the picnic table, benches, a chair, and a chaise lounge and then struck as many stick matches as it took to torch the entire ensemble; then we tore down the driveway and hid behind a Privet hedge dense enough to keep us obscured. Initially, we had it in our minds to torch the tomato garden. But Mr. Stroud could have replaced it with a few dollars' worth of plants, if not a fifty-cent pack of seeds, whereas the patio furniture would really sting. Never mind that burning wood would make a more impressive show than burning plants. And we were right; you should have seen those flames! They rose so high they licked the clothesline. But not for long: the rope incinerated; it took seconds. It was not until flames consumed the entire set that Mr. Stroud came bursting through the back door and did so like he was the one on fire. I couldn't help but admire his agility; for an older man, he could really skedaddle! Then, with fury, he un-cranked his hose from a wall mount but not before letting fly the coarsest language ever heard and in the loudest shouts ever to echo through our neighborhood. Unfortunately, he was too late to rescue his furniture; the set may not have burned to the point of cinders to the ground, but it appeared charred beyond use from our vantage point.

Richie and I laughed so heartily we nearly vomited; like two hyenas giddy over leftovers, we laughed. And despite being past dark, we could see the smoke vividly as it filled the driveway—it hovered thickly at everyone's second-story windows, and the smell of burnt wood overcame the entire block. Poor Mr. Stroud. One minute, he was well engaged in the mother of all tirades; in the next, he wilted and was silent. Collapsed to a knee, he used a hand to support a head that appeared stricken with grief. With his other, he held a hose that senselessly continued to gush water into the driveway. Mr. Stroud seemed like a man who had suffered the worst defeat and could not imagine what he had done to deserve such a cruel fate.

"We did it, Addie!" Richie crooned victoriously. "We brought the old bulldog to his knees, and it damn well serves him right. *Now* let's see him call the cops."

That night, crouched behind a Privet, spectating destruction, was my first experience arriving at the understanding that sometimes a plan may sound good, but once executed, it can leave a bad taste in your mouth … an awful taste!

"What's the matter, Addie?" Richie pressed once he realized I was no longer laughing. "Stroud got what was coming to him."

"Did he?" I peeked around the Privet at the disconsolate Mr. Stroud and tried to imagine his life. Maybe there was a good reason for his bulldog-like scowl and surly disposition. Maybe Mrs. Stroud cut him off, and he sleeps on the sofa, or worse, the poor bastard lives with intractable pain or learned months ago he was terminally ill and cannot help from feeling pissed off about it. I know *I'd* be pissed.

Next, I lamented another notion. Instead of pitting our collective wills against Mr. Stroud's, we could just as easily have played stickball in another driveway, for instance, the one behind Timmy Pytlewski's house. And playing stickball behind Timmy's house would have yielded a bonus. His mother hangs laundry outside on Saturday afternoons, and of all the adult women in the neighborhood, Cyndy Pytlewski has the perkiest breasts. We had two categories for breasts: those belonging to females old enough to drink legally and those who could not. It was not a matter of opinion but a fact: it was Theresa Delvecchio in a runaway among the junior varsity. As for the varsity, Cyndy Pytlewski—the Polish either have a consonant fetish or a vowel aversion—edged out Theresa Delvecchio's mother, Deloris. Deloris Delvecchio's breasts were more voluptuous than Cyndy Pytlewski's, but Cyndy Pytlewski's breasts were perkier and seemed to scream out to us juveniles, "Come touch us!" Okay, maybe we were delusional, but perhaps no more delusional than Father Murray, who would try his damnedest not to ogle Cyndy Pytlewski's glorious anterior when delivering his Sunday sermon. I'm telling you; it's goddamn comical! I fail to know how he manages not to stutter or lose his place reading the gospel—or, with such a keen eye for lovely-breasted women, to remain celibate. *The Lord is my shepherd; I shall not want.* Bullshit!

"Would you look at that shifty-eyed scoundrel," Cillian whispered to me in the pew one Sunday morning. "It's no secret what '*his holiness*' is doing after Mass. And I bet he's one of those creepy bastards that doesn't lock the bathroom door and dreams of getting caught." Then Cillian gave the old pump of the hand in a manner universally known as a mimic of masturbation, to which I added, "Those cassocks hide all kinds of truths." Next ensued a mild debate over whether or not wielding a boner while reading from the gospel was a sin. The discussion occurred before I pronounced myself a staunch atheist and was still attending Mass an average of once a month. Finally, Cillian and I reached the agreement: if you have a boner, to begin with, and the gospel fails to subdue your boner, it's the gospel's fault, whereas if a boner happens to occur in the course of *reading* the gospel, it is a clear indication you are not giving your full attention to what you're reading, which is hardly a sin but improper when delivering the word of God to others seated in a house of worship.

Returning to Mr. Stroud: It was a battle of wills, and it was not in our stubborn juvenile proclivity to concede. But, as I watched the black and gray swirls of smoke fill the driveway with a despairing and defeated Mr. Stroud on one knee, I wished we had conceded. You see, it is one matter to outwit someone. When matching wits and coming out ahead, one derives a measure of satisfaction: for example, when you win a debate or place someone in checkmate. It is an entirely different matter to "out-sonofabitch" someone. To defeat a sonofabitch by acting an even bigger sonofabitch makes you a worse sonofabitch, and, in the end, leaves you feeling like crap. Trust me, I know. Richie Costigan, unfortunately, did not know. Richie saw only an opportunity to revel in victory, not someone's grandfather brought to a knee. In Richie's skewed world—a world that praised cops siphoning gasoline—being a bigger sonofabitch and, therefore, a worse sonofabitch was cause to celebrate. Richie did not understand guilt, remorse, or just plain old feeling like crap because you committed a crappy act. Richie either had no time for those feelings or had them and saw them as weaknesses to which he would not allow himself to succumb.

"For Chrissake, Addie," he cried, "you look like we're at someone's goddamn funeral or something. The Strouds are loaded; the old prick'll have a new set of furniture by next week, if not sooner."

Talk about missing the point. Looking back on it, it was that very night when crouched behind a Privet beside Richie Costigan, inhaling black smoke and observing two-year-old Patrice's grandfather on one knee, that I became an atheist. Like Maryellen McNamara, Richie Costigan went to Catholic School, an institution I am convinced needs to spend less time enforcing a totalitarian doctrine and more on tolerance and civics. In other words, fewer mumbo-jumbo commandments could be whittled down to the much more succinct *do unto others* maxim. Richie and I took the low road, the one encouraging *an eye for an eye*, but our actions were more akin to a double amputation in exchange for someone bringing us to tears by forcing us to dice an onion. Religion does not necessarily equal morality, especially if its interpreter is a no-good sonofabitch. But maybe I expect too much from Testaments, old or new, that justify violence, and less should I blame their writers for failing to envision the twentieth-century miscreant. Either way, I was too guilt-ridden, thus in no mood to lay a morality lesson on Richie Costigan, and I was reasonably confident he was in no mood to listen to one. I blamed the smoke, which was beginning to dissipate, for why I was rubbing my eyes. I also cited that it was late and that I was tired. The truth was, I could have cried for how distraught Mr. Stroud appeared, enshrouded in smoke, down on one knee, and not even realizing that water continued to spill from his hose. I rose from my crouch and ambled up the driveway. I'm sure Mr. Stroud never saw me open his gate and turn off the spigot. Not until I closed the gate and was about to walk away from Mr. Stroud did he become aware of my presence. "Do you know who did this, Addison?" he asked. His voice was weak and pathetic; the old bulldog had transformed into a Spaniel.

"I think I might know the culprits," I told him. Mr. Stroud let loose an ineffectual chortle. It conveyed *it was no juvenile prank, kiddo, but a bonafide crime the culprits committed*. Since I could not confess, I had to figure out how to atone. But what could I do to raise enough cash to buy Mr. Stroud new furniture? I was hardly an entrepreneur and, by all accounts, lazy. I woke to a terrible racket at 8:00 a.m. the following day (Saturday). I threw open my window; the noise ricocheted all over the driveway, making pinpointing its location difficult. My eyes traveled first to the right, then left, stopping in each yard until they fell upon Mr. Stroud operating a belt sander. The furniture had burned but was salvageable! But why should Mr. Stroud have to shoulder all the labor? I jumped into my clothes and went racing for the door. Along the way, I told my mother not to expect me until dinnertime.

Richie and I remained friends, but we were never tight like before the night of the fire. It is strange how people reveal themselves to you without realizing it, and it can be damn sobering.

Well, Richie was Richie; take it or leave it. He was also a year older than me and was forever beating his chest about the number of girls he managed to talk out of their pants. In those days, every classroom and neighborhood crowd came equipped with a blowhard who, from a mountaintop, could not help illuminating the world concerning their sexual exploits. In our crowd, that blowhard was Richie Costigan. "I could make an anaconda cry for his mama," he would boast, then grab his dungaree-clad crotch using both hands. After all, "It takes two hands to handle a whopper."

And anytime someone dared doubt Richie about the size of his prick or the number of girls with which it had become familiar, upon getting irritated and threatening to wring someone's neck, he would get under their skin by spewing the bullshit, "Not only did I screw your girlfriend, but then afterward she bragged about it." Sometimes he would tell you that he screwed your mother or sister if you had one. But there was one girl we knew Richie Costigan never had nor would: Maryellen McNamara! There was no breaching or scaling her wall of virtue. Trust me, if there was an area in which ol' Addison Caldwell had expertise, it was that one.

CHAPTER TWO
THE SIDEWALK DEBATERS

If I've given anyone the impression I don't care much for Maryellen McNamara, allow me to set the record straight: I like her just fine and then some. I shall get to the latter or "and then some" momentarily. First, let us begin with the "I like her just fine" part. If there is one thing Maryellen is not, heading the list would be *hard to look at*, or as Cillian likes to say, "Easy on the eyes." And if you can get past Maryellen's snootiness—a condition that is not all her doing, for she was programmed and mind-fucked spending too many years among incorrigible theologians; perhaps if lured astray, the process would reverse; I'm a cockeyed optimist—you could do a lot worse when engaging in conversation, especially if you catch her at the right moment. Trust me, Maryellen and I have had some doozies recently, and I shall take the time to relay a few. However, I should warn you she is not bashful, as you may have already guessed. And I shall reiterate, if you catch her at the right moment—which comes about far less frequently than my masturbation sessions, but oftener than a biblical phenomenon—she can give you a run for your money.

Now for the latter or "and then some." Often, when I masturbate, it is Maryellen who creeps into my thoughts. Although "creeps" is somewhat misleading, it is more a case of Maryellen supplying the inspiration, desire, and all the forbidden fruit that stimulates the sweetest results. That is otherwise known as a teenager's trifecta! Why, might you ask, do I engage in this fiendish predilection of carnal worship? Her wall of virtue. It's that ideologically fortified structure repelling all comers that propels my mind to dark and forbidden places. And who could blame me? What else can one do with a paragon of virtue other than engage in feverous onanism?

Of Maryellen's many virtues, perhaps the most maddening is her discipline. Not only is she aware of what she will do the next minute, hour, day, week, and year, but every minute, hour, day, week, and year for the rest of her natural life! She is one of those rare birds perfectly content to spend all her days planning her life instead of—I don't know—*living it.* And yours truly covets an opportunity to throw a monkey wrench into her "wound-too-tight" moral compass, to induce her to do something, God forbid, out of order, unexpected, unconventional, or slightly improper—anything that prevents her from denying membership to the morally decaying West would suffice. *Addison Caldwell: the corrupter of souls.* Given her character, which involves an unparalleled sense of order and virtue, compromising Maryellen borders on the heretical, if not akin to desecrating a religious icon. And that, forgive me, is what makes imagining her garden of earthly delights so devilishly exciting. *Beware, Maryellen—as you read Psalm 23:4 for the umpteenth time—I am the valley of darkness through which you must tread.*

Many of our conversations are theological in tenor, with me beating the drum for atheism, antitheism, the wishy-washy noncommittal agnostic, or anyone else likely to piss off my red-headed friend; her list of peeves is ever-growing, but any one of the first three, given an edgy enough presentation, will do the trick. Call me Addison the Contrarian. And because, irrespective of my upbringing, I am an atheist with too many opinions—the night of the fire set me on a path to enlightenment in terms of ethos and reason only—it set the stage for numerous opportunities to clash with Maryellen. In other words, she gave my atheism purpose, a voice, one I planned to use, not squander. After all, what was the purpose of carving out a position, stamping a flag in the ground, and claiming "I'll die on this hill" if not to engage in discourse? And allow me to be crystal clear: I'm an atheist participating in debates with a girl advocating for the Catholic Doctrine to have its handprints on the Constitution, if not superseding it altogether. Imagine achieving arousal resulting in ejaculation over someone who, if they had their druthers, would un-separate the church and state, punish masturbators, and reserve intimacy for the express purpose of procreation. You would have to be pretty goddamn horny, wouldn't you? But, as I freely admitted, I have become fiendish in my honoring of Maryellen. Fiendish but still maintaining twenty-twenty eyesight!

Once, I told Maryellen, "The Ten Commandments are bull-shit." Well, maybe not all ten, but most of them. Boy, did that ever get a rise out of her! I was wise to have taken a decisive step backward before making my argument, not merely for the sake of my head but also my nuts, as Maryellen was endowed with lengthy appendages and a temper for which one must account. You never saw a pair of eyes flash with such fury. But imagine how those poor Israelites must have felt, especially after trekking over the hot desert sand for forty days and nights—or was it four years? Maybe it was forty years; I seem to recall that the Bible is particularly keen on the number four and numbers divisible by four—only to have someone inform them that murder, theft, and lying were not just ignoble virtues but not virtues at all. I bet a few in the crowd were plenty pissed at ol' Moses after he spent a month-plus rambling around a mountain, only to return to the fold lugging a couple of goddamn rocks. I know I would have had a bone to pick with Moses. After all, Egypt was not exactly the Stone Age— it was a reasonably complex society featuring sophisticated architecture, advancements in science, and courts of law—so it is fair to deduce, with more than a measure of confidence, that the Israelites, a tribe not short on IQ, had that whole murder/theft/lying dilemma, along with all the other "Shall Nots" well figured out before arriving at the base of Mount Sinai.

Then Maryellen would get all rankled and wail, "If there's no God, how do you explain *this*?" And one example of *"this"* was never enough; thus came the ever-predictable barrage of bullshit, matters that clear-cut science leaves dangling. For her, the concept of anything falling outside the parameters of the natural world, or what science fails to explain definitively, was proof positive a spiritual deity oversees the universe and that we prevail as a species in His image and on bent knees should express undying gratitude. *How does the earth go on rotating if not for the mystery of faith?*

"Science is the concerted effort to understand the natural world and its mechanisms; it was never meant to explain abstract bullshit to crackpot theologians." Upon sneering those words to Maryellen, she retorted, "Scientists are factfinders, and when searching for facts, they're also searching for traces of a supreme being—an intelligent designer."

Okay, maybe, in that instance, she made a valid point; when tapping into her inner Thomas Aquinas, Maryellen did have her moments, but accrediting all gray matter, of which there is plenty, to a supreme being or universal entity wielding an ideological component because the explanation otherwise is sketchy, is both weak and lazy. And I would be willing to wager all the money that I'm too lazy to earn that a hundred years from now, science will gain the ability to explain most of what religion swipes for itself. Unfortunately, in the mid-70s, when debating a raving theocrat, the table was not as tilted as I would have preferred.

And what gave these sidewalk debates an infuriating bent was when Maryellen would put on airs with the sort of haughtiness one might when overconfident in ownership of the moral high ground; it mattered not a lick that her logic was thinner than an unruffled potato chip. Then came the worst part. She saved it for last, like one confident they were inserting a final and decisive dagger. "John F. Kennedy was a Catholic, and so is Frank Sinatra," she would pompously intone. "And if two men like John F. Kennedy and Frank Sinatra can believe in God—and, incidentally, they are *way* smarter than Addison Caldwell—then God surely must exist. So stick that in your pipe and smoke it, buster!"

Imagine a theological debate crescendoing to a pinnacle, then nosediving because someone cited Jack Kennedy and Old Blue Eyes, and huffed that I should puff on a pipe. I doubt you could do it. But those were Maryellen McNamara's go-to guys. Whenever stuck, discovering herself on a slippery slope, or scrambling to plug the holes of a ship bound for the depths of the sea, she would blurt out that Jack Kennedy and Frank Sinatra were Catholics, as though those two bright, shining American icons, alone, could somehow eclipse the Crusades, the Spanish Inquisition, and the nineteenth century cutthroat Vatican. Whenever Maryellen would drop those two iconic names, often it was with the equivalent of a brattish seven-year-old wailing, *So there!* or *Take that!* before making a tongue and lip flapping noise some call a "strawberry." But the real madness behind Maryellen reaching for the 35th president of the United States and the twentieth century's foremost songster whenever she sensed a loss of traction: they were my parents' heroes. Maryellen enjoyed nothing more than feeling she was on equal footing with adults, especially if those adults were a friend's parents. Whether she believed it or not, she basked in the idiotic notion that the three months separating us represented a chasm no amount of reason or philosophy I brought to bear could bridge. So on she went, absurdly thrusting herself toward the highest common denominator, otherwise the world of adults, and snootily springing on peers the annoying phrase, *when I was your age*, and missing out on all the rambunctiousness and spontaneity of being a teen. What a pity. But we are still friends, Maryellen and I, despite her efforts to look down her nose at my raging hormones while I find sound reasoning to discredit Him, whom she blindly worships.

CHAPTER THREE
KENNEDY, SINATRA, AND JAGGER

I spent the entirety of my childhood bombarded by my father repeatedly telling me, "There'll never be another Frank Sinatra," and my mother, whose line of equal tenacity and exasperation was as follows: "When John F. Kennedy's heart stopped beating, so, too, stopped the heartbeat of our nation." Jesus Christ, what a drone! I never bothered asking my father whether he believed there would not be another Frank Sinatra in his lifetime or ever. I am confident that the universe will gift us another Sinatra sometime between now and our ability to venture into and colonize deep space. I am doubly sure that if my mother could somehow get beyond her near-sycophantic worship of JFK, she would revise her statement and realize it was the President's penis, not his heartbeat, that marked an ongoing concern.

They sat at opposite ends of the dinner table did these two blinded-by-fame groveling minions. The consequence was "you know who" receiving a steady diet of Frank in his left ear and Jack in his right. My baby sister, Casey, who is seven years my junior, sat across the table from me. Casey never bothered lending an attentive ear with concern for our parents' worship, and less seemed to care, not because she failed to recognize the chatter as the claptrap it was: Quite the contrary. Instead, as I would learn, none of the twaddle was for her benefit. It was not until age twelve that the light went on in my head, alerting me that my parents, Darrin and Claire, attempted to instill their different, opposite, and often skewed values by pumping up their respective heroes. I suppose many parents use what I refer to as the "bullshit-spewing method" to influence their children. Perhaps it's universal. In our abode, as it was perpetrated, the bullshit-spewing method was a power play to see which parents' influence concerning "the parodical son" would prevail.

In the Caldwell household, Frank Sinatra represents the glory days of an unchallenged Capitalist hierarchy paved by good old-fashioned well-intending Western democracy—a well-oiled system that reveres protocol and decorum but frees us to reach, strive, and dream, though not without acknowledging the importance of parameters, though it is never government or corporate entities that must adhere to these constraints but the individual, which is somewhat ironic for a nation that prides itself upon favoring the individual over the collective; and it is not so much in the abstract that these parameters exist: they are discernable lines drawn to better apply reason and logic to whatever the national agenda or narrative is at the moment; they are also used to enforce the rules of engagement, which, if one is paying attention, habitually bend to the will of the powerful; and while we are on the subject of the rules of engagement—those handy-dandy rights and articles in which we are taught to take pride—their authors have managed to convince "us plebeians" trying to navigate through society that are value as citizens is tied directly to our ability to color within the lines; though, wouldn't you know it, the lines overwhelmingly favor some while routinely kicking others squarely in the nuts. Surprised? But then take a gander upon all that the land of opportunity allows one to hang their hat: *Freedom is not free. He who loves not his country can love nothing. Men love their country not because it is great but their own. Yankee Doodle Dandy. You're a grand ole flag. Land of the free, home of the brave.* Choose your banner, young man, and welcome to "Slogan America." Isn't she grand?

In the Caldwell household, JFK represents the intellectual elite: those influential men and women who have the letters Ph.D. after their names spewing anti-establishment propaganda, setting fires under overprivileged liberals who, in turn, drag the underprivileged and disenfranchised into a fight whose real purpose they cannot grasp fully but are, nevertheless, made to feel worthwhile for having been gifted an opportunity to help rattle the establishment and satisfied for awarded a free shot at the nuts of that metaphoric monster known as "The Man." However, this whole hippie, beatnik, flower child, free love cultural phenomenon was a mere bud during JFK's time in office; it did not fully flower until after he was committed to the ground, but that mattered not to my mother, Claire Caldwell; she saw Jack Kennedy, because he was the youngest president in our nation's history, and liberal, as a man able to identify with a woman who had she not gotten herself knocked up in 1961, would have dressed like a Native American Indian, taken hallucinogens, and marched while holding some tacky homemade sign with the quasi-abstract message: *Be the Change.* But JFK had only a partial thumbprint on the quagmire known as The War in Vietnam. The rest of the hand belonged to the ever-gruff L.B.J. and Nixon, and why Claire—after seeing me off to kindergarten—joined a group of women who got arrested because they decided that laying down and blocking traffic at an intersection was a sensible form of protest.

There was much more at play in our household than politics concerning Kennedy and Sinatra. For example, Darrin was hardly a traditional conservative; he was well-centered and approached most matters with what I came to recognize as "his version of common sense," the political outcome notwithstanding. If he seemed to lean right—the tilt often occurred during the dinner hour—it was because my mother, devoid of any subtlety, made it crystal clear she would have relished the opportunity to have had her "middle-class vagina" penetrated by the nation's 35th commander and chief, if not having turned handstands to suck not only presidential cock but genuine Irish Catholic presidential cock.

"Call him a whoremaster if it pleases you," Claire hissed at Darrin, who was busily masticating a somewhat overcooked piece of London broil. No one would mistake Claire for a culinary artist. "But if word had gotten out that JFK needed playmates, yours truly would've elbowed all the other bunnies out of line." *Ask not what your country can do for you but what you can do for your country.* Claire got me thinking: With the Pope the world's most influential religious leader and JFK the most powerful leader of the free world—a clean sweep for Catholicism—had she come into the world soon enough to celebrate this lofty hierarchical exacta, might it have moved the needle of Maryellen's moral compass further right or inspired her to take up a life of debauchery? Moreover, retroactively speaking, might there be a prospective advantage to the past? But I digress; hormones have a way of causing me to stray and entertain scenarios that are not necessarily coherent.

Had Darrin Caldwell's hero been female and a beauty, say, for example, Marilyn Monroe—although Darrin thought JFK's go-to girl was a B actress, at best, and that her best performance came when she sang Happy Birthday to the president because she made the world's most sung song sound like foreplay—it might have been a fair fight. But there was no sane method to make my mother jealous of Frank Sinatra other than to claim that he was instrumental in helping to get JFK elected. Assuming that was true, it would hardly constitute jealousy. So all my father had at his disposal was to try and poke holes in Jack Kennedy's politics and character, and try, he did. On that front, JFK was a cherry-picker's dream, or so history suggests. Indeed, the ill-fated 35th president left plenty of meat on the bone for the scavengers. Those who manage lofty positions by way of elections tend to be generous.

"We had a booming economy, but then that millionaire playboy went and sold the country to the damn unions!" The acrimony with which Darrin Caldwell launched into his harangue was typical of these dinnertime volleys. "And now the country's being run by a bunch of thugs and gangsters. Damn unions are like anything else; before long, they become so big they exist for their own sake, and now our jobs are being shipped to Timbuktu!"

Darrin's final word put the exclamation mark on his mini-monologue. Next came a nod so emphatic that I expected his head to come loose from his neck and land in the instant mashed potatoes he had yet to touch. Incidentally, during these dinnertime volleys, Timbuktu rarely went unmentioned: it was Darrin Caldwell's go-to place when what he meant was overseas. According to Darrin, everything once great in America got funneled, currently resides, or is on its way to Timbuktu. Lucky them. And the reason I describe these dinnertime debates as "volleys" is because there is no such thing as an ace; a serve never went unreturned.

"Point to an era in our history when gangsters and thugs didn't run the country," Claire intoned. "One man's gangster is another man's community organizer. Hell, the Sons of Liberty were gangsters! So, making pompous declarations that government officials and union leaders behave like gangsters and thugs doesn't make it any more of a reality. And as far as that so-called 'boom economy' was concerned: three cheers for the war!" Looking my way squarely, Claire added, "World War II, otherwise known as the great savior of American Capitalism." Subtly, her eyes shifted toward the other end of the table, where Darrin finally decided to sample the instant mashed potatoes. "Not the more recent and *unjust* war. I mean, who in their right mind gives a rat's ass that a pissant country the size of New Jersey turned commie."

"It's un-American to wanna see the spread of communism unless, of course, you're a card-carrying Marxist. And if you *are* one, or a Trotskyist, it's best not to shout it too loudly or wave your banner too high; there's a reason, in the event you haven't been paying attention, that Cubans risk death to paddle or swim their way to Miami, and Russian refuseniks would sell their souls to smuggle themselves out of the Soviet Union." Darrin grinned with satisfaction. Claire made a sour face.

"What did World War II have to do with the economy?" I managed to chime in before matters further escalated. I figured if I have to strain my jaw shredding overcooked meat to where I could comfortably allow it to pass through my esophagus while bludgeoned with sexually-driven political discord, I may as well learn a thing or two.

"The war effort sent production through the roof." Darrin pounced; he must have anticipated my question. "Everyone did their share. Everyone wanted a role—a part to play—and *no one* whined about whether or not the war was unjust."

Ignoring my father's supercilious tone, my mother promptly added, "And when the war ended, everyone else had to go home and rebuild their broken cities and revitalize their scorched lands. We, on the other hand, only had to come home; not a single shot got fired on American soil, nor did a single bomb explode. In other words, while the rest of the globe spent the better part of a generation licking its wounds, America hit the ground running. Like magic, the private economy sprang from wartime government controls and policies, and before we knew it, the good old U. S. of A. had Disney Land, rock 'n' roll, burgers to go, drive-in movies, and Howdy Goddamn Doody!"

"Claire!" Darrin scolded. Darrin did not care for us using off-color language in front of Casey. When Casey was not within earshot, all bets were off. Casey, seemingly unfazed by Claire's histrionic and comical outburst, whined, "I wanna go to Disney Land."

****

So, those are my parents: Darrin and Claire Caldwell. Their allegiances, politics, and experiences are all gummed up and soused with sex and the typical neurosis and delusions afflicting most blind patriots or postmodern wannabes. However, postmodernism seems too sophisticated a term to pin on the lower-middle-class American wife of a blind patriot. To simplify the matter, my "silent generation" parents are just as screwed-up and confused as everyone else. Politics alone can muddle anything showing promise. Add war to the mix, and suddenly, everyone forgets where they are standing.

"I voted for Goldwater," Claire, on numerous occasions, made known. "I wasn't in love with his politics, but the man was a straight shooter that made no bones that our involvement in Vietnam was bullshit."

"'All the way with LBJ,' was the slogan in those days," Darrin crooned. "And I didn't give a rat's ass that he was a Texas-sized civil rights fraud who used a certain racially profane word more often than Richard Pryor; at least he didn't wanna see those goddamn commies prevail."

In '68, Darrin and Claire voted for Richard Nixon for the same reason: he promised to end the United States' involvement in the Vietnam War. Darrin was no less devoted to the concept of eradicating communism wherever it attempted to root and spread. But even he began to feel the fatigue of a war that routinely clubbed anxious Americans over the head with one horrifying news item after another. Four years and twenty thousand casualties later, again, my father pulled the lever for Tricky Dick; however, the extent of Tricky Dick's trickiness would not enter the realm of the public domain until a year into his second term. Claire went for left-wing extremist George McGovern, who, on the heels of Nixon's success in China and McGovern's party not particularly enamored with him, as was evidenced by the slogan: *Anybody but McGovern*, lost in a landslide. In '76, both Darrin and Claire went for Jimmy Carter, despite sharing the opinion: "The poor bastard is a nice guy who'll get ground-up in the gears of the establishment."

After dinner, Darrin put on Sinatra, one of Frank's many recordings with Gordon Jenkins. Darrin loved the song *It Was a Very Good Year*; it was his favorite. I had to admit the tune had depth: and those sweeping strings, Frank's impeccable phrasing, and spot-on annunciations that made every word seem poignant—if I allowed myself, I might have become a fan, but all that form, structure, and perfection failed to sit well with a young man who was a product of the 70s. But

25

there was no denying *It Was a Very Good Year* was dense with richness and refined in its texture. It also harkened back to a day, not long ago, when society was less complex and did not have so many mixed messages to decipher. In other words, a time when our nation, which once believed two oceans served as ample insulation, had fewer suspicions. So, yes, the music was good and perhaps great, but I also heard it as old-fashioned, and for a teen, old-fashioned was the kiss of death. *Sorry, Frank. I'll get around to you, say, in twenty years.*

Before long, Darrin sat alone in the living room, listening to his hero. Sometimes, I think he would put on Sinatra to chase us away so that he could be alone with his thoughts. I peeked into the living room and saw him slumped in his chair; his eyes were closed, and a blissful look came over him. It was the mid-seventies, and, unlike Claire Caldwell's hero, Darrin Caldwell's hero was alive and well and adored by millions.

Given how the dinnertime volleys would trend, it surprised me to learn that Jack Kennedy and Frank Sinatra were once bosom buddies. Then JFK was elected to the highest office in the land and, as a result—taking into account Nikita Khrushchev and Mao Zedong—became the world's most influential leader. Friendship had to take a backseat. Though unproven, Sinatra had ties to the mob, and the power brokers of the DNC could not allow any dego-stink to rub off on their Irish Catholic Prince. Sinatra felt snubbed and stopped backing the Democratic party. So, too, did Darrin Caldwell.

The following day, after Darrin rolled home from work, he found his wife clad in a zany flower-printed shirt, a headband and dancing wildly—knees and elbow flailing every which direction—to the Rolling Stones' *Sticky Fingers* album; the music was blasting from the same stereo turntable that a night ago accommodated Old Blue Eyes. Claire had her blue jeans rolled up to her knees; outlandish polish coated her fingernails and toenails; she was unnecessarily sporting sunglasses. (She had me until the sunglasses.) Her gyrations became more exaggerated and wilder when, through the blinds, she spotted a burgundy Chevy Caprice pull up to the curb in front of our house. Casey, who was dancing with Claire but dressed more traditionally for the mid-70s, had difficulty keeping up. When poor Darrin came through the door, he sneered at the stereo as though Mick Jagger's voice transmitting from the same speakers that broadcasted

Sinatra was on the order of blasphemy and that Mick was desecrating the sanctity of the air with noise too noxious for the human ear to endure. Next, when noticing Claire's outlandish getup, he rolled his eyes in what I learned was Darrin's "what the fuck" glower. Claire began strutting like Jagger—all knees and elbows—a wild turkey with too many joints but still managing some semblance of rhythm despite turning the room into utter chaos. She took hold of Casey's hands and, after half a whirl, flung her onto the sofa, then went gunning for her business-attired husband. Despite her thirty-three years and carrying three children—Claire miscarried her second pregnancy; it's why there are seven years between Casey and me—I noticed through the zany flower-printed shirt, as she yanked Darrin to the center of the living room, that this Jagger impersonator had perky tits! They were not on the order of Cyndy Pytlewski's Playtex cross-your-heart-bra model tits, but they were perky nonetheless. I do not say this lustfully; I am merely making an observation.

By way of a single deft maneuver, Claire switched from the herky-jerky flailing of Mick Jagger to the seductiveness of Salome: First, facing Darrin, then with her back to him, she oiled, slithered, and snaked her way around his person; you would have thought *Sticky Fingers* yielded to an Arabian snake charmer sitting crossed legged on the living room floor, piping notes whose purpose was to bewitch, but *Sticky Fingers* was still spinning on the turntable, and Claire was putting on one helluva show. Then, as deftly as Jagger disappeared, he returned. Claire stood on her tiptoes so that she and Darrin were pelvis to pelvis. Claire arched her back and began to mimic the back-stroke. Fearing that she might lose leverage, go too far, and fall backward, Darrin alertly encircled her trim waist and snapped her to a standing position. It drew a smile from Claire that Darrin was not bothered by her outlandish display and thought to rescue her from falling. Claire appeared aroused by Darrin's sudden burst of strength, his manhandling of her slim form. Meanwhile, Darrin seemed quite appreciative of the still fit and supple figure that could gyrate like the world's most famous rock star.

The show was not over; there was yet an encore. Claire widened her stance, raised her arms above her head, and clasped her hands together. Then, in a manner tantalizing as a feather swishing its way to the ground, she swayed to a squat. Her choreography was hypnotic and seductive and had me wondering, could Claire make herself disappear or melt into the carpet? But when Claire sank as low as she could go without gravity and her heart-shaped bottom pulling her backward, she latched on to my father and began dry-humping his leg. Next, she dragged him to the floor and then on top of her. Somehow, during the process, Darrin managed to shed his sports coat. And then there went Casey, exploding off the sofa to jump on Darrin's back.

"You're gonna kiss Mommy, arencha, Daddy—like they do in the movies?" came Casey's anticipatory croon.

"Yeah, Case." I never annunciated the *y* in Casey's name. "Just like in the movies."

CHAPTER FOUR
POOR GUY

And so it went with concern for the Caldwell hierarchy: Rock 'n' roll brought out the implike, free-spirited sixteen-year-old in Claire, and that devilish free-wheeling teen tortured Darrin's loins. Still, he strived to embrace the role of the man with too much starch in his collar or one hovering above the fray with an aversion to spontaneity. Claire made it her business to thwart his efforts and often succeeded.

It was Darrin's custom to grab *The Bulletin*, which usually landed on our doorstep at 4:00 p.m., and locate a section of the sofa before burying his nose in the front page. On the day of her Jagger routine, Claire collapsed beside him and flung her trim little feet onto his lap. Darrin, who first folded the paper in half, then quartered it, unfolded it to shield one of Claire's feet busy in its effort to induce arousal. I stood in the archway between the living and dining rooms as Darrin read items of national concern. Occasionally, he made an inane humming noise to mask that Claire's method of seduction was prevailing. Before long, all Darrin could do was hum as Claire shoved her outlandishly polished toes into his mouth before disappearing. Darrin continued to hum inanely, but it was not long before he, too, made himself scarce after carelessly tossing aside a front page that no longer gripped his attention.

And so that constituted foreplay for an interested couple in their mid-thirties with a teenager and a seven-year-old: playing dress-up, hopping around like Mick Jagger, dry humping, and forced toe sucking. And away they went!

"Where did everybody go?" wondered Casey, as the deft manner in which Darrin and Claire disappeared had just registered with the Caldwell runt.

"*We're* part of everybody," I told Casey.

"I meant Mom and Dad," she unnecessarily clarified. "Where did *they* go?"

"Hey, Case, you know how you're always whining that I'm not the boss of you?' Well, Mom and Dad thought it'd be a good idea if you had the opportunity to listen to the same bullshit."

Casey crinkled her nose in bemusement. I left her there: I was in no mood to involve myself in a discussion about how babies get made.

****

Incidentally, I'm not as indifferent to Sinatra as I may have let on, or so dense that I can't appreciate art, but the loud, raw passion, at times anti-establishment rock 'n' roll, in my opinion, is more potent. So when I select an album from the rack, I'm much more in line with my progressive, hippie, grass-toking mother.

Yep, Claire Caldwell smokes grass. Moreover, she managed to fool herself into believing I was unaware of it and ignorant of its effects. I mean, who but a stoned woman would launch into a fit of laughter when learning that Jimmy Carbone—a neighbor at the end of the block who experimented with hallucinogens and was one of those pain-in-the-ass born-again Christians—jumped out his attic window dressed as Spiderman and impaled himself on a fencepost? And who opens their bedroom windows in the middle of wintertime when it's twenty degrees? Some of my most enjoyable moments in adolescence came when knocking on Claire's bedroom door and hearing her holler out in a panic-stricken voice, "Just a minute, Addie," then scampering around the room in a mad attempt to swish away the remnants of marijuana using a bed pillow. When Darrin was in the room and feeling amorous, sometimes Claire could coax him into taking a toke. I could always tell when Darrin caved to temptation: the dreamy, imbecilic look was the dead giveaway. Three-quarters of the way through my thirteenth year—approximately the same time Maryellen learned of my chronic masturbation and condemned me to hell—I knocked on the bedroom door and told Claire, "Mom, seriously, you don't have to go through any trouble; I know. I've known for a while." As far as I could tell, the sound made by a swishing pillow ceased, and her feet had settled in one spot. I could sense relief and embarrassment through the closed door before she managed to mutter, "H-how long have you known?"

"Since last summer," I called to her from the other side of the door. I mean, who runs a bedroom window-unit air conditioner with all the other windows wide open? I did not bother hammering home that point; I did not want Claire to suffer more embarrassment than was necessary. I heard her fall backward on the bed and let out a sigh.

"You haven't told any of your friends, have you, Addie? So help me, I'll kick you in the nuts if you have. And anyway, it's just a weed—a goddamn plant. I don't care what the conservatives say."

"Sure, it is, Mom—a goddamn plant. And no, I haven't breathed a word to anyone."

Maryellen—months before celebrating my hellish destiny—upon stepping off the school bus and turning onto our block, asked, "Why are your parents' bedroom windows open? It's the coldest day of the year."

"My father always wondered what it was like to fuck my mother in an igloo, and gas is too expensive to drive to Alaska," I drolly replied.

"You're a real sicko, Addison!" Maryellen fired back. "You *do* realize it."

I thought "sicko" was a bit strong, but I would gladly take ownership of having a twisted worldview, though not without main-taining Maryellen's wall of virtue is partly to blame. Anyway, it was bitterly cold, if not the coldest day of the year, as Maryellen declared. It was also bright and clear, and Maryellen's long and luxurious fire-engine-red mane seemed to leap out from the white earmuffs she wore, and it dangled prettily on the shoulders of her white wool coat. Her face—in the summer heat, it would transform from somewhat clear to a whole galaxy of freckles—was pale yet rosy, and her elec-tric-blue eyes were remarkably vivid in the bitter cold. I wanted her to plead to me: *Hold me, Addison, I'm cold; you need to keep me warm*, and then we would share our first kiss. Yeah, I know; I was having one of my delusions. Had I tried to take her into my arms and kiss her, she would have lined me up for a swift kick in the nuts, but if you had to get kicked in the nuts, a day when your nuts had grown numb from the cold and were the size of cherry pits would be just the day.

"It's healthy to open the windows on a cold day," I added. "It kills all the germs in the house."

"So does a can of Lysol," came her sharp retort. "And besides, if it's germs they're so worried about, why aren't the first-floor windows open? Can you explain that?" I can usually think on my feet, but Maryellen had me on that one; there was no viable reason, other than the truth, for why the first-floor windows were not also open. Maryellen turned away from me in favor of the warmth of her home. *Fuck her*, was what I thought as I stood alone on the freezing sidewalk. Afterward, I went inside to disrupt my mother, thaw out my nuts, masturbate, and in precisely that order.

And while we are on the subject of the home into which Maryellen snootily disappeared, they are some interesting characters, in their own right, Mr. and Mrs. McNamara. Guy McNamara was a proponent of the war in Vietnam, a fierce anti-communist, a staunch conservative—politically, not morally—voted twice for Nixon, pulled the lever for Ford, worshiped Sinatra, and was the only one on the block who rooted for Bobby Riggs to defeat Billie Jean King. But now comes the most astonishing aspect: Guy was and continues to be the most liberal member of the family over which he resides as patriarch.

Guy McNamara is tall, slender, not an altogether bad-looking fellow, and always seen smiling. Though, as far as I can tell, I have never detected a trace of glee in Guy's smile; it seems to manifest by way of some mysterious irony that persists each day. Moreover, it's not reflexive but akin to the stitched-on smile of a stuffed animal; it's permanently fixed on his face and seemingly conveys imbecility. Guy and Darrin have Sinatra in common and, to a lesser degree, politics, and it is on those two fronts their friendship is based. Whenever their social contract gets breached and matters become personal, the outpouring invariably comes from Guy McNamara; he has divulged to Darrin many nuggets he would not dare confess to his wife, Rosemarie, and certainly not to Maryellen. Keeping in mind Guy is not a "moral" conservative, Rosemarie and Maryellen were and remained wholly convinced that Guy had suffered from a urinary tract infection when, in fact, he contracted an old-fashioned case of the clap. As a result, the poor sonofabitch was forced to drink cranberry juice every morning for a month.

"I hate cranberry juice," Guy complained to Darrin. "And worse yet, Rosemarie stands over me like a gorgon and watches me drink every goddamn drop until it's gone." But more importantly, how could Guy McNamara get away without confessing this tasty tidbit to Rosemarie, for one would assume she would have become a host to what is a dubious and transmittable condition? The answer? Upon Maryellen's birth, Guy made it known to Rosemarie that he did not care to have more children. As it would come to pass, Guy McNamara uttered those words to the wrong woman. Rosemarie McNamara is not merely a staunch Catholic but a goddamn lunatic. She reads the Bible like Claire Caldwell reads Thomas Mann and quotes scripture more often than Cillian James and I discuss Theresa Delvecchio's breasts, which, I confess, is far too frequent.

Rosemarie McNamara believes that sex should be strictly assigned for the express purpose of procreation. Period. "That's why you need to try it before you buy it," Claire, the beatnik, told me once Casey was out of earshot. Not that Casey would have understood the inference, but Claire was in no mood to tap-dance through some horseshit explanation had Casey demanded one, although sampling a new mattress or pair of shoes would have done the trick.

Poor Guy. He had no access to Rosemarie's vagina unless she was ovulating. And since he did not care to partake in the proliferation of our species beyond Maryellen, he was, as they say, shit out of luck. So, unbeknownst to Rosemarie, sly old Guy went and scheduled a vasectomy, then professed that he had second thoughts about growing the family.

"It was painless," he told Darrin. "So, big deal, now I get to screw once a month if I'm lucky. However, sharing a bed with Rosemarie hardly constitutes luck. Screwing her is the closest I hope ever to come to experiencing necrophilia. I mean, for crying out loud, can you blame me for keeping a piece on the side? If I had a son, the first thing I'd tell him: 'If she insists on waiting until her wedding night, move on to the next one.' As far as I'm concerned, the bedroom is a proving ground, and you're a fool if you let someone slide."

Whenever Darrin came away from a conversation with Guy, I used to tiptoe into the hallway, put an attentive ear to his bedroom door, and listen to him relay all those juicy tidbits to Claire, who never failed to remind Darrin of how lucky he was to "have a wife that enjoys a good fuck."

Claire avoided Rosemarie McNamara like one dodging a curbside turd left by a thoughtless dogwalker. But occasionally, she would find herself cornered and forced to agonize through a morality lesson befitting only to those who dwell in catacombs and pray ten hours a day with their heads pressed to concrete slabs or a psychotic priest who takes a cat o' nine tails to his back for having impure thoughts. Afterward, she would come stumbling through the door like a whirling dervish, too exasperated to proffer any level of coherence but owning enough composure to threaten, "So help me, Addie, if you marry the daughter of that fucking lunatic, I'll have your nuts on a stick!"

I often watched the McNamaras set off to church on Sunday mornings from the living room window. Always, it was to the nine o'clock Mass. Families are creatures of habit in that regard: often, it's for the sake of a favorite priest, or the time is convenient, though if one claims steadfast and unyielding advocacy of a religious doctrine, giving thanks and praise to the very omnipotent being upon which a dogma is based should never rate as a matter of convenience.

Rosemarie McNamara was a vision of unwavering focus; her game face was on no sooner than her ultra-conservative black buckle-up shoes hit the curb, if not beforehand. Step after severe step, Rosemarie marched onward. Her mission: to be imbued with the word of God and feel the presence of the beaten, brutalized, and crucified Jesus, His loving Mother, pitiable Mary, zealous Simon, denying Peter, damnable Judas, reluctant Pilate, weeping angels, and the rest of the usual suspects depicted in statue, stained glass, and painted onto grand architecture; and once profoundly saturated with intellectually deprived drivel, she would bask in the notion that she is an unworthy sinner but could rest assured that she would one day be saved and cleansed in the blood of the martyrs. Meanwhile, Maryellen hopped alongside Rosemarie as if she were on her way to a Girl Scout meeting. Maryellen *is* a Girl Scout. Earlier, she was a Brownie. Keeping true to her character, she lives to teach Vacation Bible School. Poor Guy: he walked two paces behind, shoulders slumped, head bowed, though still managed that same imbecilic smile for which no one could account. It was not when watching Guy slink off to Mass but in those instances when I had my ear pressed to the door listening to Darrin and Claire snicker over Guy's sex life that I would think, despite her antagonism: *Poor Maryellen. All her virtue is based purely on lunacy and bullshit.* But I would never stoop so low as to inform Maryellen that her old man philanders because her mother is batshit crazy in her adherence to religion, and the result was an unfortunate venereal episode. If ever I manage to gain entry to the proverbial promised land, otherwise known as the other side of Maryellen's wall of virtue, it will be through hard work, due diligence, and honest persuasion, not because I rocked her world and sent her reeling into my comforting arms. You see, I'm not such a bad guy after all. But until that day arrives, as Cillian James alluded to when observing the corruptible Father Murray lustfully ogling Cyndy Pytlewski's breasts, it's chronic self-indulgence for ol' Addison Caldwell.

CHAPTER FIVE
WILDWOOD DAYS

Okay, so the McNamaras, from the outside looking in or the vantage point next door, appear a bit odd, whacky, if not wholly dysfunctional. Nowadays—a decade-plus into the new century—who doesn't? Moreover, with political rancor sweeping our nation, institutional media blindsided by social media and relegating it to the role of irrational influence peddlers with a low-rent pop culture bent, and an ever-bizarre pop culture using its platform to reach those who breathlessly await its tweets, odd, whacky, and dysfunctional must be considered fortunate results.

"Artists used to encrypt their ideas and feelings into their art form," moaned Claire Caldwell. "Nowadays, they look for open mics to yammer into, and meanwhile, the music has gotten shitty, and movies are unwatchable!"

Claire's days of strutting like Jagger are long gone. Nowadays, she rides around in a flex-fuel Toyota blasting The Rolling Stones, uses both psychotropic and medical marijuana, and complains, "I still feel young at heart, but the world is drifting away from me. I can't recognize my party anymore. Where have you gone, Jack Kennedy?"

I did not bother reminding Claire that her struggles are a by-product of aging and that we tend to develop a romanticized notion of what the world was like in our youth. Once, she called me while I was away at college and whined, "When the hell did grass become weed? Why can't they leave even the *simplest* matters alone?" Just the other day, she called with a far more legitimate complaint. "Today, at the mall, I heard a teenage girl yell 'fuck you' to her mother, and the poor woman just stood there and took it. If this keeps up, before long, these overrated brats will be walking their parents around on leashes! And what's with all these gender-neutral kids? Christ, you can't even compliment a new mother wheeling around a beautiful son or daughter without receiving a rash of bullshit. Sorry to go on like this, Addie, but if this is what it means to be liberal in today's world, I say, no, thank you!"

Children scolding parents? The concept is still relatively new and, so far as I can tell, has not flowered to the point of *Lord of the Flies*. Not all change is progress.

Odd, whacky, dysfunctional, or otherwise, I grew up with the impression the McNamaras were rich—comparatively speaking. Guy drove a fully-loaded, jet-black, 1974 Buick Electra Coupe he brought brand-new, earned enough to keep a "piece on the side," and Maryellen was clad, however conservatively, in clothes purchased from Wannamaker's, and not its bargain-basement, but the women's apparel department on the second floor. And when the McNamaras vacationed, their journey always involved air travel. And the procedure was as follows: Guy encouraged Rosemarie and Maryellen to choose the destination and then dropped them at the airport—each year, without fail, an unforeseen business crisis would arise that could not be solved without Guy present—with the promise he would catch a later flight; perhaps he might join them sometime within a week. Then Guy would come rolling home in his expensive Buick, grinning like a sonofabitch, and it was never his customary stuffed teddy bear grin but a sly dog grin.

"Poor Rosemarie," I heard Darrin lament to Claire. "She was all worked up worrying about what Guy was gonna eat with her gone. It almost makes you feel sorry for the old girl."

"Maybe if Rosemarie understood that a vagina was more than an orifice through which to bleed once a month, Guy wouldn't have to fake a crisis, and, like a *normal* family, the three could go away together." Where the McNamaras were concerned, Claire Caldwell did not have a sympathetic bone in her body.

"Maybe Rosemarie's mother was too uncomfortable when it came time to explain the birds and the bees, and she needs another female—one nearer her age—to help her understand...." When Darrin realized to whom he was speaking, he broke off his thought. *Hey, lady, get your cunt out of mothballs before the goddamn thing ossifies*, was indicative of the sort of tact with which he imagined Claire breaching such a dilemma. That being the assumption, Darrin dismissively added, "Ahh, never mind."

We are not rich, not even comparatively, regardless of who you use as a measuring stick. Moreover, my hippie mother and conservative pussy-whipped father are too oblivious to realize their station—therefore, mine and Casey's—is the lower rung of the middle class. So when the time comes for us to drop out of society for a week in summer, we Caldwells—like the Costigans, Broscos, James, Delvecchios, Murphys, and all the other public and parochial school families living in what ranked primarily as a pedestrian neighborhood save for some rare exceptions—never used the term "vacation." Vacation is a pretentious word only uttered by Maryellen, who relishes the opportunity to drone on about flying in airplanes to far-flung places such as The Canadian Rockies, Bryce Canyon, and the McNamara's latest excursion, Cancun, where—and it served her right—she returned burnt like a sonofabitch; she resembled a Jimmy Dean sausage with rosary beads. For us and everyone else, vacation meant going to the seashore, and it was unnecessary to mention the Jersey Shore or, more specifically, Wildwood; both were a given. Vacation? *"Hey CJ, we're going to the seashore next week." "Yeah, us too."*

The term "vacation" is seldom used because these trips to the seashore—a mere ninety-mile destination—prevail as labor-intensive exercises. Nevertheless, it did not prevent us or anyone else from undertaking the sojourn, year after grueling year. My mother likened seashore vacations to pregnancy and childbirth, asserting, "Before the next go-around, you forget all about the pain, and then it's 'Here we go again!'"

That was the truth. Not that I knew anything about childbirth. But I thought Claire Caldwell's analogy was spot on. A year passes, and one tends to forget all the bullshit that went into accomplishing (surviving) a week at the seashore. Trust me; it was no vacation.

To begin with, Claire would start a food box a month before the trip and fill it with everyone's favorite breakfast cereal, Stroman bread, Jiff peanut butter, Welch's grape jelly, box spaghetti, sauce in a jar, and a multitude of snacks clamored from when seen on television Saturday morning while watching Bugs Bunny. Then, she would fill a cooler with perishables on the morning of the trip. Why all this preparation? Because we could not afford to eat breakfast and dinner out more than a couple of mornings and nights, we needed to cut corners so there would be enough in the till to spend on the boardwalk. *Sound like a vacation?*

As we were nearing Wildwood, we would clamor for Darrin to turn off the air-conditioner so we could roll down the windows and inhale the profusion of ocean air while driving over the sound. That blast of ocean air that filled my nostrils as a youngster has stayed with me. It's why I still crave a seashore and have come to learn that vacations are fifty percent anticipation, forty percent learning to appreciate your mattress and other creature comforts, and ten percent something else I have yet to figure out.

Darrin would coast by all the nifty-looking hotels situated near the beach and boardwalk—the ones that have fancy signs, lounge chairs laid neatly poolside and on sundecks, and swimming pools with deep ends and diving boards—then swear, "Next year, goddamnit, we're gonna stay in one of these hotels, not just drive by!" Then he would coast through a town he knew by heart to the low-rent district, otherwise, the houses that stood several blocks away from the beach— those old familiar accommodations with no swimming pools, diving boards, air-conditioners, lounge chairs (Why would there be lounge chairs if there were no swimming pools or sundecks?) or maid service. A week at the seashore was essentially recreating the drudgery of your life ninety miles southeast of Philadelphia without any of the comforts we take for granted. *Is the picture I'm attempting to illustrate taking shape?*

And then came the best part of all: the trek to the beach and the Atlantic Ocean. The house we rented was owned by Harry and Tessie Guadia, an elderly Italian couple who spoke English so brokenly that none of us understood a word they said. Yet, Darrin would stand there and offer nods of acknowledgment, smile imbecilically ala Guy McNamara, and insert polite laughter where he guessed it was appropriate. The house stood five blocks from the beach, and Wildwood's beach, for anyone unfamiliar, is like the Sahara Desert; it takes forever to reach the rim of the ocean, feel the mist of the waves spraying on your face, and spot the seagulls darting through the air overhead. It has not been too bad lately. But when Casey was a toddler—along with a beach umbrella, three chairs, four towels, floatation devices, a cooler filled with all kinds of sugar-infused drinks and sandwiches, a bag loaded with suntan lotions and various types of first-aid, and last but not least a goddamn kite! —we had to wheel a stroller packed with all sorts of baby paraphernalia, including Casey herself, and a miniature screened tent with an opaque roof, into which Casey was placed when she needed to nap or would not quit eating the sand. And all that preparation and work was for the right to get stung by jellyfish and green flies and occasionally dip in a glorified pond chock full of seaweed. Vacation? What sort of unenlightened moron would assign the label vacation to such a miserable and laborious endeavor? And yet, I would not trade it away for the world, less the fragmented family affairs the McNamaras called vacation. Those seashore weeks that required thrift and resourcefulness helped mold me into what I am today.

But it was not all dreadful because it was not uncommon—with Wildwood a popular destination because of its favorable proximity to Philly—to run into a friend or two, be it a kid from the neighborhood or a classmate. For example, I ran into Cillian the summer going into high school. What luck! And Cillian had not one but *two* kid sisters, so he was thrilled at the prospect of breaking away from his family and enjoying the seashore the way a young man was entitled to enjoy it.

I stood at the ocean's edge, feet pressing into the goopy sand. My attention was fixed on the water as I watched it pulled away from me by an unseen force of nature, only to come rushing back to crash into my ankles. Last year, Richie Costigan, the sonofabitch, had harassingly urged me, "Jesus Christ, Addie, run in and get it over with, will you!" I was never a *run-in-and get-it-over-with* kind of guy; I was more the *one body part at a time* kind of guy: ankles, knees, genitals, small of the back, and then shoulder blades, and Richie Costigan, who was anxious to have company riding the waves and getting tossed around in the surf, was losing patience with my namby-pamby oceanic approach. That was last year. Today, as I stood by the water's edge—a month had passed since I turned fourteen and had the same age number as my incomparable red-headed neighbor—I was contemplating my freshman year of high school. For fifty years, the public school I attended went from kindergarten to eighth grade, petitioned for, and was awarded a ninth grade. It meant I would get a second chance to be king of the hill. Lucky me. Anyway, I was considering my fortunes when something or some*one* came barreling into me. My mind flashed to a year ago when an impatient Richie Costigan forced me to surrender my customary ocean entry by kicking water at me. Last night, I spoke to Richie, so I knew his gas-siphoning old man, the detective, had not planned on the seashore this week. Whoever or whatever had barreled into me drove me forward several feet before tackling me into a knee-high wave. It took me a moment or two to get my bearings from such a jarring impact. When I did, I saw that straddling me and looking down and smiling like a sonofabitch was Cillian. Cillian had a bizarre but appealing smile. The corners of his eyes turned downward, while the corners of his mouth took a dramatic upward turn. I had never seen anything like it—it was a fusion of *The Comedy* and *The Tragedy*. "Addie," he cried, "we're at the fucking seashore!"

"Gee, thanks for the heads-up, CJ," I said. "If you didn't piledrive me into the Atlantic Ocean, I would swear we were at the North Pole getting mauled by Polar bears."

Cillian and I spent the day trudging through the tide and undertow. Sometimes, we would allow ourselves to drift too far beyond the breakers, prompting a lifeguard to blow a whistle, then edge toward the breakers at a point where we could catch a wave capable of delivering us to shore. Then, we would repeat the process. That night, we strolled the boardwalk like a couple of stray tomcats, making every effort to enjoy it for what it was: a wonderland of shameless honky-tonk. On the boardwalk's beachside were four piers: Sportland, Morey's, Hunt's, and Mariner's Landing. Each pier featured games of chance—some were based on pure luck, others required skill—roller-coasters, various types of funhouses, and contraptions that either revolved, rotated, ascended, dipped, darted, or oscillated with each using varying degrees of gravity and centrifugal force to achieve their unique method of amusement. Situated among these ticket-to-ride amusements were stands selling popcorn, snow cones, waffle cones, candy apples, cotton candy, hotdogs, funnel cake, and the screechy din of thousands of kids like Casey and Cillian's sisters, Karen and Stephanie, whining, "I want everything!" On the town side of the boardwalk stood tee-shirts, tee-shirts, and more tee-shirts, all sold in warped and shoddy constructed shops that were fire hazards. There rarely passed a summer that did not see one go up in flames. *Welcome to the boardwalk at Wildwood, New Jersey. One day, it'll all catch fire. Bring your own stick and marshmallows.*

"So, Addie, what's with you and that flame-headed freckled-face Catholic School bitchsicle who suffers from vaginal disassociation disorder?" Cillian was quite the wordsmith and deft at fusing two words to create one killer word meant to illustrate how or why someone was a sonofabitch. "Bitchsicle" was a gem, the perfect dysphemism to describe a cold-hearted woman who saw her vagina as the Golden Grail and guarded it with the tenacity of a junkyard dog. It was no wonder Cillian and I were friends.

"Aside from every conversation developing into a dispute, her remaining strenuously ignorant that, physically, she's more woman than girl, and reminding me I'll never get close enough even to sniff her vagina if I were the last guy on earth, and threatens to introduce my nuts to her right foot should I try, she's like silly putty in the palm of my hand." Then, I explained to Cillian the unfortunate ardency of Maryellen's Catholicism and where it derives from.

"The apple didn't fall far from the tree," I said. "And it's just my luck the tree turned out to be Missus Mac and not Mister, and she's no wishy-washy scrub pine that blows over in an August thunderstorm—the woman's a goddamn Sequoia, a tower of virtue stretching beyond the clouds! In other words, no sex or even thinking about the subject; it's a sin unless you're married and ovulating."

"A sin? Just for having impure thoughts? Jesus *mustn't* be pleased." Cillian was blistering with irony as we prepared to board the Ferris Wheel at Mariner's Landing. "Imagine getting nailed to a couple of planks, all because man caves to his compulsion to beat off. Thank goodness for the reformers who stood up to all that medieval idiocy and expelled it from polite society."

I found Cillian's perspective—incidentally, Cillian practices Catholicism—as amusing as it was illuminating and must bear it in mind for the future. You see, Maryellen never passes on an opportunity to remind me that Christ died for our sins. (Allow me to be clear: I would not dare ask so much of Jesus; if my soul was black—whether I lived in the Bronze Age or centuries beyond The Enlightenment—so be it; I'll take the consequences.) Moreover, she never specifies which of humanity's transgressions Jesus's preordained death intended to erase or adjust to ground zero. Because Missus Mac turned her into a religious loon, I assumed she meant all of them, though lumping in the pleasuring of oneself while entertaining erotic thoughts with such egregious wrongdoings as murder, rape, and theft seems to me an insult and, in a way, diminishes Jesus's sacrifice. Then Cillian said as the Ferris wheel stopped with us at its highest peak and I experienced the sensation I was unsupported—from our current position, no part of the wheel's well-scaffolded suspension was visible— "You know, Addie, you could pretend you're blind and get away with a free feel. Who knows, Maryellen might even feel responsible for your condition since she wished it on you, then offer up a sympathy fuck. If there's one thing I know about, it's Catholic school girls: burden them with enough guilt, and before you know it, their pants are down at their ankles."

Cillian was right; I had been going about it the wrong way. I should have been working the Catholic guilt angle all along. Instead, I allowed my contrarian nature to get the better of me. It's never too late to shift strategy. But I was not obsessing about my lifetime banishment from Maryellen's delightfully constructed form or it going to waste, God forbid, until she was married and ovulating. Instead, my prevailing thought pivoted to Cillian violently rocking our compartment while wondering whether someone could survive a fall from such a dizzying height. The view of the ocean from the highest point of the Ferris wheel was spectacular, and the wind, at that height, whipped through our open-air canopy. It was all quite stimulating, but I could not wait until the sonofabitching ride was over and my feet, once again, were planted firmly on the boardwalk.

It was no secret that Cillian was obsessed with heights. Still, no one ever heard him droning on how he aspired to be a special forces soldier jumping out of airplanes into combat zones or a trapeze artist defying gravity to the oohs and aahs of a crowd wringing together its nervous hands. He simply enjoyed the sensation of heights, and the more precarious, the better he seemed to like it.

****

There was a train trestle at the north end of our neighborhood. The span was approximately a hundred yards, give or take, and it traveled atop a winding road. On both sides of the road were dense woods; its trees, though quite tall and well-aged, had yet to tickle the trestle's underbelly. A train had not passed since '69, and it was a rare sight even then. In the spring of the year that Maryellen made my reservation for Dante's Inferno, Cillian walked the trestle … blindfolded!

He did not do it on a dare or bet. What sane person antes up their life as a marker? He simply decided, seemingly out of the blue, that it needed doing.

It was Friday afternoon, the last class of the week, and nearing its end. Minds were drifting; attention spans faltered; we had crossed over into weekend mode. I don't recall who among us asked Cillian, "Hey, whatcha doing tonight?" because they became inconsequential once the reply, "I gonna walk the trestle blindfolded," echoed.

His words were chilling. You see, Cillian did not deliver them in the style of a fantastical claim made with the typical chest-thumping bravura one would expect of a young man not wanting his peers to forget he was the owner of nuts the size of spaghetti squash; quite the contrary. No note of a boast or self-aggrandizement resonated in his tone. Often, when one of us made an outlandish statement, it was drenched in a *you're never gonna believe what I'm about to do*, or, *this will have everyone talking for years,* sort of tenor. On the afternoon in question, Cillian's tone echoed no differently than when he had told us that his parents were going out for the evening and he was housebound with his kid sisters, Karen and Stephanie. Moreover, he did not look any-one's way when he uttered the six words, "I'm gonna walk the trestle blindfolded." His mind seemed elsewhere. Unlike the day Sharon Mill-stein promised her body to Timmy Dwyer if he crossed all twelve lanes of Roosevelt Boulevard blindfolded at rush hour and a blowjob if he did it naked, an ominous quiet fell over our corner of the room. Sha-ron's promise had yielded laughter, as it was her way of trivializing Timmy for pestering her. Cillian seemed oblivious to the weight of the eyes pinned to him. My eyes lifted from Cillian and landed on Joey Brosco, but Joey had already turned his gaze in my direction as if to say: *you seem to know him better than anyone, Addie; is he kidding?* I answered Joey with an indecisive shrug. Though I was being kind: I knew god-damn well Cillian was walking the trestle and intended to do it blind-folded.

By the time school let out, the entire eighth grade had become aware of Cillian's plan, though he did not utter another word on the subject. Amidst all the commotion, he disappeared. He slipped away without being seen or heard. Not yet an hour after school had let out, the entire eighth grade of the parochial school knew of Cillian's plans. I had yet to reach my front door, and Cillian, unintendingly, created mass hysteria among the ranks of the neighborhood's younger teens. Richie Costigan, now a Catholic high school freshman, and Danny Murphy, Richie's seventh-grade neighbor, came tearing up the street when they spotted me. Unable to contain himself, Danny cried, "Is he really gonna do it?" Impatient for a reply, Richie Costigan smugly added, like someone owed an event of epic proportion: "Well, is he?" I gave Richie and Danny the same indecisive shrug I offered Joey Brosco. I gave the same gesture to everyone who asked me about Cillian. My goal was to discourage a crowd from assembling under the trestle, especially one I suspected enjoyed a morbid spectacle, which would come in the form of Cillian plunging to his death. I hoped I would be the only one there, that, come Friday night after everyone had eaten and digested their dinner, all the hubbub would fizzle, and the night would pass uneventfully. When I arrived at the base of the trestle, a crowd of thirty—twenty guys and ten girls seemed the approximate breakdown—were jockeying for position, but there was no sighting yet of Cillian.

"I knew he'd turn out to be a chickenshit," came a shout from a crowd that noticeably swelled in numbers in only the minute-plus since my arrival.

"So, help me," growled Richie Costigan, "if he dragged us down here for nothing, I'll wring his goddamn neck."

"No one *'dragged'* you anywhere." I glared at Richie Costigan. "No one forced you to come, and you didn't buy a ticket." Shifting my eyes upon the rest of the crowd, I said, "You all had other options tonight; no one has a right to act disappointed." Readjusting my glare to Richie, I added, "And as far as wringing Cillian's neck is concerned, I should warn you, he's no one to trifle with."

I hoped my firm tone would hasten the crowd to disperse and move on to do whatever they had in their minds to do before the school week ended, but no sooner than my hostile words filled everyone's ears, Cillian appeared. He did not appear below, as expected, and begin ascending one of the sloped paths of the hill that would bring him to the level of the trestle; he was already *on* the trestle—seemingly out of thin air, with no warning, he appeared!

It was eerie how Cillian was nowhere to be seen, then suddenly there. The ghost of Christmas yet to come would best describe the affectation of his appearance—a phantom extending a robed arm and bony deathlike finger at a grave and daring us to peek. It was unnerving how we were manipulated and victimized by our morbid curiosity. Our fragile, juvenile psyches were shredding right before our eyes.

Heads tilted upward; fingers pointed toward the dusky sky. Cillian, the spectacle, the man of the hour in our mundane lives, seemed oblivious to the crowd below. He wore a white tee shirt and cut-off blue jeans; tied around his face was a black blindfold. The blindfold rested only partway over the bridge of his nose. It marked a small consolation, one preventing my throat from constricting further, for it seemed, from my vantage point, had Cillian shifted his eyes downward—I prayed he planned to—he would know whether he was about to plant a foot on a stout plank of wood or dangle it unsupported. Still, nothing qualifying as sanity was taking place atop the trestle. Then Cillian inserted a well-placed dagger; it went straight into my heart. He grabbed a pair of sunglasses he had hidden in his pants pocket, placed them over the blindfold, and then pressed them firmly over the sockets of his eyes. His eyes could not penetrate the material or utilize their peripheral ability. And shifting his eyes downward was rendered pointless. He was utterly blind! Next came the upturned corners of his mouth. Even at a distance, with my neck straining to keep my head cocked back, I could see Cillian's mouth. Obscured, doubtless, were the downturned corners of his eyes, the signature smile of Cillian James—a strange fusion of the comedy and the tragedy. Would tonight see a tragedy?

Cillian was mocking fate, a life-or-death proposition, and us with that goddamn smile of his—a smile some loved to hate and others came to love. I just wanted him safe and sound on the other side of the trestle so I could kick the living shit out of him—administer the sort of ass whipping sure to make a sonofabitch think twice about pulling such stunts. And Joey Brosco would be right there by my side, getting in a few licks.

And speaking of Joey, he had been standing next to me all along, though I was unaware of his presence until he sauntered away. Joey positioned himself directly below the trestle and a few paces ahead of Cillian. Joey, slowly but steadily, was walking backward and making what seemed, given the occasion, idle chitchat. It took a minute, but I finally caught on to what he was doing or hoping to accomplish. I nearly rushed to his side to join him to make it a collaborative effort, but it occurred to me—and thank goodness it had—if ever there marked an occasion when one voice was better than two, it was tonight.

"Hey, CJ, Carlton is going against Seaver tonight," Joey began. "You won't wanna miss it; their pitching duels are always epic. I brought along my radio, so afterward, we can hike the neighborhood and listen to the game; you, me, and Addie—just like always."

Baseball! It was perfect! A genius idea on Joey's part! Cillian would never catch on to Joey's goal, which was to get Cillian to follow his voice.

"Yeah, that sounds great, Joey; you, me, and Addie—just like always. But how'd you know where to find me?"

I was praying: stay on point, Joey. Don't say anything that will get Cillian rattled or excited. Talk about Schmidt's home run pace, Carlton's earned run average, Theresa Delvecchio's tits—anything you can think of that will keep him walking a straight line!

"Don't you remember, CJ? You mentioned it during our last-period class," Joey reminded him.

I was a bit premature in anointing Joey Brosco as a genius. His effort was veering off course, and I was back to a constricting throat, anticipating a tragedy. *Goddamnit, Joey, don't challenge him!* Like Carlton fastballs, I hurled subliminal messages through the air.

"I did?" Cillian intoned. A clear note of surprise rang down from the trestle. Next, Cillian shrugged. He had no memory of mentioning the trestle and his mad intentions. More clearly than the surprise ringing down from up on high was the notion it was not a show or daredevil stunt we were witnessing. What transpired at a death-defying height was strictly between Cillian and himself. The crowd below, its anxious handwringing notwithstanding, was irrelevant to what engendered Cillian's madness. Then Cillian said, "Hey, Joey, do ya think I'm good enough to try out for the Flying Wallendas?" For Joey's benefit, and mine too—Cillian sensed I was part of the handwringing crowd—had made a plausible attempt at a lighthearted moment. But what transpired atop that trestle was not light of heart and more poignant than a high-wire act. I could sense it, as could Joey.

"Yeah, sure, CJ," said Joey. "I could see you as a Wallenda. But the ballgame is starting in a few minutes."

"I gotta tell you, CJ," I began once our seat reached the bottom and we were preparing to deboard the ride, "I think my Ferris wheel days are over."

"Addie, if you weren't such an atheist, you wouldn't worry so much about dying." Next came Cillian's signature smile: the comedy and tragedy. This time, it was unobscured.

CHAPTER SIX
THE THREE FRESHMEN

For as long as anyone could remember, a particular time-honored tradition persisted at our neighborhood learning institution. None but the highest grade was deemed worthy of entering the school each morning by way of the fire tower. The privilege marked why the rest looked upon eighth-graders as the chosen elite, though it was not an earned privilege unless you consider *not* flunking seventh grade a worthy achievement. Watching from the perspective of an envious kindergartner made it seem that eternity must first pass before walking in the shoes of those who stampeded through *the majestic tower.* Then it happened. One day, you woke up an eighth-grader, buzzing with anticipation and poised to claim your birthright, only to suffer the rudest of introductions: an earthy stench comprised of chalk dust and urine that had accumulated in an unventilated vertical passageway for seven decades. It was a rare combination: chalk dust and urine. Blackboard erasers routinely clapped clean in the fire tower, explained the chalk dust. The urine? Concerning uncouthness, the teenage male has no rival. So much for feeling like the chosen or elite. Worse yet was having to hold your breath first thing in the morning throughout the effort required to climb six flights of stairs, and God forbid you got boxed in behind some fat bastard huffing and puffing after a single flight. It may not have occurred often but could be a real sonofabitch when it did. And after the second flight, wouldn't you know it, the bastard's shirt came untucked. Though thank goodness it had because, after the third flight, a shirttail marked the only barrier between me and the crack of his ass as his pants and boxers faltered. Next came the fourth flight. I could feel heat and sweat emanating from his rotundness—I was swimming in it! By the fifth flight, I developed a hatred for the poor, near-breathless sonofabitch—by the sixth, his parents. Trust me; if there was one thing you never wanted to have happened while still digesting breakfast, it was getting stuck behind Augie Belts in the fire tower. By the end of October, though, I was getting used to it—not Augie Belts, the collaborative stench of chalk dust and urine. And occasionally, for posterity's sake, one felt obliged to leave behind a sample when no one was looking. "Updating the décor" was how we uncouth adolescents described this foulest of practices. It is in no way justification, but if first thing in the morning we had to gag on concrete stairs and subway-tiled walls that have spent the past seven decades absorbing teenage piss, we felt less repulsed, knowing a bit of it was ours.

And so now yours truly is a freshman, a member of the first-ever ninth grade at our proud neighborhood institution. And that old fire tower, which had welcomed deposits of urination since 1906, would have to accommodate double the traffic!

We were a couple of hundred-plus kids gathered in front of a fire tower door in what bore a loose resemblance to a line. It was a lazy line; it staggered and shifted—perhaps "line" is a poor choice to describe what was essentially a cluster. Upon arriving, it was not a conscious effort that Cillian, Joey, and I gravitated toward one another and that this impalpable force that kept us aligned in a tight triangle seemed to divide us from the crowd. We were immersed in the cluster but not part of it. Moreover, our presence created the impression the line, in its psychology—assuming lines can possess such manifestations—was comprised of two factions: us and everyone else. And no air of snobbery was afoot; we did not hover above the fray, less allege any peer unsuited to lengthen or penetrate our triangle; the only prevailing theme was that Cillian James, Joey Brosco, and I were inseparable. We were not a clique, fraternity, or society of three but a triangle of brothers. It would remain as such, not just for as long as some waited while others malingered before entering the fire tower or until lunchtime, for what remained of the day, the first week, or month, but for the entire school year and many years beyond. We did not understand it at first, nor did we seek to capture any attributable essence; we simply allowed whatever was between us, palpable or otherwise, to develop and take whatever shape it was destined to assume. Apart, we were the same old Cillian, Joey, and Addison, but collectively, and in ways that we did not struggle to define, there prevailed a sense we exceeded our years. One might assign the term synergy or some other imperceptible force that generated the undefinable energy that drew us together and sprang from our collectiveness. Nevertheless, it was not present unless all three of us were together—it took a triangle to create the secret sauce.

Joey never said so—not in so many words—but he attributed the uniqueness of our triangle to the night Cillian walked the trestle. Aside from claiming he aged ten years, Joey was never heard bemoaning that night and subtly illustrated that it was the origin of our symbiosis—that despite the madness, something clicked. As each school day unfolded—each day supplying its typical teenage mini-dramas—on the way to becoming a week, and weeks became a month, and a month many months, Cillian, Joey, and I became more aware of the world beyond our immediate scope and the mechanisms of society and, as a result, the basis of our friendship became clearer.

Then, the night of Thursday, January 20th, 1977, arrived: Jimmy Carter made his inaugural speech. The triangle of brothers developed an interest in politics. It was an abstract interest; we did not beat the drum for a particular party or ideology but followed the campaigns of Carter and Ford closely. We did not favor one candidate over the other but could not wait for the debate; it promised to be exciting—it *would* be historical—as it marked the first time presidential candidates agreed to debate on television since Kennedy and Nixon. Okay, it was not Muhammad Ali versus Smokin' Joe Frazier in *The Thrilla in Manila* or Ali versus George Foreman in *The Rumble in the Jungle*; it was two middle-aged white guys, neither of whom appeared capable of throwing a punch, much less taking one, though I recently learned Ford was an athlete; he played college football. Nevertheless, a debate is a contest, a competition, and anything promising a winner and loser is bound to generate excitement.

We decided to watch the debate at my house. After dinner, Darrin listened to Sinatra, Casey and I did homework, Claire toked a little grass—a typical night at the Caldwells—and before long, Cillian and Joey were ringing the doorbell.

The debate began. Claire and Darrin made no attempts to wield any influence; they freed us to take in and process all that was said and draw our own conclusions. Much was discussed on the subject of balancing the budget. Carter championed the concept of taxation as the solution; Ford promoted a less constrained market to generate the necessary revenue. As expected, the notion of market capitalism, a less tethered entity, resulted in Claire squirming how when forced to muddle through an encounter with Rosemarie McNamara. However, concerning the issue of budget-balancing methodology, Ford sounded the more optimistic of the two candidates. Then, like a flash, it hit us: the triangle of brothers understood a debate was a game, and a game is not without gamesmanship and tactics. Gerald Ford was the incumbent; it was his job to sell America the concept the country was in solid financial shape, whereas Jimmy Carter, the challenger, needed to instill a measure of fear and negativity—he had to be mindful of sounding too negative—but that he could rescue us from going to hell in a handbasket or whatever euphemism represents an abyss.

Carter sounded self-assured and intelligent when the debate switched to the topic of energy; there was genuine conviction in his rhetoric. But then he scared the living shit out of everybody when he told us we would run out of oil in thirty-five years. Each of us did the math in our heads and came up with the year 2011, then calculated our respective ages.

"Christ, I'll be *seventy!*" cried Darrin. "Tell me what I might have to do without tomorrow or next week, not in thirty-five years."

I'm with Darrin on that issue. Two thousand and eleven was too far-flung a concept to grasp, especially for a fourteen-year-old in the autumn of 1976. My most pressing concern was when I would be granted access to explore the body of a young female, not when the world would have torn through its supply of fossil fuel. What would Maryellen be like in 2011? Would the world still have Catholics? But Carter did have the right idea—to explore new sources of energy—though it was hardly a needle-mover, politically: Greenhouse gasses and the climate were not hot-button topics in the mid-1970s, a time when we, as a nation, had yet to shake off the ill-effects of our Vietnam entanglement and white-knuckling our way through The Cold War. Carter was also wrong with his "thirty-five-year" prediction; there would be plenty of oil in 2011, but crude—it had entered its fifth decade since becoming a geopolitical dilemma—was falling out of favor.

"I bet we'll have battery-operated jetpacks by 2011," said Joey Brosco. "So, who cares if there's no oil?"

"Or transporter beams," added Cillian.

Both those ideas may sound farfetched, but from a 1976 perspective, eleven years into the next century was not just the future but futuristic! Looking back, it amazes me that we have gone beyond much of what three freshmen, two adults, and a seven-year-old were able to imagine in a living room in the fall of 1976. Hell, even the props once used in science fiction movies and television shows nowadays appear hokey. Captain Kirk's communicator was essentially a flip phone. Who, anymore, has a flip phone?

But it was yet 1976, and the age of technology, as we would come to know it, be it digital or cloud-based, was not in the foreseeable future. But since we are on the subject of technology, when Elizabeth Drew—one of four debate moderators, along with James Gannon, Edwin Newman, and Frank Reynolds—with eight minutes remaining in the debate, asked Jimmy Carter about laws governing federal agencies, we lost the audio feed. Panic tore through the room; even Casey, who favored the challenger because she knew him to be a peanut farmer, was beside herself. We watched NBC, and Claire yelled to me, "Quick, Addie, turn on ABC!" Still, there was no audio. It was the same on CBS; Jimmy Carter's mouth moved, but we could not hear a word.

"Goddamn Japanese televisions," grumbled Darrin. Glowering at Claire, he added, "I told you we shoulda bought an RCA!"

Then, suspecting it could be a technical issue affecting all three networks, Darrin catapulted from his chair to go next door to the McNamaras. He made it to as far as the front door when there stood Guy, wondering whether the issue was with his set or the networks. Both men were grateful their TVs were intact, but no one was happy, and Jimmy Carter was still yammering, one could only suspect, about laws governing federal agencies. Then Carter stopped. The candidates, moderators, and audience were made aware of a technical issue. Before long, David Brinkley broke in and explained to the portion of the nation tuned in to NBC, "The pool audio from the Walnut Street Theater in Philadelphia has been lost." The veteran anchorman could not explain the reason for the loss of audio but hoped restoration would come soon.

"That's *just* dandy," griped Claire. "The nation will have yet another reason to laugh at Philadelphia: first, we throw snowballs at

Santa Claus, then botch the first televised presidential debate in six-teen years!"

Claire had a right to be pissed. We all did. Nineteen hundred seventy-six was the year of the bicentennial; every time you turned around, it seemed Philadelphia, the birthplace of our nation, was staging an event of epic proportions. Thus far, we have done our-selves proud. Tonight, however, was a calamity; it was the political equivalent of the Heidi Bowl. Remember the Heidi Bowl? With sixty-five seconds remaining in what many agreed was an epic battle for the ages between the Oakland Raiders and New York Jets, NBC switched from the game to a previously scheduled program featuring a young girl and her grandfather in the Alps. I do not doubt that Heidi was a lovely girl, but she became public enemy number one as far as American football fans were concerned. The Raiders scored two touchdowns in a span of nine seconds, and no one outside the Oakland Coliseum saw it.

David Brinkley was in the foreground of our television screen and doing his darndest to fill air time. But what could he do? He was no sportscaster. Moreover, Brinkley had to be careful not to give away too much debate analysis; the debate breakdown was what he had planned for the 11:30 nightly news. Meanwhile, the candidates remained behind their respective podiums, stiff as boards and trying to appear unflappable, unlike Richard Nixon in 1960. You could liken them to mannequins or hood ornaments: their podiums were at slight angles pointing toward one another, and they stared straight ahead and did not engage—not each other, the moderators, or the Walnut Street Theater audience—for twenty-six minutes!

"Maybe they're partaking in audio failure protocol," said Cil-lian, "and blankly staring like imbeciles is what they're supposed to do."

"I think Carter is having a worse time trying not to move," said Joey.

The debate resumed, but the mojo was gone. "It's difficult to regain your edge after sitting idle for twenty-six minutes," Darrin told us. The remaining eight minutes were anticlimactic. There was no knockout, knockdowns, standing eight-counts, or reasons to sum-mon a cut man or ring doctor; experts believed Ford won the debate in a split decision.

****

At school the following day, we learned that aside from Sharon Millstein and the faculty—the latter overwhelmingly favored Carter (We would come to understand the world of academia as it relates to politics) —we were "it" as far as who watched the debate. We attempted to discuss it with our "capable educators," but their political views seemed, dare I say, parochial to the point of juvenile. According to them, Democrats are the champions of the weak, poor, sick, underprivileged, and all minority groups—in other words, a band of Robinhoods in neckties; whereas Republicans are malefactors—a sinister clique of elites whose very fiber is comprised of corporate greed owning a prime directive to make sure all the nation's wealth is steered away from workers and funneled to industrial magnates who harbor contempt for the poor and minorities of every stripe.

"Abraham Lincoln was a Republican," Cillian James reminded Mrs. Corcoran, our American History teacher. Thirty heads jerked in Cillian's direction. He managed to do what neither Carter nor Ford could do last night: land a haymaker. Thirty sets of eyes were spinning in their sockets over the notion that the party that spawned Tricky Dick also produced some good guys.

"Where politics is concerned, it's a 'pick your poison' proposition," Darrin told Cillian, Joey, and me after the debate. "It's either corporate greed or union thuggery; don't waste your time looking for good guys or heroes." During our time of political baptism, the Triangle of Brothers learned quite a bit. Knowledge is power, and Cillian wanted to wield it. "It was the Dixie*crats* that held up the passing of the civil rights bill, not the Dixie-*cans*." Cillian was on a roll, and it got everyone's head nodding as if to say: *What about it, Mrs. Corcoran?* Before Mrs. Corcoran dared to open the door to a debate with a bunch of raging hormonal adolescents on the virtues of one party versus the other, she had our noses in a textbook that neither promised to inspire nor provoke. After all, why bother engaging in civil discourse when one has access to a ninth-grade history book?

That left only Sharon Millstein if we wished to confer with anyone over the debate. Sharon was a pretty girl, but not—pillowy lips aside—to the extent of posing a distraction; a guy could engage in a genuine conversation with Sharon without his mind wandering off into dark or forbidden places. It is a helluva skill we guys are pressed to develop: keeping our eye on the ball when our true objective is devouring the hurler of the ball; it's a real high-wire act and one for which we do not receive enough credit. But I digress.

Sharon watched the debate in its entirety and had plenty to add but was anticipating the second debate—the one in San Francisco that would feature the issues of foreign policy and national defense. The candidates were sure to get grilled on the Arab boycott, the threat of an oil embargo, and Israel. Like us, concerning politics, Sharon was still in the process of cutting her teeth and looking forward to steak. She examined issues and policies, *not* from the slant of a party line but like she was taking a blind taste test, and she was not a "fierce" Zionist but did tout a spark for a faraway land that, every day, seemed to make the news.

"Why shouldn't Jews have a state all their own?" Joey Brosco contended. "Catholics have Vatican City; Muslims have Mecca."

Joey made a fair point: the other two monotheisms have a place of pilgrimage; why not Judaism? But Cillian and I assumed, however sincere, Joey was using his modest geopolitical acumen to finagle his way into Sharon's pants.

"I'm just curious to learn whether or not I can tell which of the two candidates, if either, is sincere in their affection for Israel and which is just pandering for the Jewish vote," Sharon said.

Sharon, as would I, failed to detect any pandering. The keen eyes of Joey and Cillian arrived at the same determination. And why would we have suspected otherwise? It was television, time to sharpen the ol' presidential persona for the performance of a lifetime; if anyone lacked a genuine spark of Zionism, or beneath a well-constructed persona there lurked an anti-Semite, it could get revealed tonight in San Francisco should every detail no matter how small, not receive due vigilance; preparation was paramount, nothing would get left to chance: how to stand, positioning of the head, body language, and, lastly, the conviction and measure of resoluteness with which to respond when probed and given a chance for a rebuttal; there is no margin for error in a presidential debate; it's Sinatra nailing it on the first take, or else! After the Nixon debacle in 1960, there was no chance the handlers of these candidates would see their man's antiperspirant fail. Like Al Pacino's icy glare had us all convinced he was Michael Corleone, Jimmy Carter and Gerald Ford would exit the stage having convinced America each could guide her toward a promising future.

The third debate was staged in Memorial Hall on the William and Mary campus in historic Williamsburg, Virginia. The telecast began with, "Good evening, I am Barbara Walters," and ended with Barbara Walters reminding the nation that election day was only eleven days away. Ford pardoning Nixon would prove the kiss of death. The analysis was as follows: instead of distancing himself from Tricky Dick, Ford jumped right back into bed with him, thus rendering the Republicans hopelessly corrupt. For the Democrats, Nixon was the gift that kept giving. Moreover, with Ford facilitating the collateral damage, Jimmy Carter did not need to inspire voters like JFK to get chauffeured to Pennsylvania Avenue.

"Maybe it mattered, maybe it didn't," Claire said. "After Vietnam and Watergate, the country needs a new toy to kick around, and Jimmy Carter doesn't have any dents on him."

The inauguration was a real snore; it was the Oscars without tits. *What do you get when you strip from the Oscars gowns accentuating coveted female anatomy? An inauguration!* Following Carter's address came a parade: it featured a motorcade, color guards, a brass band playing typical patriotic fanfares, our nation's last cavalry platoon, and floats from each state—the floats were either *somewhat* representative of each state or how a given state hoped to alter its image. For example, the Montana float featured Native Americans of the Crow tribe. The Mississippi float represented diversity: the antebellum South was keen on clarifying that civil rights were more than lip service and believed a float in a parade would do the trick. The Kentucky float featured Colonel Sanders. We thought the face of a fast-food chain representing a state known for basketball and horse racing was cheesy. With 184 years of history under its belt, why would Kentucky send a fictitious colonel to Washington, D.C.? It was the equivalent of California and Florida sending Disney characters, which they did not. Then Cillian pointed out, "The Colonel does bear a resemblance to Uncle Sam, and if you were to add that shit-eating grin that causes folks to check if their wallets are still in their back pockets, I doubt you could tell them apart."

Claire was right: we were an angry, unsettled nation—whose recent past was checkered—longing for a pristine future, and Jimmy

Carter hadn't as much as a blemish, never mind any dents. The dents would come. They always do.

And so that ended the political baptism for three inseparable freshmen: two campaigns, three debates, one election, and the pomp and circumstance of an inauguration. We took from the process what we could, then formed the philosophy: Society is a complex archetype comprised of tiers. "It's like a stadium," Cillian illustrated, "only the nose-bleeders and expensive seats are inverted." Indeed, it is a carefully devised system or predetermined pecking order, with all things trickling from the top tier to the bottom, making several stops along the way, and getting picked over until all that's left is bare-bones. This multi-tiered society included a whole menagerie of actors: corporatists and bankers; politicians and union bosses; community organizers and career criminals; educators and clergy; parents and rebellious teens; and, lastly, young children and the feeble. And what is the compulsory outcome of this trickle-down system? Everyone must breathe in what those a tier above exhale, if not forced to stand knee-deep in what they excrete. It's called passing it on or paying it forward. If "The Man" exercises its dominion within the hierarchy, an affected group will take a pound of flesh from those below, often with malice. It's the law of the jungle—take it, or else. Among our peers, Cillian, Joey, and yours truly were the first to the party concerning the laws of the jungle.

We imagined that society was a house of cards, one tier tenuously sitting atop another; it made, in effect, the dominated—the deprived and often unwitting compliers of society—the pillars, the supporters. It is a curious chain of command. Moreover, what would happen to such a structure should a person stray from the collective, fail in their job as a pillar, and dare to become an individual? Worse, what if three had dared—dared to be different, to swim against the current, ignore procedure, refuse to conform? We were neither radicals, Cillian, Joey, and I, nor progressives beating the drum for social justice. And so far as conservatism was concerned, there were no particular virtues or values that we wished to conserve, aside from the basic principle: we wanted no obstacles placed in our path, and, in exchange, we would not serve as obstacles in the paths of others. It seemed a fair-minded ethos, our democratization of the maxim of reciprocity: Let free spirits run free, and they shall not themselves act in any way an impediment. In other words, get the fuck out of our way; we got shit to do!

"I thought I 'stepped in it' by marrying a conservative," Claire lamented. "But now I've gone and raised a Randian!" Claire seemed to be fretting over the question: *Was it me, or was it the world?* before adding, "Can you explain to me, Addie, how *that* happened?"

My predictable reply, "What the fuck's a Randian?" did not settle well in Claire's ears. I was midway through my fourteenth year and on my way, or so I alleged, to becoming fairly astute in matters, but the term "Randian" was unfamiliar. Claire stomped her foot and pointed at Casey, who, in turn, cried out, "Mom, Addie should get a good ass whooping for using the "fuck" word." Claire's effort to glower at Casey for pointing out my foul language by using foul language of her own and then repeating my foul language was comical. The result was the three of us erupting in laughter. "Okay," Claire began—the hippie was making a plausible effort to restore order— "just not in front of your father; we wouldn't want to offend his delicate sensibilities."

Afterward, Claire explained the rudiments of objectivism, otherwise known as the philosophy of Ayn Rand. I told Claire, "I consider myself a Jefferson liberal and a Thomas Paine 'Rights of Man' kinda guy." In other words, human rights are a matter of natural order, not something doled out by a political system or a monarchy. Suggesting that rights "are given" implies they can also be stripped away. After Claire's dismissive shrug to my claim that "Collectivism was bullshit" —for we did traverse the full breadth of the Randian to Marxist or poststructuralist arc—she followed by saying, "You'll change your mind a dozen times between now and the time you're old enough to vote."

Claire's flippant charge annoyed me more than I bothered to express. It seemed to suggest either I did not know my mind (Who wants to hear that concerning their sociopolitical acumen?) or my current stance—given that I was still in the spring of my years— lacked relevance, which was equally demeaning. However, to keep on course what proved a worthwhile dialog, I did not submit too strong an objection. As we were nearing the end of our tete-a-tete, Claire confessed to not being "a fan of Ms. Rand's or objectivism" and that my father had yet to read her books, nor was he up to speed on the philosophy, politics, and life of Ayn Rand. Naturally, Claire's dislike and Darrin's ignorance of Ayn Rand prompted me to dash off to the library for a copy of *The Fountainhead*. Claire called out my name as I was about to run off, but I feigned not being within earshot. Upon arriving at the library, I understood why she called out to me: to warn me—for she had guessed my intentions—that *The Fountainhead* was a 727-page volume. Nevertheless, I brought it home. I may have had to recheck it a time or two, but I read it cover-to-cover—every goddamn word. Did I appreciate every morsel? I was fourteen: the complexities and perverseness of the love triangle that Ms. Rand weaves into her tale of objectivism were, at times, out of reach, but I understood more than enough of *The Fountainhead* to regurgitate the prevailing aspects of the story to Cillian and Joey. I also read aloud to them the courtroom summation of Ms. Rand's hero for objectivism: a man who defended himself against the power brokers of society and the establishment and won. Howard Roark, a fictional architect inspired by Frank Lloyd Wright, became our hero.

But life was not all about presidential elections, heroic architects, or three young men the first among their peers to grasp the laws of the jungle, which state: Everyone must breathe in what those who hold dominion over them exhale and be wary that society's oppressors regard underlings as little more than houseplants to be fertilized with carbon dioxide and a steady diet of bullshit to ensure they develop into obedient servants before venturing off into the world. We were prone to as many lighthearted moments as the rest of our freshman peers. For example, who could forget that day in Mrs. Monk's science class? Poor Sharon Millstein. Incidentally, it was no easy feat to pull one over on Sharon, and she could dish it out as well as she could take it. On the day in question, she turned beet-red and flushed for a week when having to endure our company. As I stated earlier, Sharon was not "tongue to the floor gorgeous," which was Cillian's stock phrase when describing a female able to rouse his saliva glands, but had an unfortunate endowment for one who had to exist among obnoxious hormonal males: unusually plump lips. It should not require explaining why such a feature on a first-year high schooler was more a curse than an asset.

We sat six to a table as the matronly and inexhaustibly dull Mrs. Monk made every effort to dole out the virtues of the biological world.

She was not a subpar purveyor of information, Mrs. Monk. Nevertheless, freshman boys require inspiration, and the 19th century Fraulein and Mary Poppins style dresses Mrs. Monk wore, along with those goddamn orthopedic shoes and the opaque stockings that sagged at the ankle, engendered episodes of abrupt hormonal recession, as did her steel-gray hair pulled back and gathered into a tidy bun. However, her oversimplification of coiffing did smoothen every crevice in her stern and rapidly aging face. If there was even a woman born to wilt an erection, it was Mrs. Monk. Worse, if you came strolling into her classroom flashing anything possessing the facility to amuse: for example, a basketball, soccer ball, pet rock, Swiss army knife, baseball cards, yoyo, magazine, forget about walking in wearing a ballcap, and Heaven help you if you wore it backward, it got instantly confiscated with no chance of retrieval until Friday, and if you dared to protest, the following Friday.

Back to Sharon: Cillian and I told our unsuspecting thick-lipped friend to look under the table upon unzipping our flies and peeling out our eager-for-action shlongs. Did I mention that Sharon turned beet red? Perhaps she thought we were trying to alert her to the presence of a mouse or an untied shoe. You should have seen her face when Sharon resurfaced. And then, of all things, she went down for a second look. Did Cillian and I know it was a doubletake—a knee-jerk reaction to the unthinkable—otherwise, a moment to process another of incredulity? Of course, we did. But all is fair in the world of freshman pranks.

"At least you bastards are circumcised," she fired back at us.

"Was it the first look or the second when you noticed our gentile penises were up to snuff?" Cillian continued to taunt.

"I'm not sure," said Sharon, "but I would have gagged if I saw doinks with screwed-up jackets. I might gag anyway!"

"Sharon," Cillian cried, mustering pride-infused indignation, "I've been growing this goddamn thing for nearly fifteen years; it's way more than a doink."

Afterward, we asked Sharon why Jews bothered making a ceremony out of what was essentially genital modification. We learned Sharon knew as much about what motivated her bullshit monotheistic-based superstitions as we did ours, which was not much. Also, it should get duly noted: despite the intensity of her redness, which led to hiding her face behind her hands for being easily pranked, then frothing over with the laughter of embarrassment, Sharon was a good sport and someone Cillian, Joey, and I, considered a true friend.

It was Cillian's idea: the ol' whip it out under the table trick. He could be a real prankster. But within our triumvirate, he was the most intellectual; Cillian's theories tended to dabble in the abstract— or, as people say nowadays, *he's a real outside-the-box thinker*, but sometimes his mind wandered off to dark and mischievous places. As for yours truly, I supplied the wit and irony. And now for Joey: God only knows how, but he managed to complement Cillian and me; he was the glue that held us together or prevented us, given our dispositions, from becoming a supernova. Somehow, Joey kept us grounded and out of trouble. For example, he convinced us that beating off into a napkin did not qualify as a science project. Joey failed to imagine two wads of jism on a napkin, even if the napkin was a Vanity Fair doily, holding up well against exhibits such as orreries, homemade volcanos able to simulate an eruption, or other elaborate gadget-like projects. "We're not aiming to win first prize for Chrissake," we told Joey. Still, he frowned upon the idea of bodily secretions entered in a science fair.

"What if we forego the napkin and use a slide and microscope; won't that make it a legitimate entry?" I thought I made a persuasive argument, but Joey countered with, "When Mrs. Monk looks into your microscope, she's bound to recognize it for what it is: the cum of two prankster teens! I'm guessing she won't be amused."

"It'll also be the closest she'll have come to jism in decades," I said. "She might be grateful."

"Grateful enough to expel you and CJ," Joey added.

Cillian and I compromised. We drew a diagram of a sperm molecule and called it a day.

There was a fundamental utilitarian aspect to Joey as a leg to our three-legged stool, and it was one for which Cillian and I should have expressed more gratitude. Why? Joey had an innate sense where the proverbial lines in the universe are drawn and would allow us to get close to them—often, Cillian and I teetered on a razor's edge— but never let us cross. Call it intuition, but Joey was born knowing when, or if, a sonofabitch's buttons could be pressed, how often, and when enough was enough. Joey also functioned as a peacemaker, arbiter, and intermediary and understood that certain people could remain in one another's orbit only so long without violently colliding. Whatever Joey lacked in size, and size-wise, he was what the prideful Irish Cillian would call "a wee lad," he more than made up for with instinct. And Joey also had a subtle way of letting you know when he was disappointed in you. I mean, when he wanted to, Joey could make you feel like shit, and it was unlike how you felt when, for example, your parents expressed disappointment. After all, they are your parents; you're supposed to clash and afterward not give a rat's ass. With Joey, it was like having your favorite uncle or grandparent tell you that you were a no-good sonofabitch. It would really sting!

****

On Tuesdays, Wednesdays, and Thursdays, Cillian, Joey, and I granted ourselves permission to skip Spanish class. We were the first-ever ninth grade at our seventy-year-old institution, and many of us had a class—be it health, gym, Spanish, or art—that, simply put, we mailed in. Our school of thought concerning Spanish was as follows: Class on Monday, finagle our way through the next three days, test on Friday. We considered it a waste of time to be pinned to a wooden chair for those three hours conjugating verbs, sometimes saying them aloud in a bullshit Spanish accent, when all the necessary information was in a textbook and would require seven minutes of study and that's if you were un-caffeinated. Some classes make the procedure of sponging up information in a fixed location seem antiquated, and Spanish marked one. My theory was as follows: if speaking Spanish were our true destiny, God would have made us Spaniards. Cillian and Joey appreciated my rationale but reminded me, "You're an atheist, Addie; God had nothing to do with your creation."

Okay, so maybe I occasionally referenced God when I required an assist to hammer home a point; that hardly makes me a theologian, and I sure as hell am not a closet worshipper, if that's what you're thinking. But the real reason we skipped Spanish class and not health, art, or gym? Mr. Valdez. Since Spanish saw its introduction to the curriculum, he was the school's first Spanish teacher who owned Spanish as a first language, thus had an opportunity to represent the welcomed change everyone desired—it was refreshing to finally hear Spanish flow effortlessly instead of the strenuously cobbled and mechanical version Mrs. Fritz used to speak—but Mr. Valdez was repulsive. He was displeasing to look at and worse to be near. Either he never washed his coffee-brown hair or combed Crisco through it; we were unsure of which, though both were sufficient reasons to grimace. His mustache was too big for his gaunt face—a face never unblanketed with the stubble of a five-day-old beard, which included noticeable flecks of white. But worse than his hair, oiliness, and gauntness—features loaning him the appearance of a tramp not unfamiliar with spending nights beside an exhaust vent—was how painfully obvious Mr. Valdez tried to mimic the mannerisms of Vito Corleone; he must have spent hours studying the character. What made his effort laughable? Mr. Valdez was all knees and elbows, making him much better suited to mimic Fredo; he even sounded like John Cazale, if you could imagine John Cazale speaking Spanish, though the person the swarmy Mr. Valdez put everyone most in mind of was Cheech Marin.

Mr. Valdez would hand out mimeograph papers: a column of verbs requiring conjugation was on the left side. Afterward, he would say the verbs aloud. Then, like good Spanish aspirants, we would parrot him, cumbersomely rolling our tongues to fight through our Philadelphia accents, hoping to develop a more suitable Spanish one. Handwriting a list of conjugated verbs was not so bad when Mr. Valdez, as he was prone to do during the course of the day, sauntered across the hall to Ms. Moskowitz's room, where we imagined him coaxing her into a coat closet hand job. Ms. Moskowitz taught Greek Mythology and was thought a suitable match for Mr. Valdez, who seemed quite flirty whenever she hovered. When remaining with us, Mr. Valdez developed the annoying habit of strolling the room's aisles; he would stop and lean over our shoulders—you could sense his chin inches away—and his breath was in accord with his appearance. And those teeth! The man must have drunk God knows how many cups of coffee per day and smoked a thousand cigarettes! The stench hit us no sooner than we breached the doorway to the classroom; it was set in his clothing and Crisco-combed-through hair, creating an aura that would have given the CEO of Philip Morris a boner!

So off we would go to the gymnasium, Cillian, Joey, and I, skipping out on an imposing hygienic catastrophe every Tuesday, Wednesday, and Thursday. At the gym, we would unroll a mat, and on it, Cillian and I would beat the living shit out of one another. We enjoyed wrestling, grappling, getting clinched up, and going mano a mano. I suppose adopting wrestling as our chosen method of expending all our surplus teenage energy and anxiety qualified us as a couple of Neanderthals. And we went "full tilt" when grappling on the mat; it was a real take-no-prisoners affair; we scrapped with fury and passion until our bodies were battered, wrecked, our lungs near breathless, thus rendering us unfit to crawl off the mat and mimicking horseshoe crabs washed up on the shore. Strange, but these donnybrooks were a tribute to our friendship and how we expressed our affections. Neither of us would dare hold back. If one of us gained an edge in a match, we rode the advantage unmercifully. Holding back and showing mercy would equate to a lack of trust in friendship or that our bond was not strong enough to survive a good old-fashioned ass-whooping. Cillian and I would have preferred getting pinned in ten seconds than to lose that undefinable *whatever it was* that made our friendship special.

Bent and broken, the horseshoe crabs would press Joey, the referee, to render a decision. Aside from the rare instances when one of us got thrashed, Joey weaseled out of rendering a verdict and declared the match a draw.

"I was too busy refereeing to tell who had the advantage," he would moan. If we continued to press him, he would say, "CJ, that was some armbar you were riding," or, "Addie, I didn't think CJ would ever break that half nelson, the way you had it locked up." But he never awarded either of us a match unless it was an all-out thrashing, and then we didn't require a decision. Then, before heading back to class, to make him feel included, Cillian and I would grab Joey and rough him up a bit; sometimes, we would roll him up inside the mat and threaten to leave him. He suspected it was coming but was a good sport. But I should warn you: Joey Brosco is no one to trifle with. Pound for pound, he's as tough a sonofabitch as you'll find. With all his gnarliness and hairiness, he's akin to a piece of scrap iron, and everything concerning Joey Brosco's appearance screamed Sicilian; he was getting disposable razors in his Christmas stocking before he knew how to beat off.

So that was Cillian James, Joey Brosco, and yours truly: the best thing we had going for us in those days was our three-way friendship, which we valued and honored equally.

CHAPTER SEVEN
REVEALING MY SUMMER PLANS

The calendar turned and ushered in the year 1977. On his way out the door, President Ford pardoned Iva Toguri D'Aquino, otherwise known as Tokyo Rose. "Tokyo Rose" was a name that allied troops fighting in the South Pacific during World War II gave to a group of female English-speaking radio broadcasters spewing Japanese propaganda. The only "Tokyo Rose" the U. S. Department of Justice was interested in was Iva Toguri D' Aquino, a woman whose radio handle was "Orphan Ann." An American citizen, Toguri D' Aquino—before the attack on Pearl Harbor—traveled to Japan to care for a sick aunt, only to find herself trapped there because of the outbreak of war. Moreover, because of her American status, she was ineligible to stay with relatives, nor could she receive aid or provisions from her family as they got placed in an internment camp in Arizona. So Iva Toguri D' Aquino took a job as a typist at a radio station before getting promoted to the airwaves.

"The poor woman flies halfway around the world to care for a sick aunt, and before she knows what hit her, she's charged with treason? If ever there was a circumstance that careened out of control and kicked someone in the teeth, it was that one," I told Cillian and Joey.

"Sounds like a case of relatives in Japan not especially keen on going out on a limb for her," said Joey. "I mean, for Chrissake, Germans, at the risk of being shot on the spot, hid Jews in attics and cellars; how goddamn hard could it have been to hide a Japanese American woman in Japan!"

Not to be outdone, the incoming president, before his first presidential cup of coffee had a chance to cool, assuming Jimmy Carter drinks coffee, pardoned Vietnam War evaders. Upon reading this news, Darrin shrugged and conceded, "I guess it's the right thing to do. After all, who wanted to cough up his life over what many, nowadays, acknowledge was a mistake."

"Gee, look who finally showed up at the party," Claire ironically intoned. "Mr. *Death to All Communists* naps through an entire movement and wakes up with a burst of clarity. Who says old dogs can't learn new tricks?"

Claire was in rare form when learning President Carter pardoned the Vietnam War evaders. Euphoric, rhapsodic, in a state of orgasmic joy that a wrong she championed against was finally put right best described her mood. And I could feel it coming. Claire would begin gyrating around the dining room table like Jagger any second. She did not disappoint; however, it remained to be seen if this latest episode would end similarly to all her spasmodic episodes: the massacring of dinner.

Unfortunately, war is a human consequence with an inevitability rate only paralleled by death, taxes, and gravity. The North Vietnamese were back on the warpath: this time, they were squaring off against forces that had allied with them against the U.S.-backed South Vietnamese.

"It's hard to imagine they have enough soldiers left to begin another initiative," Darrin intoned. "It seemed like we killed the population of North Vietnam five times over."

"And that's precisely why a jungle war with a country allied with China marked a prime example of stupidity," Claire retorted.

If the Vietnam/Cambodian affair seemed convoluted, it was because the nations themselves were convoluted. Vietnam invaded Cambodia, or Democratic Kampuchea—the new name given by the communist faction "The Khmer Rouge" —and removed The Khmer Rouge from power. Which side was reading from the playbooks of Marx, Lenin, and Mao, and whether Communism, National Socialism, or fascism was the prevailing theme: who knows? What did we learn? Three hundred thousand died, not including God knows how many from starvation. The U.S. had no involvement.

"That's the way to handle Communism," said Cillian. "You leave it alone and wait until it trips over its own weight. It's like chickenpox—a disease that has to run its course. So you sit and wait, and before long, watch them kill each other over the bones in the street or hunt cats and dogs, assuming the cats and dogs haven't already cannibalized one another."

"What about when Communists acquire yellowcake uranium and know how to build nuclear warheads," Joey asked. "Do you still sit and wait?"

Joey Brosco had a knack for lowering the boom on a discussion. So from Southeast Asia—where, according to Darrin, what hastened Communism was an overreaction to French colonialism—to the Soviet Union, our Cold War adversary, we went, the U.S.S.R. representing the one place on earth capable of striking genuine fear into the hearts of Americans. The perception was as follows: if the Far East symbolized an occasional flare up of gout, the Middle East a case of chronic angina, then The Soviet Union was cancer, the big C, and Joey decided we were staring into an abyss, otherwise a King Kong-sized dose of radiation. We were terrified the Soviets had better weapons than the U.S. and convinced their scientists, who had names we were unable to pronounce because they utilized every goddamn consonant in the alphabet, knew more than ours. The Cold War was a game of high-stakes poker, and not knowing what the Soviets had in their hand or up their sleeve loomed as a terrifying proposition.

And then Elvis died: not the day we were fretting over the possibility of a nuclear holocaust; "The King" would die later that summer when Cillian, Joey, and I were hundreds of miles away on a farm in Western Pennsylvania, where, as I stated at the outset, the unimaginable happened. Darrin called to talk about it and began with the glum question, "I guess by now you heard." I could hear the sadness in my father's voice. Also, I detected a trace of alarm, leading me to assume David Berkowitz, a.k.a. The Son of Sam, who had been in police custody for six days, escaped.

"Heard what, Dad?" I asked.

"Elvis died," he said.

"How'd he die?" I asked. There was silence on the other end. What followed was several inarticulate grunts. Then Darrin uttered, "You know how it is nowadays … the way people die."

People have always died and managed this inevitability in all sorts of ways. Were they doing it differently "nowadays?" Was there an "in" way of achieving this human certainty? I decided the phone call marked an occasion that called for sensitivity—for taking the high road; thus, I would not force my father to spell out for me in plain English that "The King," Elvis Pressley, a man who became the face of a movement—rock-n-roll—that swept my father's generation and gifted it a slice of Americana they embraced passionately, died senselessly from a drug overdose.

"Sorry to hear it, Dad," I said.

"Your mother is inconsolable." I had never heard my father sound so glum. Doubtless, Claire was locked in their bedroom, employing a dainty thumb to tamp down the pinch of marijuana she had placed in her handy bowl and was getting ready to fire up. To interject some lightheartedness and buoyancy into the conversation, I said, "Dad, isn't Sinatra your go-to guy?"

"Frank," Darrin began—my father and Sinatra were on a first-name basis— "is, and always *will* be, my go-to guy for sheer musical pleasure. But Frank was only good enough to get you to first base. But if you were a young man with a set of wheels and had aspirations of getting to second base or seeing what was under the hood, you better hope Elvis's voice was broadcasting." The cheesy car and baseball metaphors meant that Casey was nearby if not right at Darrin's elbow.

Elvis's iconic status never diminished, but as the body count mounted in Vietnam, the pendulum swung from rock stars able to sing girls out of their skirts toward rockers whose principal themes were antiestablishment or anticapitalistic—otherwise, music with an intellectual and thought-provoking bent. It never occurred to me to wonder whether Maryellen was an Elvis Pressley fan. Nevertheless, it's challenging to imagine songs like *Love Me Tender*—which sounds more like a funeral dirge than a ballad—inspiring a separation of girl and skirt. I would think a number such as *Love Me Tender* would strand a guy at first base, if not lull him to sleep to where he might get picked off and have to slink back to the dugout to a cascade of boos.

Speaking of getting stranded on first base or picked off, Joey Brosco began the typical northeast January "hot under the collar." If you knew Joey, you would understand why. The Phillies parted company with their all-star second baseman, Dave Cash. You could cite Dave Cash being Joey's favorite player as cause for his huffiness; after all, no one ever likes to see their favorite player traded away; it nearly broke my heart two years ago when the Phils told Willie Montanez it was time to pack his bags; though, eventually, I learned to appreciate

Gary Maddox and saw the value of the trade. *Thanks for your service, fella, but I think we can do better.* Dave Cash departing after instilling a winning attitude by way of Pittsburgh—Cash infused an organization and fanbase that were perennial cellar-dwellers with the slogan: YES, WE CAN—marked additional cause for a disgruntled Joey Brosco. But what was the real reason behind Joey's rankled state? Joey had shoeboxes upon shoeboxes of baseball cards and a system in which he had them arranged. Concerning seasons past, Joey had players placed in either number order—each baseball card is designated a number—or by position. Joey organizes the current year's cards by team, and the order is as follows: manager, coaches, starting lineup, bench players, starting pitchers, and lastly, the relievers, all nice and tidy in rubber bands—Joey is careful that the rubber bands are not so tight that they damage a card. The current year's shoebox was like a miniature filing cabinet featuring dividers labeled National League East, National League West, American League East, and American League West. Also, teams were not haphazardly placed in their respective divisions but in the position where they currently stood in the standings; thus, this mini filing cabinet required constant updating. And then, as sometimes happens, a player gets traded and screws up Joey's system. It especially rankled him when a player got dealt after the current year's cards made it to print. Dave Cash, rubber-banded in with a bunch of Expos while in a Phillies uniform, did not set well with Joey. Moreover, the Phils' quest for a new second baseman gave Joey a Dodger-blue-clad Ted Sizemore and a red and white uniformed Johnny Oates migrating to the Dodger pile. For Joey, this was chaos on too grand a scale.

"What the hell do the Phils want with Sizemore, anyway?" he griped. "He's a .260 hitter on his best day. Cash could hit .260 standing on one leg, for Chrissake!"

You could tell Joey that his house was on fire or someone kidnapped his dog, but don't tell him a ballplayer got traded in-season or after the current year's cards were printed.

Joey was not the only one showing the wear and tear of aggravation in recent days and was not shy about lending it a voice. Ol' Darrin Caldwell has been treating his family to what Claire Caldwell referred to as "Your father's nightly bitch-fest."

"And here I thought only women were cursed with menstrual cycles." Those were the words Claire uttered while looking my way after Darrin finished ranting: "We've got double-digit inflation, you can't buy a house unless you're a millionaire, national pride is sinking like the Titanic, we're spending a fortune on The Cold War, the Saudis have us over a barrel—no pun intended—Detroit's getting its ass kicked every quarter by the Japs and their tin rat traps with lawnmower engines and go-cart wheels, nowadays you can't even apprehend a serial rapist without someone hollering 'police brutality,' and what do you hear out of the mouth of every Tom, Dick, and Harry? 'Did you see Star Wars?' All day and every day, it's the same bullshit! While the country's going to the dogs, all its citizens are at the goddamn movies!"

Either the United States is the world's worst country or has the best dogs. I must confess to not wrestling with this dilemma for long because Claire, with her gaze now turned squarely on Darrin, distracted me when crooning: "Aww, poor baby; did the office girl forget to give you a hand job today? I *must* have a talk with her." Before Darrin could respond to Claire's condescending irony, she added, "Does your little wifey need to take care of her big, strong hubby right away, or can it wait until after dinner?"

Claire sprang from her chair, stood over Darrin, and dipped her hand below the table for what must not have been the friendliest of squeezes if my father's face was any indication, and Darrin was no poker player.

"Go ahead and laugh if you must," Darrin continued to gripe, "but kids are coming out of college and going right into the old man's business because they're not finding the opportunities promised, entrepreneurship is sagging, and between the Soviets, Arabs, and Japs, treating us like a pinata, our nation's resolve is beginning to wither— our once-robust country is starting to resemble your sister." Claire's sister, my Aunt Jessie, was one of those women subscribing to the philosophy: you can't be too rich or too thin, so she hoarded away every penny she came by and dieted and exercised her way to a flat chest and boney ass. Secretly, I believed, Aunt Jessie despised being a woman. In that respect, she was ahead of her time. Moreover, had the medical procedure been accessible to the middle class, Aunt Jessie would have been my uncle. Then Darrin further ranted, for, evidently, our nation hyperbolically characterized as a geopolitical pinata was insufficient,

"Half the globe is lining up because they think they have a free shot at our nuts!"

"Yes, dear," Claire broke in, making every effort to affect a mocking tone. "If there's one redeeming feature upon which the 70s can hang its hat, it isn't the 60s."

"Damn right, the 70s isn't the 60s! Especially if the measuring sticks are jobs and economic growth," Darrin crowed. "It's also been a bit lean concerning assassinations." The last remark was not as much an add-on as it was a stinging retort by Darrin Caldwell, and down went Claire Caldwell's all-time favorite president, attorney general, and civil rights leader. The trifecta!

Claire, momentarily, was too dumbfounded to point out that increased government spending by an average of three percent per year to fund social welfare programs, plus the Vietnam War, resulted in low unemployment and a stable economy. In contrast, the war ending created a scenario for inflation, and when piling on an energy crisis, the result was a noteworthy economic recession. But Claire Caldwell did not remain buried for long. Recovering nicely from the ironical manner in which Darrin alluded to the lives of Jack Kennedy, Robert Kennedy, and Martin Luther King cut short, she intoned, "Did you have anyone in mind? Is there anyone you feel deserves a fatal bullet?"

It was no rhetorical question that Claire posed; she was rightfully curious to learn whose life or lives her husband wished to see snuffed out. It stands to reason such knowledge would rank among the many items one might care to discover about the person with whom they routinely bed down. Knowing who someone wants dead can speak volumes about a person. That's always been my theory, one from which many inferences can be drawn and gained. But instead of disclosing to Claire a shortlist of those he idealized for a worldly exit, Darrin let loose a throat-clearing sound clarifying his exasperation. Then, shifting his eyes in my direction, he offered a sneer. Why, might one ask? According to Darrin, I had shown myself remiss in displaying an appropriate measure of guilt and shame. In other words, I failed to grind through my day like the weight of the world was sitting squarely on my shoulders, nor had I aligned myself, if only ostensibly, with his numerous vexations. *How dare I!* I shrugged back at Darrin in a manner sufficiently intimating: *Am I no longer living in a free society? Is it not within my right to look and feel happy? Must I stress over double-digit inflation or go to pieces on the chance that the Soviet nuclear arsenal might be better at obliterating the planet than ours? Would it somehow serve the greater good if I walked around wringing my hands with dismay that the Japanese were giving the world what it wanted: fuel-efficient cars? or bleeding out of my eyes because I reside in an energy-dependent country, frustrated that Arabian oil barons control the flow of their assets and manipulate the market?* Indeed, not only does my citizenship grant me the right not to live in a constant state of fretfulness, but I also wield the right not to breathe in what others exhale nor stand knee-deep in whatever they excrete.

It seems that because the land of opportunity has yet to reach the pinnacle of perfection, it must suffer denigration from everyone with a tongue in their mouth; the whole nation, from the Atlantic to the Pacific, from the Mexican border to the Canadian, wakes up in bitch mode, and we have managed to convince ourselves that our gripe du jour is something everyone within earshot cannot wait to hear. If someone isn't spouting the notion that *the government is a corrupt, self-serving entity*, then its *ballplayers are making too much damn money*. Everyone wants a first-class education and five-star service but with as little appropriation as possible. In other words, the country should run on pixie dust, and no one should experience a moment's inconvenience.

Casey had just walked into the room when I announced to Darrin and Claire, "I have a job lined up this summer." Casey's appearance and the sharing of new information thwarted Darrin and Claire's political tete-a-tete before it reached the point of exhaustion.

"You do?" Incredulity chased away the vexations responsible for Darrin's sour demeanor. The sudden shift from assassination, interest rates, and worldwide instability to employment also caused him to lurch forward in his chair. Bewilderment surfaced not because I had a job lined up but because I took the initiative and made an effort before he had the opportunity to hound me over what I planned to do this summer other than slumming. "Slumming" was Darrin's stock word for doing nothing, which I mostly did with my "do-nothing" friends last summer. Sure, I did some odd jobs. We all did something for a bit of spending cash, but I didn't commit to anything steady. Concerning work, I was not what you would call "a commitment" kinda guy. The upcoming summer would mark a paradigm change.

Aside from incredulity registering on Darrin's otherwise pale, conservative American face, condescension also resonated. *So, hotshot, tell us all about this "job" you landed* were the words encrypted in the succinct reply, "You do?" Perhaps Darrin assumed I signed up to clean the park stables with free horseback riding as compensation or had agreed to tutor girls in English literature in exchange for hand jobs? The latter would not be an altogether bad proposition, given that nowadays, they don't play Elvis on the radio as regularly as they did back in Darrin Caldwell's heyday. Next, I noticed Darrin taking a moment to examine me. His eyes began at the floor and slowly shifted upward until they reached that blank area known as a forehead, although that area, at the moment, was furrowed in thought. What did he notice? I no longer had the face of a boy. I was no macho man, either; it was a case of subtle changes elbowing boyishness aside to make room for the early stages of manhood. Joey Brosco, the hairy sonofabitch, would perform thorough examinations of my face probing for a single whisker. He would go about it with the diligence of an explorer searching for some lost tribe of the Amazon, only to regretfully intone, "Sorry, Addie, not yet. But there's the tiniest dot on your chin where a hair might sprout... say, in six months. A tweezer will do the trick; I'm sure you can borrow a pair from your mother."

Okay, so I wasn't ready for Gillette, but my face looked more masculine than a year ago. As Darrin continued to take stock of his firstborn, he also realized we were the same height, though I still had a wiry teenage frame compared to his thicker-set adult one. Recognition and pride flashed in his eyes. What followed was a look of bemusement. *When did all this occur?* was what I managed to gain from his expression. *Doubtless, while you were busy distressing like a mental patient over the Soviets, Arabs, and Japs passing around a stick to beat a pinata commonly known as the United States,* I would have been inclined to answer had he posed the question aloud.

"So where will you be working, Addie?" Claire finally asked. I should not be so hard on Claire; she showed genuine enthusiasm that I would spend my summer working: Working, earning money, learning responsibility—in other words, growing up.

"On a farm in Western Pennsylvania," I unhesitatingly blurted out. I expected Darrin and Claire to shrug me off, a gesture expressing: Okay, Addison, nice joke, but where will you *really* be working this summer? But there was no shrugging or gesturing of any kind accusing me of dismissiveness. Instead, you could almost see the air leaving the room and how its absence made Darrin's and Claire's chests heavy. Finally, Casey, who seemed insensible to the abrupt shift in mood, wondered aloud: "Western Pennsylvania, like where the Amish people live?"

I was unaware that Casey knew about Amish folks, never mind where they lived. I was impressed with my kid sister, and it made me sorry to disappoint her that the farm upon which I would spend the summer exerting myself was a bit farther west than where the clan-like Amish of Pennsylvania huddled.

"Western Pennsylvania, as in fifty miles north of Pittsburgh," was what I apologetically told Casey. I kept my eyes pinned on my kid sister. Why? It was unnecessary to look Darrin's way or Claire's; their reactions, however precious, were predictable.

Upon recovering a portion of his wits, Darrin managed to formulate the question, "Just how in the hell were you able to apply for, never mind land, a job on a farm three hundred miles away?"

Aggressively, Claire lurched forward in her chair. The purpose behind her abrupt action was clear but rare: to display solidarity with Darrin. Claire did not come out and verbalize the cheesy add-on: *Yeah, hotshot, how'd you pull that one off?* She was not one to excel in the role of the lackey gangster parroting the command of their boss. *Whudda, you, a wise guy? Hey, you heard the boss; are you a wise guy?* Often, Claire Caldwell lets her actions speak for themselves.

"I didn't need to apply," I said, nodding first to Darrin, then to Claire. "The job, you might say, fell into my lap."

The opportunity to act cryptically does not often arise. Revealing my summer plans gifted me an occasion, so I indulged in it. Did I milk it beautifully? I sat back, arms folded, grinning like a son-ofabitch, and watched Darrin and Claire exchange one perplexing glance after another. *What could he possibly mean by not having to apply for a job and it falling right into his lap? He can't be serious! That sorta thing can't happen. Can it? And a farm three hundred miles away; a city kid: what does he know about farming?* Their glances conveyed all that and more. For a switch, it was amusing to watch them struggle to draw into their lungs and utilize for oxygen what ol' Addison Caldwell had exhaled while standing knee-deep in what yours truly excreted. Life, if we show ourselves alert, giftwraps its share of surprises.

"How can a job so far away as fifty miles north of Pittsburgh fall into yours or anyone's lap?" It was a legitimate question Claire posed, and it deserved a sincere answer. For how *does* one, particularly a young man going into his sophomore year of high school, land a job clear across the state? Anyone would allege the notion as wildly far-flung. But then, right on cue, Darrin went and fucked it up by growling like a goon, "Yeah, how?"

Poor Darrin; whenever Claire took the initiative, he slid neatly into the role of the lackey gangster—a typical minus-80 IQ parroting subordinate; the poor man could not help himself any more than rain can change its trajectory. I let loose a near-inaudible chortle backed by the sort of smirk deserving of a backhand. Darrin knew my laugh and smirk were at his expense but not why, which made it beautiful. But I had carried the gag long enough; it was time to unfold my arms, assume a humbler posture, and come clean.

"CJ has people over in Western Pennsylvania, and they have a farm," I began. "The old man, CJ's Uncle Dave, kicked the bucket recently, and his Aunt Leila, who was Uncle Dave's second wife, needs help this summer, and so she called CJ's folks, hoping to recruit him and that he could convince a couple of his friends to cough up their summer."

"Second wife?" Why Darrin became fixated on this Leila woman being Cillian's dead Uncle Dave's second wife was beyond me. Whether she was the first, second, or tenth, any wife would still be an aunt through marriage.

"Men *have* been known to remarry," Claire interjected.

Claire broached the subject in a coddling manner; the intention was to mock Darrin's conservatism and illustrate that men tend to remarry and do so swiftly because they are quick to evaluate the extent of their inadequacies once widowed. It's their shortcomings that hasten the acquisition of another mate. "Men are all penis and ego," Claire asserted. "If either or both aren't constantly stroked, a man becomes miserable and tyrannical—his chemicals go rancid, and his brain heats until it cooks itself."

"Oh yeah?" Darrin countered. "Well, I know a few stone-faced widows that would benefit greatly from having what to stroke!"

The conversation took an unexpected turn in the form of Darrin and Claire bickering over the dual dilemma of who would be swiftest to remarry or carry on most effectively without the other. Then again, perhaps it was not so unexpected. Claire and Darrin had a knack, a gift, for engaging in what began as an all-inclusive discussion and whittling it down to the two of them going toe-to-toe over territorial bullshit. It took Casey asking me, her face twisted in consternation, "You'll be gone for the whole summer?" to get us back on topic. "You mean you won't even be able to come to the seashore with us?"

It never even occurred to me that Casey would miss me. I was nearing the end of my freshman year of high school and, like most young men at this stage of their life, I was wrapped up in writing my coming-of-age story, which thus far included the camaraderie of good friends but was a touch light concerning a sexual awakening. Lately, I hardly noticed Casey; I cannot remember when last I asked, *Hey, Case, how was your day?* or engaged her in anything that qualified as a meaningful exchange. Of late, it's been, *pass the potatoes*, or, *how long are you gonna be in the bathroom*, and little else. Christ, I was feeling guilty!

"Hey, that's right!" Darrin interjected. Nearly parroting Casey, though without sounding like a lackey gangster, he added, "You *won't* be able to come to the seashore with us, and it wouldn't be worth your while, at such a distance, to come home on weekends. And if you did, you'd spend half your wages on bus fare."

"So when will you be leaving us?" Claire asked.

Claire's words had no resonance of a woman anxious to be rid of her teenage son for the better part of a season; less were there any lingering notes of curiosity in her tenor. On the contrary, thus she sat patiently awaiting my reply, her eyes swollen with anticipation. Claire's anxiousness over the day of my departure stemmed from wanting to know how much time we would have together. Claire Caldwell may have toked grass, strutted like Jagger, and has yet to learn of a protest she would not back, but first and foremost, she was a mother and, by all accounts, a good one.

"I leave the morning after the last day of school and won't return until just before Labor Day," I told her. My words were resolute and confident; I strung them together without hesitation. I felt myself surging, my status elevating to near adulthood. After all, I was traveling hundreds of miles to join the ranks of the gainfully employed. My posturing caused Darrin and Claire to recoil.

"That's your entire summer vacation!" I was unsure why Darrin deemed it necessary to indicate that the day after the final day of school until Labor Day would account for my whole summer. Perhaps he wanted to plant second thoughts in my head or preferred that I work stocking shelves in one of the local food markets. Then, with a wave of a hand and a lighthearted tone meant to bring the room back into harmony, I said, "It'll do me good, for a change, to have a new experience, to get away from the city."

It did the trick; the restoration of harmony ensued; even Casey was climbing on board with the notion of her big brother gaining a new experience. But just as the party was breaking up, I was reminded that I was still at home and that my last name was Caldwell. Grinning like a sonofabitch, Claire turned to Darrin and stated, "Just for the record, Old Blue Eyes wouldn't be worthy of an assassination—in *either* decade."

CHAPTER EIGHT
CATCHING THE LATE TRAIN

It was late May. I believe it was a Tuesday, though it could have been a Wednesday; I am only sure of the month. I swing by Cillian's place; he is waiting for me outside; there is no doubt concerning that detail. Why am I sure of this seemingly inconsequential aspect and not the day? Cillian seems anxious and jittery, as if he cannot flee from the vicinity of his house fast enough. I grow sensitive to the misgiving of Cillian waiting outside—he is leaning on the porch railing and facing the street—that he does not want me anywhere near the front door. Either he fears I might disturb something or become troubled by what I might witness should I make it to as far as the door and ring the bell. I do not press Cillian on this matter. There is no need; it figures to be a long night, and if he wishes to unburden himself, there will be ample time and opportunity. We are on our way to Joey Brosco's place for supper.

Originally, supper at the Brosco's was not part of the plan, but the more we thought about it, the more appealing it became, and ultimately, it would prove to be a bonus.

The three of us skipped school the day before. Sometimes, we would do that, take a day to ourselves. When you are an adult, it's called *taking a personal day*; teenage boys have yet to assign a name for this practice and thus are stuck with the delinquency: cutting class. It was no big deal these self-awarded "personal days." Because our attendance record was solid, we could afford an occasional luxury, though this latest episode saw us miss a pop quiz in English literature. And there we sat, the three of us, after school, in Mrs. Hargrove's class, where we were each assigned a desk on the room's perimeter, our coordinates forming an Isosceles triangle. It was overkill, and Mrs. Hargrove knew it. If we sat in the same vertical row, a desk apart, it would have proved sufficient to discourage cheating, but Mrs. Hargrove's goal was to deliver a stark message to us indulgers of self-assigned privilege. Either that, or she was on her period. With some teachers, you knew the second you crossed the threshold into their classroom whether or not they were menstruating, and there was nothing more unnerving than being issued a makeup exam by an irritable, bleeding woman constrained in a power suit.

At most, it was a half-hour exam—assuming one was conscientious—consisting of nine factual questions, three divergent questions, two higher-order questions, and an essay question on Steinbeck's *Of Mice and Men.* The order of the questions was scattered, but the essay, as always, came at the end. For fifteen minutes, no one made a sound. It was not until I heard Cillian's humming, which was on the order of puttering, that I realized it joined another incoherent noise: the one I was making. I was unsure whether we were humming independently or if one of us subconsciously followed the other. Then, of all things, Cillian blurts out, "Number nine's a trick question."

My head snapped upward with such force I was astonished that it remained on my shoulders. Warily, I shifted my gaze to Mrs. Hargrove, expecting to witness daggerlike sparks shooting from her eyes. To my surprise, she was calm. Had she failed to hear Cillian raise his voice? She mustn't have. So much for my ability to gauge a woman's menstrual cycle. I glanced over at Joey and could tell from the position of his hand he had yet to reach the ninth question, which asked: *Curley's wife is not given a name. What is the most likely reason Steinbeck does this?* All the choices involve Curley and his wife's character, and they are a couple of real sonofabitches. Curly was your typical Napoleon-complex-type bully who could push everyone's buttons because his old man owned the ranch. In Depression-laden America, if standing between you and starvation was taking shit from a rancher's son, you kept your mouth shut and bucked your barley. John Steinbeck, it seems, knew a thing or two about breathing in what others exhale and standing knee-deep in what they excrete; one could claim he wrote the manifesto on the subject. Curly's wife played the role of one ostensibly innocent, characterizing a poor oppressed girl who married too young, got stuck with a bully for a husband but was more treacherous than an icy one-lane road curving around a mountainside with no guardrail; she was a nameless representative of a sort who, if a fellow was not wary, supremely intuitive, or owned a pair of eyes in the back of his head, could get him killed then act mystified over how it happened. But there was no all-of-the-above listed as a choice, which meant Cillian was right; it was a trick question. Once again, I glanced across the room at Joey. He seemed satisfied with whatever answer he chose. Then he says, still looking down at his test, "How about a ballgame tonight? Carlton's going against Sutton."

On nights when we were not strolling the neighborhood with a transistor radio, Cillian, Joey, and I would trek down to The Vet and sit way up in the cheap seats—the nosebleeders.

"Sounds good," I said. The Phils versus the Dodgers, Carlton versus Sutton; I needed no convincing that tonight would be a good night to sit at the ballpark. Then I grimaced like one would when bracing for a tirade. But it never came.

"Yeah, sure," Cillian added. "Count me in." Then, feeling brave, I called over to Joey, "Incidentally, Teddy Sizemore's hitting .290, and he and Bowa have become one of the best double-play combos in the National League."

"They're every bit as good as Morgan and Concepcion," Cillian chimed in. "And way better than Lopes and Russell."

On we went, filling an ether known as a classroom with talk of stats, standings, and league leaders while trying to ace *Of Mice and Men*, and all the while, Mrs. Hargrove wore an amused expression, like she wanted to join in the banter but held back; I watched her struggle to maintain the integrity of the teacher/student barrier. Then Joey said, "The Phils need a winning streak; they can't let the Cubs get any further out in front." That's when Mrs. Hargrove broke rank and stunned us by categorically stating, "The Cubs will fade. They always do. There's every reason to believe they're cursed. But superstition aside, the Phils will be sitting in first place come the fourth of July."

The Cubs will fade? They always do? Did I hear right: Mrs. Hargrove was a baseball fan *and* historian? In a flash, I could see beyond a power suit and aura of bitchiness—the latter I assumed was the byproduct of nine menstrual cycles—to discover an unguarded baseball fan, a woman who, most nights, was doing what we were doing: rooting on her team! Aside from Mrs. Monk, whose age and matronliness disqualified her, Mrs. Hargrove was the teacher we assumed was the least relatable to freshmen boys. But as often is the case, life is full of surprises. Unfortunately, we would only have Mrs. Hargrove for another month. Had we only known this side of her sooner—the side that couldn't wait for seven-thirty, the first pitch, and the voices of Harry Kalas and Richie Ashburn bringing nine innings of Phillies baseball to the region—we would have saved our A-game for English literature.

****

Joey lived closest to the train, so we decided dinner at his place made sense. We would meet Joey at the train in the past, but today, he told us, "When my folks make spaghetti and meatballs, they make enough to feed a small army. And all homemade!"

I needed no arm twisting. Claire Caldwell could boil noodles and twist open a jar with the best of them—but homemade? I would be a fool to pass up dinner at the Broscos. Cillian, offering the quip, "My mother knows where the kitchen is; I'm confident she's walked past it a time or two," was equally enthused. I mean, who decided that fish in the form of breaded sticks, mashed potatoes from a box, and cut green beans boiled to mush accounted for dinner?

We entered the Brosco home, and it hit us: the aroma of homemade gravy; the air was warm and thick with it; we barely penetrated a step into the living room and found ourselves delightfully enveloped. Yessiree, we had gained a passage into Dego Heaven. I felt inspired to holler out something appreciable in Italian, but the only word that came to mind was *abudanza*. I was afraid it might serve as an expression more suitable for complimenting a girl endowed with huge breasts and not one used to praise someone for creating wonderfully aromatic cuisine. *Hey, CJ, there goes Theresa Delvecchio parading in a halter top. Abudanza!* I was wise to hold my tongue. I mean, if you think there's even a ghost of a chance of making an ass of yourself the first time meeting folks, it's best to play it safe; that way, neither of Joey's parents, on the sly or afterward, would have to ask: *Which one of your asshole friends walked in yelling abudanza?*

No sooner did we reach the kitchen than we learned it was no phenomenon how Joey received his miserly endowment of height. Both Mister and Missus Brosco must have come from awfully short tribes. Poor Joey; he never stood a chance. Not even by way of a fluke might he have reached an average height a product of his folks. For example, a homely couple, because each may possess, however subtle, a redeeming feature or two, on a rare occasion, for instance, a planetary alignment, can produce a girl that every guy in the neighborhood dreams of diddling. Trust me; I've seen it happen, though Mister and Missus Brosco creating a six-foot son would be on the order of a draft horse birthing a unicorn.

Aside from a lack of height, another noticeable feature was the multiple generations between Joey and his folks. At a glance, one might readily assume that the Broscos were Joey's grandparents— some kids, for numerous reasons, live with grandparents—but the resemblances were too remarkable; Joey was a perfect fusion of his folks. It was in the kitchen that Cillian and I received our introductions to Mister and Missus Brosco: Mister B was stirring gravy; Missus B was straining spaghetti.

"Fellas, you'll have to excuse us," said Missus Brosco, "Italian families have a habit of cramming themselves into kitchens, no matter the size of the kitchen or family."

As Missus Brosco spoke, her lips—although characteristic of a much younger woman's, for example, Sharon Millstein's—captured my attention but not in an inspirational way. And if there were features that betrayed Missus B's age, it was the dark circles accenting her eyes and slate gray hair: the latter was nicely trimmed, though a bit too boyish. And, Christ, was she short! A well-proportioned dwarf was my first impression. Okay, maybe not quite a dwarf, but she was hardly anyone's interpretation of "normal." Moreover, she looked up at Cillian and me with lenses so thick they created a funny glare that made seeing her eyes beyond the dark circles difficult. I liked Missus Brosco right off the bat; the woman had spunk.

When examining Mr. B, it was clear that he and his Missus patronize the same barber: the ol' around the corner, no appointment necessary, everybody walks out looking the same barber. His speech was low, raspy, and hurried; when Mister Brosco spoke, it seemed he could not get the words out fast enough, and although intelligent, because his mouth had a habit of false-starting and racing out ahead of his brain, he sputtered a fair amount of the time. His eyes were soft like Joey's. How Mr. B's diverged was that they seemed to possess a lifetime's worth of sorrow, coalescing with more experience and wisdom than anyone would care to collect. He stood stirring gravy while tucked under his arm was a crutch performing the task of the leg that went missing. Mister Brosco was a touch taller than Joey and thicker around the middle, but they probably weighed the same, given that his left leg was amputated just above the knee. I cannot begin to explain my obsession with this morbid tale of the tape; perhaps lunacy would be a good place to start. Also, I made every effort not to stare at Mister B from the belt down, but honestly, how many one-legged guys do you see stirring gravy at a stove? It was like a goddamn freak show: parents resembling grandparents, cooks with missing limbs, and dwarfs looking through coke-bottle glasses, though a kinder and more welcoming household one would never find. If you were agitated, hurried, or stressed before entering the Brosco domain, its ethos would vanquish those ill-tempered feelings; you could not wield vexation in the presence of the Broscos had you tried. And that they were practicing Catholics was a point of emphasis—the Broscos, without fail, gave the Lord the one hour a week they believed He was owed—but their true religion was the seven nights a week they sat down together to break bread.

It started to make perfect sense, Joey's conservative approach to life: always preaching the reward must outweigh the risk, understanding that within nature, there exist such matters as balance and laws of averages, and perhaps most importantly, human beings are no less fragile on their best day than they are on their worst. Joey Brosco was a product of a young man born to older parents, instead of, for example, a hippie mother who opens the windows in the dead of winter to toke grass in her bedroom. But Joey could be a real hothead. I've seen him blow his stack on a few occasions, and the result saw guys much bigger, wisely taking a step backward. But Joey was known more for his thoughtfulness than hotheadedness. However, I could not fathom why he neglected to forewarn Cillian and me about the condition of his old man. A father having one leg is not a matter likely to slip someone's mind. *Sorry, did I fail to mention dear old Dad is missing a limb?* And what was the likelihood that Mr. B lost his leg sometime after Joey left for school this morning? But the more I thought about it, the more sense it made that Cillian and I ventured unprepared. That way, we went to the Broscos to have dinner with Joey and his folks, not meet a dwarf and a one-legged man. Sometimes, it's that which we fail to mention that best expresses our pride for the ones we love.

As we were positioning ourselves around the dining room table and preparing to dig into a glorious feast, one matter, aside from the mouth-watering aroma of the food, was apparent: The dreaded brown paneling, gold drapes, mundane wall-to-wall carpet, and veneered furniture so lacquered-up it looked like plastic—unfortunate stylistic debacles abundantly present in the 60s and 70s—were not on display at the Broscos. Joey's folks, concerning home décor, managed to avoid the abovementioned decades, keeping with two-toned walls divided by chair rails, blinds and elegant valances for window dressings, and area rugs accenting furniture of a classic style made with genuine mahogany. Not a shred of tackiness or tastelessness was present. In other words, the place looked as good as it smelled. Next, we joined hands, and Mister Brosco, in his raspy and hurried voice, prayed: "Bless us, O Lord, and these Thy gifts, which we are about to receive from Your bounty. Through Christ our Lord. Amen. And from the bottom of my heart, I thank You for our old friends and for keeping us around to meet new ones."

I was hoping that was the end. Hell, I was terrified that since I was a guest, I might get called upon to add a liturgical sentiment to the dinner prayer. What would I say? What possible invocations could I make? Please, O Lord, give Carlton the strength to out-duel Sutton after this feast, and tomorrow, let me find my way into Maryellen McNamara's pants. Hail Mary was the only prayer I had memorized and could recite confidently. Father Murray, the infamous ogler of Cyndy Pytlewski's breasts, had me repeat ten of them after my first confession. And what an idiotic affair *that* turned out to be. I was eight; what the hell does an eight-year-old have to confess? I was shaking like a leaf walking into this coffin-sized, darkened closet. On the way in, I raced through the Ten Commandments, grasping for any infraction, all for the sake of having something to say once I stepped inside the dark, cramped space I was about to share with a closeted sex maniac. Murder, adultery, bearing false witness, coveting thy neighbor's wife: these were sins way above the pay grade of an eight-year-old sinner. So, I did what came naturally; I made up a bunch of bullshit, including selling Casey for Phillies tickets. As I said, the result of this farce was Father Murray sending me to a pew to recite ten Hail Marys. And Cillian and Joey wonder why I'm an atheist.

As it came to pass, Mister Brosco was just as anxious to dig in as I was and did not call upon Cillian or me to add to his prayer. I could not venture a guess as to how many times Mister B said grace. By now, one would think it was routine, like running a load of laundry, taking out the trash, or any other compulsory household chore. Not a chance; Mister Brosco's words possessed all the weight of naked honesty—the impact of a humble soul surging with gratitude. I felt a twinge of guilt for being a nonbeliever.

My guilt vanished no sooner than I took the first forkful. Then I lifted my head. Across the table, I watched Cillian shoveling food into his mouth with a zeal comparable to a competitive eater, or that never again would he see an opportunity to consume such superbly prepared cuisine. *Ballgame? What ballgame? A Carlton versus Sutton pitcher's duel would be just fine on Joey's transistor radio.* Next, my eyes fell upon Mister Brosco, who sat at one of the table's heads, then Joey, seated beside Cillian. Father and son mirrored one another's actions and pace; it was the damnedest thing I had ever seen. First, they sliced their meatballs into four equal pieces using their forks, then took a full minute to chew and swallow each piece. Talk about savoring every morsel? Joey and his father, at dinnertime, were akin to a sloth dealing blackjack at a casino; your money would last all night; the only risk would be falling asleep and off your stool.

Then, it finally happened. I could sense Cillian's thoughts— it was like he had a cartoon balloon hovering above his head, and inside it, the words were flashing—and it was not just the synergetic nature of our friendship that helped me intuit what he was thinking. Mister Brosco, too, sensed Cillian's thoughts because he slapped his stump and announced, "World War II, fellas. Left the rest of her in the South Pacific."

Left the rest of her in the South Pacific? And here I thought yours truly was the king of irony and black humor, although I'm not so sure Mister Brosco's goal, in this instance, was humor, black or otherwise. Nevertheless, with the lighthearted and ironical manner in which he regarded his leg, one might come away with the impression the missing portion floated from the shore of Guadalcanal, got nibbled to the bone by a school of fish, or was lost somewhere in the thicket of a jungle and was made a meal of by a cluster of maggots.

Then it occurred to me that Mister B was thirteen years longer without his leg than he was with it; thus, he could broach the matter lightheartedly, similar to how one would a pair of gloves or accessory of little consequence that went missing. *I left the damn things in a bar but got too drunk to remember which one.* Then he added, in his typical hurried, sputtering manner, after swallowing a morsel of meatball that spent more time in his mouth than it took Muhammad Ali to knock out Sonny Liston: "Between the war and holocaust, thirteen million people got whisked off the planet. All I had to do to keep freedom and democracy alive and safe was cough up half a leg. I'd say that makes me lucky; *damn* lucky, in fact."

Now there goes a man with some goddamn perspective! I'm sure anyone would agree, with concern for gaining an outlook on a situation, that Mister Brosco had a few things figured out. So, there I sat on a train taking me to watch Carlton and Sutton, ace hurlers of their respective staff, duel at the Vet while my true hero was a one-legged man with whom I had just become acquainted. It proves, yet again, life is chock full of surprises, some more surprising than others.

Darrin Caldwell was lucky: His birthday placed him in a nice, tidy window—one that made him too young for Korea and too old for Vietnam. As a youngster, I had asked my father, after my Uncle Terry was sent away to that agent-orange-riddled jungle in Southeast Asia: "Dad, were you ever in the army?" Darrin eyed up his six-year-old son, not wanting to lie nor seem cowardly, and said, "Nope, but I used to be a cowboy."

Imagine my delight: I could brag to my friends that my old man was once a genuine cowboy, had a horse, and rode the range! By my next birthday, though, I had a few things figured out but never bothered to approach Darrin to ask: *Hey, Dad, could you run that whole "cowboy thing" by me again?*

We sat in the last row of the seven-hundred level: first base side. It was the perfect place to sit if you were someone appreciative of plenty of leg and elbow room. We did not mind trading distance from the field for roominess, and ticket prices were also a factor; the last row of the seven-hundred lever marked the least expensive seats in the park. My head was in the game, but not to the extent that there was no room to dwell on Joey and the dissimilarity of our lives. For example, I had a sister who was seven years my junior; Joey had one, Gina, who was twelve years older than him and made him an uncle by the ripe old age of nine to a baby girl named Connie. For all intents, Joey was an only child—an only child with a one-legged father; thus, it was unlikely playing catch on the front lawn was as routine an occurrence at the Broscos as the nightly dinner prayer. Mostly, Joey took his basketball to the playground—why, at his size, he opted to become proficient at basketball, I'll never know—or lost himself in his baseball cards. With concern for the latter, there was no such thing as a statistic of which Joey was unaware; it mattered not if it was an obscure player on an also-ran team; Joey could tell you how many bases he swiped back in 1971 or doubles he whacked in 1975. Cillian and I followed baseball as closely as anyone—not a day passed that did not see our noses in the sports section of the Daily News—we knew the position of the standings and league leaders by heart. But Joey? It was astonishing how he could rattle off stats, including the earned run averages of every top pitching prospect in the minor leagues. His statistical proficiency earned him the nickname Encyclopedia Brosco.

Come the fourth inning, we headed for an exit that led to the six-hundred-level concourse. The storm we hoped would pass came, followed by the grounds crew—frantic little men springing into action with the urgency of firefighters on the way to an inferno—who seemingly appeared from out of nowhere and, with legs churning similarly to mushing sled dogs, rolled out a tarp to cover the infield. From the perspective of descending stairs from such a height, the procedure was reminiscent of a nineteenth-century fire drill. We did not mind the rain delay; it gave us more time to spend at the stadium. During a delay, the Vet transforms into a commune for the hardcore fan—those willing to endure anything short of the fallout from an atomic bomb—and chases away those delicate souls who decide too quickly the prospect of resuming play is unlikely and thus make a beeline for the exits. Those who remain—strangers whose commonality is a passion for a ball club—are chattering away in the concourse about a team that, in '74, won the heart of a city with the upstarts Mike Schmidt, Greg Luzinski, Larry Bowa, and Bob Boone, and presently appear on the threshold of greatness. Pockets of conversations meld together, and for the span of a rain delay, there is no such thing as a stranger; it is fascinating to witness what sports can do. As for Cillian, Joey, and me? We huddled in a breezeway connecting the amphitheater and concourse and gazed at the rain pouring into a concrete doughnut called Veteran Stadium. Before long, Cillian said, "It won't be long now." We understood he was not referring to the rain delay but our journey across the state to a farm in Western Pennsylvania.

"I never met my Aunt Leila," he told us. "Never even seen a picture of her." A trace of consternation registered on Cillian's face before adding, "It's gonna feel strange visiting an old, familiar place with all the old, familiar people gone." It sounded strangely like an admission that Cillian, all along, harbored suspicions concerning his Uncle Dave's second wife or, recently, had developed some misgivings for his newly widowed Aunt Leila. Another option was that Cillian had second thoughts about spending an entire summer away from the city.

"I've never seen Maryellen naked live *or* in a photograph," I said. "If anything, that only makes my desire to see her all the more intense."

"That's hardly the same thing," Cillian argued.

He was right; my analogy was weak. Still, I was keen on the three of us spending the summer away, breathing clean country air, and enjoying the benefit of farmgirls who would treat three city slickers with more generosity than their city counterparts. That scenario repeated in my head for weeks, and I was in no mood to entertain its demise.

"My Aunt Phyllis died less than a year ago," Cillian told us. "Then, my mother—she's my Uncle Dave's younger sister, incidentally—gets this phone call not quite two months later. It was Uncle Dave telling her that not only did he remarry, but he got hitched to this Leila woman no one had ever heard of who's an entire generation younger. I mean, who gets remarried after only being widowed two months? Though, in the end, what did it matter: Uncle Dave was gone before springtime; his little trophy wife, it would seem, proved too much for him, and now the farm is all hers." Cillian shrugged contemptuously, adding, "I imagine my cousins, Wayne and Jack, have a few questions concerning their stepmother, a woman young enough to be their sibling and is now the lady of the very farmhouse in which they grew up."

"So, you suspect this Leila woman, who you never saw or met, is some sorta black widow?" Joey theorized. "That maybe she's a serial killer who offs men once she convinces them to add her name to certain vital documents?"

Cillian's gesture was a self-deprecating shrug, for when hearing his "Aunt Leila theories" articulated aloud, he reconciled how farfetched they seemed. Next, I added my pragmatic two cents. "Maybe it was more a case of Uncle Dave reconciling his imminent death and wanting to spend whatever time he had left banging a young piece of tail. But let's say, for the sake of argument, Aunt Leila is a black widow or a deranged killer that offs husbands to acquire property: there's three of us and one of her."

"How old did you say this Leila woman was?" Joey asked.

Cillian had not mentioned Leila's age, only that she was a generation younger than Uncle Dave. "Twenty-eight," he tersely replied. It means poor Uncle Dave, with the breadth of a generation being twenty years, kicked the proverbial bucket sometime in his late forties. Kinda tragic, I would say. Moreover, Cillian had yet to learn how Uncle Dave died; he only knew he had, that a modest-sized private service was held to honor his life, and that the only attendee in Cillian's immediate family was his mother. Perhaps Missus James did not want Mister James, Cillian, and the twins, Karen and Stephanie, around when she gave Leila a piece of her mind if, indeed, that was her primary reason for trekking to western Pennsylvania at a time of year when the weather was still frigid.

I suppose you cannot blame Cillian for his mind traveling to dark corners where Uncle Dave and Aunt Leila were concerned. A death, followed by a hasty marriage and another death, could get anyone's wheels turning.

Cillian had not seen his Uncle Dave in three years but has fond memories of many Thanksgiving dinners on the farm—a time before his older cousins, Wayne and Jack, whom, as a youngster, Cillian idolized, married, and moved on. Cillian also recalled for us days when his Western Pennsylvanian kin sat around the Thanksgiving table and lauded the Pirates and Steelers—days when the Phillies and Eagles were also-rans—while he fought for enough air to put in his two-cents on behalf of the teams at the other end of the state. His last Thanksgiving on the farm—it being a year before Aunt Phyllis began her steady decline—Cillian came to dinner prepared to boast about the Broad Street Bullies and the Stanley Cup, only to learn that Western Pennsylvanians, in those days, had little regard for hockey. Cillian did not either, nor does he nowadays, but when you are determined to shove something up someone's ass, you can only shove what is available. If you lived in Philadelphia in 1974, the Flyers were the only offering.

"My cousin, Wayne, told me that Lord Stanley was a 'locker room ankle-grabbing fruitcake,'" said Cillian, "and that if the Penguins brought home the Stanley Cup, he 'wouldn't as much as piss in it.' With him, every conversation was about the Stillers. The Stillers. Franco Harris, Mean Joe Green, and the goddamn Stillers! And what's the deal with Western Pennsylvanians; none of them can pronounce a long *E*."

"Apparently, neither can Philadelphians," said Joey, who reminded us that half the city, especially those living below Cottman Avenue east of Roosevelt Boulevard, calls the Eagles the Igles. *Yo, how 'bout dem Iggles!*

Cillian's favorite part of the day was the hour between Thanksgiving dinner and dessert. The entire family, the women included, went off into the field for a game of two-hand touch. My lean, athletic friend had his very own rooting section—Cillian was a hero to his twin sisters, Karen and Stephanie—and made sure they had plenty of reason to cheer.

We circled the concourse until we arrived at the breezeway leading us back to our seats, only to find the Zamboni machine still making straight lines in the spacious outfield as it vacuumed up water from the artificial turf before depositing it into a drain. Next came another nineteenth-century fire drill, only in reverse, which ended with the grounds crew dumping sand and raking it onto the dirt cutouts around the bases and home plate.

The rain delay had lasted over an hour, enough time to shelve Carlton and Sutton for the night. Ozark and Lasorda would have to muddle through the remaining five innings using their respective bullpens built for the rigors of a pennant race. It is not the scenario one hoped for when aces toe the rubber, but nature had other plans. The Phils had made a little noise early when Jay Johnstone homered but entered the rain delay down 2 -1. Warren Brusstar is standing on the hill for the Phils; Charlie Hough will hurl for the Dodgers.

Ol' Charlie Hough is one of those pain-in-the-ass knuckleballers. To be fair, Hough seems to have more control over his knuckler than the most famous knuckleballer, Phil Niekro, has over his. Either that or Steve Yeager does an exceptional job catching knuckleballs. Most catchers prefer not to see knuckleballers; they tend to make catchers look like bush-leaguers—and what major leaguer wants to look like a busher? Every time I watch a knuckleballer pitch,

I'm reminded of that silly Ray Milland movie *It Happens Every Spring*. Milland plays a college professor who doubles as a scientist working on a substance to repel insects and, in the process, discovers a formula to rub on baseballs, thus making them wood-repellent. Knuckleballs tend to come floating toward home plate like an indecisive butterfly, but with far greater velocity and seemingly rubbed down with leather-repellent. So tricky to catch cleanly are knuckleballs that often they hit the heel of the catcher's mitt and go bounding away, thus turning the catcher into a Labrador Retriever and making what many allege is the most challenging job in all sports impossible. More important than the catcher's difficulties—keeping in mind, he's the dumb bastard squatting behind the plate calling for the knuckler—were the Phillies' woes; ol' Charlie Hough, historically, gave the Phils hitters fits, though Gary Maddox managed to triple in a run. But then, wouldn't you know it, again came the rain, this time in the seventh inning. Cillian, Joey, and I scurried to the concourse after helping ourselves to five-hundred-level seats after the crowd thinned from the first delay. As we scampered, little men appeared, seemingly from nowhere, simulating a nineteenth-century fire drill.

"It's gonna be a long night," Joey intoned. "But I'm glad to be at the stadium instead of home with my radio." A thoughtful look came over Joey. "My father has never missed an inning of a ballgame," he added as though no more extraordinary deed could a man hang his hat on. "Rain delays, extra innings, west coast games that don't start 'til 10:30; it doesn't matter. He's a fan with a firm grasp on the importance of every pitch."

"I wish my old man were more like yours," I said. "All he watches are game shows after listening to Sinatra. Imagine getting excited watching plump middle-aged women jump up and down, their breasts jiggling, because Johnny Olson told them they won a brand-new refrigerator. And then there are these overdressed supermodel wannabes unfurling their arms, smiling with ten pounds of lip gloss, and flashing capped teeth. I feel sorry for those women. They were likely farm girls from Nebraska who went to Hollywood thinking they could be the next Rita Hayworth and ended up posing next to a goddamn appliance. But my old man thinks they're all stunners, so every night it's thirty minutes of Sinatra, then game shows."

"Oh yeah," Cillian intoned. "I can top that, Addie. All my old man ever watches are John Wayne movies. 'The Duke,' he calls him. Drives us up the wall! I mean, if it isn't sweaty, stubbly, dust-covered cowboys grumbling dialogue and riding around on horses for two goddamn hours, it's smudge-faced men in combat fatigues, crouching in foxholes and tossing grenades. Talk about a *you-seen-one-you-seen-'em-all* proposition! When I was eight and told the old man I signed up to play little league baseball, his reply was, 'What's wrong with the Cub Scouts?' He figured Cub Scouts would lead to Boy Scouts, ROTC, the army, and a commendation for performing admirably in combat. But I guess that's the primary function of fathers, to shove their heroes up the asses of their sons. So far, we got Sinatra and John Wayne." Cillian's eyes fell on Joey.

It was beautiful how Joey grinned, like when someone cannot wait to answer but still possesses the discipline to hold you in suspense. Nevertheless, it would be a challenge to cite a hero—Cillian's and my feelings aside—more iconic than John Wayne and Frank Sinatra, assuming we were keeping to American culture.

"My mother told me, if needed, my father would've crawled—despite only having one knee—to Connie Mack Stadium whenever the Cardinals were in town. Which means his hero was none other than Stan Musial. And not to minimize the effort, but back when Stan 'The Man' was still playing, my folks lived at 26th and Lehigh, making it a fairly short crawl."

"Still," I chimed in, "for a guy with one leg, just crawling into the next room would be a sonofabitch."

"My mother went to Connie Mack Stadium with my father until Gina became old enough and learned to love baseball or was convinced she should love it. Whether Gina got introduced or indoctrinated, who's to say? Anyway, my father never bragged about it. But my mother told me numerous times how, before the war, he was a damn good ballplayer—played second base for an American Legion team that went undefeated."

"That's going pretty damn far, especially for a guy your father's size," I said. "I bet he was one of those tough, aggressive players like Bobby Grich or our very own Ted Sizemore."

"Leave it to you, Addie, to fuck up an otherwise perfectly good compliment," Joey groused.

"Joey, you have to learn to face facts," I said. "Right now, Teddy Sizemore is outperforming Dave Cash."

"It's because Cash is playing for the Expos. If you plug him into a championship line-up like the Phils or Dodgers, he'd be hitting .330!"

Joey could knock you over with how vehemently he argued for Dave Cash.

"What's even more amazing," Cillian said, bringing us back from our digression, "is how accepting your old man is about his leg. I know guys who've acted bitter for years over a whole lot less. For example, my neighbor, Buzzy Winston: the sonofabitch used to walk his dog every day but has refused to walk it since his wife left him. At first, we thought his wife must've taken the mutt with her, but then we heard ol' Sparky yapping. Why punish Sparky because your wife found greener pastures or because you were a shitty husband? Anyway, it just goes to show you how some folks handle adversity."

"Stan 'The Man,'" I uttered with a note of reverence. "We must remember to ask Mrs. Hargrove about *her* baseball hero. I'd sure like to know who it is."

Learning the favorite ballplayers of older folks fascinates me. My across-the-street neighbor, Mr. Paschal, a real crusty old sonofabitch, has told me to the point ad nauseam, "There'll never be another Joe DiMaggio. Now there, young fella, was a ballplayer!" Mr. Paschal points and shakes a bony, gnarled old finger at me when he states this claim; I suppose the authoritative gesture further validates the claim's indisputability. I remind him, statistically, that Musial, Mays, and Aaron have all surpassed The Yankee Clipper. Upon listening to my statistical analysis argument, Mr. Paschal narrows his eyes and grits what's left of his umber-colored teeth, thus causing his jawbone to appear as though it might protrude through his crusty, blotchy old skin accented with a million blue spidery flecks which are the result of half the capillaries in his face having erupted—it's a real ugly old man scowl that Mr. Paschal flashes; the sonofabitch resembles everyone's first attempt at an omelet—then he hisses contemptuously, "Numbers! They only tell part of the story; you gotta rely on the eye test as well, and I'm tellin' ya, DiMaggio glided through the game like an artist. No one who ever played the game had his instincts, certainly not any of the mercenaries that play the game nowadays."

Typical of men of Mr. Paschal's generation, the oldster holds to the flowery and romantic notion that the ballplayers of his youth cared not what they made and played only for the love of the game. Yessiree, green grass, day baseball, and the minimum wage; they only played the game to be heroes to kids and entertain adults. Money? What money? Mr. Paschal nearly blew a gasket when I informed him that, while Joe DiMaggio earned one-hundred-thousand-large in 1949, Reggie Jackson, after whacking 47 dingers twenty years later, in 1969, took home a paltry twenty-grand. That's less than four hundred and thirty bucks per round-tripper! Incidentally, Joey supplied me with these juicy tidbits with which to go to war against Mr. Paschal.

To be fair, Mr. Paschal's viewpoint was not without reason. Everybody thinks the ballplayers of their era or youth were the best to have ever played. Doubtless, one day, I'll be a crusty old prick pointing a bony finger at some poor bastard and bending his ear about Mike Schmidt and Steve Carlton. And speaking of dominant left-handers, Guy McNamara—the philandering prick—insists Sandy Koufax was the greatest of them all.

"But Carlton has already surpassed Koufax in career wins, is right behind him in strikeouts, and still has a good seven or eight years to pitch," I respectfully pointed out to Maryellen's old man.

My logic was flawless, or so I assumed. How could Guy McNamara fail to see it? Incidentally, Maryellen subscribes to the theory the baseball *tête à têtes* I have with her old man is my sly way of attempting to curry favor with her. She is not *entirely* wrong. Moreover, she flashes me one of her typical snooty *Don't think I'm not on to you, Addison* sneers from inside the front door whenever her father and I debate over Carlton and Koufax.

"But you had to have seen Koufax the last six years of his career," Guy McNamara would stress. "He struck fear in the hearts of even the most daunting lineups—teams were mentally defeated before they stuck their noses out of the clubhouse. I'm telling you, Addie," he would add with reverence," you had to have seen Koufax to believe it."

Again, with the eye test. Naturally, it matters, but it makes it challenging to talk baseball with older folks; everything flows through their prism. The tables are tilted.

"According to my Uncle Dave, no one played the game better than Clemente," said Cillian. "Uncle Dave revered Clemente as a ballplayer and as a man. Aside from my Aunt Phyllis dying, the worst day of his life was New Year's Eve 1972." Cillian need not elaborate; Joey and I were well aware of what the last day of the calendar year 1972 meant: Roberto Clemente died in a plane crash while en route to delivering aid to the earthquake victims of Nicaragua. Cillian's Uncle Dave was not the only one who lost a hero that day.

With the mention of poor, dead Uncle Dave, the conversation returned to Western Pennsylvania and the summer hovering on the immediate horizon—a summer that would set the stage for the unimaginable. "Do you both realize," I began, with far more graveness than the subject required, "the summer will pass without us feasting our eyes on a scantily dressed Cyndy Pytlewski hanging laundry and the even scantier dressed Theresa Delvecchio parading around in a halter top and short shorts? Has that kernel of non-fiction yet registered?"

No one would mistake Philly for Vero Beach or Santa Monica in the summertime, so Cyndy Pytlewski and Theresa Delvecchio were a big deal for us.

"Of course, it has," said Cillian. "But I didn't wanna be the first to ruin the day by mentioning it. Incidentally, I came this close to confessing to Terry Dell that it's her to whom I dedicate my nightly tributes."

Theresa Delvecchio did not seem to mind the haircut her ethnic-sounding name received from us neighborhood guys. In fact, she appreciates the nifty snip.

"Missus P. is an adult goddess," I said, "but my mind won't let me jump generations when the issue is onanism."

"Score one for the Italians," said Joey, who went on record describing Theresa Delvecchio as a longer-haired, fifteen-year-old version of Sophia Loren looking like she did in the movie *Houseboat*, starring Sophia and Cary Grant. It is a targeted description Joey makes, though hardly inaccurate. The reason I know this to be so? Joey pestered me unmercifully until I agreed to watch the flick. And when muddling through what amounted to typical romantic-comedy claptrap distributed by Paramount Pictures in the late 1950s (1958 to be precise), no fewer than a half dozen times, Joey hollered to me,

"You see Addie; I told you so." The first time was when Cary Grant and Sophia Loren appeared on the boat's deck at night. There was every indication they were about to share a kiss, if not for one of Cary Grant's pain-in-the-ass kids (his daughter) bursting onto the deck and complaining about a bad dream or toothache—I don't remember which. Then comes the scene when Sophia appears wearing a gold evening gown and looking so scrumptious that her date—Angelo Donatello, played by Harry Guardino—becomes nervous his cherished bachelorhood could be in jeopardy and runs off, leaving Cary Grant to escort Sophia to the dance. It amazes me the horseshit Hollywood got away with before the 1960s, with all its dissent and anxiety, ushered in the age of realism. It amazes me how one war (World War II) could ring in an age of innocence and prosperity while another (The Vietnam War) introduced distrust and brokenness. It amazes me how war, even when not a single round of ammunition went off in our country, in one way or another, wields the capacity to shape a nation by getting it to look gratefully outward or regretfully inward. Then we arrive at a scene that sees Sophia posing in a doorway at night: moonlight illuminates her skin, and her eyes convey a look I would describe as primally alluring. My atheism suffers its first minor dent—one of those parking lot bumper jobbies—for I am convinced that Sophia Loren is the work of the Devil.

"How 'bout it, Addie," Joey called to me.

"When you're right, you're right," I called back. Indeed, our neighborhood goddess looked like Hollywood's goddess could have birthed her.

Theresa Delvecchio or Terry Dell if you prefer: a girl with long, shiny, luxurious coffee-brown hair, sporting a flamboyant personality when free from restraints—bands, barrettes, and clips, how could she!—and permitted to bounce; it commands the attention of every man, woman, and beast. From September through June, she sports a complexion of the loveliest olive; throughout summer, golden brown. Her skin radiates, glows, and, when perspired, stirs evocations requiring a noteworthy poet of romance to arrange. Equally inspiring is the frosty gloss and shadow gleaming upon the fullness of her lips and lids of her Sophiaesque eyes, and the coolness of those colors project themselves from a radiant sea of golden brown in the midday sun and later at dusk. But Theresa's most affecting quality, assuming it is possible, amid such abundance, to whittle it down to one: She hasn't a clue what a teen goddess she truly is. Moreover, as Cillian so brilliantly expressed, she's oblivious to her capacity to send clusters of young men to their beds to engage in "tributes of savage-like onanism." Indeed, Theresa had a fan club of raging hormonal warriors. Yet, if she was aware of it—how could she not be? —Theresa remained unfazed and humble. One could submit that she had gone out of her way to be another face in the crowd.

So, why, one might ask, aside from the obvious, am I gushing about the virtues of Theresa Delvecchio when it is Maryellen McNamara to whom I have, on numerous occasions, engaged in feverish onanism? For starters, Theresa and Maryellen are the same age. Moreover, they entered the world the same day, less than an hour apart.

"Theresa and I are both Tauruses," Maryellen was fond of crowing. "That means we're reliable, dependable, and always willing to give others a helping hand."

That was Maryellen at age ten. And it was then that she began her inexhaustible quest of pointing out the various conducts that qualified me as a no-good sonofabitch. But what did I care about reliability at age ten? Was I to run straight to Father Murray and confess that I was unreliable—thou shall not act unreliably—lacked dependability and demonstrated a reluctance to help others? Theresa, at age ten, did not seem the slightest bit concerned that I was a typical self-centered ten-year-old prick. And speaking of one's age, it would never occur to Theresa Delvecchio to waste a second of valuable time wielding her age—especially as it pertained to her peers—as a means of superiority. She is far too busy with verve and buoyancy, thrusting herself into the world with enviable results to worry about age-related bullshit. Also, between Terry Dell and Mary Mac—once inseparable Catholic Schoolgirls—only one of them, with supreme haughtiness, treads upon the path of the righteous while making sure others alleged unworthy are duly repelled. Meanwhile, the "other girl," although grateful for the education Catholic School provides, reserves the right to have doubts—doubters represent the healthiest believers, remaining intellectually curious, fearlessly wandering from cul-de-sacs in which religion tries to imprison them, and welcoming debate—and, with gusto, embraces the many layers and complexities that form a society. So, this brings us to the ultimate question: Why would yours truly, Addison Caldwell, discounting stupidity as an overarching factor, obsess over what many would allege is the wrong girl? I could cite that I'm a young man who appreciates a challenge, but that would imply that Theresa Delvecchio was a pushover. Despite sporting ensembles meant to torture—halter tops, short shorts, and toe-loop sandals—she was no patsy to her male peers. In matters of the opposite sex, I could also cite both an affinity and appreciation for lassies, given that I am of Irish descent; unfortunately, my experience is too limited, and it is nonexistent when disregarding the relationship between my hand and imagination. I could further cite masochism piggybacked by self-denial as a means of building character. Doubtless, it has been tried, and perhaps successfully, but realistically, what percentage of young men finishing up their freshman year of high school with their minds already in summer mode are taking stock in the content of their character? So here goes it: Behind all her tumbling red hair, pale skin, freckles that in the summer sunshine will become the dominant feature of her pretty face, shoes with buckles, Catholic School uniforms all cleaned and neatly pressed, and an unnatural adherence to a doctrine that takes joy in its capacity to inhibit and oppress, I believe there exists a tiger—a sanguine jungle cat that for years, while trapped inside, has been pacing back and forth hoping to find a way out, hoping to locate an orifice through which it can unleash itself upon the world. Sadly, though, this creature remains caged, stuck, and frustrated—a tyrannized and subjugated beast—and all because her mistress lives in fear that, should she yield but once to the long-denied felinity that resides within, it might mean having to say goodbye forever to buckled shoes, fastidious uniforms, and existing tidily above the fray. In my heart, I cling to the notion that this tiger will one day know the light of day. And I want to be there when it emerges, to witness its debut and experience its thrust, its presence, even at the risk of this allegorical largest of all jungle beasts ripping off my nuts.

And there goes the Zamboni machine, vacuuming what Mother Nature deposited onto the artificial turf and funneling it into a drain. Welcome to major league baseball circa 1977: concrete doughnuts and fake grass. I wonder what Babe Ruth, Ty Cobb, or Mister Brosco's hero, Stan "The Man" Musial, would think of a machine designed to vacuum rainwater from a synthetic field? And look, some-one must have pressed the rewind button, so if anyone missed it the first time, they would get a chance to watch a nineteenth-century fire drill in reverse.

We settled ourselves in the first row of the three-hundred level, third base side. The second delay was not nearly as long as the first—maybe a half-hour—and not long enough for Lasorda to shelve ol' Charlie Hough and his knuckleball. Larry Bowa, Richie Hebner, Mike Schmidt, Bob Boone, and Ted Sizemore went to the plate, flailing away like a bunch of bush-leaguers; only Jay Johnstone and Greg Luzinski appeared as if they had a clue what to do with a knuckler. The final result? The Phils bit the dust, losing 6-4. Worse yet, they lost a game in the standings, as the Cubbies, who Mrs. Hargrove insisted would begin the process of fading, beat the piss out of the piss-poor Padres 23-6! Who scores twenty-three runs in one nine-inning ball-game? The Phils did not plate twenty-three runs all week! Goddamn Wrigley Field, with all the wind, can turn Major League baseball into a circus minus the clown cars and Keystone Cops. Hopefully, the fade Mrs. Hargrove promised will begin tomorrow.

Two rain delays, four appearances by the grounds crew, and nine innings of hardball resulted in us not exiting the stadium until a few ticks north of midnight. We rode the Broad Street subway from Pattison Avenue into the center of town. Exiting the subway, we walked a quiet and eerily desolate concourse to an even quieter and eerier underground train platform at 15th and Market. It was 12:30—a time when young men, out on their own and left to their own de-vices, are prone to come up with hair-brained ideas. The Frank-ford/Market line ran steadily from 6:00 a.m. until 10:00 p.m., but you could wait a spell in the hours beyond midnight. A *long* spell.

"Christ," I half moaned, half yawned, "we'll be here all night and with no place to sit." Then Cillian said, "Forget the train. We'll make better time walking the tracks. Trust me; it's safer than walk-ing through town at this hour."

If it was not yet a year since the date of Cillian's high wire act, also known as "the trestle episode," it was damn close. I have suffered many instances when, in a twilight sleep, I am too late to recognize that Joey—his voice below the trestle is guiding Cillian to safety—has be-come tongue-tied, and the result is Cillian walking off the edge and plummeting toward his death, and me running to break his fall. These episodes cause me to jolt, spasm, and contemplate what might have happened: Cillian, a human missile, coursing straight for Earth, and me running to a given point, then looking away upon grasping that intercepting this missile is an exercise in futility. I try to place my thoughts elsewhere to get beyond a twilight doze to deep sleep. Sometimes, it works; sometimes, it doesn't. So why did I, as too did Joey, unhesitatingly jump down onto the train tracks?

Walking underground train tracks beyond midnight may have been a soberer affair than walking a train trestle blindfolded. Yet it rendered no advantage. The likeliest scenario was that we make it a stop or two down the line without getting mangled between steel rails and the wheels of a train, hoist ourselves up onto the platform, and then board the same train that we would have back at 15th Street—otherwise the one that potentially kills us. But when it is well past midnight, and you are in your mid-teens, not every aspect of life is required to make sense. Cillian and I finding the act of beating each other senseless on a wrestling mat easier than echoing the sentiments, "I care for you" or "Your friendship is something I cherish," hardly qualifies as an epistemic tour de force, especially for anyone faint of heart. Our unique brand of affection notwithstanding, sometimes— if only for the sake of feeling alive, tempting fate, testing the theory of natural selection, or simply being a defiant sonofabitch—the logic branch of epistemology must take a back seat.

Like a family of geese, we walked single file: Joey took the lead, I was in the middle, and Cillian held up the rear. Cillian took the initiative of assigning positions; after all, it was his hair-brained scheme. "If a train comes, I wanna make sure I'm the one that gets run over," he said. I'm guessing Cillian had Mister Brosco in mind when he placed Joey in the lead but did not elaborate. Instead, he said, "Come on, Joey, you take the lead; you're the most valuable."

It was a noble gesture—at least the intention was noble— and uttered affectionately; on that front, I'll give Cillian his due. But if a train comes, and we are caught in no man's land and do not have the presence of mind to leap over the partition onto the westbound track, all three of us would end up railroad stew. I did not bother pointing this matter out to Cillian. Why spoil an act of valor, however futile?

The outcome of our stunt aside, Cillian placed himself in what ostensibly seemed the least envious position. However, if truth be told, we did not think for one second that getting ground up under the wheels of a speeding train was a viable possibility. We were still young and stupid enough to believe, cosmically, that our lives were too meaningful and thus incapable of being snuffed out by what we perceived as harmless teenage foolishness. If teenagers had their own sections in cemeteries, and their causes of death were inscribed on their stones, it would doubtless read like a slapstick comedy a network executive would salivate over, with the boys, primarily, and all their daredevil bullshit, providing the punchlines. For example, recently, a young man named Robert—surname withheld—met his end when he went over Niagara Falls on a jet ski. Robert planned to deploy a parachute, but parachutes do not react well when doused with tons of water. Another, Rodney—surname also withheld—upon attaching jumper cables to a 110-volt outlet, tried to jump the battery of his water scooter with it still resting in Lake Washington. The result was instant electrocution. Topping the list of Darwin award winners for most comical deaths was Dave. Dave stole one of the protective mats used to cover the metal poles along a ski slope. Upon utilizing the mat as a sled—you guessed it—he crashed head-on into the pole with the missing mat and died on impact. I saw headlines flashing before my eyes: *Three Teenage Boys, Run Over by the Same Train. Foolish Stunt Proves Fatal; Three Dead as a Result.* Doubtless, we would make the national news, and, from coast to coast, the criticisms would pile up: Goddamn Philadelphians; they throw snowballs at Santa Claus, screw up presidential debates, and now they're getting mashed to death in train tunnels!

Philadelphia is an old city, perhaps the oldest in the country. Its transportation system is also old, if not the oldest: the railroad ties have long since ossified, the rails themselves are of equal age, and each has withstood who knows how many trips from Bridge and Pratt to 69th Street—the first and last stops of the Market Street and Frankford Avenue Line. So redolent was the smell of old wood and steel mixed with machine oil, and when walled inside an underground tunnel, the concoction of odors coalesced to deliver a dense earthiness and mustiness, one that sparked a memory from my early childhood. A few years before Casey was born, I used to sneak downstairs to Grandpa Alexander's dark, damp cellar on Girard Avenue to tinker with his old tools (Grandpa Alexander was a carpenter) and other cobwebbed relics no longer in use but capable of captivating a youngster. Before long, the memory faded. I was no longer down Grandpa Alexander's cellar; instead, I was in a subterranean tunnel, and the mustiness accentuated by the concoction of wood, steel, and machine oil—otherwise stagnated air—was edging me toward the possibility that should I allow myself to become ill-composed over the idiotic position in which I had placed myself, I might choke.

We must have been halfway between stops. No longer could I see any light from the 15th Street platform or light up ahead announcing that we were nearing the 13th Street station. Christ, it was dark! Our eyes, though, were beginning to adjust to the darkness. Also, there were a few lights scattered throughout the tunnel—they were similar to the lights that mechanics positioned over car engines—helping us see with enough clarity the partition dividing eastbound and westbound should it become necessary to leap onto the westbound track. Still, it was too dark for my liking.

Finally, we saw up ahead the light emanating from the 13th Street station and then the platform itself. Turning to the left, I spotted the dim lights inside the bargain basement of John Wannamaker's, a nine-floor department store. Its basement was where all the really expensive shit from the second and third floors that failed to sell within a year ended up. This bargain-basement demotion was the only way families like the James, Broscos, and Caldwells could afford to shop at Wannamaker's. So how does a teenage boy wrapped up in writing his coming-of-age story know about the bargain basement of a department store? My Grandma Elizabeth works part-time in the coat department on the main floor—the same main floor that features the famous 2,500-pound bronze eagle statue and where every Christmas season, folks by the hundreds, gather for a light show accompanied by the famous Wannamaker organ playing Christmas carols. When I was a youngster keen for a Saturday adventure, against my father's wishes—my hippie mother did not seem too concerned one way or the other—I would wind my way to the train (the same one I'm praying won't run me over), ride it into downtown Philly and Wannamaker's, and surprise Grandma Elizabeth. She was always delighted to see me and would wink as one might when understanding a youngster had done something against a parent's wishes but was a good keeper of secrets. Then, in grandmotherly fashion, Grandma Elizabeth would slide me the seventy-five cents required to purchase a Wannafrost, which was Wannamaker's version of a custard cone.

Although unintentionally and without anyone manipulating the result, grandmothers represent a most curious phenomenon within the circle of human relations. They begin their matriarchal tenure as the greatest thing since sliced bread, only to end up the least stimulating person in the room. Perhaps the female amygdala past a certain age, turning grandmothers into worrywarts, best explains the phenomenon. Anyway, what's strange is that the transformation process goes undetected from a grandson's perspective. It is only at its conclusion that a grandson becomes enlightened that a change has occurred. Moreover, it is uncertain whether this unfortunate transition occurs over a year, a month, or overnight, but it does happen.

We left the dim lights of Wannamaker's bargain basement and the brighter ones of the 13th Street platform behind, electing, although without putting it to a vote, to tempt fate, press our luck, live on the edge—choose the most fitting idiom—and head on to 11th Street. Then it happened: We knew, eventually, it would, as we would have continued pressing our luck if not for an intervening force. We found ourselves at the halfway point, otherwise known as no man's land—where the lights ahead or to the rear were no longer visible—when we heard the roar of an onrushing train filling the tunnel. I felt my heart sink with a thud and then race like never before. I recently read that a sudden burst of adrenaline can create enough stress to induce a heart attack; the article also mentioned fibrillation, oxygenated blood from the lungs not adequately reaching the heart, and a bunch of other technical bullshit I had difficulty grasping. But I figured my heart could withstand the strain at my current age, three months younger than Maryellen, four younger than Cillian, and five younger than Joey. Then I heard Cillian make a cheesy analogy that compared the tunnel to the vagina of a girl looking to lose her virginity and the train to the prick of a real horny sonofabitch with loads of experience not seeking a commitment: in other words, a one-night stand, a one-and-done affair, a cold and unemotional business transaction. Cillian failed to mention our role in this brief and somewhat amusing parable, though I could not claim to hold a keen interest.

As it came to pass, all three of us panicked. Instead of leaping over the partition onto the westbound track, our instincts took over, and they screamed out the command: *Run!* But sprinting through a dark tunnel with the added trick of negotiating railroad tracks made about as much sense as being down there in the first place: None! Then, the onrushing roar that hastened our faulty instincts came to a stop, doubtless at the 13th Street platform, where we should have been standing and preparing to board. Hell, for that matter, we should have been back at 15th Street all along and currently experiencing the view of the 13th Street platform from a window. But that's not what we were doing. Instead, we were running for our lives, and Jesus Christ, when I tell you Joey Brosco was no track star, I'm not kidding! What the hell was Cillian thinking by putting him in the lead position? Life is supposed to be about survival of the fittest: the slowest wildebeest gets eaten by the lion; the careless marmot gets swooped down upon by the hawk and ends up a tasty meal; the impetus behind our placings may have *seemed* magnanimous, but possibly Cillian's goal was to get us all killed. All sorts of wild thoughts were flying at me. Mixed in with the wild ones was a flicker of sobriety, and, thankfully, it prevailed: You do *not* try and pass a guy while running on railroad tracks when the tracks are in a dark tunnel; for sure, someone will fall, and the result would not be pretty, especially for the poor bastard whose responsibility is to clear away mangled body parts from rails; although, it is unlikely that someone holds this position, specifically. Nevertheless, in these rare instances, when humans attempt to interact with trains, someone must get stuck with shit detail.

Finally, we spotted a glow of light coming from the 11th Street platform. But then the train started up; we could hear its departure from the 13th Street station, that old familiar hydraulic train wheezing before gathering a head of steam, working its way up to maximum speed, and filling the tunnel with its onrushing roar. We were not far off, almost there; all that remained was the outcome, and there were only two: We would arrive at the platform before the train reached us, or the train would get to us before we arrived at the platform. It could not be simpler. More thoughts began flying at me— unrelated thoughts over which I had no control—ones that, given the circumstances, lacked congruency: How could the Cubs score twenty-three runs in a single ballgame? Just wait until I see Mrs. Hargrove tomorrow! *Would* I see Mrs. Hargrove tomorrow? Would Mrs. Hargrove and thousands of other Philadelphians hear this morning's lead story about the three morons who got run over by a midnight train? My grandmother is the greatest. Jeeze, I really love Casey! I swear to the god I never believed in, worshipped, or prayed to, if this train spares turning me into a plate of scrambled eggs, I'll fall on my knees before Maryellen and confess it is her vagina that inspires my maniacal self-indulgence; hence the mysterious ooze Mr. Hubert warned us of two years ago in sex-ed class. Indeed, Maryellen, every time I spout jizz, it's for you, baby, all for you!

The train's roar echoed menacingly in our ears; we could feel its breath on our necks—this far superior force that, with ease, could outrun us *was* outrunning us, and its unmistakable gains introduced an unparalleled sense of terror. It could not think this mechanical monster, nor could it experience empathy. Moreover, it had a one-track mind with a single function: to pursue and its inexorable and implacable pursuit caused me to doubt the outcome and wish that my heart was ill-equipped to withstand the strain and explode; thus, I would perish in stride without a shred of awareness. But wait, not so fast: I had arrived! I made it to 11th Street, and there was still time yet if only the diminutive Joey Brosco could hoist himself atop the platform by way of his own effort. Before I could fully consider the consequence should Joey struggle, he was home free, aided doubtless by a burst of adrenalin. Not a full second later, I joined him.

On our backs, Joey and I lay. Glaring down at us are the lights from the station's ceiling. I stared into them until I felt my eyes stinging; I wanted to sense whatever palpable proof was available that I was still alive; even chunks of the ceiling collapsing on me, I would have greeted with welcome. Lying there, we made awful convulsive noises—strident and dissonant caws—that were part hysterical laughter and cries of joy, a poignant fusion that rang like the laughter of the insane. Indeed, they were not celebratory sounds echoing through the concourse, for we had gained nothing; we merely retained what should never have been anted up in the first place: Our lives! Next, we jerked ourselves to a sitting position and surveyed the platform. Where was Cillian? Then came the silver bullet, our soulless tormentor, blaring into the station; its roar, during this period of desolation, was deafening.

The windows of each car flickered past, and the cars, save for a few stragglers, were empty. The train settled, and after making the deafening hydraulic yawning sound that it produces when completing a stop, Joey and I screamed for our friend: "CJ! CJ!" Once more, we surveyed the empty platform as though there stood a possibility that Cillian could appear out of thin air. Again, we screamed out Cillian's name; our voices reverberated throughout the empty station—from the eastbound side to the westbound side and then back—but following our ricocheting calls, there came no reply. With a hiss, the doors of the train flew open. The universe fell ominously silent; the train, at rest, seemed more menacing than when it was hunting us down. The doors zipped shut. No one exited. On this night, at this late hour, 11th Street was no one's destination unless the goal was to grapple with mortality. But this was Philly, a big city, a rough town: if it was mortality one sought, plenty of places were more than willing to accommodate someone owning such a dubious ambition.

As the train made its departure, Joey and I kept our eyes fixed straight ahead at the windows flickering past us like the images on an old film projector. We could not bear to look down, as we might witness what the underbelly of a train does to a human body. Finally, when the train cleared the station, there was Cillian, standing on the partition that separated the eastbound and westbound tracks, perched with arms folded and grinning like a sonofabitch—it was that goddamn comedy/tragedy smile of his we saw from the platform, the one where the upturned corners of his mouth meet the downturned corners of his eyes.

"Why the faces, laddies?" he called, using the Irish brogue he often intoned whenever a situation called for irony. "Did you think me dead, bejesus?"

"Get the fuck over here!" I bellowed. "Or, so help me...." Cillian hopped down from the partition and meandered across the tracks, not like someone who narrowly escaped death by the skin of his teeth but like a young man strolling through a sun-drenched field whose only concern was picking dandelions. As he hoisted himself onto the platform, I grabbed him by the back of his shirt and threw him forward so that he landed sprawled between the tracks and the tiled wall. Next,

I pounced; I managed to place Cillian in a chokehold, and while maintaining this debilitating maneuver, Joey peppered his belly and chest with a flurry of punches. It was the most profuse outpouring of love Cillian had ever experienced. Nothing says "I love you" more plainly than friends beating the living shit out of you because, for a few weighty and portentous moments, they suspected you were a goner.

When I eased up on my hold, Joey's flying fists faltered. He fell backward, huffing and puffing from the exertion. Then Cillian said, "The next stop is 8th Street. I bet we could make it with a half-hour to spare."

We sprawled out on the 11th Street platform and laughed ourselves to a state of delirium. When riding the train homeward—it did not arrive for nearly an hour, proving Cillian's calculation that we would have reached 8th Street with a half-hour to spare—it seemed an eternity passed since handing Mrs. Hargrove tests proving how much *Of Mice and Men* we had retained. It was a long day that proved one of the most stimulating of my life. After eight months, I learned that the woman enlightening me about the literature of my language, who at her warmest was stoic and otherwise menacing, was a baseball fanatic. Who would have imagined? I learned to admire and feel much richer for having met a one-legged man; if there was ever someone with an admirable perspective on life, it was Mister Brosco. While many lost their lives ensuring that democracy and freedom remained viable substrates, all he had to do was "Cough up half a leg." Lastly, I learned that one of my two best friends—although I reject the notion he is suicidal—has a death wish. The question was, why?

CHAPTER NINE
SAYING GOODBYE TO CASEY AND MARYELLEN

It was 2:35 a.m., or so said my tacky Pink Panther wristwatch, when, at last, I planted my feet on my doorstep. It is anyone's guess what whirled in Darrin's head the previous summer when he decided a Pink Panther wristwatch was just the item for a fourteen-year-old. It was one of those objects you pick up long enough to say, "Gee, that's cute," not, "I gotta teenage son who's gonna love this!" I took a moment to glance upward. More specifically, my fixed upward gaze targeted my parents' wide-open bedroom windows. And why shouldn't the windows have been open; it was nearly June. But the fresh night air was not the objective as it smelled like Claire was up to her old tricks; doubtless, she was fit to be tied that I was so late coming home—I did give her a courtesy call concerning the multiple rain delays—and it provided her all the excuse she needed to fire up a 2:00 a.m. doobie.

An inner sense of bliss surged within me; it engendered feelings of confidence and friskiness—I heard that almost getting mangled by an inner-city commuter train can trigger all sorts of odd sensations—and this mix of emotions emboldened me such that I marched around back and bounced pebbles off Maryellen's bedroom window.

"Maryellen," I repeatedly called. Let the record state that Maryellen did not dash to the window as might an expectant maiden awakened from a blissful dream of her betrothed sweeping her off her feet and setting her atop a white stallion, though, upon first recognizing her unexpected late-night suitor was none other than me, she did call out, "Addison?" in a tone that seemed to resonate with curiosity and delight. It was, indeed, a lovely timbre that rang out my name. But not a moment later, upon gathering her wits, Maryellen hissed, applying appropriate middle-of-the-night volume: "Addison, you idiot! It's 2:45 in the morning!"

"Maryellen," I began; a note of unmistakable earnestness gushed. "I wanted you to know that tonight, I almost died." I omitted the explanation of how this near-miss came to pass; doubtless, her reaction would not have been to froth with sympathy. Nevertheless, as I should have suspected—and what might anyone expect at such an hour—sympathy was in short supply. Instead, Maryellen hollered down in a razor-sharp tongue, "Yeah, well, *almost* dying doesn't count, Addison; let me know when you *really* intend to die, and if you have any say in the matter, die in broad daylight, not in the middle of the night!"

Dropping to a knee, I spread my arms. "But I love you, Maryellen," I profess. "You are the sun by day, the stars by night, my true guiding light." Do I realize that I am playing Cyrano de Bergerac to Maryellen's Lady Roxanne and that my effort is farcical? If Maryellen suspected that I was using farce to mask sincerity, she made no accusations to indicate as much. Either way, she lowered the curtain on me by slamming shut her window before returning to bed. Farce notwithstanding, I walked away feeling quite the lover, a true champion for romance. Unfortunately, unlike Cyrano, whose rivals were the Baron Christian de Neuvillette and Comte de Guiche, my rivals were the core principles of a nineteen-hundred-year-old doctrine. In other words, compared to what I was up against, Cyrano, despite his schnoz, had it made in the shade.

It was no sooner than I had taken to my bed that I felt that old familiar rush of blood. Like usual, my flaming, red-headed, freckle-faced, unsympathetic neighbor invaded my thoughts. I suppose where Maryellen was concerned, I was akin to the dog who made every effort to win the affections of the one family member unimpressed by his cuteness.

The following afternoon, Cillian, Joey, and I let Mrs. Hargrove know that teams poised to fade don't typically make a habit of posting twenty-three runs in a single game, to which she retorted: "You boys are old enough to have been following baseball since when,1971? Maybe 1970? I've been through more pennant races than I care to mention." I couldn't pinpoint Mrs. Hargrove's precise age, but she cut a nice enough figure to where she ought to be proud of her age— whatever it was. Mrs. Hargrove put me in mind of Joan Crawford, minus the tragic eyes and copiously applied lipstick. "And you can rest assured," she added emphatically, "the Cubs will fade." After citing numerous examples of the Cubs racing out to leads only to plummet in the standings, I left convinced that Mrs. Hargrove knew history like Joey Brosco knew statistics, which was saying something!

During these last fading weeks of the school year, we got close to Mrs. Hargrove. It made saying goodbye difficult. "Come back for a visit in late September," she told us. "By then, we should have a good idea who the Phils will be going up against for the pennant." She had us swelling with confidence. Of course, the Cubs will fade!

Meanwhile, on the home front, Darrin was lauding the completion of the Trans-Alaskan Pipeline. "Seven hundred thousand barrels of genuine U.S. crude, every day, is gonna pass through that sucker!" he intoned

"At a total project cost of eight billion dollars, 700 thousand barrels a day had *better* trickle through that pipe," Claire retorted.

"Rain on the parade if it makes you happy," said Darrin, "but that pipeline will pay for itself before you know it."

"It'll be a few years, yet, before it's running at full capacity," Claire reminded Darrin. "And when it is, I doubt we'll see the Saudis shuddering in their sandals."

A day later, Claire was bleeding from her eyes because the Supreme Court ruled six to three that neither the Constitution nor Federal Law, as it currently stands, requires states to spend Medicaid funds for elective abortions. The ruling does not mandate states to "bar" funds for abortions, only that if states wish to, and their constitutions permit it, they can bar the use of public funds and facilities for "nontherapeutic" abortions. As only she can, Claire launched into the mother of all rants that nothing brandishing a penis should have permission to rule on a woman's reproductive rights. "If a woman, in her first trimester, does not wish to carry a pregnancy to term, no governing body with its bullshit legislation should wield the power to see that she does! What are we, brood sows? Pack mules?" Claire was penis hunting tonight, and by the time she was through with her tirade, she had poor Darrin convinced he was one of the six vilified Supreme Court Justices who came down on the wrong side of the issue and, as a result, was forced to forfeit all bedroom privileges. "As of right now, you and Wally Johnson—Wally Johnson was Claire's pet name for Darrin's penis—are on probation."

Darrin could not get a word in edgewise. He went next door to visit Guy McNamara. The Supreme Court's ruling would have no bearing on Guy.

And then came the final day of school. The Cubs had yet to receive the memo concerning their manifest destiny. In other words, there were no signs of a fade on the horizon.

"They don't hand out pennants in June," Mrs. Hargrove reminded us.

I had become a mental patient over the predicted fade insofar that I required daily reassurance. The last day of school also meant yearbook signings: Sharon Millstein wrote in Cillian's yearbook, and in mine, the encoded message: *Thanks for the memories, no matter how small. Love, Sharon.* One day I'll have a wife, and she will ask, "What did she mean by 'no matter how small,'" and I shall admit to once being a scoundrel who tricked a girl into looking at his penis. As for Sharon? You have got to love a girl with a sense of humor, and Sharon was loaded; humor was her version of tits, and like tits, it showed up every day, and she learned to use it effectively to tame her male peers. Okay, maybe you couldn't accentuate it with a form-fitting top, but it never disappointed, nor was it devoid of sex appeal. Sharon wrote in Joey Brosco's yearbook: *I'm proud of you, Joey. I know it wasn't always easy, though somehow you managed to keep "our boys" in line. Best of luck, Love Sharon.* Cillian and I had a keen sense that something was brewing between Joey and Sharon coming down the home stretch of our freshman year. I heard somewhere that Italians and Jews—perhaps it's the superstitious bent ingrained in their cultural DNA—get along well together. Anyway, that's what I heard. It's just unfortunate that Joey will be gone all summer. Bad timing, I suppose; however, summers tend to fly by, and if the feeling keeps, Joey and Sharon can pick up what they started in September as sophomores. I would feel more confident betting on Joey and Sharon than on the Cubs fading.

"*So*, about this Leila Bennett person, or Aunt Leila, or whatever you're calling her these days," Darrin began. He decided it was high time to don his "concerned father" hat and brim over, ostensibly, with misgivings at the proverbial 11th hour, otherwise known as the night before my departure. "Has she told you yet what your pay rate will be? And concerning your responsibilities, will you do actual farming, maintenance, or grunt work—otherwise common labor? You are getting paid, aren't you? It isn't one of those screwy summer camp deals, I hope. I heard about these working ranches people visit instead of taking a typical vacation; Americans are always shopping for new experiences."

At times, the predictability of Darrin Caldwell could be downright comical. For example, because Claire was still ill-humored over the latest Supreme Court ruling—a ruling that led to Darrin's frustration and forced him to breathe in the hot, acrid air that Claire was copiously exhaling—he, in turn, decided to pay it forward by assuming the role of an authoritarian father. But yours truly is an understanding son well aware of the universal mechanisms present in modern society. Most notable is a bodily organ not yet assigned a name but apparently secretes an enzyme carrying the instruction: whenever we have been shat upon and cannot retaliate in kind, we must seek out someone upon whom we *can* shit.

My empathy for Darrin's situation notwithstanding, I had a sound mind to reply: *A working ranch would be a walk in the park compared to some of our beach vacations.* Instead, I said, "You got me, Dad; it's all been a ruse; there's no ranch, no farm. The U.S. had gotten involved in some far-flung international incident. It was all very hush-hush and, to say the least, convoluted, but to make matters right where national security is concerned, we must send three youths to a Siberian penal colony, and Cillian, Joey, and I drew the shortest straws. Hey, but you know how it is, Dad: in one way or another, we all must serve our country."

I did not go so far as to remind Darrin of his days as a cowboy; that might have been considered a low blow or cheap shot. After all, it was not ol' Darrin Caldwell's fault that he was born too late to serve in Korea and too soon for Vietnam. Moreover, I was not inclined to unleash a barrage of farcical sarcasm upon a benevolent patriarch who, currently, like his son concerning matters of the vagina, is on the outside looking in. However, it seemed no sooner than the bell dismissing me from the school year to summertime reverberated that a line of people antsy to give me a piece of their mind concerning my summer plans had formed. And friends, I was quick to learn, tend to be exceedingly generous when opining over someone breaching abstractions known as "the boundaries of others," though I suppose I shouldn't be too hard on my peers for exhibiting typical human behavior. Anyway, it just so happened that dear old Dad was the last in line, and by the time Darrin and I engaged in our little tete-a-tete, I had suffered enough irritation. Finally, and before the matter had a chance to become too contentious, I checked my tacky Pink Panther wristwatch and said, "Isn't it about time for Sinatra?"

Richie Costigan, the sonofabitch, was my first challenge of the day, sniffing me out just as I turned onto my block, and the entanglement occurred not long after coming from a delightful session of hugs, handshakes, and sincere well-wishes during yearbook signings.

"Dumping all your old friends for the summer, are you, Addie?" Richie began. "Neighborhood not good enough for you anymore?"

No one could spew antagonistic bullshit better than Richie Costigan. His efforts usually consisted of questions teetering between legitimate probes and broaching a confrontation. It was typical Irish cop-bullying bullshit; I had long since become familiar with Richie's tactics. He accosted me as might a nationalist suspecting someone of joining the communist party. So I decided to play along—to engage Richie.

"You got me, Richie," I said. "I've grown tired of my old friends, and the neighborhood sucks."

"Always a smartass, arencha, Addie?"

"Look," I began with the understanding I was a smartass and enjoyed being a smartass— "smartass" is the term that best defines me. But I also understood that Richie Costigan needed defusing. I was not looking to rekindle a friendship; my only goal was to avoid making an enemy. "I needed a summer job and jumped at the first offer. It just so happened it's at the other end of the state, end of story, and it's a story that lacks mystery or motive." Next, I wished Richie a good summer, made every effort to sound sincere, and then walked away. I could not hazard a guess as to why Richie got his horns all twisted. Maybe he is jealous of my friendships with Cillian and Joey. However, I cannot imagine why: my friendship with Richie ran its course a while ago. Some friendships come with an expiration date, and Richie and I had reached ours—a fact both of us were aware of. And our breakup did not warrant a discussion; breakups are not the sort of thing guys hash out over coffee. Meanwhile, Richie and I have maintained some civility but prefer not to hover in one another's orbit longer than necessary.

Upon enduring additional bullshit from other *so-called* friends, I had a much more civil go-around with Timmy Pytlewski. I have yet to encounter a more affable acquaintance than Timmy; he was akin to jello—there was always room for Timmy—in that he could no more adversely affect the dynamic of a situation than jello could your stomach. Timmy was a peacemaker, had a kind word for everybody, and was perfectly at home making himself the butt of a joke. "The neighborhood won't be the same without you, Addie," he said. "For sure, it'll be missing some humor." My exchange with Timmy ended with me in the arms of Missus Pytlewski for what I supposed was an affectionate goodbye for the summer embrace. Okay, so maybe she was not attired in one of her scrumptious-looking *hanging the laundry in summertime* outfits, but, goddammit, it was still Cyndy Pytlewski; I could feel her renowned bosom pressing against my chest. For a fleeting moment, the embrace felt loving—a split-second chock-full of possibilities—thus I soared to some lofty place, a quantum leap beyond Mary Mac and Terry Dell to the top of the world where I rode a wave sure to land me in the big leagues. But then Missus Pytlewski went and fucked it up when she took a step backward and tousled my hair in a motherly fashion. And there was no mistaking it was a *remember to be a good boy this summer, Addie* type of tousling. In other words, it was not in the least bit reminiscent of how Sharon Millstein pressed her lips to Joey's—a kiss carrying the message that Sharon planned to keep herself pure until her hairy little gentile returned.

From Cyndy Pytlewski to Claire Caldwell, I went. Claire was waiting for me at the front door, or so it seemed, assuming her demeanor was any indication. Her mission was clear: to annoy me in a way only a mother can. She handed me a piece of paper known as "the dreaded checklist" and then proceeded to go over it one strenuous item at a time, and the list was longer than my goddamn arm! Next, Claire escorted me to my bedroom, where, waiting for me atop my bed was an open suitcase surrounded by an apothecary smorgasbord: eyedrops, nasal spray, mouthwash, nail clippers, sunscreen, ointment in case I forgot to use the sunscreen, aspirin, Band-Aids, talcum powder, and a dozen other items including what first captured my attention: a flat, rectangle-shaped yellow box containing anal suppositories. Able to follow my gaze, Claire defended this idiotic purchase by citing, "The water is sure to be different on a Western Pennsylvania farm, well water, most likely, and if you're not used to well water, it's liable to irritate your bowels and cause you to have some difficulty … down there." Claire shilly-shallied with a schoolgirl's embarrassment when pointing at my posterior; it was all very un-Claire-like. Then she unnecessarily added, as though somehow it could have slipped my mind: "Remember, you're a city boy."

I held my ground while wearing my game face; my expression was akin to Carlton glaring in at a nervous rookie. I rarely display such discipline. But had I let loose even a single utterance, the matter of the flat rectangle-shaped yellow box might have qualified as a conversation, and whatever misadventures that could potentially befall my hindquarters three hundred miles west of Philadelphia was not a subject I was willing to broach. Then, upon listening patiently to Claire's rationale in support of her first aid *just-in-cases* and *what-ifs*, I handed her the checklist and escorted her from my bedroom. As I expected, she got all huffy and moaned, "Fine! I was only trying to be a good mother. But if you don't want me to be a good mother, then hell with it!"

For a second, I felt a pang of guilt for having pooh-poohed Claire's due diligence concerning motherhood, then called to her in the hallway while reexamining the smorgasbord, "What's the matter; was the drugstore all sold out of Trojans?" If ever there was a *just-in-case* or *what-if* item meant to travel with a teen on his first summer away from home, it was a box of Trojans. Moreover, it was challenging to imagine Claire Caldwell too embarrassed to have condoms rung up at the local apothecary, which meant that she had every reason to suspect that I would begin and end the summer of '77 a virgin.

"It's not too late, Addie," she called to me from the hallway, somewhat apologetic for the oversight. "I can still run out and get some if you think you'll need them."

"Never mind," I sourly replied. I did not want condoms as much as I wanted Claire to believe I needed them.

I flung my suitcase back in the closet and reached for my duffle bag with the shoulder strap and side pockets. I rolled up three changes of clothes, some deodorant, toothpaste, and a toothbrush. I owned a razor, but my whiskers were hardly worth the effort. If it turns out that my face rapidly matures this summer, I'll return Labor Day weekend bearded. Cillian's provisions would be similar. Joey, however, would be adding a razor, *cans* of shaving cream, and several blades; the sonofabitch from the neck up was an Italianized version of the Marlboro Man. Joey would also cram shoeboxes of baseball cards into his bag: doubtless, some vintage or premier collection that he reserved for such occasions—like being away from home for two months—and the current year's cards, his 1977 collection featuring Dave Cash, Ted Sizemore, and Johnny Oates not in their current uniforms.

Next came dinner, followed by the earlier-mentioned exchange I had with Darrin. At last, I had successfully navigated a thicket, withstood a gauntlet, survived copious amounts of that pervasive social currency known as bullshit, displayed generosity when besieged by the more frequently spent social currency stupidity, shown myself crafty in avoiding a potential altercation hastened by envy, delivered stinging invectives to morons too moronic to understand that I was not handing out compliments, was Mr. Smooth—if I don't say so myself—when determining mollification ranked as an essential theme, and an acerbic prick—a role that better suits my persona—when a situation called explicitly for that asset. Aside from the above-mentioned, it was a typical, uneventful day in the life and times of Addison Caldwell. And now, with it all behind me, I decided to spend what remained of this typical day, my last night in Philly, not with friends—though I had plenty of offers: Danny Murphy, Timmy Pytlewski, and Theresa Delvecchio among them—but with Casey. I took her for ice cream. We had a parlor in our neighborhood called The Sweet Shop, and they had a butterscotch vanilla-flavored ice cream that made me swoon.

"You're looking at me weird, Addie," Casey said as we sat on The Sweet Shop's high stools and went at our ice cream with those long cocktail spoons necessary to reach ice cream at the bottom of those tall, glass flutes ice cream parlors typically supply. "Why are you smiling like that?"

"You're gonna be a real heartbreaker, Case; you know that?" Casey's face twisted such that the only discernable interpretation was confusion. I did not offer any explanation. Instead, I tousled her bangs similarly to how Missus Pytlewski had tousled my hair earlier. Casey's bangs rest just above her well-shaped eyebrows. When unveiled, they are exotic, though not until tonight had I honored them with any attention. As I continued shoveling ice cream into my mouth, I took stock of my kid sister's assets. She had what I would describe as an adorable overbite. Other features worth noticing were eyes that possessed all the fire and energy of youth and legs already shedding their childlike spindliness and taking shape. She had just turned eight, had Casey, and could claim, however briefly, to be only six years my junior. The fleeting spell notwithstanding, having that claim available made her sit up straighter and act less like a child. Casey's birthday effectively engineered a tide that raised her ship, whereas my birthday reintroduced the low tide that caused her to feel every bit the runt that she was. But I would be gone all summer. I wondered what kind of girl I would return to come September.

"Hey Case, because I'll be away all summer—and that's a heckuva long time—there's a good chance I'll get lonely, even with CJ and Joey for company. So do you know what I'm gonna need? More than anything else, whudda you think I'll need?"

Casey ceased gobbling her ice cream. She rested her spoon on a napkin and lurched forward on her stool. She appeared anxious for my words, as one would when anticipating that what was about to get revealed would not just prove vital but that there stood every possibility they were a prevailing factor. "More than anything, Case, I'm gonna need a pen pal—someone willing to write to me and with whom I'd enjoy reciprocating. But, of course, you wouldn't happen to know someone keen to be my pen pal, would you? And it can't be just anybody; it would have to be someone I'd want to hear from and enjoy writing *to*—someone who appreciates my sense of humor and isn't shy about expressing themselves, even if it means disagreeing with me."

Those beautifully shaped eyebrows of Casey's arched and then broadened. The fire in her eyes flashed brilliantly. Like most young girls whose collective molecules were bursting and ascending toward forming a rousing pinnacle, she was especially pretty when smiling.

"Now, don't get me wrong," I added, "I don't want you inside bogged down with pen and paper all summer. Let's agree to write to each other once per week. That way, we'll have loads of interesting things to report."

Casey echoed her agreement that writing on a once-per-week basis was a good idea, although something in her fiery eyes conveyed she, conservatively speaking, would double my output.

I felt guilty for largely ignoring Casey these past eighteen months. With thrusting myself into a teenagerhood that involved developing a healthy preoccupation with the opposite sex and cultivating meaningful friendships, I lacked all cognitive awareness that my kid sister became collateral damage, got relegated to nothing more than a piece of furniture I thoughtlessly walked past, an inanimate object I all but forgot was there; and now not only would I rank as an absentee brother for this summer, I would not be with my family at the seashore. What awful timing!

If that night in the tunnel, which saw me nearly mangled by a train, served a purpose, it alerted me that Casey Caldwell was a person and a damn meaningful one. She was not someone I loved by way of default, but a person I truly loved. We tend to overlook siblings and devote either a meager amount or no effort to what, ultimately, are vital relationships. But it all changed that night at The Sweet Shop for Casey and me. Indeed, the tunnel episode may have placed me on a path of enlightenment, but the night in The Sweet Shop shined a light and showed me the way forward. We could sense the change—Casey and I were akin to architects of time itself, and minute to minute, word by word, we were making time unfold in perfect harmony and symmetry. It was beautiful.

"Thanks, Case." I always dropped the *y* in Casey's name, altering it from a nifty girl's name to an inanimate object. I should not be so lazy and honor the neat name. Cillian and Joey took to calling Casey Caldwell, my baby sister, CC.

"For what?" Casey, in this instance, seemed every bit a young woman when she shrugged. "Did you really think there was a chance that I wouldn't want to be pen pals with my big brother?"

"No, not for that," I said. "Thanks for being the only sane person I've spoken to since leaving school this afternoon."

It was nearing nine o'clock. The Sweet Shop would close in less than ten minutes. We took an irregular route when making our way home. The goal was to avoid people, particularly those I knew, like Richie Costigan or anyone else who were liable to endanger the perfection Casey and I created tonight. When we arrived at our front door, Casey, who was more worn out from our excursion than she was willing to admit, looked up at me with hopeful eyes and asked, "The Cubs are gonna fade, aren't they, Addie?"

****

The following morning, I woke up extra early. My plan? To avoid a long, drawn-out bullshit goodbye—the sort one might receive when about to be deployed halfway around the world to deal with a foreign entity the U.S. government perceives as an enemy of democracy and freedom (in other words, a threat to our economy) but, wouldn't you know it, ol' Claire Caldwell was already up, well caffeinated, wearing her mother of all motherly game face, and wasted no time starting in with: *don't forget to do this and don't forget to do that*, and, *are you sure you don't want to take the suppositories?* The poor woman developed an obsession that I make my Philadelphia departure equipped with something to shove up my ass. She would need to get over it. Not a minute later, Darrin came creeping down the stairs, and his appearance was followed by Casey's. Yessiree, it was a goddamn feeding frenzy, and yours truly was on the menu.

Casey's slinky arms felt pleasing around my waist; her subdued and loving morning presence almost made Darrin and Claire's alternating onslaught palatable. Casey remained with her arms snugly around me; doubtless, she intuited what her role should be this morning and had an even keener sense of my appreciation. She came up to the top of my chest. In returning her embrace, my arms rested on the tops of her shoulders, my chin on her head. The grin on my face was reminiscent of Guy McNamara's; it would remain unchanged until Darrin and Claire had exhausted their bombardment of redundant verbiage. Casey whispered in my ear on her tiptoes, "I already miss you." I whispered back, "I already miss you, too. But, by tomorrow, I promise they'll start behaving again." Before being tempted to take Casey along, I broke our embrace and reached for my duffle bag.

"What about breakfast?" Claire whined. Breakfast was never made, cooked, or prepared in the Caldwell household: bowl, cereal, milk, spoon, end of story. Trust me, it was not a story steeped in pragmatism or minimalism but in the principle of good old American "smash-and-grab" convenience. Often, breakfast was a condensed pajama-clad version of dinner, featuring Claire—her nose stuck in the front page of the *Inquirer*—lambasting some poor Republican because she equates fiscal conservatism to falling short on women's rights, and Darrin, ironically, reminding her that Jack Kennedy was "all about equal opportunity for women."

"We're having breakfast at the Broscos," I told her while reaching for the door. Upon flinging it open, I discovered rolled up and in a rubber band the *Philadelphia Inquirer*—otherwise the source of our morning antagonism. I reached, grabbed it, and then sent it sailing through the living room to Darrin, who was standing in the archway of the dining room. "Nice catch," I said, then pushed the door shut. Next, I raced down the first set of steps—the ones we shared with the McNamaras—to the landing. Before I descended the steps that led to the curb, I paused. Why? Out of the corner of an eye, I spotted Maryellen. Yesterday, she was the one person who failed to share her unsolicited and undesired opinion concerning my summer absence. The reason? I did not see Maryellen yesterday. In fact, it had been days since I managed a glimpse of my neighbor and all her flowing red hair and summer freckles, now the dominant feature of her pretty face. Never let it be said that I am a man who is unappreciative of saving the best for the last. And Maryellen could pretend, all she wanted, that reading the newspaper on the front steps at 7:45 in the morning was a matter of routine. But I knew, as sure as playing in train tunnels was dangerous, she planted herself there to see me off before I made my summer-long departure. The question was, why? Perhaps she intended to engage me civilly—that there were some kind words Roxanne wished to share with Cyrano before he hastened along on his journey—or there was some lingering issue over which she was keen to antagonize me, and it could not wait until September. Maryellen tossed aside the newspaper she was pretending to read. On second thought, I should give her credit; maybe she was reading the rag after all. I did manage to glimpse a headline, one containing the name Karen Ann Quinlan, a woman who, because she had been resting in a vegetative state for two-plus years, had all the "right to die" folks all charged up enough to oppose the conservative Catholics who cling to the notion of miracles. Maryellen, naturally, was a staunch supporter of the latter. She rose to her feet and met me at the landing. It felt strange. If nothing else, it marked a departure from the norm. In each of our encounters, which were too numerous to mention, I—the bold seeker and initiator—approached *her*. But now there she was, planting herself on the front steps as might a lost puppy, then launching herself in my direction. It was too good to be true.

If it was not too good to be true, it was too good to bother being true, as it was the morning of a departure followed by a two-month separation. Whatever prompted Maryellen's momentous break from protocol—assuming we had a social contract into which written were bylaws and procedures—would have to get placed on the proverbial back-burner for ten weeks with the hope it would not grow stale.

The timing notwithstanding, what marked both an unexpected and unprecedented aberration served to elevate Maryellen to a plateau reserved for those wielding the capacity to fascinate and impose; she even stood taller than I remembered despite standing barefooted. Her outfit presented an additional anomaly, though an unimposing one. A typical summer outfit for Maryellen was white sandals, Capri style pants—the kind that comes just below the knees and has ties—and a stylish but maddeningly unrevealing blouse. This morning, she was sporting jeans modified to the point of short shorts and a halter top exposing her midriff in totality. This delightfully skimpy ensemble made her appear curvier and hippier than I imagined when alone and paying her carnal homage. Moreover, what marked a welcome departure from the usual revealed her as *"all woman"* and one capable of causing a guy to second-guess his status or become wary of biting off more than he can chew. First, my eyes were drawn to the freckles dotting Maryellen's bare shoulders—never before had I an opportunity to glimpse her bare shoulders. She cut a surprisingly toned and athletic figure, similar to a swimmer or track and field athlete. And the summer redness in her face—that annual fieriness that manifests every June and blazes throughout the summer—was well-apparent and lent her a look of wildness; it was an *I dare you to try and tame me if you think you're man enough* sort of look. I was swimming in a sea of desire, each stroke carrying me closer to the brink of improbability—otherwise, the unleashing of the allegorical tiger I maintained Maryellen has kept unjustly imprisoned. It would be just my luck that the long-suppressed jungle cat would debut on the very morning I was to begin a journey that would keep me away from the city and Maryellen for the entirety of a season.

Despite all there was to feast upon— and, trust me, there was plenty—I was drawn, primarily, to the flatness of Maryellen's belly and, in particular, her navel. Why? I had never seen it before this morning. Things I've been denied visual access to in the past, even if they are body parts common to both sexes, tend to fascinate me. What can I say; it's how I'm wired. The result was Maryellen's navel prevailing as my most recent source of titillation—a commanding fixation; thus came upon me the rapidly developing and bizarre notion that Maryellen's copious physical gifts plus the lure and mysterious nature of not just *her* womanhood but the profound and inscrutable nature of femininity since the Garden of Eden originated from the tiny hollow at the base of her lovely abdomen. And Maryellen had a sexy innie, a slight vertical oval well exposed above the waist of her dungaree short-shorts. A horizontal oval would have been inconsistent with her lengthy midriff. And I never cared much for outies; they tend to creep me out. An outie belly button compels me to entertain the concept that a little creature is trapped inside and, to avoid suffocation, is attempting to thrust its nose through an accommodating orifice. An outie on a girl would be a deal-breaker, mainly because all that lure, mystery, and inscrutability would go right out the window, along with the lint that fails to collect due to the odd configuration.

Okay, there is every possibility my mind is melting; numerous thoughts are flying in every direction and losing shape before I can adequately think them through. But one matter should not get overlooked: Maryellen practically leaped down from the top step to greet me at the landing; it marked a momentous action I cannot overstate. As far as probability was concerned, it may not rub elbows with the Amazin' Mets, Joe Namath and the Jets defeating the Colts in Super Bowl III, or Augie Belts lugging himself up the fire tower five days a week for two years without suffering a cardiac arrest. But, in the life and times of a young man about to turn fifteen looking for an experience, it was unparalleled.

"So, Addison, you're gonna be a big working man this summer," Maryellen intoned. It was more a statement than a question and a rather condescending one that reduced me to an eight-year-old whose job was to ensure the neighborhood newspaper made it safely to every doormat. Maryellen had her methods, and making declarative statements dressed up as questions to express haughtiness ranked as one of her more annoying devices.

"*I*, on the other hand," she snootily added, "will be teaching Vacation Bible School, which means I'll be working with young children to reinforce the virtues of Catholicism through various games and crafts. It's done strictly on a volunteer basis, naturally. I can see why one would want to earn money, but passing on life's virtues through a religion's core principles is far more rewarding, but it's unlikely an atheist like you would understand."

What, one might ask, can wilt an erection faster or more thoroughly than a woman droning on about the extent of her virtue? Nothing! No force known to Earth, natural or otherwise, wields such capacity. Nevertheless, you have got to appreciate a girl with versatility. First, she causes my loins to throb; then, she ices them over. Anyway, my response to Maryellen's Vacation Bible School lecture and what an atheist "like me" fails to understand was to do the unthinkable: I allowed my duffle bag to slide off my shoulder, down my arm, and onto the ground. Next, abruptly—never could I have predicted anyone prompting me in this fashion—I fell prostrate to the ground where, rapidly, repeatedly, and perhaps in mimic of one whose cranial matter is not in good order, I pecked away at the pale tops of Maryellen's feet. It was not a form of maniacal worship I performed, though that was how it must have appeared to anyone leaving for work or going for their morning newspaper, as was the case with Mister Paschal and Missus Stroud. Mr. Paschal was making for his car; Mrs. Stroud, her newspaper. Instead, I was mocking whatever magnitude, virtue, and authority Maryellen purported to have possessed or thought to have gained through the corpus of her faith. Doubtless, my display was a bit theatrical, but sometimes, histrionics are required to make a point. When I got back to my feet, having uprighted myself explosively, thus personifying the virility I always hoped Maryellen's imprisoned tiger possessed, I informed The Goddess of Virtue, "Just for the record, I blew past number five hundred ages ago and closing in on a thousand. What's more, you have inspired every effort. And, incidentally, because I wouldn't want you to misspend your concern: I'm a goddamn eagle eye. So don't you go losing any sleep over ol' Addison Caldwell."

I reached for my duffle bag. Softening my tone and with sincerity I had readily summoned, I wished a visibly stunned Maryellen a good summer, then walked away. Upon reaching the curb, I noticed a somewhat mystified and anxious-looking Mister Paschal peering back at his front door. I could sense his dread: he was praying Missus Paschal failed to witness my manic display, which an onlooker could have construed as adoration bending toward worship. Had Missus P done so, Mister P feared she might expect similar treatment as compensation for all the salty bullshit she spent decades enduring. I offered the poor bastard a derisive shrug, then, in a tone matching the gesture, I called out, "That's what real men do nowadays. Give my regards to DiMaggio." Missus Stroud, meanwhile, had the look of a woman convinced that Maryellen must have bewitched me or cooked up a potion and was praying she would share the ingredients. I like Missus Stroud but had no time to explain what transpired. Instead, I offered her an idiotic grin to interpret before wishing her and Mister Stroud a good harvest this summer.

CHAPTER TEN
THE DIVE

Upon leaving three people frozen in stupefaction, I headed toward Cillian's place. It's a banner day when you can stupefy one person, never mind three, so I had amassed some equity. I was a block from my house before realizing the familiar smell stuck in my nostrils was that of fresh nail polish. Apparently, Maryellen woke extra early this morning to pretty the tips of her appendages just for yours truly. I should be flattered. However, while engaged in a moment that left three people agape, my only concern was the symbolism of my gesture, not the appearance of Maryellen's toes. The latter might have proven a bonus was I not otherwise occupied illustrating that my antagonist's Neo-Catholic conservative virtues required the sort of modification that would hasten her familiarizing herself with the ethos of her generation or brushing up against it to the point of being sullied and wielding a worldview based on experience. Then again, had I not gotten swept away in a moment of psychopathy, there was little chance I would have discovered myself on all fours mimicking a demented woodpecker. But I'm a young man in his mid-teens, otherwise a real piece of work, which means I could go either way mentally. Anyway, I could always write Maryellen and tell her that the effort of waking at sunrise to polish her nails did not go unappreciated. I hear that women appreciate men who are in touch with their feminine side.

As expected, Cillian was waiting for me on the porch, leaning against the front railing and facing the street. After I turned onto Cillian's block and he spotted me not less than fifty yards away, he jumped down from the porch with cat-like agility. I stopped and waited for him. I could not pretend to know what goes on in the James household, less hazard a guess. Neither Joey nor I had yet to set foot inside Cillian's house, and Cillian ensured we never reached his front door. It was not a subject we breached, not with Cillian. Doubtless, Cillian must have had his reasons for keeping us away, for wanting his family life to remain a private affair. Out of respect and affection for our friend, Joey and I pretended not to notice what had become a painfully conspicuous effort by the summer of '77. If Cillian wished to introduce the subject, it would be on his terms, in his time; we would not push him but would permit him all the space he required concerning his family and whatever it was about them that engendered his hesitancy. Besides, the three of us would have the next two months to bring any matters weighing on our minds to the surface. Something was bound to wiggle its way free during the days of laboring in the summer swelter.

Cillian rigidly expressed gratitude for the opportunity to get away this summer. However, concerning his words, gratefulness was only palpable at face value; his intonation was hardly indicative of someone brimming with appreciation. His march was resolute for a spell, though the more distance we put between us and his house, the more his rigidity waned. Before long, his words began flowing with the fluidity I was accustomed to hearing them, and his steps were more leisurely. We were on our way to Joey's place.

Despite all my reveries, in which Maryellen McNamara and Theresa Delvecchio were present, individually or in tandem, I have reconciled that the kitchen at the Broscos was Heaven on Earth. In the kitchen, Claire Caldwell could not accomplish on four legs what Mister Brosco could on one with a hand tied behind his back, and with the ever-capable Missus B only an arm's length away, they were to culinary arts what Batman and Robbin were to crime fighting.

Our farewell breakfast consisted of hot sausage, sweet sausage, bacon, scrambled eggs made with grated provolone cheese and seasoned with pesto, omelets made with Monterey Jack cheese and diced ham, sliced honeydew, and cantaloupe, two kinds of juices, and Belgium Waffles not oozing with stick butter and pancake syrup, but with fluffy tub butter and genuine maple syrup made by an Algonquin tribe. Are you kidding me? Algonquins! And let us dare not forget to mention the coffee. For as long as I could remember, poor ol' Darrin Caldwell, every morning, has poured boiling water over Taster's Choice or Nescafe. Instant coffee! Mister Brosco had this old-fashioned stainless-steel drip contraption that screwed together: Water went into the lower cylinder; coffee grinds, which Mister B ground himself, went into a micro-screen insert, then the upper cylinder was screwed on. The upper and lower each came equipped with a handle. When the pot whistled, Mister B took hold of the handles and inverted them. A minute passed, and I did not have a cup of coffee pressed to my lips—to suggest as much would have been an insult—but a genuine experience!

"This is the aroma and taste I wanna experience when Jesus comes for me." The grand expression belonged to Cillian when first sampling Mister Brosco's a.m. potion.

Sometimes, Cillian and I lent too much hyperbole to occurrences and situations considered commonplace, if not mundane. An example would be my ruminations upon glimpsing Maryellen's navel. It was an inane routine that developed last summer on Wildwood's boardwalk when evaluating what seemed to hyper-vigilant adolescents an endless parade of tits and asses and saw its full flowering by midterms. Admittedly, it was vaudevillian but occasionally showed wit—a moment or two of potential. Sharon, who could roll her eyes like a champ—no one could execute an eye roll better than Sharon; she claimed to learn the gesture while watching reruns of the Jack Benny Program—did not share our enthusiasm and would remind us, "Drama class was yesterday." Sometimes, she would say, "Context, ladies, context," then pat our heads and remind us, "You're at an age when grappling with matters beyond your penises could prove too great a strain."

My thoughts turned to Sharon as I sipped Mister Brosco's coffee. I'll miss her this summer; it's a bonus when a girl can be a true friend, not just someone you routinely fantasize about. I hope, come September, Sharon and Joey can make something out of what they started; I like the notion of Sharon occupying meaningful space in our weird little world.

Mister Brosco sprang up from his chair to brew another pot of coffee. "Won't be more than a minute," he promised. "I know you boys are anxious to get on the road."

I *was* anxious to get on the road, but I also wanted to savor every sip and bite of what was available on the Brosco dining room table. And why would I not? I could count on the hand of Three Finger Brown when fed this well; the last time was a month ago, sitting at the very same table and chair. (In case you were wondering, Three Finger Brown's full name is Mordecai Centennial Three Finger Brown. He pitched during what was known as baseball's "dead-ball era" —an era that began in 1900 and ended in 1919—mainly for the Chicago Cubs. "Mordecai," because his parents liked the name; "Centennial," because he was born in 1876; and "Three Finger," because the sonofabitch had only three fingers on his pitching hand and, somehow, being minus two digits helped his breaking pitches break more sharply. How do I know all this, you must be wondering? Because Joey Brosco knows everything there is to understand about baseball, not just the game fundamentally, but its history, which officially began shortly after the Civil War. Mrs. Hargrove, insisting "The Cubs will fade," sent Joey into hyperdrive to collect all the historical data available on the team that makes its home at Wrigley Field. The last time the Cubs won the World Series? You guessed it: Three Finger Brown was the ace of the staff!)

We rode the train, the one that came within a whisker of running us over, to 30th Street Station. It's Philly's version of Grand Central Station in that it is big and has no shortage of hustle and bustle. The plan was to purchase three one-way tickets to Pittsburgh, buy them, and wait for the next train heading west. Then, from Pittsburgh, we would board a bus to New Castle. Upon arriving in New Castle, we call Aunt Leila to pick us up at the station. That was the plan, or so it was assumed. Then, no sooner than we arrived at 30th Street Station, amid all the Philly-style hustle and bustle, we learned that Cillian had another idea—a slight alteration.

"Relax," he told us. "I already squared it with Aunt Leila. We'll purchase tickets for the first train heading west to Pittsburgh … tomorrow morning. Meanwhile, we owe ourselves a time of adventure."

Joey and I took a decisive step backward, then glared at our friend with eyes brimming with suspicion. Next, with arms folded to our chests, our gazes met in a manner that conveyed to Cillian that the math was against him.

"For crying out loud," he cried, "we'll be working every day until the end of the summer; we deserve a day of freedom—freedom from every known constraint." Then, using the brogue of a Dubliner, as he often did when pleading his case, he cried, "For fuck's sake, a body'd be a fool to squander such a chance, bejesus!"

Admittedly, the idea was attractive: to take full possession of a day and experience the full thrust of freedom: no responsibilities or time limits, nothing but three young men untethered with a few bucks in their pockets and all of downtown Philadelphia to use as a playground. And whether or not, as Cillian pleaded, we were deserving, he was right; it would be foolish not to seize hold of a single day and own it entirely.

"Okay, CJ," I said, making an effort to sound more distrustful than inspired, "but you've gotta promise us one thing: Whatever you have in mind, it won't involve railroad tracks."

"Addie, I swear to the God you don't believe in and never pray to; no aspect of my plan will involve transportation beyond our legs." Despite the irony that Cillian so slyly inserted, he did sound earnest. "In fact," he added, "if by chance we stumble upon a railroad crossing, you can tie me to the rails just like villains used to do in silent movies, cheer when the train comes, and laugh when I shit my pants."

On that note, we purchased three tickets, checked our bags, and then trekked from 30th Street Station to Boat House Row, where we began to hike the pathway skirting alongside the Schuylkill River, which mirrors the East River Drive. Our destination is Valley Green, a section of Wissahickon Valley, a park seven miles long with a bridle path called Forbidden Drive that stretches uninterrupted for every valley mile. It was a hike from 30th Station to Boat House Row. Wissahickon Valley was an additional four miles, and Valley Green was yet another four. Nothing says exercise like a hike to get to a preliminary hike before the actual hike.

"I guess the plan is to walk holes in our shoes," said Joey.

A scene including the famous boat houses, statues along a river, the river itself, the architecture of the many bridges spanning the river, rowing crews swishing by in dragon boats, bikers, runners, a lush landscape, and intricate rock formations shadowing our trek: in totality, it was reminiscent of a guided tour; thus, the effort of four miles was over before we knew it. Part two of our journey ended with a sign that read *Forbidden Drive*, the entrance into a valley called Wissahickon.

"You're gonna love it here," said Cillian. "It's one of those places that, once you're there and breathe it in, you won't wanna leave."

Joey and I yielded to "our friend the tour guide" and enjoyed the sights and sounds of the many lesser-known aspects of our old city. Seldom had I been a passenger in a car motoring along East River Drive, and not until today had I hiked it. Thanks to Cillian's persuasiveness, I was blessed with a day affording me the titillation of knowing life beyond a familiar threshold. The result? I felt alive, liberated, and in control of my destiny; thus, what prevailed was a consciousness that I was bigger than my person and had a bounce in my step one might experience when the world as it pertained to human potential awaited the grasp of my hands.

The same could not be said of Joey: he was the pragmatist to Cillian's far-flung nature, a string to a kite reminding the explorer that his feet must remain on the shoulders of ancestral wisdom while venturing into a world of novelty. I often settled somewhere in between and could lean either way depending on the day, hour, or adventure we undertook. As much as his pragmatic nature allowed, Joey seemed agreeable to how the day was unfolding, despite his mind stuck back at 30th Street Station, where it dwelled on the train we were supposed to have boarded. Doubtless, Joey was thinking: although the trail along the Schuylkill River and the bridle path through Wissahickon Valley has proved magnificent, so too would have the scenery from the vantage point of a train heading westbound through Pennsylvania. Joey also expressed concerns about where we planned to spend the night and what would happen if we failed to return to 30th Street Station to catch the 8:00 a.m. train to Pittsburgh.

"Relax," Cillian urged. "Nothing has changed. Western Pennsylvania is still our destination. We're just taking a slight detour, a minor deviation." He paused; I could see his wheels turning. "Imagine that our next twenty-four hours are a typical day at the beach. We swim out into the ocean at the point where the breakers form, then go for a ride. We don't question what the ride will be like; we take it. Sometimes, we catch a smooth wave and coast nice and easy back to the shore; other times, we catch a wave that kicks our ass, the kind that gets us all twisted and makes us feel like someone's shoving us into a meat grinder. Add a strong undertow, and this lunar-controlled pool we call the Atlantic Ocean is dragging our chins on the floor. The point is that no matter the surf's condition or what time of day or season you ride the waves, you always end up in the same place: the shore."

"We're wave riders; is that the idea?" It was not a question Joey posed but an acknowledgment of the all-for-one-and-one-for-all unity that the three of us have enjoyed since the night Cillian walked the trestle and that together, we equaled a force of nature.

Cillian was right; Valley Green and the many miles of Wissahickon Valley added up to paradise—a long and winding oasis within a bustling city.

"My dad used to take me here when I was a kid. We'd spend the day hiking the trails, covering every inch of the valley, and once, we rented a horse from the stable next to Valley Green Inn. Wrangler was his name; I still remember him. But then the twins came, things got hectic, and what was once easy became too difficult."

Cillian stopped. I could tell there was more that he wanted to say, but he reined himself in just shy of revealing anything that qualified as an invitation for Joey and me to pry into the part of his life he so safely guarded. But he did loosen the cap. Perhaps before long, unlike Maryellen to her tiger, he'll twist it off and generously pour out what he has kept suppressed.

"Come with me," he said, "I wanna show you something," and led us from the bridle path over a stone bridge that placed us on the other side of the valley. The bridle path or Forbidden Drive—named Forbidden Drive because the seven-mile artery was once accessible to automobiles, then in the 1920s, the volume of car traffic grew to the point of necessitating its prohibition—was wide enough to accommodate horseback riders, bicyclers, dog walkers, joggers, and hikers. But once you branched off the drive onto the trails, which coursed through dense woods at an elevation, agility was paramount, thus making it necessary to walk single file. A half-mile past the stone bridge and with the creek fifty feet below, we came to a clearing—a concave area that nature took millions of years to carve into a hill.

"Devil's Pool," Cillian announced. "That's what they call this place."

I looked to my left, in the opposite direction of the creek. What prompted me was the sound of water cascading over several tiers of rock before spilling into the body of water that Cillian called Devil's Pool. We seemed to have entered a gorge within a valley, and the mist produced by water cascading over rocks within the concave formation made it noticeably cooler.

The pool was approximately twenty-five feet in diameter; surrounding it was a wall of rocks—few were jagged, most were flat—making it a five-foot jump or dive. Recessed further back were higher rock walls by which one might enter the pool. These higher and further away walls would require additional bravery (or stupidity) and ample leg strength to make a safe plunge. Also, there was a thick rope well secured to a stout tree limb, and if one were properly motivated, they could ascend through the tree's scaffolding, grab hold of the cord, swing their way to the center of the pool, and let go. It was a helluva drop, maybe twenty-plus feet, otherwise the equivalent of jumping off the roof of your house, thus a bit too daunting for yours truly, I do not mind admitting.

"It's called Devil's Pool because it has an undetermined depth," Cillian told us. "Some say it's fifty feet; others say a hundred. Predictably, you have the occasional moron swearing it goes all the way to the center of the Earth or even Hell. Well, what are you two waiting for, an invitation?"

"But we don't have our bathing suits!" Joey protested. "We'll have to walk around the rest of the day in wet clothes!"

"Joey, you dumb bastard, lose the goddamn clothes!" Cillian was already shirtless when castigating poor Joey. Joey sagged, then sighed for being foolish enough to think Cillian meant for us to swim attired.

"Relax," I told Joey. "We're having a helluva day so far, aren't we?" Joey smiled. And why wouldn't he? We were sharing a day young men lived for.

We shed our clothes until we stood naked as jaybirds, located a flat rock suitable for diving, and plunged into what doubtless was the coldest water on Planet Earth; it took our breath away. Despite being at a higher elevation than the creek and bridle path, we were still immersed in a valley so densely wooded it impeded sunlight from penetrating and warming the first few feet of what some alleged was a fifty-foot-deep, hundred-foot-deep or bottomless pool.

"What are you feeling around for?" I asked Joey.

"Just curious to see how small my nuts got," he said. "I went from a wet teabag to a walnut in the time it used to take Cash and Bowa to turn a double play."

"I don't remember my last erection because it's a chronic thing with me," I admitted, "but I'm praying it won't be my last."

We spent minutes blathering about the water, its coldness, and its effect on our more delicate parts before we grew to where, if not comfortable, we could tolerate it. It was then that we realized Cillian was not sharing the pool with us. I glanced over in the direction where we left our clothes, suspecting it was all a practical joke and that Cillian had gone, disappeared, leaving us clothesless and naked in the pool. It would be just like the sonofabitch to pull such a stunt while Joey and I were in a disadvantaged position, but our clothes were still in the same rumpled piles where we left them. Across the way was another pile of rumpled clothes belonging to Cillian. I surveyed the pool's perimeter—otherwise, the rocks responsible for its formation. There was no Cillian; he was gone. But where to? Where could he have run off? It was unimaginable that he would have taken off through the woods without a stitch of clothing. Indeed, we were in a deep valley yet still a city park, and because school was no longer in session, we were hardly the only three making use of the place.

****

The year is 1974: Heiress Patty Hearst is kidnapped outside her Berkeley, California apartment by the Symbionese Liberation Army; Hank Aaron takes Al Downing's second pitch deep over the left-field fence of Atlanta's Fulton County Stadium to eclipse "The Babe" as Major League Baseball's all-time home run king; Richard Nixon, amid the pressure of the Watergate scandal, resigns; and a ribbon got cut opening a new amusement park called Great Adventure in Jackson, New Jersey—a mere thirty miles from Philadelphia.

And it was no ordinary amusement park: Great Adventure featured rides, a safari, shows, gardens, a sports complex, a shopping district, horseback riding—even a campground with a beach! It was no wonder excitement echoed throughout the neighborhood when we learned the new park—some touted it as the northeast corridor's version of Disney Land—was about to open. Not since the Phillies moved from Connie Mack to Veteran Stadium had we frothed with such anticipatory buzzing. ("Buzz" was too weak an idiom to describe the climate in Philly when the Flyers brought home the Stanley Cup. "Mayhem" was more suitable.) Maryellen was the first in our neighborhood to experience Great Adventure; she went with her Girl

Scout troop the day it opened and returned only to describe the experience as "Unspectacular," proving that even at age twelve, she was snooty. Perhaps instead of exciting shows like the one exhibiting dolphins every bit as trainable, intelligent, affectionate, and communicative as canines, Maryellen was expecting a reenactment of the first Pentecost festival—Biblical garb included. But the same could not be said of five-year-old Casey Caldwell: my kid sister oohed and aahed throughout the dolphin show. Claire oohed and aahed at the dolphins too but was a sucker for rollercoasters; she rode each one, and because Casey failed to meet the height requirements, Darrin had to remain behind; he and Casey licked ice cream cones and cheered when the rollercoaster zoomed past them. Darrin, meanwhile, was excited about the safari; however, back in '74, instead of being tram-toured through New Jersey's version of the Serengeti, patrons of the park were required to tour the safari using their own vehicles, and baboons tore the living shit out of the vinyl roof of Darrin's '71 Chevy Nova.

Riding rollercoasters, cheering for marine mammals, and having the more docile creatures of the animal kingdom press their slobbery snouts against the side windows of our car while wondering *who are these fuckers, and how did we come to end up in New Jersey?* was all well and good. But I went to Great Adventure for one reason: to see the magnificent Don Columbo, a Villanova graduate and U.S. Acapulco cliff-diving team member.

We had all seen the team dive the Acapulco cliffs on Wide World of Sports, and, for a while, these cliff-diving daredevils, led by world record holder Don Columbo, were all the rage. I was sitting next to Casey, and just the sight of the ladder—a narrow, perpendicular spire stretching to the sky—caused me to wring my hands together. I could not imagine climbing something so narrow as that ladder to such a dizzying height; a person would have to be a lunatic. Perhaps Don Columbo was a lunatic. Then the world record holder, one rung at a time, began his one-hundred-foot ascension. I raised my eyes until they came to rest on the platform from which Don Columbo would plummet. Although "platform" was too generous a word, it was a perch and one barely suitable for a large bird, never mind an adult-sized human. I tried to imagine how the pool appeared from the vantage point of that one-hundred-foot-perch—doubtless a helluva lot smaller than it did from where *I* sat. And what would happen should Don Columbo overshoot the pool? Would hidden safety nets magically appear? I was making myself crazy nervous. Next, the world record holder stepped onto his one-hundred-foot-high perch. He remained with his back to the crowd for several seconds, then turned to face us—hands held high above his head, stretching, breathing. As I continued wringing together my hands, Casey took to strangling my arm—I could feel the nails of her dainty little fingers digging into my biceps. Meanwhile, Darrin fidgeted and hummed some Sinatra strain, and Claire's nervous twirling of a lock of her hair put its elasticity to the test.

The moment of truth was finally upon us. From the clouds, Don Columbo launched a three-position gainer. Swift and true, the diver came coursing back to earth; a hundred-mile-an-hour javelin pierced the pool. Seconds later, Don Columbo emerged unharmed to applause. The applause for a spectacle is different from when Mike Schmidt hits a late-inning go-ahead homer. Instead of being greeted with *leaping from our seats frenzied* applause, it's more of an *ooh and aah, thank goodness the daredevil is alive and can dive another day* type of applause. I spent the remainder of my Great Adventure wondering what compels someone to turn themselves into a Nolan Ryan fastball launched from the sky. Three years later, at Sea World, Don Columbo would up the ante: he would dive, successfully, from 156 feet! But in 1974, despite not out-swatting the "Sultan of Swat," failing to go down in disgrace, or neglecting to get kidnapped, Don Columbo made the biggest splash … literally.

****

After exhausting the pool's perimeter, my eyes came to rest on the one tree whose trunk emerged from behind the first tier of rocks. I followed it until it narrowed, and its scaffolding began. Ten feet, twenty feet, my eyes continued rising until they came to rest at a thick knot at the end of a rope; doubtless, it was where Philly's Tarzan wannabes positioned their feet before swinging their way over the center of the pool and letting go. Next, my eyes traveled the length of the cord, stopping at the limb to which it was secured; to the left of the limb supporting the rope arched another of equal thickness but higher. It was on *that* limb that Cillian stood.

"Joey," I said quietly and gravely while subtly pointing to draw his eyes skyward.

To not startle Cillian, Joey matched my soft tone and graveness when he exclaimed, "Jesus Christ, from where he's standing, it's a fifty-foot drop if it's an inch!"

It was the night of the trestle all over again. Clusters of thoughts raced through my mind, or perhaps just two: Would I be burying a friend or traveling to Western Pennsylvania marked one. The rocks surrounding the pool, which I found fascinating in color and shape minutes ago, suddenly seemed menacing, marked the second and prevailing dilemma. Joey and I had the same idea: swim to the pool's perimeter and latch onto one of the rocks. Why? We were too bound up with anxiety to continue treading water. For that matter, we were too nervous to do anything other than remain still and quiet while Cillian tightrope-walked a tree limb arching fifty feet above our heads. Why must he do this? Was the impetus purely thrill-seeking, or was a far more profound and existential reason compelling his madness? I thought I noticed a knee buckle, but if one had, Cillian managed to regain his balance as quickly as it became compromised. I tried but could no longer remain quiet.

With no alarm in my tone, I called up to Cillian, "You could always straddle the branch and shimmy your way back to where it's safer."

He disregarded my words—I suspected he would—and proceeded to inch his way further out on the limb. Finally, Cillian reached a point on the bough where he could successfully plunge to the pool's center should he manage to thrust himself forward. It was also a point where, should he slip, he would clear the rocks, although barely. He stood balancing himself on a limb, savoring the moment, this cheater of death. Joey tried but could no longer restrain himself; his nervous tension needed a voice.

"CJ, will you jump in the fucking pool already!"

Cillian poised himself for what would prove the mother of all dives; not even Don Columbo would be foolhardy enough to attempt a fifty-foot dive from a platform so unsteadying as a tree branch. Carefully—his feet positioned single file on the limb—he bent himself to a slight crouch. I could see him calculating the effort; otherwise, the necessary thrust required to reach the pool's center. Then he flung himself upward and outward from the limb. Feet first, hands stretched high overhead and pressed together, Cillian, a human missile coursing downward from a dizzying height and about to slice through icy water, had plunged. The speed with which he plummeted was astounding. Equally impressive was the force with which he pierced the water. It was hard to imagine the pool had enough volume to prevent him from reaching its undetermined depth with some measure of force.

Joey and I each let loose a decisive sigh that Cillian was not lying sprawled on the rocks below a mangled, twisted, bloody mess, having suffered head trauma, massive internal bleeding, with several bones protruding through his skin, and likely dead—and, if not dead, death would be kind, for we were deep in a valley, far from help, assuming help could do any good should we manage to procure any.

Okay, so we would not have to tackle *that* scenario. But another thought occurred to us, one not as horrifying but no less disconcerting: What if the so-called undetermined depth of Devil's Pool was not fifty feet or one hundred, never mind the center of the Earth or Hell? What if it was all a myth, bullshit, and the actual depth was a mere fifteen feet, or worse, ten? Granted, either was a far friendlier proposition when juxtaposed with landing and instantaneously splattering on a rock. Still, I could not imagine a ten-foot bottom being kind to a diver plummeting from a fifty-foot perch. It kept flashing through my mind, the altitude from which Cillian had descended and the velocity with which he entered the water. Admittedly, it was spectacular, but now fifteen seconds have elapsed—more than ample time to emerge from a dive regardless of the pool's depth, and Cillian had yet to surface. The height, the missile-like plummet, and the blur of an entry, collectively, equaled spectacular, but as the seconds ticked away, spectacular equated to frightening, as we imagined Cillian in agony, his limbs broken, his person a twisted mess at the bottom of Devil's Pool.

"It's been thirty seconds," said Joey. In his head, Joey had been counting off the seconds since Cillian entered the water. He was not the only one. In some ways, it was worse than the night of the trestle; then, we had eyes on Cillian and, as Joey had done so effectively, could communicate with him or, if necessary, yell had he swerved too close to the edge. But this scenario? It was a goddamn nightmare! Joey and I had the same idea: to plunge below the surface and search for our friend.

The pool was comprised of water originating from the Schuylkill, and the deeper we dove, the colder and darker it became. It was not long before we reached a depth where the water's murkiness made vision impossible. We swam to the surface for a breath, then right down again we sank, plunging to the water's murkiest point and beyond—to where we could not see past our respective reaches. Still, we swished our way through the darkness, feeling around while praying that our hands would locate Cillian so we could swim him, however broken, to the surface. As I swished and searched, dread overcame me, thinking Cillian was stuck instead of wrecked— his forceful plunge pierced an object lodged in the earth, and he could not pry himself free. Doubtless, there must be stout tree roots waiting to ensnare an arm or leg, and who knows what other surprises were lying and waiting to entomb someone whose dive took them to an ill-advised depth. After all, it was Devil's Pool; anything was liable to be down there. My hands found what unmistakably felt like human flesh—live, supple, animated human vigor potentiated by pulsing blood. My heart surged, thinking I had stumbled onto Cillian, alive and well, but not a second later, I realized my hands were mingling with Joey's. I could sense that Joey had experienced that same surge before sagging with dismay. We had made our second plunge from opposite ends of the pool, and after who knows how long we had spent scavenging and swishing through cold, murky water using our fingertips as eyes, we swam right into one another. Now, facing us was a defining moment offering two options: We could abandon the search or remain underwater until hypoxic and allow Devil's Pool to claim us as well.

I know what it is like to run from a speeding train and suffer a moment of uncertainty as to whether I would prevail; it marked one of those moments that can stay with a person for years; it can travel well into adulthood and occasionally jolt them from a restless slumber. Now, I know how it feels to swim to the surface of a pool once all hope is lost. In the span of six weeks, I accrued two experiences that, in their respective moments, using measures too critical to remain bound by rationality, forced me to take stock of my life. I swam beside Joey, someone for whom I had a great deal of affection; how I wished that he and Sharon, come September, would fall deeply in love and that we would never stray from one another. I love Casey and tried to envision what my eight-year-old kid-sister was doing while this impalpable force known as *grieving a friend* strangled my heart. Before long, though still submerged, I spotted a glimmer of daylight. My thoughts turned to Maryellen. Despite how she and I antagonize one another, there is something between us that we shall explore one day when the time is right, and she is prepared to embrace the world beyond the ecclesiastical. That was life after Cillian, as I tried to rationalize it.

Joey and I surfaced, huffing and puffing; our distressed lungs screamed for air. Moments later, when breathing became less effort, we wiped the water from our eyes and beheld a vision. There, on a rock, arms folded as though he had been waiting too long and growing short on patience, sat Cillian, grinning like a sonofabitch—his customary comedy/tragedy smile with the corners of his mouth pointing north and the corners of his eyes south.

"Goddammit, we shoulda known!" I moaned. Joey was a touch more expressive as his eyes fell upon the sight of Cillian looking too smug and comfortable for his liking. Those *Italians*, I have come to learn, have a knack for conveying their feelings. Joey began with, "You shanty Irish cocksucker;" his voice rang through the valley. His tirade ended with, "Slide your no-good Celtic ass into this pool!"

Cillian shimmied his way down from the rock and into the water; he knew pulling such a stunt would come with consequences. Joey and I swarmed; we were on Cillian like piranhas days denied food. I positioned myself behind the prankster and executed a debilitating chokehold. I also managed to lock up his legs, thus leaving him vulnerable so Joey could land a flurry of punches. Naturally, punches thrown below the water's surface are not nearly as effective as ones thrown on land, and Cillian, the sonofabitch, laughed like someone tortured by way of tickling; it further enraged Joey, who proceeded to throw a flurry of openhand shots to Cillian's defenseless head. Next, we forced Cillian's head underwater; we held him down long enough that we were confident we made our point, and still, he came up grinning and laughing. A moment later, all three of us were yucking it up and had forgotten about the frigidity of the water or how deep Devil's Pool may or may not be. We took turns performing a variety of dives from the first tier of rocks.

"Better take it all in," said Cillian. "Who knows whether we'll have an opportunity to swim this summer?"

I did not reserve much thought to whether we would have an opportunity to swim this summer. Every city has its share of community pools, but we would not be in a city. Moreover, who knows what passes for recreation in rural western Pennsylvania? I began to imagine all sorts of activities peculiar to city boys, including small game hunting, log sawing contests, and jumping off a barn roof into a pile of hay.

Following our swim, we each claimed a flat rock to lay on, allowing the cool valley air to dry our bare bodies. It was, so said my idiotic Pink Panther wristwatch, four-thirty when we began dressing. With Cillian in the lead, we continued hiking elevated trails that wound to the bridle path that took us to Valley Green Inn, once a pre-Civil War Hotel, now a restaurant with a world of charm, primarily because of its unusual location for modern times. It was with reluctance that we departed Valley Green and Wissahickon Valley. But we had miles to trek, many on the bridle path of Forbidden Drive, more on the track that divided the Schuylkill River and East River Drive back to Boathouse Row; from there, it would be on to 30th Street Station. We were three teens trapped between boyhood and manhood who could lean either way, depending on the day or hour. But there was also a sweet spot upon which to land, to ground one's reality. Call it a sliver of space or threshold separating boyhood and manhood preventing these periods from colliding, overlapping, or evolving into an unnavigable mishmash; and, in light of this miserly sheard likely an abstraction only occupiable for a day, I prayed for more generosity, for example, a summer or season to bask in the sensation of feeling untethered without risk.

If we learned anything today, nature is inspiring and capable of turning smartass teenagers into philosophers diving into the rubrics of many isms. And while enveloped in an earthy flora, we began the gamut, first debating whether the universe had an ideological component and, if so, what role it played in our lives. Predictably, I advocated on behalf of skepticism; Cillian beat the drum for deism and Joey theism. Belong long, we moved to the more complex question: *Should* an omnipotent entity exist? That opened up a whole other "can of worms," especially since humans have weaponized matters concerning revealed wisdom to mitigate authoritarian ends. Migrating from the deific to the cosmological and their possible fusion led us to debate whether time is a function of space or is space a function of time. Eventually, and perhaps it was predictable after walking so many miles, we whittled down the rousing matter of the time-space continuum to the inane question: What did Chicago mean when they sang the lyric *25 or 6 to 4*?

Upon clearing Forbidden Drive, we found ourselves on the pathway mirroring the Schuylkill River and the East River Drive. I sensed that Cillian hadn't yet exhausted himself; plenty of debate still simmered.

Although slyly, Cillian has been attempting to convert me since last summer in Wildwood after deboarding the Ferris Wheel. Don't get me wrong, Cillian, unlike Maryellen, is no pain in the ass; it's only occasionally—for example, tonight—that he reminds me, "Addie, not every matter has to be a potential 'intellectual problem,' and not every intellectual problem is a dilemma that needs solving. Sometimes it's easier just to say, fuck it, I'm going to accept the wisdom handed down and call it a day. Who knows, it might even get you laid faster."

"What about it, Addie?" said Joey, suspecting that the thrust of my atheism stemmed from relishing the role of Devil's advocate, embracing my contrarian nature, and the thrill of turning myself into a human missile seeking to upend the irrational, otherwise the wisdom of mystics. Joey's tenor also implied: If my future were to include Maryellen's vagina, I needed to, if not fully surrender, keep an open mind concerning abstract matters.

"Look," I began, "I don't know who the dude was who coined The Golden Rule: 'Do unto others as you would have them do unto you.' But whoever it was nailed it; there was no need to take perfection and dice it up into Ten Commandments, then spin them into a religion that a thousand years later would spawn another and five hundred years later yet another—this isn't television, which first featured *All in the Family*, then spun off *Maude* and *The Jeffersons*. And in case you haven't been paying attention, all this doctrinal spawning has delivered a world filled with bullshit theocrats recklessly swinging their elbows; now everyone's trying to carve out space or mark territory to enforce their version of 'ultimate truth.'"

"Once upon an eon, in neolithic times or the Stone Age, there was only one religion, one culture," said Cillian. "Now there are hundreds of cultures practicing multiple religions, and it's given the world character and variety and yielded several pathways to salvation."

"Fine," I countered. "But people don't prophesize culture or go to war on its behalf. And there won't be much salvation if we all kill each other in the name of God. If there is a God, I bet He's livid over all the nonsense done in his name. Any minute, we should expect a flood."

"Confucius," Joey managed to chime in. "He was 'the dude,' or at least the most famous coiner of the 'Do unto others' spiel. Leviticus had his version, too, but The Golden Rule might go as far back as the Middle Kingdom period in Egypt. Some like to call it 'The Maxim of Reciprocity.'"

"Encyclopedia Brosco strikes again!" Cillian intoned before turning to me and hissing, "All right, laddie boy, any moron prone to doubt capable of forming a sentence can take potshots at religions; it's low-hanging fruit for a *self-appointed* free-thinking intellectual. But let's see you sing for your dinner: Can you reach the berries on the highest branches and take down 'The Big Kahuna?' I'll wager that you can't even send Him to His corner for a standing eight count, much less knock Him out."

So, Cillian issued his challenge, had laid down his gauntlet: no longer was it satisfactory to poke holes in the perceptible nonsense perpetrated by self-serving demagogues pretending to advocate for The Man in the Sky; I was to take down the Big Kahuna Himself! Where to start? We had miles to go, thus plenty of time. I remember hearing the idiom, 'The sins of a father get passed onto his son.' It came from Claire, who cautioned Darrin of karma once they made it to the car and realized they had gotten away without paying for a set of steak knives at Woolworth's. "One day, Addie will end up in handcuffs for something he *didn't* steal," Claire predicted. Although a fascinating concept to contemplate, karma is based on a cosmic and abstract principle, otherwise another instantiation of bullshit. Nevertheless, I thought it was an excellent place to start: torpedoing The Old Man through His victimized Son.

The night sky was clear with a gibbous moon shining over the Schuylkill and had, for company, an abundance of stars. Maybe it's typical of the night sky at the juncture of the summer solstice; I could not say.

"Look up," I urged Cillian and Joey. "Do you see all those stars? We're gazing at a mere micro-fraction of our galaxy, the Milky

Way, never mind an infinite universe. There are billions and billions of stars across the galaxies, and each one, like the one we call 'the sun,' has enormous mass, gravitational pull, and satellites, if not revolving planets. And on one planet in each star system, there are bound to be conditions suitable for intelligent life—some more intelligent than us, some less. So, let us assume, for the sake of debate, under a common omnipotent, all-powerful-creator-of-the-universe-and-everything-in-it God, that societies, regardless of what their beings look like, have developed throughout the galaxies. As they have—unless they're morally superior—it stands to reason either these beings were, currently, or will sometime in the future be subject to the same primal desires that have repeatedly led humans astray: greed, lust for power, war, oppression, slavery, you name it; sin after mortal sin they no doubt will commit. Do you understand what that could mean? Either there are infinite Jesuses, and each one is doomed for crucifixion on countless planets—or, since God supposedly had but one Son, maybe it's a case of the same Jesus crucified billions of times over on billions of planets ad Infinitum. But regardless of which option you choose, I reject the notion God fucked up our design by saddling us with a prefrontal cortex and an amygdala that seldom cooperate, then took His eye off us for a few millenniums, only to cry, "Jesus Christ, quick, You need to get down there and die for these crazy bastards; they've gone off the rails!"

"All right, Mr. Astronomy, so you brought a gun to a knife fight, and You Know Who will need a tougher chin than I expected. But…" —Cillian's intonation implied wavering— "I'm still not convinced."

"Jeez, Addie," said Joey, "that was like the result of John Lennon and Galileo brainstorming while puffing on an opium pipe; I can tell you've been thinking about this for a while."

The irony and humor of my companions notwithstanding, I decided to go in for the kill. After all, the far-flung concept of crucifixion times infinity only would have served to rock Maryellen's world—it placed theism, as it pertains to Christianity's perception of an Almighty Master of the Universe, on a ship and sunk it—but did little in the way of disproving godlike omnipotence.

"When you apply the concept of a spiritual deity in a way relevant only to our world and the corpus of human history, it can almost make sense. *Almost.* But the story starts to fall apart when you factor the concept of God beyond our world, into the galaxy, and across an endless universe. For example, Rigel, the brightest star in the Orion constellation, is seventy times larger than our Sun and forty-thousand times more luminous. Let that sink into your heads for a minute." I paused. "Now, despite Rigel's size and power, it can get sucked into a black hole as though it were nothing more than a goddamn ball of fuzz. So, if possible, imagine that the same force responsible for such wondrous entities as Rigel, black holes, supernovas, and galactic event horizons also commanded Abraham to slay his son and Saul to murder all the Amalekites. I don't think you can do it! So why can't we agree that God, or the concept of an almighty master of the universe, is simply the coalescence of time, space, and energy and call it a day? The reason we can't? You won't find many priests willing to bend a knee to time, space, and energy, never mind folks willing to fork over their hard-earned wages on their behalf. More than anything, God is an industry, and there's nothing supreme or divine about industry."

"For fuck's sake, laddie, me poor head's spinning faster than a dwarf planet ready to explode, bejesus!" Cillian cried. "No wonder you can't get into Little Red Riding Hood's pants. But even were you to succeed, after steamrolling her with all that intellectual claptrap that sucks the spirituality from the universe, her vagina would probably turn to sandpaper!" Turning to Joey, Cillian added, "But the sonofabitch has convinced me; there's no God."

"Like hell, there isn't." As I stated, Joey can get a little hot under the collar, especially when you stroke his fur the wrong way, and my turning Cillian into an infidel qualified as *the wrong way*. "Charles Darwin or no Charles Darwin, you can't go from pond scum to Beethoven's 9th Symphony, not in a million years, not fifty million. And just for the record, Beethoven was deaf when he composed what arguably stands as the greatest musical composition ever written. I don't know, fellas," —Joey's intonation turned whimsical— "but it sounds like divine intervention if you ask me." Reigniting his harangue-like tenor, he added, "If I'm a betting man, I'm laying my money on a creator, an intelligent designer. And that goes double for the cosmos. I don't give a rat's ass if the universe is made up mostly of gas, dust, and wormholes; someone had to put them there."

Tonight's debate marked an instance when having parents two generations removed was a plus, as Joey had a broader frame of reference than most fifteen-year-olds. Attempting to prove God or advocating for the principles of revealed wisdom by citing the abilities of Frank Sinatra and John Wayne would have resonated as utter inanity—God Himself might have belly-laughed. But Beethoven, having composed his grandest work, the majestic Ninth Symphony, with the life-affirming *Ode to Joy* movement, while entirely deaf? I must admit, Joey loaned some genuine credibility to the notion of the human spirit hardwired to a supreme entity.

"You know, Addie, Joey has a point," said Cillian. "Maybe we are attached to a vast spiritual being, and some among us—the supremely gifted and hyper-intuitive—can tap into that open channel."

"CJ, make up your goddamn mind!" I crowed. "It's either philosophy or religion; astronomy or astrology; chemistry or alchemy: you can't have it both ways."

"But there's a helluva case for both arguments. So, just like Joey declares all our wrestling matches a draw, I think we should declare this debate a draw."

"I'll accept a draw for now," said Joey. After a lengthy pause, he added, "But whether or not a spiritual God is responsible for supernovas and galactic event horizons, it's quite possible that He is a She."

Okay, so that was a bit of a jolt and, ostensibly, an abrupt departure from the topic. Perhaps Joey theorized that because women are assigned the responsibility of birthing the human race, an omnipotent "She" must have birthed the universe; it is not a concept at which a faith-based person should scoff. Or maybe the nature of his reasoning was simple and pragmatic, beginning with how Missus B worked two jobs back when Mister B was still getting acclimated to life with one leg or how years later, again, she took a second job when funds got tight, or how, despite her diminutive size, she epitomized a *bottomless pit of energy*. One might imagine the effort required for Missus B to walk to a bus; she had to ambulate with thirty percent more agility to do anything within the same timeframe as a normal-sized person. Although the abovementioned went a long way in explaining Joey's reverence for women, I was clueless as to how it pertained to our debate. Moreover, Joey, because of his unique relationship with statistics, had an affinity for practicality and was thus more appreciative of discussions that wound their way to decisive conclusions, not open-ended bullshit that, if not getting bogged down in a thicket, tends to meander until out of oxygen and lost in the wilderness. In other words, he may have found these theological and philosophical intersections fascinating but ultimately unsatisfying and decided it was time to steer us in a different direction.

"Considerate it for a minute," Joey urged. And so, Cillian and I pondered the concept of a female master of the universe. "Whether or not we care to admit it, women control how we think."

Finally, a light went on in our heads. Joey was not alluding to women as an abstraction or in totality, which includes mothers, teachers, and other women of authority, but young women—our peers or "puppet masters" as we were beginning to understand them when mulling over the subject of a "She" God. Classrooms and friend groups are microcosms of society. Among the young men who help comprise these mini societies, there are sure to be an athlete or two, comedians, intellectuals, and so on, and whatever the girls happen to favor for the moment is what steers male aspiration.

"Christ, it makes so much sense it's scary," cried Cillian. "Us guys are nothing but a bunch of square pegs forcing ourselves into round holes all for the sake of the vagina, anatomy's version of the Holy Grail."

Where teenage boys were concerned, indeed, the vagina was the Holy Grail. Perhaps it still was for crusty old pricks like Mister Paschal; it certainly was for Guy McNamara.

Keeping to our generation: if the girls seemed titillated by athleticism a particular week, the boys would go to any length to prove themselves through means of speed, strength, and agility. If it were comedy they seemed to favor, invariably, the boys would begin hurling witty insults at one another for the sake of a laugh; every girl appreciates a guy who can make them laugh. When it was "brain week," boys dove into their respective acumens for methods to display their intelligence. The "Holy Grail" turned us into minions, shifting from one station to the next, hoping to land in someone's garden of earthly delights.

"They hold the hoops and, like trained seals, we jump through them," Cillian moaned. Ironically, he added, "We should give ourselves credit for having the fortitude to endure such manipulation."

I draped my arm around Joey and told him, "No loving God would create such evil creatures."

I landed what I thought would prove the decisive blow, but then Joey countered, "Not only does God exist, but there's also a devil, and there's a damn good chance both are female."

So that was where Joey was steering the narrative: it was the ol' *if there's a god, then there too must be a devil* philosophy—otherwise, the ol' *you can't have one without the other* principle. And Joey, quite cleverly, I might add, used Satan's power manifesting through women—the all-powerful, omnipotent vagina—to illustrate his point. Just wait until I tell Maryellen! Just wait until she learns that to exorcise the devil residing in her bosom, she must take mercy upon my weak maleness and surrender.

"A virtuous woman and manipulative woman fighting for universal supremacy, and a couple of billion undisciplined penises caught in the crossfire," Cillian intoned. "I don't know about you, laddies, but I'm beginning to feel a bit diminished, subjugated—like a rodent traversing the Serengeti with hungry hawks circling above, bejesus."

We walked in comfortable silence for several minutes before coming upon the lights of Boat House Row, casting seemingly thousands of sparkles into the Schuylkill River: a river with its very own star cluster—its motion creating a galactic orrery. While Joey and I were mesmerized by this simulated galaxy, Cillian offered what seemed like passing words: "My mother is crazy."

Initially, we did not mindfully dive into what we alleged was an ephemeral affectation. Instead, we allowed Cillian's words, which seemed to carry a sense of whimsy—neither Joey nor I detected the weight that often accompanies matters of poignance—to float past our ears. Besides, the parents of those slated to graduate in 1980 were late additions of the silent generation; otherwise, a sect that got swept up in baby boomer culture, which meant everyone I knew, Joey Brosco notwithstanding, was sure to have had one crazy parent. Moreover, it was 1977—Post-Vietnam War America—one crazy parent to a household seemed a prerequisite: Clare Caldwell tokes grass and blows it out the bedroom window when it's nine degrees in January; Richie Costigan's old man, in Nixon's America, used to siphon gasoline; Guy and Rosemarie McNamara rewrote the manual on what it means to conduct a dysfunctional marriage. But then Joey and I sensed that Cillian was no longer with us—that he had stopped walking. We turned and looked back at him. He did not have the bearing of a young man whose mother was simple of mind with how she tried to hide a mari-juana habit or had other annoying but reasonably sane peculiarities. We walked back to where Cillian stood. Though his eyes were closed, he sensed we were near—that we had come to rescue him from an abyss. He began to speak:

"Years ago, when it started, she would go an entire day, all twenty-four of its hours, without getting out of bed. My father used to tell me, 'Your mother is under the weather,' or, 'Your mother is over-tired; don't worry, come tomorrow, she'll be fine.' I was a kid; I ac-cepted what my father told me: if he says she'll be fine tomorrow, she'll be fine tomorrow. Then, sometimes, I'd catch my mother sitting in the living room staring straight ahead, lips slightly parted, not responding to anything: us, the TV, the telephone, the doorbell; it would go on for hours, this strange state where she appeared incapable of sounding out words. Often, I would leave the house; that glazed-over look that came over her terrified me. Later on, it got worse: she would stay in bed for many days and go that long without uttering a word or bathing. Finally, my father stopped making excuses and placed her in Friend's, the psy-chiatric hospital on Roosevelt Boulevard across from Sears. She wasn't there quite a month and came home fixed and feeling better than ever. My father had a wife; I had a mother; life was good. Then, a year passed, and it started again. So far, my mother has had three stints in Friend's Hospital. She's a disaster, which means I'm the son of a dis-aster, and you know what they say: the apple doesn't fall far from the tree. It scares the living shit outa me."

As the Steve Miller classic goes, Ol' Claire Caldwell was "a mid-night toker." That is her choice. I can choose differently. Unfortunately, Cillian may not have the luxury of choice. I have lost sleep thinking my best friend—although I do not subscribe to the theory, he is sui-cidal—has a death wish: The blindfolded walking of the trestle, the gamble that he could reach the platform before the train reached him, a death-defying dive; suddenly it all began to make sense. Who would want to reach adulthood knowing that by the time you arrived, you would be ready for the looney bin, or worse, go through what re-mained of your teens antagonized by what being "ready for the looney bin" looks like? And Cillian was too bright for a bullshit pep talk. Re-gardless of what Joey and I might tell him, the fact remained: children do not take after strangers. Like it or not, parents are both a gift and a curse. But not having a bullshit pep talk available does not mean logic should go to waste. Joey and I reminded Cillian that, in all likelihood, his mother was not the originator of craziness or "nut gene" and that "the curse" was an unfortunate inheritance.

"You have four grandparents, don't you?" I reasoned. "So, the chances of you ending up like your mother are only one in four unless, of course, both your mother's folks were looney bin material; then it's fifty-fifty, and what are the odds of that being the case? Slim to none, I would suspect."

The three of us had our arms draped around one another and were brought to tears by what we alleged to be a shrinking probability of an undesirable outcome. What I assumed would take half the summer was out in the open on day one.

"She did give me my name, my mother," Cillian told us. "My father wanted a junior, but she insisted that I have a strong Irish name, which I appreciate."

"My father was so thrilled for a son that there was no question I would be a junior," said Joey.

"Your father is heroic, Joey," said Cillian. "He deserves a junior."

"Claire Caldwell was obsessed with Kennedy. It wasn't until recently that I discovered JFK had Addison's Disease and figured it was the reason for my name; it'd be just like my hippie mother to name me after a dead president's disease. But then I learned it was only a year ago that Kennedy's Addison's became part of the public domain. So, I asked my mother, 'Why the unusual name?' She told me, 'Your father wanted you to have a difficult time pissing your name in the snow.'"

From the brink of tears, then laughter. Then Joey and I said, our eyes piercing into Cillian, "The three of us are gonna have a helluva summer. Next year, too, and the year after." Cillian knew what we were hinting at, and it prompted the reply: "Like the great philosopher, Jim Morrison, once said, 'The future's uncertain, and the end is always near.' But all right; no more trestle walking, underground midnight rambling, or high diving. You have my word: from this day forward, I'm gonna bore the living shit out of you."

We located a pizza parlor on Market Street. Afterward, we returned to 30th Street Station, claimed our bags, and used them as pillows when lying on benches to sleep. There would be no midnight rambling—under or above the ground.

CHAPTER ELEVEN
AUNT LEILA

I can now report firsthand the experience of waking up in a train station: no hellos, good mornings, or cordial greetings of any kind, just shifty and suspicious eyes all wondering: *Are they bums? Runaways? Are they gonna cause trouble, these three sleepy, disheveled-looking characters?* It's funny how you can hear thoughts louder than when folks shout them into the ether. And poor Joey, God bless him, felt pressed to explain to everyone who cast their distrustful eyes in our direction that we were not squatting in the station or scrounging miscreants with eyes peeled for an opportunity but had an appointment with a train. If Joey sensed someone was less than convinced, he would whip out his ticket as if to say: *See, we have a right to be here, just like everybody else!* I'm poking fun at Joey, naturally, and it was often that Cillian and I rode him for what we called his *what will the neighbors think* mentality. But we did respect Joey Brosco's sense of decorum, a gift from parents two generations removed, otherwise known as "old-school" folks.

We yawned and stretched, then washed down a bagel with coffee. Next, we boarded a train, appearing like three wrecks that failed to attend to hygiene of any sort.

"Coffee stimulates my bladder no sooner than it finds its way there," said Cillian before taking the liberty of divulging to us his morning rituals, some of which were hardly conducive to train stations or any public domains, assuming the sharing of perversions was not a goal. He closed by adding, "I hope there's a bathroom on this train, or *someone* is gonna be miserable."

"It's not a commuter train," I reminded him. "I'm sure somewhere in the car is a receptacle suitable for collecting piss and other material specific to a penis should someone prove unable to control certain urges."

Alluding to Cillian's morning rituals, Joey, his face twisted with incredulity to the point of comical, uttered, "You beat off *every* morning?"

"I couldn't extricate myself from a mattress without first beating off," Cillian admitted, as though there was no loftier source of pride to which one could cling. Joey looked my way, hoping to see that I had matched his disbelief, only to discover the contrary.

"It's necessary for brain function," I told him. "*Especially* in the morning. I couldn't find the refrigerator door if I didn't first beat off." Joey's reply was a rolling of his eyes that would have made Sharon Millstein proud.

Before long, we sat watching the world go by from the windows of a train. It was a source of amusement until we left behind the familiarity of our city and the somewhat lesser familiar suburbs in favor of rural Pennsylvania. Scenic Penn's Woods, with its forests, rambling hills, and farm vistas, before long, became monotonous; its landscape, like the background in a Hanna-Barbera cartoon, was a series of endless repetitions, and so I closed my eyes and set my mind adrift. After all, how many tree-dotted hills and farms can you look at without concluding they all look the same? Besides, I needed to make up for that "beauty" of a night's sleep I had on a wooden bench in a train station that never fully settled. I was not aggrieved about the inconvenient accommodation; I would not trade yesterday for the world—not even for a compliant Maryellen!

Unfortunately, in each instance, when I slipped into a twilight sleep that threatened to become a bonafide snooze, the vision of Cillian teetering on a tree limb fifty feet above my head caused me to stir and shudder. Moreover, the wearier I became, the more surreal and insane the episode seemed. I kept imagining the result of Cillian's bare body smashing against one of those charcoal-gray, stone-aged rocks—rocks that have been around since the dawn of time—after a Tarzan-like plummet from a treetop. I looked over at Cillian sleeping peacefully, then at Joey. It seemed ages ago since yesterday morning when we breakfasted at the Broscos. I gazed out the window at a landscape stubborn to change. I repeated this cycle numerous times until the train chugged into The Steel City.

Upon stepping off the train, our first order of business was purchasing a newspaper. We set aside most of its sections and went diving into the sports page, pacifically the baseball box scores, only to discover that the Phils coughed up another clunker, this time to the Cards, 7—1. Five hits and one lousy run were produced not by a base hit but by a measly sacrifice fly by Luzinski. Even had Jim Lonborg pitched a gem, which he did not, it would not have made any difference. Meanwhile, those notorious faders, the Cubs, shutout the Mets 5—0 to go 7 1/2 games up on the Phils.

"So much for the big fade Missus Hargrove assured us was coming," I bemoaned.

"If anything," said Cillian, fearful that if the season continued at the current trajectory for much longer, it could end up a lost cause, "the Cubs seem to be gathering steam, while the Phils are grinding out one listless effort after another."

"So far," —it was Joey's turn to lament the situation— "they sure as hell don't resemble the team that last season won a team record 101 games: not without Dave Cash batting lead-off and playing second, they don't."

As the old-timers are fond of saying, they don't hand out the pennants in June, no matter how well a team plays. For the moment, though, it was hard to feel encouraged despite the Phils' most recent acquisition: Bake McBride. McBride was brought over from St. Louis to sure up what was a shaky defensive outfield. Despite the offense that Greg Luzinski and Jay Johnstone generated—both terrific hitters—the Phils could not continue flanking Gary Maddox with two players that ambulated with no more agility than the grazing cows I glimpsed from the window of a train. Luzinski and Johnstone's lack of defensive prowess led to the expression: Three-quarters of the world was covered by water; Gary Maddox covered the rest. Kinda funny, huh? Not only would Bake McBride change the outfield defense for the better, but he was also no slouch at the plate. With Luzinski supplying half the Phils power—Mike Schmidt provided the other half—Jay Johnstone, or "Jaybird" as many like to call him, or "Flakey Jay" as he was also sometimes known, despite his popularity with the fans, would be the odd man out.

"I *like* the McBride deal," I chirped. "Dane Iorg and Rick Bosetti are marginal players at best, so all the Phils coughed up to get Bake was Tommy Underwood, a decent pitcher with a low ceiling."

"It's a steal as far as I'm concerned," said Cillian. "Underwood has already hit his ceiling. Meanwhile, McBride has star potential."

"I have to rearrange my goddamn cards," Joey griped.

We tried to convince Joey, with the operative word being "tried," that with the Cardinals sporting red and white uniforms and red caps, McBride would not look terribly out of place in the Phillies' stack. It would be a stretch to suggest that Joey bought the aesthetics angle of our logic but saw the upside of the trade.

Cillian called Aunt Leila to let her know that, within an hour, we would be boarding a Greyhound Bus heading toward New Castle. New Castle, we were told, was fifty miles, give or take, from the bus station. I equated that to mean another hour on the road. It seemed daunting. Anything would have after sleeping on a wooden bench using a duffle bag for a pillow. Hopefully, a Greyhound seat will prove friendlier than an Amtrak. Hopefully, I won't imagine Cillian and all that could have gone wrong yesterday and that the result will be a recuperative snooze, not a series of twilight dozes that only served to remind me how exhausted I am.

It took every minute of the hour before a Greyhound heading toward New Castle was available to board. We spent much of the time speculating about Aunt Leila—a woman exceedingly swift in swooping in to fill the shoes of someone's deceased wife. Entertaining theories concerning such a matter seemed only natural. Besides, we were about to spend our entire summer vacation at her home and in her presence; we would be foolish not to view her as a person worthy of speculation. If nothing else, this woman called Aunt Leila was an unknown, a mystery, but of what nature? Moreover, Uncle Dave remarrying no sooner than the sympathy cards had arrived at his mailbox is not a matter one should overlook. Such a scenario marked plenty to provoke anyone to raise a suspicious brow, especially when piggybacked with the reality that Uncle Dave went and joined Aunt Phyllis not long afterward. Then a notion struck me, one based on pragmatism: this Leila woman, all along, was Uncle Dave's side piece—knowing Guy McNamara as I do, the idea seemed more than plausible. Given the expedience with which Uncle Dave remarried, it was likely that Leila had been—however discreetly—in the picture for years rather than a random encounter, and Uncle Dave decided she represented his just reward for proving himself a worthy caretaker to a sick wife. Keeping a piece on the side is no one's interpretation of honorable behavior when caring for an ailing spouse. However, on that front, I shall reserve my judgment, for there is every possibility that Aunt Phyllis, aside from being realistic about her fate, was a selfless woman who encouraged Uncle Dave to find someone because she could not bear the thought of him alone. Lastly was the more intriguing but nefarious scenario: This Leila woman was hovering, lurking, and had poor Uncle Dave sized up and pounced before he had ample opportunity to grieve. Adding to the intrigue, Uncle Dave dies shortly thereafter, and Leila inherits the farm. Be it altruism, adultery, or deviousness baked into the web of a Black Widow, it made for plenty of intrigues on the summer menu.

"How'd your Uncle Dave end up in Western Pennsylvania?" Joey decided to ask. The question veered us slightly off-topic—Joey had a habit of asking questions that diverged from the root of a discussion—but his curiosity, in this instance, did not lack merit and was somewhat related. And now that the question fluttered about: how *did* Uncle Dave, a man who grew up in Philadelphia—a city steeped in culture and history, was a true wonderland of museums and parks and had four professional teams to boot—wind up in a section of the keystone Claire Caldwell dubbed "podunkville?" (I should not judge too harshly: New Castle, Pennsylvania may not be so "podunk" as I imagined, though the possibility did weigh on my mind. And should it turn out that New Castle is but an oasis of silos and cornstalks—discounting work and Cillian and Joey for company—what was there to do in a "spit of a town" fifty miles north of Pittsburgh? How would I spend my free time? Would there *be* any free time? It was a little late in the game to mull over such concerns, but one matter I knew with some certainty: yesterday would be tough to top.)

"He enlisted in the army," Cillian told us. "After a tour of duty in Korea, Uncle Dave got stationed in Carlisle, where he met my Aunt Phyllis, and as the story goes, he fell *out* of love with Philly and *in* love with rural Pennsylvania."

"I *suppose* such a case can occur," said Joey, who, upon ruminating geographic love scenarios, could only imagine the inverse.

The Greyhound was marginally more comfortable than the train, but the sleep I so desperately craved still eluded me. I did the next best thing available: staring blankly out of a window, daydreaming, imagining, and romanticizing my life in the future before pestering Joey for the sports page, but not until allowing him the ample time required to memorize every box score, statistical league leaders, and standings.

Never was there born a human so enamored with numbers as Joey. It is impossible to separate baseball from numbers; numbers measure a player's value and have marked the game's storied history. And although Joey could not say with certainty, I'm guessing numbers led him to baseball, not the contrary. And don't bother arguing with him over who led the league in homers, runs-batted-in, and batting average a particular year or the result of a game played on a specific date; he could reach into his brain and summon it instantly; his recall ability was uncanny. I'm telling you, Joey could spew numbers and results as readily as Maryellen could the sacraments and with the accuracy of a paid assassin. If I didn't know better, I'd swear the entire history of baseball was tattooed on Theresa DelVecchio's body and that Joey had a pair of binoculars with an unobstructed view into her bedroom.

At a glance, New Castle was hardly Philadelphia, but neither was it podunkville.

"Not half bad," said Joey.

"It'll work," said Cillian, who hadn't seen much of New Castle beyond the outskirts of the farm.

We exited the bus, dropped our bags on a sidewalk, and stretched before searching the area for a two-toned—red on top and mustard-colored on the bottom—1975 Ford F-350 Ranger Super Cab. We were tired and a bit bleary-eyed but snapped to attention when we heard the impressive horn blow that could have only come from a vehicle such as the above-mentioned. And if that horn were not enough to garner our attention, the figure that stepped down from the behemoth pickup would prove unfailing: the three of us turned our gazes upon one another like we just won the Irish Sweepstakes. All we were thinking was—and when I tell you our thoughts were unified, less challenging to read, I am not kidding—please let this woman be Aunt Leila and not a woman on an errand who we would not see again until it came time to drop us at the bus station come September.

"Hey, fellas," the woman called from the other side of Butler Road; her tenor rang with enthusiasm before waving us over to her truck.

From as far as the other side of the road, I could tell that she, who we prayed was Aunt Leila, was not just tall for a woman but the same height, if not taller, than Cillian and me. (Cillian and I stood five feet ten inches tall and weighed a buck fifty.) My estimate was accurate, for we were eye to eye when standing beside this glorious creature we prayed was Aunt Leila. If anything, she may have been a whisker shorter, though it was difficult to tell with her donning a cowboy hat, an accessory that suited her handsomely. On her feet were work boots—the kind you would expect one to wear when driving such a behemoth as a Ford F-350 Ranger Super Cab. Her pants were blue jeans, which she had taken a pair of scissors to and modified into short shorts. The white blouse she sported contrasted the boots but was well in accord with the "farmer's daughter" sex appeal she so liberally exuded. A mane of wavy blonde locks tumbled down from her cowboy hat; it was too heavy to swell in the summer heat and thus stretched silkily below her shoulders. She—and this is me being conservative—was an eyeful.

"You must be Cillian," she chirped. "I can see the family resemblance." She extended a hand at the end of a sinuous and athletic-looking arm and crooned, "I'm Leila Bennett."

By introducing herself as "Leila Bennett," the woman we prayed was, and indeed turned out to be, Aunt Leila, made it known she did not favor the qualifier Aunt. After blurting out her name, our smiles transformed from the acceptable, predictable, and typical fascination men are expected to reveal when in the presence of a female stunner to boyishly idiotic. What rescued us from a prevailing first impression that we were green adolescents let loose in society was the surprising strength of Leila Bennett's handshake; it straightened us up promptly. You expect a firm handshake from a man, not so much from a woman. Leila Bennett's handshake was not just firm; it was the most rigid handshake I had the pleasure of experiencing. I suspected she was overcompensating, which made perfect sense when you are a solitary woman about to spend her summer with, for all intents, three strange young men. *I'll show these three bucks that Leila Bennett is no one with whom to trifle.* It became apparent they were not compensatory handshakes we had received. Simply put, her handshake was an extension of Leila Bennett, the woman—an unabashed, enthusiastic farmgirl, unapologetic for her farmgirl ways. We were impressed.

Leila's hands were proportionate to her height but hardly masculine, nor did they appear or feel—despite what work boots and a cowboy hat might imply—roughed up from labor, though her broad and robust-looking wrists seemed well suited for tasks involving strength. Other noteworthy features were a physique sure to keep a sculptor working overtime and eyes possessing the clarity, brightness, and energy of a girl unabashedly celebrating the vivacity of youth. Indeed, Leila Bennett, with her long, strong bones, set-back shoulders, and eyes that had the talent to smile while probing, was a fusion of femininity and raw country-girl charm. And despite Leila being a half-inch shorter than Cillian and me, she seemed a helluva lot more imposing in her work boots and cowboy hat. Suddenly, the death of Uncle Dave seemed less mysterious. *Rest in peace, Uncle Dave. Doubtless, it was worth it.*

"This is some truck," Joey intoned once we were all seated inside the behemoth two-toned Ford, with Leila and Cillian in front and Joey and me in the back. I purposely sat behind Cillian; I wanted a more advantageous angle from which to view Leila.

"It's strictly my utility and errand vehicle," said Leila. "She's got pep, she does, and enough power to plow through a brick wall without losing a drop of speed. In other words, when I signal to change lanes, you won't catch no smartass thinkin' he can floor it and squirt by me." Using a closed fist, Leila rapped on the top of the dashboard to accentuate her claim of what her truck could do to a brick wall or demonstrate what would happen to anyone assuming too much ownership of the road. "For leisure, I ride a '77 Harley Shovelhead Chopper. She's royal blue and trimmed in black. Now *that* sonofabitchin' thing cooks! Lots a folks around here ride Harleys. Rex Hadley's got *him*self a Shovelhead; all red and chrome, his is. A wicked-looking sucker; but I think royal blue suits me better. Do folks ride Harleys where you fellas are from?"

"Mostly, they ride the bus," came my droll reply.

"Right," said Leila. "City folk. Y'all don't have much need for motorcycles unless you take 'em for Sunday rides in the country. But that's all right, Addison; I'm a girl who appreciates a sense of humor." Her head turned slightly to the right, and she delivered a wink that went straight to my loins. I think it's fair to say that our first impression of Leila Bennett was that we liked her. Very much, indeed.

The Bennett farm was not in New Castle proper but located on the outskirts of town, which made perfect sense—it was where a farm's location was likely to stand—but this did not bode well for three young men hoping to have access to a bit of hustle and bustle when it came to spending their free time. In other words, being cooped up and isolated could prove problematic, doubtless sooner than later. But, at the moment, we had a more pressing concern; it was past five o'clock, and all we had thus far today was coffee and a bagel at 7:45 a.m. We were starving. Right on cue, Leila guessed, "I bet you boys are good an' hungry about now?"

Leila drove us to get takeout pizza at a place called Barney's. What were the odds a sonofabitch named Barney could make pizza worth eating? He couldn't: the pie was garbage, just as we suspected it would be, but we ate it; we were starved, and starving people, unless imbeciles, do not complain about the food, especially when someone else dips into their purse to pay for the shitty food. We expressed proper gratitude, then went at the shitty pizza like wolverines lacking confidence nature would cough up another meal. However, in the future, without seeming too bold or ungrateful, we will request something else.

While en route to the farm, I could tell by the look on Cillian's face he had no idea Uncle Dave and Aunt Phyllis were not actual farmers but owned the land and the house and, long ago, had entered into a farmland lease agreement. "I just assumed all these years that Uncle Dave was a farmer; he always sounded so proud whenever he talked about the farm."

"And he *was* proud," Leila told Cillian. "But it was your Aunt Phyllis who was the farmer—or, at least, because she grew up in Carlisle, knew some basics about farming. As for your Uncle Dave? Hell, he was a city boy like you, Cillian. In other words, livin' on a farm ain't the same as knowin' how to farm. But he learned a thing or two along the way your Uncle Dave did—but only a thing or two. If truth be told, his goal was never to learn how to farm but to save up enough scratch to buy Elk's Tavern. You mighta seen it when we were driving through town; Elk's was the place with the big yellow moose head painted on the front window. It's on account of that yellow moose that the tavern's become a landmark. So it was pretty smart of your Uncle Dave to have a moose head painted in the window. It woulda been ten years this fall since he owned the tavern. Anyway, it was never *my* dream to own a tavern, but I don't mind, not especially. I'm there most days and even a few nights. As for the farm? Your Uncle Dave always had a fixed lease: it kept the farm on its toes to make sure it turned a certain profit margin, but with your Uncle Dave gone, the house long since paid for, and the tavern, a reliable source of income, I base the farm strictly on production and keep it capped to the farmer's advantage. After all, a girl can't be greedy. Now, if one of you fellas wouldn't mind raisin' the garage door…."

All three of us leaped down from the truck like our hair was on fire. It caused Leila to chuckle and point out, "The door only has one handle, fellas."

In the garage went the truck. To the right of the Ford sat a John Deere. Leila Bennett's prize possession stood to the tractor's right: her '77 Harley Shovelhead Chopper; it was a stunning machine.

"Don't worry," she said, "we'll take her out for a spin soon enough." She led us inside, made for the kitchen, threw open the refrigerator door, tossed each of us a can of Schlitz, and said, "There's still plenty of daylight left if you fellas wanna walk the grounds. After being cooped up all day long in trains, buses, and trucks, it might do youse good to get out and stretch your legs for a spell."

It was unanimous: Leila Bennett had us smitten. However, we had one lingering concern as we crushed our empty cans of Schlitz against the top rail of a fence that divided the uncultivated land around the house from the farm. With the farmland leased, thus the work spoke for, what was the purpose for our trekking to Western Pennsylvania? We would find out soon enough.

CHAPTER TWELVE
THE CONFESSION

Summer nights in Northwestern Pennsylvania are markedly cooler than they are in Philly. I'm guessing it's attributable to the altitude combined with the breeze coming off Lake Erie versus the humidity that densely hovers over a city that is essentially a valley. But I'm no climate scientist or meteorologist. Whatever, delightful night air came pouring in through my bedroom window. It was quick to flood the room, and the result was yours truly sleeping like a babe: Not an altogether bad perk when measuring the contrast between a young man set loose in a big, diverse city versus a subdued and isolated country. As the days unfolded, we would discover other perks and unexpected delights. Among them, with New Castle so close to Pittsburgh, we could pick up the feed for Pirates games on television and radio. Spending the summer away from home but near enough to a city where played a division rival that figured to be stiff competition for our Phils kept us well connected to a prevailing interest.

On morning number one, mixing well with the cool 7:00 a.m. air that otherwise would have kept me pinned to the mattress, was the smell of bacon seconds after hitting a griddle. Some aromas can fill a whole house no matter its size, and bacon sizzling in a skillet marked one. When I reached the kitchen, I discovered Leila already had an audience: Joey. He sat there in an undershirt gazing up at our twenty-eight-year-old hostess did the dark, hair-laden sonofabitch. Meanwhile, all I had to offer was a typical pubescent chest and not one discernable whisker. It was the Marlboro man versus Richie Cunningham.

Leila's wavy, tumbling blonde mane was disheveled in typical morning fashion. Moreover, she had yet to apply a stitch of makeup but looked more youthful and alive than last night; perhaps it could be attributed to well-rested eyes and skin that appeared more toned in the early portion of the morning. She was flipping pancakes and cooking bacon—the latter overwhelmed the aroma of the coffee she had already brewed—and had squeezed fresh orange juice. She appeared unhurried and methodical. I felt an arm slithering around me; its goal was to place me in a half-nelson. "Morning sunshine," Cillian teased before adding, "One thing's for sure: Uncle Dave didn't starve to death."

Leila winced. It was difficult to tell whether Cillian's words or spattering bacon grease was the cause, but it was the first time the unhurried and methodical cook had altered her expression since I entered the kitchen.

"There're lots a folks starving in the world nowadays, but none around these parts." Her tenor seemed a clear and firm recommendation that the subject of how Uncle Dave made his earthly departure in his late forties was a closed one. And just like that, the notion of Leila as a mystery—which, last night, we dismissed as foolhardy stupidity once finally acquainted and while downing cans of Schlitz—again whirled in our heads. Cillian's mother had traveled west for Uncle Dave's funeral but never revealed how he died, even when Cillian pressed her on the subject.

"It doesn't make any difference how he died; dead is dead," was all my mother offered.

Thus far, the subject of Uncle Dave's death remained a closed one. But now begs the million-dollar question: Just how does a woman with the looks of Leila Bennett fall into the lap of a man two decades her senior—a man only widowed long enough for a cup of coffee to cool—and then, with no explanation, the man in question fails to see the first day of spring? As far as suspicion was concerned, there was enough meat on the bone for everyone to nibble their way to a full belly. In other words, it did not require an overactive imagination to wonder what may or may not have transpired between Dave Bennett and his recent widow.

No sooner than I began obsessing over nibbling my way to a full belly with scandal for food, Leila's chirpy order, "Dig in, fellas," rang out sweetly. Her mood, which shifted just long enough for me to embrace a sensibility of distrust, swung back to the woman I first woke to this morning—the same woman who emerged all smiles from that behemoth 1975 Ford F-350 Ranger Super Cab at the bus station. Thus, I dismissed what I concluded was faulty intuition and went with the theory that it was nothing more than the combination of grease spatter pelting Leila's skin and me in an unfamiliar setting responsible for turning the wheels of suspicion in my head.

But the kitchen was hardly an unfamiliar setting for Cillian—numerous times he had sat at this very table—yet I knew, with certainty, what raced through my mind also ran through his, Joey's too. And whether or not there was a mystery to get to the bottom of, Leila, and the opportunity to fill our bellies brought the room back into balance.

"With your Uncle Dave, a recent newlywed, and before that, having the responsibility of taking care of your Aunt Phyllis, there's a whole list of chores that, putting it kindly, got put on the back burner." Even though Leila spoke directly to Cillian, Joey and I picked up our ears; we sensed a matter of shared relevance was about to be revealed. "Then your uncle went and left us," Leila added. "And there I was, a twenty-eight-year-old widow, scrambling around to settle his affairs. I wasn't expecting any help from your cousins, Wayne and Jack, and they didn't offer none. First time I met 'em was the morning of the funeral, and I ain't seen either since. And as sure as I'm sittin' here, that's how certain I am your Uncle Dave was wearing his Rolex watch the morning he was laid out. It ain't unusual for a fella or lady wantin' to get buried with something personal, something they cherished, like a favorite piece of jewelry. Uncle Dave never said so, specifically, that he wanted to get buried with his Rolex, but he loved it, and it looked real smart on 'im, too. But, come the afternoon, didn't I look over at that casket and notice the dang thing missing? Rex Hadley told me Wayne and Jack hocked the watch and used the money to pay for a road trip, and no one's seen hide or hair of 'em since.

"I never settled anyone's affairs before. Talk about baptism by fire? I was flyin' by the seat of my pants and scared I was gonna get taken advantage of. And I'm not the sort to complain—so don't take this the wrong way—but I sure didn't envy myself. Then, one day, I took a good look around, and it hit me: this old place, like no one's business, needed a heapin' helping of TLC! That's when I remembered Dave tellin' me about a nephew he had in Philly. Then, at the funeral, I met your mama, and she told me all about Dave's family from the other end of the state. So, because your mama and I had gotten to talkin' and were gettin' kinda friendly—even though I could tell she disapproved of her brother remarrying so soon—I figured, why not give her a holler and ask if you wouldn't mind coming out for the summer and bringing a friend or two. But don't worry none; you fellas'll get a crack at the farm. Meanwhile, this old place needs all the care she can get."

And so began our first full day in Western Pennsylvania, of what we learned would mainly be a summer of home improvement. Our first task was to scrape the house in preparation for painting. The house had not seen a coat of paint since who knows when—maybe from as long ago as when Uncle Dave was in the army and stationed at Carlisle—and the old paint was well chipped, peeling, and needed scraping away before applying a new coat. It promised to be a job that, unless having the benefit of friends with which to engage in banter and invent off-color song parodies and occasional glimpsing of a long, shapely woman who dressed according to her assets, would prove unrelentingly strenuous and dull. But, as luck would have it, we had the benefit of both the former *and* the latter.

Two scraped from the ground, while the other scraped above from an extension ladder on another wall, so the scrapings did not fall into the eyes of the two working below. Every hour, we alternated positions. Twelve-thirty arrived, and we got called in for sandwiches and cans of Schlitz. Come one o'clock, we were back at it. From the upper rungs of a ladder, I watched, with more than a passing fascination, Leila seated on a tractor, making straight lines up, down, and across the lawn. Her short shorts, hair gathered in a ponytail, sunglasses hiding her baby blues, and long, shapely golden-brown arms that flexed when she turned John Deere's steering wheel supplied all the inspiration I could desire. Not before today had I merged tractors and beautiful women in the same thought; they are entities, one might assume, incompatible if not worlds apart, and yet Leila Bennett operating a tractor seemed as natural as a boy with a baseball glove, although perfection, in my view, was not too generous a term; at least it appeared the case in Western Pennsylvania. Perhaps life is all a matter of geography: If you were born in Philly, you might have seen a tractor on a television commercial—I tried imagining ol' Darrin Caldwell sitting atop a tractor, but my mind's eye is limited concerning absurdities—if you were born in Western Pennsylvania, you end up tinkering with one. That was as philosophical as I could get while scraping peeled paint perched on an extension ladder.

Unlike Leila, I did not have the advantage of eyes hidden behind sunglasses. I did my best not to gawk at a woman who, despite manipulating manly equipment, seemed ever-mindful of her assets. And why shouldn't Leila Bennett display an awareness of her bountiful riches, especially with a captive audience afoot? It was her right, and far be it from me to deny a country gal her rights.

Into the garage rolled John Deere, and out rolled Harley Davidson. A woman and her toys; Christ, it was titillating! Leila revved the engine, and once it settled to a low rumble, she called to us, "I'm off to the tavern; I'll be back sometime between six and seven. And I'll have food!" Again, she revved the engine before coasting to the main road. She paused for an unknown reason. As she rode off, she freed her mane of hair from whatever had it so neatly imprisoned. I stopped my scraping to honor this action, to properly watch her luxurious, tumbling mane waving in the headwind. I was at a loss to explain the reason, but there was something about the movement of Leila's hair from the seat of her Harley that made me sad for her departure and long for her return. Perhaps her heading to Elk's Tavern—thoughtlessly leaving behind young, captivated men in favor of spending time with grown men—was the source of my experiencing a momentary pang of emptiness. Whatever the cause, Leila Bennett on her blue Harley was a fusion of a *Sports Illustrated* swimsuit cover and Lady Godiva. It was three o'clock. Three hours, maybe four, until she returned.

Scraping, scraping, scraping, and more scraping: scraping high and scraping low; scraping from a ladder and scraping from the ground; paint chips fluttering every which way; decades of sunbaked and frozen-on dirt getting stirred up and filling our nostrils; elbow grease from the right and elbow grease from the left; hour after hour of mindless, unvarying labor—the sort of labor parents warn children about so that they take school seriously. And this was no country cottage or bungalow; it was a goddamn farmhouse—a sizeable structure that had me cursing my best friend's dead uncle—and we were only at the halfway point when came the roaring thunder of Leila Bennett's '77 Harley Davidson Shovelhead Chopper. She turned off the main road and came coasting down the driveway. On her face, she wore a satisfied grin. Perhaps we had exceeded her day one expectation—or, progress was no factor at all, that it was more a case of Leila taking pleasure knowing three not altogether bad-looking young bucks were laboring on her behalf. In a world devoid of delusions, the former made more sense. However, my gut—the same faulty, impalpable entity that missed the mark earlier at breakfast—screamed otherwise. And although Leila's grin hadn't a trace of superiority as she coasted onto the driveway sitting regally atop her Harley, the perception was that she was our queen bee and that we were her loyal and grateful subordinates.

I came climbing down from the upper rungs of an extension ladder; it had been my third "tour of duty." I saw, anchored with a bungee cord to the back seat of Leila's Harley, a flat, square box. I cringed, thinking we labored all day in the sun for Barney's Pizza, but when Leila brought her Harley to a stop, she hollered above the low rumbling of the engine, "I brought home pizza from the tavern. How 'bout we call it a day." It was 6:45 p.m.

The tavern's pizza may not have been Santucci's or the boardwalk pizza we city rats were accustomed to devouring at the seashore in Wildwood, but it was decidedly better than Barney's.

"Not bad," Cillian intoned. Cillian was emphatic in his praise; he wanted it known that if takeout was what would pass for dinner every night, it should come from Elk's Tavern.

We devoured dinner as if competing. Our rapacity made Leila grin. Afterward, we migrated to the living room. Cillian was decisive in taking the straight-back chair; I assumed it was where he usually sat when visiting his Uncle Dave and Aunt Phyllis. Joey and I collapsed on the couch. Leila settled in a recliner; her long, shapely legs, at the end of which were surprisingly delicate feet, supplied a feast for the eye. Leila Bennett is a gift that keeps giving. A console television was the room's focal point, but the Pirates were home against the Expos; the game would be a radio broadcast.

We had arrived at the part of the day I had spent last night pondering before cool air and exhaustion eased shut my eyes: The evening. How would we whittle away the nights in the country on a farm, far removed from anything resembling what city folk call "hustle and bustle?" I need not have wasted time wondering; I had my answer. We were too goddamn bushed to do more than sitting and talking, and even *that* seemed taxing. But then Leila cracked open the door, thus inviting a probe by alluding to a time in her past—unlike Maryellen, she did not snootily croon when I was your age—in a manner implying it was a lifetime ago in another place. While I was busy imagining what Leila looked like at fifteen, Cillian asked, "Where was it you said you grew up?"

Leila had yet to mention her hometown.

"Woodsfield, Ohio," she readily chirped. Leila seemed unbothered that Cillian interrupted her yarn by calling attention to her oversight. Looking my way, then Joey's, she asked, as though issuing a challenge, "Betcha never heard of Woodsfield?" Before Joey and I could admit our geographic shortcomings, Leila forgivingly added, "That's okay; most folks never have."

She pressed the recliner's footrest into place, converting it into a rocker, and lurched forward. "It wasn't a bad place to grow up. A town of less than three thousand, it was. In a town that size, you know everybody—or, if you don't know 'em, you at least heard of 'em. My folks ran a dairy farm, and I spent most a my girlhood pullin' my weight; helped out plenty, I did. Though, it got to where Mama was doing most of the managing and me the milking. Daddy? He started having some trouble with his Jack, though I think his difficulties started long before he met Mama. Whenever Mama would complain, he'd tell her: 'If this stuff weren't no good for you, Lynchburg wouldn't a honored Jack Daniels by puttin' up a damn statue of 'im.' He'd always finish by crowin', 'He was a great American, Jack Daniels.' And when he got in the last word, he'd take a bigger swallow than usual as though a bigger one proved his point." Leila shrugged before adding, "You know how it is with some men and their drink. No sooner than alcohol hits their brain, it gets their wires all crossed, and then there's no tellin' what can happen."

With what seemed resignation, Leila fell against the back of the recliner. No longer did she appear vibrant and alive as she had this morning when assuming the role of a short-order cook, or later when operating her John Deere, or when she set free her hair before thundering off to Elk's Tavern. In recalling days as a youngster spent in the presence of "Daddy," discernable tiredness and haggardness came over her. Cillian rescued the room from slipping into a state of strained silence when he asked, brightly, as he was brimming with curiosity, "How does a girl who grew up milking cows in Woodsfield, Ohio, come to meet a man with a farm in Pennsy?"

It was not a question aimed to dig or probe but a simple matter of curiosity that prompted Cillian to ponder what hastened what anyone might allege an unlikely union. Joey and I were equally curious: just how *does* a gal from Woodsfield, Ohio, come to meet a widower, or a soon-to-be widower, whatever the case may have been, from New Castle, Pennsylvania? Not that the two towns are that far apart—I would later learn less than seventy miles separate them—but a man caring for a sick wife, one would imagine, does not get around.

"First, let me tell ya, straight up," Leila began. "There aren't many Dave Bennetts walkin' around. I don't care how hard you shake a tree; there ain't a one that's gonna fall out; he was a rare bird, and, try as she might, a gal won't find a kinder, gentler, or more considerate man. But, if truth be told, *I* didn't meet Dave Bennett, *he* met me, and it was a damn good thing he did, though I'll always believe it was the good Lord that sent him my way, and for it, I'll be eternally grateful."

My eyes roved a house that, despite the TLC required, was a fine place to live by most standards. Then I looked through a window at an expanse of farmland, including the livestock of which Leila Bennett was now the sole owner. Eternally grateful would be one way to describe how she should feel that Uncle Dave came into her life. But there I go again: one minute, Leila Bennett is a dynamic woman able to fascinate me with every twist and turn of her body, and in the next, I have her as an opportunist or worse.

"Ya see," Leila continued, "girls are born clinging to the silly notion that somewhere out there in this wide world is a prince just for them, and he's searching high and low the whole world over, and if a gal waits, is patient, that prince is sure to find her—he'll swoop right on down and rescue her, and it'll be magical. Then we put on a few years and realize it's all a bunch of bullshit; there are no princes. But then, outa nowhere, comes Dave Bennett—better late than never. By the time he found me, I had already crossed over to the wrong side or 'gone to the bad,' as some like to put it. It happens. And I don't make no excuses for myself neither." Leila's last words were snapping. Then she grimaced before adding, "Ya don't imagine it could ever happen, but one day ya wake up, and you're there. Worse, when you're a woman and don't have much in the way of resources, once you drive that tractor into the ditch, it's hell gettin' her back on the path." Leila's face softened when intoning, "But Dave Bennett, God bless 'im, could see past all my sins and into what was truly in my heart. 'If Jesus could forgive Mary Magdalene, then I can forgive you,' was what he told me. I'll never know a lovelier man. And I'll never know what drove him to commit his final sin, but there but the grace of God go I. That said, may he rest in all the heavenly peace he deserves, which is plenty."

I watched Cillian straighten in his chair. Joey and my reactions were similar. We all sat on the edge of our seats, posed unnaturally erect in a room that suddenly grew chilly. Next, our eyes searched for one another. Before long, I brought my gaze back to Leila. She was staring off into the distance or wherever her mind travels when forced to dwell upon unpleasant matters. Then, without warning, she snapped from her momentary stupor and was on her feet. She went prancing toward the kitchen and returned with her hands full. "Here," she said and handed Cillian a transistor radio. "Turn it to 1280 AM for the Bucs game." Next, she passed me a yet-to-be-opened fifth of Jack Daniels; perhaps, like Leila's father, it was Uncle Dave's liquor of choice and his final purchase, judging from the bottle's condition. "Take it easy," she warned us. "Drink just enough to take the soreness out of those muscles that worked so hard today and not a drop more. It'll also go a long way in helpin' y'all sleep."

We watched Leila retire to her room without another word. Then, with a radio and bottle, we went and made ourselves a seat on the upper plank of the wooden fence that separated the yard from the farm. We positioned ourselves so that that farm was our view. The setting sun was comfortably at our backs and setting ablaze the field. It was a splendid country scene.

"Okay, could someone please enlighten me, in the event my brain has turned to scrambled eggs, to what the fuck just happened in there?" It was Cillian, naturally, because he was more akin to the situation, who uttered aloud the very words resting on my lips, Joey's too. The question ranked as rhetorical. Nevertheless, when one has had thrust upon them an unexpected reality, an explanation is required, if for no other reason than to assure the afflicted party that they have not stumbled into an alternate reality and are still bound to the same atmospheric properties and conditions as those around them. Subsequently, without hesitation, I blurted out, "We just learned we're in the service of a former prostitute and that your Uncle Dave decided to end his life." It was a lot to take in; thus, I clung to the idiotic notion that "decided to end his life" instead of the harsher term "committed suicide" would resonate more palatably. But no words, regardless of how gentle, would ring with favor, with only forty-eight hours passed since Cillian opened up to us about his mother.

"The math hasn't changed, CJ," Joey resolutely asserted.

"Joey's right, CJ," I added. "It's not etched in stone that your mother has to follow Uncle. Dave.

And you're not doomed to follow either of them."

We kept hammering home the "four-grandparent theory" and the fact that the fate of Uncle Dave in no way altered the percentages. "And, so big deal that, while caring for your aunt, your uncle snuck out for a little nookie," said Joey. "That's hardly the crime of the century."

Piggybacking on Joey's viewpoint, I added, "Really, CJ, men have committed far worse transgressions. Although I'll grant you, it's likely uncommon for a man to fall in love with his prostitute and then marry her once his wife croaks, but who are we to judge a situation from the fringe?"

"Drink just enough to take the soreness out of our muscles and not a drop more? Is she kidding me? I haven't even started, and already I need another bottle!" The disdain in Cillian's tenor was sharp but not bitter. It meant Joey and I had reasoned well. Moreover, we employed no means of trickery, placating, or bullshit. Plain, simple, and honest reasoning were the tools in our kit. It was what our friendship was based on: the truth, no matter how brutal, and the truth, at times, can be tricky to swallow. Before long, a state of calm prevailed. What hastened it was advocating the notion: if all there was to the universe were three friends sitting on a fence, passing back and forth a bottle of whiskey somewhere in the middle of Western Pennsylvania, with a ballgame for company, that would be fine by us.

And speaking of the ballgame: The Pirates were beating the shit out of the Expos. Meanwhile, we learned the Phils were in a tight one with the Cardinals, and the Cubs were also in a tight one with the Mets. Unfortunately, the night would not end well. The Bucs finished off the Expos behind Bruce Kison 10—2; the Phils, despite Carlton going the distance, lost 3—2; and the goddamn Cubs, who Missus Hargrove promised would fade, won again, this time 5—4. The Pirate's win and Phils' loss dropped the Phils into third place, eight-and-one-half games behind those notorious faders. Darn, that Missus Hargrove; she really had us convinced.

The light in my Pink Panther wristwatch finally went kaput; I could not tell what time it was when our fence party broke up, but it was well after the twenty-seventh out went into the books. Joey made straight for his room. He had yet to handle the pressing issue of Bake McBride rubber-banded with his former team, the Cardinals; it was imperative that Bake get placed with his new teammates, otherwise known as "the third-place Phils." Joey had conked out last night before tending to his cards. I had my arm around Cillian while walking toward the house. I could tell he was still dwelling on all he had learned tonight. It does not matter how supportive your friends are; some issues are too weighty to shrug off, good company, a ballgame, and top-shelf booze notwithstanding. Tonight would not go down as the best night in the life of Cillian James. I could only hope his exhaustion, plus the whiskey, would prove kind.

CHAPTER THIRTEEN
SETTING UP THE ROTATION

Another chilly night; cool air floods my room, and despite a multitude of stars studding the sky—a greater galactic profusion than had shone over the Schuylkill River two nights ago—from the window of a farmhouse in the furthest western reaches of Pennsylvania, the night seems much darker than it does in a city of clustered together streets and avenues, much darker and stiller—decidedly stiller. A cityscape, despite a constant symphony offering numerous crescendos and climaxes, from the onset of the night until the wee hours of the morning, the whooshing of cars, tooting of horns, skidding of tires, and clanking of trucks pulling heavy loads are more discernable, more distinguishable, and often more jarring than in the bustling daytime when these sounds blend to produce the phenomenon white noise. The country also offers a nocturnal symphony featuring instruments: for example, the mile-long freight train that takes forever to pass a given point. The seemingly endless repetition of a freight train chugging in the distance amid the darkness and stillness of night can provide comfort that the Earth is still turning and thriving because forces are minding their responsibility. It was this peculiar luxury—a faint industrial symphony and what it represented—along with the cool night air that delivered me into a peaceful slumber.

But then I was awakened. Why was this? It was no less dark, still, or cool. Had I dozed only for the duration of a freight train chugging its way past my window, then was stirred by what my subconscious perceived as an unsettling quiet? No, I had been asleep for much longer than it would have taken a train to ride into silence; of that much, I was sure, though *something* had awakened me. But what? If not the absence of faint distant chugging or the echoing of unknown clusters of katydids throughout the farm, something caused me to stir. Perhaps another presence in the room? Cillian? He could not sleep. What transpired tonight—matters that could not wait until morning—proved too weighty, and he needed to unburden himself. I felt the mattress's perimeter sink; what caused it was someone applying their weight. My blanket—that cozy barrier separating me and the night air I had tucked under my chin—I could feel peeling away. Slowly, someone unveiled me, and how this maneuver unfolded should not have ranked a source of distress. Still, it did distress me, or at the very least alarm me, for I was confident Cillian would not perform this seemingly innocuous action with such gentleness. Next, I felt a hand on me—a probing hand.

"Shhh. Don't be afraid, Addison; it's just me."

Leila? It was her voice; that much, I was sure. And her hand? Did she mean to place it where it was presently resting? But wait, Leila's hand had not rested; it searched, blindly probed in the dark until it came upon what it had set out to discover. Next, it clutched, moved, and slithered; its touch and the manner of its movement caused me to suffer a momentary bout of paralysis, not from fear, but because what I suspected was about to take place traveled far beyond what I had thus dared to imagine. I was treading in uncharted waters in the dark of night!

Where Leila's hand had frolicked, I presently felt the warmth and moistness of a flickering tongue—a wickedly skilled tongue. Next came the warmth and wetness of a mouth equally adept; Leila was devouring me. But then the heat, moistness, skill, and pleasure it brought abandoned me, but not Leila herself; she still hovered in the dark, preparing to introduce another of her delights. With one knee already on the bed, she swung a leg over me and planted her other knee alongside my hip; she had effectively straddled me—had pinned me to the bed. Next, with her help—there was no mistaking who wielded dominion—I felt myself slip inside her; I was a prisoner to Leila's heat, her will, the verve of her desire.

"Stay with me, Addison," she said. Although a gentle command, there was no mistaking the thrust of its authority. I could feel Leila's breath on my face; it was not unpleasant. "I need you to last and not let go until I say."

Strange, but what came over me, with a measure of discomfiture, was the notion that Leila and I were not making love, nor were we engaged in what an experienced couple might acknowledge as a casual fuck, less were we enjoying anything that might qualify as intimacy. The prevailing theory? Leila was using my penis to masturbate. Her goal was simple: to achieve an end while maintaining a given emotional distance or detachment. In other words, I was there but not there—or, it was more a case that the majority of my being had little if any consequence. Perhaps it was my inexperience hastening this assertion. But wait, how well did I know Leila Bennett? There stood every likelihood I was experiencing what, according to her, qualified as frothing over with intimacy and emotion. Though if my prevailing theory ended up being the case, why should I care? I was a male, the baser of the two sexes, or so Claire Caldwell had instilled in me. But tonight, I was in there with a jungle cat—a pro—a hired gun, which I could not begin to match in baseness, much less experience.

I reached up and found Leila's shoulders, then allowed the feathery touch of my fingertips to glide down the length of her willowy, well-toned arms to her hands—hands that were pressing on my chest and mirroring each well-timed thrust. With this subtle display of intimacy, I sought to make the experience seem less animal and more human, though I suspected Leila failed to take appreciable notice. Then, just as my fingertips reached her hands, I could feel Leila stiffen. Next came shortened thrusts in quicker intervals that quickened further yet: she was manic, rapacious, in the throes of a frenzy, and it led to her convulsing, and her plummet from this rousing pinnacle ended with the collapse of her head in my chest and hair flinging forward in my face. I went to wrap my arms around Leila; the notion was to coddle and soothe her following the force of a violent carnal episode. But no sooner than the thought occurred to me, she reassumed her perch of dominion akin to someone who suffered the pitfalls of a hill only to reclaim the summit to lead a charge. She raised from my chest; the sway of her back arched beautifully; Leila appeared as regal as when seated atop her royal blue Harley. She shook her head vigorously, flinging her luxurious mane—it had hung sultrily about her face—behind her. Her hands were again pressing on my chest and matching what were presently composed thrusts when she whispered—a husky and hurried resonance belied her composure—"Come on, Addison; cum for Mama."

Leila, referring to herself as "Mama," nearly caused me to wilt. What saved me from the sort of crisis known to shred the male ego was not an action of which Leila was conscious or anything I had thus far the opportunity to imagine. The prevailing factor, or saving grace, was Leila leaning forward just enough so I could feel the heat emanating from her body; the sheath of sweat blanketing her skin intoxicated me—I was swimming in it! Also, a tendril of her lovely mane fell forward and stuck to the moisture on her face. The latter was so simple and yet potent.

"Atta boy, Addison," she said as I squirted inside her. "Get it all out."

Afterward, Leila playfully tousled my hair. And although the gesture reduced me to a dog who performed admirably for a treat or an "atta boy" who satisfied "Mama," it was the first moment since entering my room that Leila put me in mind of the woman who picked us up at the bus station. However, not even a second's afterglow did she afford me. Leila hopped off me as though I were as familiar to her as an old, beat-up bicycle she had ridden for years—the sort of bike so old and faithful it had been years since its owner employed the kickstand, as time after time, the poor sonofabitchin thing thoughtlessly fell to the ground after a hurried dismount. In other words, I was chewed up and spit out by a cougar. And just like that, she was gone.

****

And now begins our second full day in Western Pennsylvania. Yours truly did not make it to the kitchen until, God forbid, 7:15 a.m. My smart-ass friends greeted me with the predictable *"good afternoon, sleeping beauty"* bullshit one tends to receive when making a tardy a.m. appearance, assuming a lousy fifteen extra minutes qualifies as sleeping in. My tired eyes found Leila busy flipping omelets, toasting bread, and brewing coffee; she wore no indication that she found Cillian and Joey's humor amusing or decided it was wise to conceal that she had. I received a cordial "good morning" from Leila, which I politely returned. Next, I rubbed my eyes to where they saw clearer and again rested them on my middle-of-the-night seductress. Talk about a poker face! I would not want to play cards with Leila Bennett; neither her face nor body language revealed that anything beyond the ordinary occurred last night. Moreover, neither stiffness nor stoicism marked a prevailing deportment. To act this evasively after such an occurrence as the previous night demonstrated uncommon restraint, I thought. Not that I expected to come strolling into the kitchen to an excitable Leila crying out, "CJ, Joey, you'll never believe who I fucked last night," but I would have appreciated a subtle wink.

The longer the morning wore on, the more I considered the possibility I had imagined the whole affair. Between being driven to distraction by Leila on a tractor and Harley and my exhaustion, and each condition aided by whiskey, the prospect is not one I should be too quick to disregard. Another scenario was that Leila was prone to walking while asleep. If Claire Caldwell can be a midnight toker, Leila Bennet can be a somnambulating fuck-monster; each of us has our quirks.

Before we took ourselves to task, I managed to ask Cillian— it seemed reasonable that I should, given what happened last night— "How'd you sleep?"

"Wasn't the soundest I ever slept, but I managed." His manly pat on the back meant *thanks for asking.*

"Yeah?" I intoned, swelling with curiosity. "Nothing happened? Nothing out of the ordinary?"

"I didn't have any nightmares or get abducted by aliens if that's what you mean by 'out of the ordinary,'" he said. I shrugged to indicate that I was satisfied and dropped the subject.

Leila made only one visitation and not, for lack of a better term, "the rounds." Not to sell Joey short, but had he received a middle-of-the-night visitor, he delivered a better acting performance than Leila.

Scraping, scraping, and more scraping: scraping from an extension ladder, then from the ground; scraping from stepladders to reach areas not quite the second story but above the first; bonding over elbow grease, sweat, and peeled paint chips pried loose and sent fluttering through the air; Leila coming and Leila going; Leila in a truck and later on a Harley; Leila with her hair up and later with it down and dancing delightfully on her bare shoulders; Leila in short-shorts, prancing about first in work boots, and later in sandals. As we labored, we received the full and torturous gamut of all things "Leila," including sandwiches to fill our bellies and cans of Schlitz to quench our thirst, and it was all aided by the sort of teenaged banter that helped work seem less laborious.

Later, our "queen bee" returned to the farm on her thunderous Harley with Elk Tavern pizza in tow. From there, the night took on a near-identical form of the night before: we housed a pizza in what seemed seconds, migrated to the living room for conversation—tonight, we managed to avoid suicide and the confessing of sordid pasts—then Leila handed us a transistor radio, a bottle of whiskey, and encouraged us to enjoy the night air and drink only enough to rid our muscles of any lingering achiness.

We retired to what would become our nightly universe: the top plank of a wooden fence. We would sit facing the farm with the setting sun at our backs and tune into the Bucs games. We sipped, talked, and listened, and most nights, we failed to notice the sun's disappearance and the night sky darkening until the sun had long since taken its bow and the galaxy reflected its glitter overhead. Tonight, the Phils shutout the Cardinals 2—0 behind Mr. Quick Pitch himself, Jim Kaat. The Phils' two runs came on solo homers by Mike Schmidt and Gary Maddox. The win pulled them a half-game in front of the Bucs, who lost 6—3 to the Expos, but they gained no ground on those notorious faders, the Cubs, who beat the Mets. Although the season was not quite half over—there was still all of July, the dog days of August, plus September—at what point do you start to worry? Incidentally, I never understood the term "dog days," why they are in August, and how they apply to baseball.

"Keeping pace beats losing ground," Joey maintained. "Don't worry, we'll catch the Cubs; the Phils are the better team, and it'll prove out before the end of the summer."

Joey was right, and we knew it: but a baseball season is a one-hundred-and-sixty-two-game grind, and if you are a fan of the team doing the chasing, the season, instead of buoyantly in rhythm, can unfold at an agonizingly slow and choppy pace. And since I broached the subject of "agonizingly slow and choppy," that was just how the night passed, as each creak that old farmhouse made caused me to stir with anticipation that it was Leila en route to my bedroom. But she never came, and hours had passed before I reluctantly surrendered to my exhaustion.

****

And now begins our third full day in Western Pennsylvania. Sleep or no sleep, come the morning, I made sure I was first in the kitchen. At 6:45, all was clear. For better or worse, as my kitchen skills began and ended with asking, "What's for dinner," I put on a pot of coffee, which launched an appreciative Leila from her pillow. Joey followed shortly thereafter. Not Cillian: he did not make his tardy morning appearance until 7:30.

"Jeez," I intoned, glancing down at my idiotic Pink Panther wristwatch, "lucky for you, we saved you some leftovers."

"Hardee-fucking-har," he groused. But the real hardee-har-worthy moment came when I observed Cillian's face: his dreamy eyes and idiotic smile were all the evidence I needed to know that he was incapable of holding a lucid thought in his head.

"French Toast, CJ?" was Leila's chirpy offer.

This morning, Leila did not wear a poker face. Moreover, she let loose a girlish giggle when setting her eyes on Cillian.

Now perfectly aware of the reason behind yesterday morning's brief inquiry, Cillian, while wearing what Darrin Caldwell would describe as "a shit-eating grin," intoned the nifty question using an Irish brogue, "Well, ol' paddy o' mine, still a non-believer, are ya?"

Grinning like a sonofabitch, I replied, "Aye, laddie; at the very least, I'll give ya the devil, though I never imagined she'd hail from Ohio."

We were through scraping old, peeled paint. Today (Saturday), we will take on the task of pressure washing the house and replacing exterior sills that are too rotted for a fresh coat. We went rummaging through the shed and discovered plenty of suitable wood. As for tools? Uncle Dave was armed to the teeth.

"Your uncle must've been a real do-it-your-selfer," I theorized.

"Either that," said Cillian, "or he was a collector; these tools don't look to have suffered much wear and tear."

We agreed on the latter: this handymen's haven we penetrated, once we brushed away the cobwebs, looked too clean and organized. Moreover, everything we needed was in plain sight: workbench, clamps, ninety-degree chop saw—we would not be making any angle cuts—drill, electric sander, and six-inch wood screws; and because we attended public school, instead of studying impractical matters such as theology, we benefitted from hours spent in a wood shop, thus replacing a few exterior window sills would prove a cinch.

The workday ended early but too late to begin painting. Besides, we had to let the house dry before sloshing on a new coat. So Leila garaged her Harley in favor of her behemoth Ford, and the four of us rode over to Elk's Tavern for dinner. We mingled with some locals, including Rex Hadley, who did not mind showing off his Harley, and Stu Larson, who owned one of those seed and feed stores that supply farmers. Jimmy Ringo kept the bar, and none of the Elk's Tavern faithful would have known if his skills ranged beyond pouring mugs of beer and shots of whiskey. Steel mill workers, coal miners, loggers, and local businessmen made up the clientele of Elk's— the same folks that tailgated outside Three River Stadium hours before the Steelers kicked off. After dinner, Leila remained behind but coughed up a few bucks and pointed us toward the center of town.

"There's a fountain, a nice town square, and a main street all lit up," Leila told us after we were through eating. "And there's a shop to get some custard cones if y'all feel like dessert."

It was a bizarre feeling, to say the least, to be doled out cash for ice cream by a woman who, two nights ago, pummeled me into a mattress. But, from here on, while in western Pennsylvania, I would be wise to expect the unexpected: Money for ice cream, whiskey for achy muscles, and vagina whenever.

Not by a longshot did downtown New Castle resemble Philly. But after three consecutive nights isolated on a farm, we welcomed any change of scenery. Before heading back to the tavern, we kicked around for a couple of hours, which was more time than downtown New Castle required. Then Leila rode us back to our universe: a wooden fence, a view of the farm—it was well past dark by the time we arrived—a bottle of whiskey, and a Bucs game, which we did not join until the bottom of the sixth inning with the Bucs trailing 6—1. That was how it would end; the Pirates never mounted a threat. Meanwhile, the Phils beat the Mets 4—2 to keep pace with those goddamn Cubs who have developed an allergy to losing. Although, as Joey never fails to point out, it was still June. But it would not be much longer; the month was creeping to a close, and the Cubs had become strenuously uncooperative. And speaking of Joey, Cillian and I wished him luck when our fence party broke up.

"Good luck tonight, laddie," we called to him as he began ambling toward the house. Joey turned about just as Cillian and I had hopped down from the top plank of the fence. The expression on his face was precious; it was one of those head-scratcher looks, though he never reached for his noggin.

"I'll be fine," he called back to us. "I think I can remember how to fall asleep."

"Whatever you say," Cillian replied.

But then I got to thinking: despite graduating from rattles to razors in record time, perhaps Leila, who was tall for a woman, did not favor guys so short as Joey Brosco. I hear women can be fickle about such matters as the height of a man. I cannot say that the prospect of whether or not Joey would get laid tonight kept me tossing and turning; however, it would make for an awkward summer were Joey, wittingly or otherwise, denied access to Leila Bennett's vagina. Cillian and I, friends that we are, would not stand for it; we would have to explain to Leila: either the game includes all or none of us, assuming, of course, that Leila planned to extend her promiscuity beyond last night. After all, it was her vagina; she could slam the door on us at whatever point she wished.

The summer of '77 was in its infancy; thus, I had no idea what to expect concerning Leila's north-of-midnight visitations. I thought it made perfect sense that since Leila had already sampled two of us, she would want to make it a clean sweep, though far be it from me to dare apply the principles of equity to a woman's vagina. As it would come to pass, neither Cillian nor I would need to approach Leila on the subject of Joey having a bite at the apple; we had our unequivocal answer come the morning—at 7:45! I heard Leila, busy at the stove, mutter under her breath while shaking her head in mock dismay: "They keep gittin' later an' later, these young bucks."

After breakfast, without question, we followed Leila into the garage and piled into her truck. It was not until we reached the end of the driveway and about to turn onto the road that Cillian thought to ask, "What's the game plan, Leila?"

"Whudda ya mean, 'what's the game plan?'" An unexpected note of indignation rang in Leila's tenor. Seemingly appalled by our ignorance, she cried, "It's Sunday, ain't it?"

The irony was unimaginable; it nearly caused me to fall out of a moving truck it was so damn unimaginable. Leila fucks all three of us, one at a time, on consecutive nights, then carts us off to church! The summer of '77 breached all known boundaries in its quest to prove one thing: the world must be an asylum because its inhabitants are batshit crazy.

"I should warn you, Leila; our Addie is an atheist." I wished Cillian hadn't opened that can of worms. Not to imply that I'm someone afraid to own up to his convictions, but it was a little early in the day to begin twisting horns, if you know what I mean.

"What's that s'posed to mean?" Leila intoned. "Like he don't believe in goin' to church or something?"

Had Cillian let it rest there, I might have been in the clear; many God-fearing and God-loving people don't bother with the weekly ritual of attending services. But Cillian saw it necessary to chirp to Leila, "Nope; with Addie, it's the full-monte; he's got no faith that there's a Man Upstairs!"

I thought Leila was going to veer off the road, perhaps test the stoutness of her Ford against a utility pole. "Whudda ya *mean* he don't believe in God? How could someone not believe in *God*?" Leila directed her words of incredulity and outrage at Cillian. Then I saw her searching the rearview mirror and shifting to set her eyes of disbelief and fury upon me.

"Addison, if you don't believe in God, what *do* you believe in?" It was apparent from Leila's tone that her question was neither rhetorical nor a fact-finding probe. On the contrary, she could not have cared less about what I believed in; her only concern was why I lacked faith in a spiritual deity overseeing our lives. Moreover, if needed, she was prepared to rescue me from eternal damnation or plunging into a fiery abyss by steering me on the path of salvation, even should the effort require hogtying and dragging.

I was praying Cillian would not further agitate by mentioning Rigel, black holes, or anything pertaining to galactic event horizons, supernovas, and the time/space continuum in front of a woman poised to launch into an Evangelistic harangue. Unfortunately, I did not pray hard enough: Cillian went full-tilt, ripping off a torrent of cosmic blather—he paraphrased my soliloquy from four nights ago—before diving headlong into typical Darwinian mumbo-jumbo, neither of which Leila had any appreciation, less comprehension. It was no wonder I imagined how much less contentious this moment would have been had Cillian walked off the trestle, I had fallen out of the Ferris wheel, or all three of us got mashed by a speeding train. And because not a shred of science or reason had resonated less registered, Leila felt compelled to cry, "You're not one of them crazies that practices witchcraft or voodoo, are ya? 'Cause if you are, Addison, I got an FYI for ya: this ain't the most liberal part of the world if you catch my drift. So, if you're into anything too weird, you might oughta keep it under your hat."

"On my honor, Leila, no witchcraft, no voodoo; I never even sacrificed a chicken."

Leila drove to the next crossroad without uttering a word. But I could tell she was growing antsy; her shifting eyes searched for me in the rearview mirror. "Addison, if you don't believe in the Lord," she bemoaned, "then that also must mean you don't love the baby Jesus!"

There was a mixture of astonishment and pleading in Leila's Midwestern twang: *How could you?* she was essentially saying. *How could you be so monstrous as not to love a child who would grow up to become our savior, the world's redeemer?* I could see it in her eyes; it also rang in her tenor: I was Addison Caldwell, the baby hater. It made me recall a Sunday morning in recent times when flipping through television stations and stumbling upon Jimmy Swaggart, the sonofabitch. Tears welled up in the Evangelist's eyes as he professed his undying love and passion for "the baby Je-yee-yee-yee-zzzusss!" It seemed that among those lunatic Revivalists—Billy Graham and Jerry Falwell among them, not to mention some of those black preachers whose fondness for hyperbole is unrivaled—there was a common belief that the longer they reverberated Jesus's name, the sincerer they sounded in professing their love and devotion, or that it would better serve to convince others to express love and devotion in the form of donations. Although mildly amusing, as the onus seemed more on showmanship than faith, they sounded more like a bunch of snake oil salesmen than men of God. In contrast, because they lacked histrionics, Catholic priests could preach the same strain of bullshit but make it sound more authentic—more learned.

"Hey, Case," I called to my sister, "come check out this sonofabitch."

"Addison, watch your language around your sister," Darrin reminded me for the umpteenth time. Claire stepped out of the kitchen and leaned against the arch dividing the dining room and parlor to see what prompted me to summon Casey. "Seriously, Addison?" Her tone was laden with irony and reproachfulness. "You think watching church on television will get you into Maryellen McNamara's pants?"

"For Chrissake, Claire," Darrin shrieked while gesturing toward Casey to remind everyone that the family runt, who was snickering, for she had grasped the innuendo, was still in the room. "Soon, we'll be a family based on free love and hippie nonsense and with no moral compass to follow!" Claire, who had little appreciation for being told she, more or less, was the corrupting influence behind our moral decay, mocked Darrin by singing a verse of Sinatra's *My Way* horribly out of tune with the lyrics:

> *For what is a snob*
> *what has he got?*
> *If no tight ass*
> *then he has naught…*
> *To utter words*
> *the masses feel*
> *As they gather 'round*
> *to watch him kneel*
> *He dodged the blows*
> *and so it goes*
> *He did it theirrrrrr way*

Darrin retaliated by delivering the stinging insult, "Hey, Jackie, would you mind sleeping in the guest room? Marilynn's coming over tonight," in a New England accent—a not altogether bad JFK impression, I must admit, though it sounded more like Bobby. Following his final word, Darrin went overboard by tactlessly mimicking a bullet going through his head. Meanwhile, Jimmy Swaggart was still going strong, rambling on, as do all typical theists claiming to know what God has bestowed upon us and expects in return. Then it occurred to me, as though struck by something unseen: Bullshit is an art form. Moreover, it's artistry that deserves respect. Okay, maybe you can't hang it in a museum alongside Dali or Picasso. But Jimmy Swaggart could spew bullshit into the ether every bit as effectively as Rembrandt once spread paint onto a canvas—the man was a true savant, a genuine maestro able to hold an audience in his thrall as Stokowski once had when conducting Bach transcriptions. I harkened back to days, not all that long ago, listening to Father Murray's humdrum as he sifted through the crowd in search of Cyndy Pytlewski's tits, only to conclude that there was a vast difference between delivering a sermon and oratory. As sure as I was sitting there, I knew that Jimmy Swaggart was a snake oil salesman, and yet I could not look away; his convictions were powerful, his declamation potent.

Did I not love the baby Jesus? It was a trickier question than I first realized. After all, who relishes seeming contemptuous or indifferent when the subject is an infant? I agonized over rendering a reply that would guarantee getting us to the church in one piece. Finally, I told Leila, "I never think of Jesus as a baby, only as an adult who was arrested and crucified for political reasons."

"Political reasons!" Leila shrieked. "How could Jesus dyin' for our sins have had anything to do with politics; there ain't no mention of that in the Bible. I don't know, Addison, but it sounds to me like someone's been feedin' you a line."

It mattered not that I was sitting behind Cillian; I could feel him smirking over the notion I was standing in a hole, and, as a lifeline, some smartass handed me a shovel. The Bible and Leila's love for the baby Jesus made her insensible to logic and reason. One must understand when they are barking up the wrong tree. "Either way," I said, "whenever I think of Jesus, I tend to think of the 33AD Jesus, not the babe." I hoped that would lay the matter to rest.

"That's a shame, Addison," Leila said as if my eternal soul was in jeopardy. Moreover, she seemed genuinely plagued by the notion that I was irredeemable and frothed with sincerity when adding, "'Cause if I had one wish in this whole wide world, it would be to kneel at that cradle in Bethlehem and see the light of God on the face of that babe, my Lord and Savior. It makes me tingle all over just thinking about it."

Regardless of its speed, falling from a moving truck was more than a viable option; it was the only option. Nevertheless, I managed to say to Leila politely and with as much earnestness as I could muster: "It's nice to feel that way about something," and not another word. I mean, really, where could I go from there if not out a window?

And so, to Cillian and Joey's amusement, I agonized through an hour of madcap Evangelism. The pleasure my friends derived ended up more agonizing than the service itself; it rained down upon me like the wrath of a biblical plague. And if they poked me in the ribs once, they poked me fifty times to ensure I honored Pastor Flynn with proper attention. I pretended that Pastor Flynn was an actor auditioning either for Father Barry's role in *On the Waterfront* or Father Flanagan in *Men of Boys Town*. Eventually, I ignored Pastor Flynn and the sharp elbows altogether and amused myself by allowing my eyes to rove the congregation. I noticed many in the pews were also present last night at Elk's Tavern, where, according to their sagging lids and faltering posture, they squandered a generous portion of their wages. It just goes to show that sobriety and religion tend to misalign.

After receiving the word of God from Pastor Flynn, who taught us how to accept, properly, both the baby and the crucified Jesus into our hearts, we spent the afternoon taking Harley rides. Then, we settled in the parlor with cans of Schlitz and watched the Bucs on television: it was a Sunday doubleheader. Sometime during the games, both of which the Pirates would lose (6—1 in the first game and 13—3 in the second; meanwhile, the Phils kept pace with those notorious faders, the Cubs, who won an extra-inning affair), we reached a resolution and managed the effort without it resonating like an endorsed congressional policy or structured schedule. No longer would we receive visitations from Leila; instead, we would go to her room in the same order she visited ours: yours truly, Cillian, then Joey. I would go to Leila's room on Mondays and Thursdays, Cillian on Tuesdays and Fridays, and Joey on Wednesdays and Saturdays, sometime between the hours of ten and midnight. Sundays, we would rest. Just as God created Heaven and Earth in six days, and on the seventh day He rested, so, too, would we rest on the seventh day. Fuck-fuck-fuck, fuck-fuck-fuck, then church. Just following the Commandments, the way we see 'em. Admittedly, one might be hard-pressed to find a more athletic interpretation of the Bible, but many have traversed "the good book" using a skewed lens.

Because we were in there with a real pro, our cocksmanship ascended to levels we never imagined. Understand, we did not necessarily see this newly developed skill as a virtue but rather an exploit, one in which we could take pride and hopefully have opportunities to recreate at the other end of the state come the fall. With that in mind, we compared ourselves to the great pitching rotations in baseball history: Seaver, Koosman, and Matlack; Palmer, Cueller, and McNally; Koufax, Drysdale, and Osteen. Then Cillian, because Joey had spouted off great pitching rotations beginning from as far back as the 1890s, playfully put him in a full nelson, which rendered Joey immobile, and bellowed, "How 'bout Spahn, Sain, and pray for rain? Huh; how 'bout that one, Encyclopedia Brosco?"

As the story goes, the Braves, years ago when they played in Boston, had but two reliable pitchers: Warren Spahn and Johnny Sain. Hence, the jingle, Spahn, Sain, and pray for rain. Joey had little appreciation for having pinned on him the "pray for rain" part of our rotation but took the gibe well enough. Once Cillian released him from the wrestling hold that had him immobilized, Joey stretched his diminutive frame back into shape and proceeded to tell us the history behind the chant: *Spahn, Sain, and pray for rain*. We listened. We always loaned an attentive ear whenever Joey was in the mood to offer a free history lesson. *Spahn, Sain, and pray for rain* was a jingle every baseball fan knew, but few our age—Joey being the rare exception—knew its history. Thus, we learned of the epic and superhuman performances that Warren Spahn and Johnny Sain put forth in pitching the Braves through September and into the 1948 World Series, and also the poem that spawned the famous chant written by a sportswriter of the Boston Post during the September pennant race:

> *First, we'll use Spahn, then we'll use Sain,*
> *Then, an off day, followed by rain.*
> *Back will come Spahn, followed by Sain,*
> *Followed, we hope, by two days of rain.*

Then Joey crowed, "How 'bout Wynn, Lemon, and Feller?"

Historically, it was the best rotation named, as Early Wynn, Bob Lemon, and Bob Feller became enshrined in the Hall of Fame—Bob Lemon, most recently. But we decided to ignore history in favor of keeping current; thus, we anointed ourselves the penile equivalents of Tom Seaver, Jerry Koosman, and John Matlack, ready, willing, and able every third day to serve our queen bee. Indeed, our universe, which thus far included a wooden fence, a bottle of whiskey, a transistor radio, and a view of a farm in a fading sunset that would surrender to a star-studded country sky, would extend to Leila Bennett's vagina by way of a fixed rotation—rainouts notwithstanding.

Sex with Leila was nothing like how I imagined sex would be with Maryellen. With Maryellen, there was romance, discovery, tenderness, and more foreplay than we could ever have had time for before our bodies ended up in a tangle with me inside her. The fragrance of Maryellen's hair would intoxicate me, rousing me to thrust deeper, and my virility would reflexively send her neck arching back, thus exposing her moistened throat over which I would glide my tongue. With Leila, it was none of the above. Our "sessions" were far more succinct and akin to the following: that's your penis; this is where you're supposed to put it; now let's get down to business; class need only last so long, and you had better have handled your business before the dismissal bell. In other words, Leila schooled us not in the art of lovemaking but the art of good old-fashioned fucking, and, goddamnit, she was good! What do I mean by good? You would expect a former prostitute to be somewhat cavernous, but Leila had the kegel development of a gymnast; she could juice a lemon until all that remained was a limp piece of rind. And although she turned Cillian, Joey, and me into virtuosos in almost no time, the process was methodical: we were, with optimum efficiency, to bring Leila to a swift climax, climax ourselves, then skedaddle from her room. Leila's heart may burst with love for the baby Jesus, but concerning sex, she was emotionally impoverished. Perhaps it was a residual from her past life—her pre-Uncle Dave days—that sex no longer ascended to the realm of exploratory idyll but remained grounded as a means to an end, and the aim was simply to "get off," and the swifter, the better. And although inconsistent and unpredictable, there were occasions when Leila revealed herself susceptible to compliments—how could anyone not gush with praise when in the presence of a goddess-like physique? —and would allow us to feast upon her perky, well-formed breasts, the loveliness of her curvature, and the dazzling suppleness of her graceful length: from her fresh farmgirl face to the tips of her slender toes, Leila Bennett was a smorgasbord, a dessert tray, an ice cream bar with every flavor of the month.

Aside from the obvious, what lent the summer of '77 its bizarreness? Leila displayed a warmer and friendlier demeanor when outside her bedroom walls. Whether on her Harley with her hair flailing about, sitting atop her John Deere with her long, sinewy arms flexing with each turn, or high up in the cabin of her behemoth Ford, she was radiant—she sparkled. When her feet were on the ground, she pranced about like an earthy, innocent farm girl, unaware of her facility to torture men. But in her bedroom, the sparkle in her eyes vanished, and in its stead came a predatory glare—the simple farm girl would transform into a ravenous and dangerous cougar. Then came the arrival of Sunday with Pastor Flynn and the baby Jesus.

****

The Fourth of July fell on a Monday (my night) in the summer of '77. We were on our way to Owen Burkhardt's farm for fireworks. When we arrived, Owen Burkhardt's driveway and lawn looked like a parking lot that only permitted Harleys and pickups. Cillian, Joey, and I were about to learn that they know a thing or two concerning fireworks in Western Pennsylvania; the town of New Castle manufactures nearly half the world's celebratory explosives. The result? By 9:30, you would have thought you were in the middle of a goddamn warzone. From as far north as Route 80 to as far south as the Allegheny River, all you saw were trails of light followed by spectacular explosions forming giant multi-colored glittery umbrellas. We oohed and aahed while sipping beer from mugs after gobbling barbecued ribs. Owen Burkhardt supplied the keg; Rex Hadley the ribs; Leila brought additional fixings from the tavern; it all aided in a loose and rowdy celebration of independence had by rough-looking men and scantily dressed women.

We did not arrive back at the farm until a few ticks shy of midnight. Leila practically hogtied me before dragging me into her room. She was all amped up from the fireworks and seemed racked with urgency concerning the time; I could not hazard a guess what it might mean should we fail to climax after the clock indicated it was Tuesday, nor did I ask. From the outset, our session was an all-out manhandling, though, in this instance, it was the female displaying bestial traits. Leila was akin to a drill sergeant with a whistle; I could not shed my clothes fast enough and was still wearing an article or two when she pushed me back onto the mattress and promptly straddled me; the latter maneuver came following a dive that saw Leila's knees, thankfully, crash-land atop the bed and not on my more delicate parts. It was reminiscent of our first night, only far more savage. Leila was

Mean Joe Greene, and I was some poor, immobile quarterback protected by a shitty semi-pro-offensive line.

"Stay with me, Addison, stay with me." Leila's breathy words, however pleading and demanding, were unnecessary, for by now, I knew better than to let go before she reached the promised land. And were her thrusts ever quick! They seemed more vibratory than arriving in forceful, rhythmic drives with discernable intervals. Pelvically speaking, Leila was a force of nature, a phenomenon; I'm confident she could create enough friction to spark a fire but settled for successfully masturbating using my penis. Then came her sudden collapse, which saw her head falling to my chest and her hair flinging forward into my face. It was followed not by the regaining of poise—thus far, poise was nonexistent—but Leila's initial sign of composure in what would stand as our briefest encounter.

"Come on, Addison, come on," she urged. And just like that, our session ended.

The following night, with Cillian and Leila upstairs occupying one another and Joey in the living room reading the sports page from front to back and memorizing every statistical morsel, I sat at the dining room table, composing a letter to Casey. Thus far, I had failed to hold up my end of the bargain, and my weak output weighed on my mind. Not since my second night in Western Pennsylvania—mere hours before my first encounter with Leila—had I written a word to Casey. I recounted how Cillian, Joey, and I turned our journey to Western Pennsylvania into an adventure but stressed "mum's the word," as I did not wish to send Darrin and Claire into a fit, suspecting I had become reckless. Since then, I have received two letters from Casey: the second politely reminded me that the summer was barely underway, and we were already out of turn. It bothered me to think that Casey might view her big brother as someone big on words but not so hot when it came to following through with promises, but what could I write and tell my eight-year-old sister: I represent the Tom Seaver of a three-man rotation that fucks the same woman? *Dear Case, I fuck a twenty-eight-year-old former prostitute every Monday and Thursday night, sometime between the hours of ten and midnight. I've become morally bankrupt since leaving home, but I manage, if you can believe it, to keep the seventh day holy. P.S. Don't tell Mom and Dad, especially the part about going to church.* Naturally, that was not a letter I would dare send; I just wanted to put those thoughts on paper to determine better just how absurd they were; it gave me a chuckle before I crumpled the paper and tossed it aside.

"*I* could use a laugh," Joey called to me from the living room.

"It's nothing," I called back. "I was just laughing at my own stupidity."

"If that were the case, you'd be doubled over."

"Hardee-fucking-har!"

What to write? I was pressing and coming up empty. After all, did Casey want to hear about scraping peeled paint, pressure-washing and painting old wood, and replacing rotted sills? Then it finally occurred to me, after crumbling up another piece of paper, that Joey, all along, had his hands on the answer. According to her selected activities, Casey was no tomboy but bled white with red pinstripes for the Phillies, and the past few days provided me with plenty of material! *What a difference a week makes* was how I began. *Since May, it seemed all the Phils were doing was winning just for the right to remain eight-and-a-half games behind the Cubs, who were winning every way imaginable. Now, look at us! Only three games back; can you believe it? By listening to the Pirates games every night, we've been able to follow the season no less attentively than had we been home. But I must tell you, Case, the Pirates broadcasters, Milo Hamilton and Lanny Frattare, although good, are not Richie Ashburn or Harry Kalas. We Philadelphians are spoiled. Aside from seeing my kid sister, the one thing I'll be looking forward to, come September, is listening to some hometown broadcasting!* I rambled on about Harley rides, fireworks, the coolness of the evenings, and that the eating, particularly breakfast, was A-plus.

Former prostitute or no former prostitute, I did not know what to say about Leila on a personal note other than to mention she was tall, country pretty, and a helluva short-order cook. And with what little I mentioned Leila, I was careful to refer to her as "Aunt Leila." Not to suggest I composed the sort of lines in which, if read between, subtle messages and implications were detectable, but I figured it was best to play it safe and not give Casey anything to wonder about. *Love, Addison. P.S. Give my best to Kennedy and Sinatra. Better yet, tell Claire that I'm suffering from hemorrhoids. Trust me; it'll make her day.* I had filled three sheets of paper and then prepared to have them sent off. That night, I was last to turn in.

The following day, we applied the final touches—red shutters against a white house—having transformed a dull old farmhouse into a structure that, from the roadside, sparkled. It may not have been ours, but we took pride in its appearance. Afterward, Cillian and I decided to celebrate the end of a job well done by having one of our famous lovefests; it had been nearly a month since we last grappled. I suppose painting those damn shutters was such fine and tedious work that it left us with muscles aching to explode and apply maximum force to anything capable of matching it with equal resistance. In other words, it seemed an appropriate time to beat the living shit out of one another. Joey stood nearby, refereeing. We would call upon him to make a clear and decisive judgment, which, as usual, he would weasel out of by citing specific holds and maneuvers that Cillian and I applied adeptly before determining, once again, making every effort to sound plausible using the typical line, "This time I think it really *was* a draw."

Poor Leila. Never witnessing anything like the unconventional manner in which Cillian and I express affection for one another, she burst through the back door and hollered at Joey, "They're killing each other! They're killing each other!" Flummoxed by Joey's casual bearing or mistaking it for indifference, she cried, "Arencha gonna do something?"

"I *am* doing something," Joey told her. "I'm keeping score."

"Addison, CJ, you two stop that…." Leila faltered, and her momentary hesitation caused her to become tongue-tied. During this period of lingual failure, she tried to determine what Cillian and I were doing: wrestling, fighting … rumbling? Finally, her tongue righted itself, and she managed to blurt out, "…this instant!"

"They're almost done," Joey told her. "At the current pace, they won't last much longer."

"Since you two refuse to listen to me, then go ahead and kill each other! See if I care. I'm fucking Joey tonight, anyhow."

Leila stormed back into the house with child-like foot-stomping rage. Strange, but even with every muscle in my body screaming from the strain they were forced to endure, I detected a note of jealousy in Leila's tirade. Suddenly, mixing with all my strained muscles was a twinge of compassion that Leila understood what was transpiring between Cillian and me but that this small-town Midwest hick, who, for reasons I had yet to learn, was led astray and married a customer, hadn't a true friend. She survived an alcoholic father and an awful career choice, and the fortuitous result, or perhaps not so fortuitous result, was the acquisition of a farm and tavern. But where were Leila's friends or the one person she could pour out her heart to without judgment? Most girls have the former, and every girl has the latter. Leila wanted to become part of us in a way she could not. Consequently, she became part of us the only way she knew how.

"Well?" Cillian and I both, through huffs and puffs, deferred to Joey. Joey threw his hands in the air and shrugged as if to say, *Well, what?*

"Tell us who won the match, for fuck's sake!" Cillian bellowed.

Joey hemmed and hawed as only Joey could until finally, he declared, "I didn't see an advantage either way, but it was a helluva match, one of your more exciting ones."

Hours later, we were back in our universe. Three young men sat on a fence. What can pass for a universe when the right company meets limited options can be magical. Three young men perched with their backs to a fiery sunset, facing a farm, watching it pass into darkness. Three young men passed back and forth a bottle of what Leila Bennett called hooch while Milo Hamilton and Lanny Frattare, one pitch at a time, took them through the unfolding of nine frames of hardball. The first month of summer disappeared; nights were getting warmer but did not possess the same mugginess we had grown accustomed to at the other end of the state. The Phils and Cubs were leading late: it appears no ground would get gained tonight, but you cannot knock a win—a win is a win, and tonight, we would have to go to our beds satisfied with a three-game separation. In other words, we must not be greedy but honor the concept it is a long season featuring a process no one can rush. The grand old game, if nothing else, teaches patience, that pesky virtue no one sees as a virtue but remains one of life's more annoying necessities. As for the Bucs? They were fading in the standings but remained within striking distance. If nothing else, the Bucs could still bring the lumber and play the role of the spoiler.

Cillian was quiet tonight. Not just as the Bucs were running out of outs; he seemed subdued throughout most of the evening. I would go so far as to submit he was more than quiet. Quiet means one has failed to make themselves heard or had little to say. Cillian, however sparse, did manage a few utterances. But it was not his lack of output that had Joey and I concerned. Had it only been that, we might not have noticed his meager contribution. After all, a man is entitled to be tired and, consequently, quiet. What was clear was that Cillian's mind was elsewhere; thus, his limited utterances amounted to ineffectual and halfhearted fragments that neither added nor subtracted from our exchanges.

It was not long after our arrival that Cillian, it seemed, nimbly hurdled the emotional stumbling block known as Uncle Dave's suicide and the knowledge that his once dear uncle had gone tomcatting while poor Aunt Phyllis was on her way to an appointment with either the baby Jesus, hailed-with-hosannas Jesus, or Good Friday Jesus. But a sour emotional state, like a case of indigestion, has a knack for repeating. And while we are on the subject of family dysfunction, Cillian has not mentioned his mother since our second night on the farm, though it endured as a dissonant note bound to reverberate unkindly. First, we noticed his jaw clenching. Next, we watched him squeeze his brow. He was struggling and, for whatever reason, making an effort to keep it to himself. If left unconfronted, he might swallow the poisonous feeling and pray he could digest it without lingering consequences. Joey and I hopped down from the fence and faced him. Cillian sensed it was not an arbitrary action; he felt the weight of our collective gazes.

"You shoulda beat the living shit outa me and walked away." Cillian's voice quaked. "Goddamn, you two; why didn't you do what you were supposed to and leave me on that platform? It was your right. Didn't you understand?"

My head jerked. It was a reflex. For a fleeting moment, I was expecting to see, in the dark, several thousand tons of public transportation bearing down on me. But, as quick as the moment came, I recovered and told Cillian, "We weren't obligated to follow you into the tunnel; we chose to go."

"Addie's right," said Joey. "It was our choice. We coulda let you go alone."

"Addie's wrong. And so are you." Cillian hopped down from the fence. "If I ran through a wall of fire, not knowing what was on the other side, you would trail after me, and I would do the same for you. Because that's who we are. And it's for that reason I had no right to borrow against our friendship. It's the shittiest thing I ever did."

I could tell Cillian failed to feel the tears streaming down his cheeks. I did not feel mine either. The three of us stood huddled together like we had by the boathouses when hiking back to the train station.

"All right," I said, summoning some equanimity. "Starting from this moment, there's nothing to atone for; the score is dead even; it's the top of the first tied at zero. We'll begin holding one another accountable tomorrow."

We were all in agreement. Moreover, any lingering guilt or resentment over what happened that night in the tunnel had lifted. It was strange, especially when juxtaposed with how we spent our summer evenings, but it was the first night we felt fully enveloped with intimacy.

"There's only one problem," said Joey. "Just how in the hell am I supposed to pitch after this outpouring of emotion?"

Poor Joey. Leila made it crystal clear earlier that it was his night when Cillian and I were grappling on the grass. Moreover, there was no "praying for rain;" Joey was the Jon Matlack of our studded rotation; thus, from the beauty and intimacy of great friendship to a mindless fuck he must traverse. Somehow, Joey would have to dig deep and find his way. But one matter was for sure: Leila Bennett, with little effort, could be downright inspirational.

"Quit yer whining, laddie, and get in there and screw like a champ, bejesus," Cillian urged. Before long, Joey rejoined us in our universe, grinning like a sonofabitch.

CHAPTER FOURTEEN
THE KISS

Whether on Philly's crowded and steamy streets, watching the heat rise from the tar and off the hoods of a sea of automobiles, or in the wide-open spaces of Western Pennsylvania, summertime grows wings and flies by, and the warmest season of '77 would prove no different. There is no getting in front of the summer, less pushing back against it—it comes rumbling down the avenue, all avenues, like an unforgiving steamroller, and everyone must take heed and hasten their good times while the getting is good.

We blinked, and the first day of August was upon us: twelve games had come and gone from the Major League schedule since the night Cillian broke down, and together, Joey and I helped him vanquish the lingering guilt over the night in the tunnel, and still, those notorious faders, the Cubs, were riding shotgun in the National League's Eastern Division.

"They just won't go away," I moaned, wringing my hands together in the dark, under the stars, while perched in our universe, as Milo Hamilton updated scores of games still in progress and others about to end. Then Encyclopedia Brosco reminded us—historian that he was— "On this very day, in '69, the Cubs were holding six-and-a-half games on the Mets, 'The Amazins,' and from there, we all know how the rest of the story went. So, relax and try not to cut off the blood supply to a vital body part; there's still a ton of baseball yet to be played."

Relaxing, demonstrating patience, and reconciling "there's a ton of baseball yet to be played" is all well and good. But some of us would find the here and now no less exciting—thank you very much— if permitted to glimpse the future to acquire a better reading for predicting an outcome. Only having picked up a game-and-a-half in the standings over the past two weeks was not my idea of efficiency; the view would appear much rosier from the position of a game-and-a-half in front. And besides trailing those notorious faders, the Cubs, the Bucs, once again, were right up the Phils' ass, only a game behind—their front bumper was laying on our back and nudging us out of the way. Less than three games were separating three teams; the chase was on!

We had spent the waning days of July cleaning out an old shed and barn. Both were aged structures, as old as the house and every bit as worn from the elements. We rid each of their obsolete tools, materials, and objects Leila deemed unsalvageable. Lord knows the last time Uncle Dave had set foot in either structure; perhaps he never had or hadn't for a decade; we guessed the former. Upon emptying both structures, one thing was evident: every bug and insect in Lawrence County had routed themselves to the barn and shed of the Bennett Farm to perish. We were a full day dragging everything each structure had housed for who knows how many years, with Leila deciding which items went into the "junk pile" and which the "stay pile." Day two began with ridding both emptied spaces of an impressive thicket of dead bugs, rodent droppings, and cobwebs on top of cobwebs before we wiped down all the material in the "stay pile" and restocked it. The material with the likelier utility we designated for the shed; everything else went in the barn because of its proximity to the house. Next came—you guessed it—exterior scraping, pressure washing, and painting; perhaps if word gets out, we'll start a restoration business.

There were plenty of fun days, too. Taking Harley rides and cruising in Leila's two-toned behemoth pickup truck armed with six-packs of Schlitz and blasting rockabilly music on the radio passed for recreation. "Come on, fellas, we're goin' hellraising!" she would bellow when in the mood for the latter, and she need not twist our arms. Leila sporting a cowboy hat and western-style boots, singing outlaw country, and finding every plausible excuse to holler "Hell yeah!" out the window qualified as an activity. Yessiree, no Sinatra or Rolling Stones' Sticky Fingers for the gal from Woodsfield, Ohio. Often, those Harley rides and hellraising excursions would end with a backyard barbecue, and frequenters of the tavern would come by for a bite. Other times, we would pack a picnic lunch and drive until we spotted an inviting meadow to spread a blanket and laze away the afternoon.

Like anyone else, Leila could be complicated and sometimes erratic. Often, these traits did not surface intentionally. Moreover, it was apparent that Leila was unwitting of her less appealing characteristics and phases. At times, while managing her equilibrium, she sometimes appeared to drag the weight of all her twenty-eight birthdays through a given day. It was understandable for someone with limited experience, responsible for the day-to-day operation of a tavern and overseeing a farm, to get overwhelmed. Yet, she maintained a level of competence, and the acknowledged effort ranked her unmistakably as our queen bee and reinforced that we were her loyal drones and trusty subordinates—in *and* out of the bedroom. In the bedroom, to a degree, but not entirely, we shed our identities to keep intact the single multi-faceted organism featuring interchangeable parts that Leila drafted into service; thus, our foursome became Queen Bee Leila and her court: an establishment comprised of three young men seemingly of one mind and one goal orbiting one magnetic creature. We were helpless to act otherwise. For three hormonal young men thirsting for exploration, tits are akin to gravity or any entities capable of enforcing the laws of physics, and when packaged with blonde hair, blue eyes, and a long, sporty frame, the term "transcendental" is not hyperbolic. And it mattered not that Leila was an old farm girl, former prostitute, and Woodsfield hick; she was also twenty-eight, a beauty, and exceedingly liberal concerning how she shared her bountiful assets with three young men from Philly.

Outside the bedroom, there were instances when the gap between Leila, the businesswoman, and her three loyal subjects would whittle away inexplicably or shrink without warning. Sometimes, the gap would close altogether, leaving us a foursome: three city boys and their country gal sidekick. When Leila, the country gal, smiled, her eyes held within them the surprise of a young girl on Christmas morning; it was a thing of beauty, inspiring. Then Cillian, Joey, and I would catch ourselves doing, precisely, what we swore never to do: vie for Leila's attention and affection. Between Leila and us, it had to be all for one and one for all, an egalitarian orgy—literally. There could be no competition, no aperture through which the principles of a market economy, with its winners and losers, could emerge; otherwise, there stood every chance the summer of '77 could evolve into a season of discontent for everyone concerned.

Did I mention we blinked, and it was already the first of August? August the first was a Monday: my night. Thankfully, the Bucs lost; they have been hot of late and seemed poised to wrestle first place away from the Cubs before the Phils.

"Okay, Tom Terrific, go and git 'er," Cillian urged. "No changeups or curves. Tonight, it's all fastballs. Show 'er that ninety-five-mile-an-hour heater!"

When penetrating Leila's domain, she sent glaring eyes my way. Unlike the predatory glare I became accustomed to receiving, it was more akin to a *where the hell have you been* glower fixed in her gaze.

"The game went into extra innings," I somewhat lamely explained. "The Bucs coughed it up in the eleventh."

Her scowl softened. "Four to three," she said, rattling off the score. "You fellas aren't the only ones around here interested in baseball, I'll have ya know. Been following the Bucs since Mazeroski hit the Series winner against the Yankees."

I did the math in my head: Leila would have been eleven when Bill Mazeroski stunned the baseball world by sending the Yankees home in defeat. The Bucs make sense for Leila: Woodsfield is 100 and 150 miles nearer to Pittsburgh than Cincinnati and Cleveland, respectively.

Leila was seated at her vanity. It was a switch. Often, I found her sitting up in bed with her nose in a magazine. Leila was not much for novels; she favored magazines, particularly ones featuring hotrods, Harleys, pickup trucks, John Deere tractors, or any type of apparel and equipment suitable for outdoor adventure, whether it be camping, hunting, or fishing. With concern for fashion and interests, it was rare that Leila betrayed her origins as a Woodsfield hick.

"Hey, Addison, how 'bout hittin' these shoulders for me, would you?" Leila pulled her robe down just far enough to expose her shoulders; any further, I might have become too distracted to do what she asked with any measure of usefulness. Like everything else connected to this glorious creature called Leila Bennett, her shoulders were fine features, sinuous and well-toned, but tonight, they were rigid. After Leila drove her John Deere onto a ramp, she positioned herself underneath the tractor, then disassembled and sharpened the blades. Her next task also saw her working from the ground; the Ford had her all twisted and contorted. She raised the behemoth using a jack suitable for lifting a semi or raising a house to put on stilts, then positioned herself to replace the front brake pads.

"These dang things are squeakin' like a sonofabitch," she grumbled.

Two such tasks would give anyone a pair of stiff shoulders, yet it did not make the break from protocol seem any less anomalous: First, Leila was seated at her vanity; second, she exhibited what I alleged was a trace of vulnerability and it was not just apparent in her tenor when requesting a shoulder rub that a weakened state prevailed; it was palpable in her overall demeanor. Whatever happens in the moments ahead, tonight's encounter already marked a satisfying departure from the usual *I'll cum, you cum, then out you go* affair.

As my fingers kneaded Leila's shoulders, my nostrils filled with the scent of her hair; it was still moist from her shower, and her skin was warm. My eyes shifted from my busy hands to spying on Leila through the mirror. She appeared dreamy and unaware of the purring sounds she made; both indicated she was content to have my hands on her. She lowered her robe further and leaned forward—the gesture was a tacit request that her back receive equal attention. It pleased me more than the weeks of mindless fucking, to be a participant in this new game Leila was playing. I turned my gaze downward; Leila was sagging, wilting, delighting under the strength of my hands. I allowed myself, mistakenly, as it would turn out, to lapse into a state of reverie, for it made it that much more jarring when she said, a note of authority snapping in her tone: "Okay, big boy, that was real nice, but now it's time to get down to business."

Off came her robe; off came my clothes. Before I knew it, I was kneeling between Leila's legs, gazing down at a collection of angles, protrusions, and curves—a confluence of superlative womanhood, the potency for which few men were a match. Tonight would mark one of the rare instances when Leila granted me time to know her skin, to explore her body. Only twice before had she permitted these moments of worship, and, as in the past, it was followed by her wickedly and authoritatively informing me, "Candy store's closed, Addison; now fuck me like ya mean it, how I taught-cha."

Once Leila guided me inside her, I matched, if not usurped, her authority. My objective was to overwhelm her wickedness, reclaim the control I had when standing over her wilted form when applying my hands to her rigid shoulders, and conquer the dominion this maker of rules so liberally heaped upon herself. Thus, I began thrusting like a primordial beast deprived of every aspect of human refinement. Boldness merging with wildness would best describe how I surged ahead. But soon, I became mindful of the unsustainability of my pace and the consequences of sprinting versus running. Failing to last would be the kiss of death when in there with an experienced cougar like Leila, who demanded nothing short of satisfaction. With the gal from Woodsfield, there would be no *don't worry, you'll do better next time*; always looming was the prospect, should my cocksmanship fail to meet the challenge, there would be no "next time;" it's *back to the minors for you, kid; we don't tolerate any bush-league play in the majors*. With the fear of demotion, I steadied myself and delivered firm, deliberate thrusts. *Fuck me how I taught-cha*. With this subtle yet noticeable shift toward restraint, I deluded myself into believing I was in control of myself and over what transpired.

Delusional or not, I sensed the breadth of Leila's pleasure; it further emboldened me. Thus came my ascendence to captaincy, and Leila Bennett was the ship I commanded—a vessel that, based on my will, I could steer to wherever I desired.

My pace had further slackened; my effort became more measured. And just as I had when acknowledging Leila's pleasure, I savored each sustained thrust. Before long, I became sensible to Leila's bedroom, noticing features that escaped me in earlier sessions: the Aztec design knitted into what I could tell was a homemade afghan draped carelessly over the back of a chair; a chest of drawers painted blue—its color and hardware did not match anything else in the room, least of all the vanity; my guess, it was sentimental—a rifle, its butt end I noticed days ago protruding from under the bed now stood erect in a corner; and lastly, a photograph of a woman placed conspicuously atop a nightstand. How had I failed to notice it before tonight?

The woman in the photo was too old to be Leila's mother; perhaps she was a grandmother. The frame was wooden; its design was of a bygone era. In a way, these simple artifacts I scanned served to humanize Leila, soften her, and fling her authoritative command of "fuck me like ya mean it, how I taught-cha" clear out of my head. I sensed that, if cobbled together in some fashion, these objects told the story of Leila Bennett's life—a subject in which I had developed more than a passing interest. Not since shortly after our arrival had Leila mentioned her alcoholic father. And whenever we watched her sharpening tractor blades or had her head inside an engine, she was quick to cite "Mama" as the one responsible for all her knowledge concerning matters in which few women care to dabble. But whatever became of Leila's mother or, for that matter, the Woodsfield farm?

Tiny beads of moisture formed on Leila's upper lip. I did not watch them develop; they appeared, and their sudden arrival loaned more softness, more humanization to accompany the painted blue chest of drawers and photograph of someone who once had or still mattered. Moreover, the hardness that Leila displayed between ten and midnight—those predatory glares that marked the essence of her late evening persona, the sex for sex's sake that, until tonight, reigned as the prevailing dictum—receded like an ebb tide and exposed soft edges that Leila may not have wished to reveal.

I pushed against the bed and, in doing so, peeled my chest away from Leila's breasts. The subtle maneuver created the necessary separation I needed to gaze down at Leila and the moisture glistening in the hollow of her throat and between her breasts. I wanted to taste her sweat, to know the sensation of my tongue gliding over her dampness in those areas. The desire burned, but the effort failed to materialize as Leila's long, sinuous arms snaked their way around my buttocks, and with the benefit of her lengthy appendages, she forced me deeper inside her and had ample strength to hold me there.

Tonight was not the first time I experienced the imposing strength of Leila's grip. Her limbs were formidable, vise-like; their ability to hold and constrict someone entangled with her was akin to finding oneself in the clutches or jaws of a giant beast; to struggle against Leila's sex-driven physicality was, in a word, futile.

To be clear, I did not relinquish my captaincy willingly; Leila took it from me, stripped it away; the ship was steering itself—mutiny! Then, inexplicably, similar to how a blood pressure cuff relinquishes its grip, Leila decompressed. Her pelvis, which was capable of anchoring a tug-o-war, relaxed. Next, I watched her eyes, which were open to slits, go all aflutter, her mouth idyllic. I never imagined anyone looking so soft and lovely while entangled and ravenous; it was so unlike Leila, and the departure inspired me to lower myself to where I could probe for her lips; I wanted to taste her mouth.

Soft as a whisper was how I kissed Leila. What happened next was unimaginable.

Leila's hands, which were clutching my buttocks for leverage, with the speed of an electrical impulse or snap of a taut piece of elastic, were in front of me—her palms pressed flat to my chest. It was a peculiar reaction, I thought—a knee-jerk response to a gentle kiss. Moreover, Leila appeared as one might when braced to thwart an attack. The anomaly had me wondering whether I had breached a trust. But of what nature? Assuming it could reassure her, I leaned on her defensive hands and kissed her again.

It seemed unimaginable that Leila perceived me as a threat or that she—immersed in a summer theme she nurtured—felt violated; the very notion must rank as bizarre and incoherent. Nevertheless, she hoisted me off her, accomplishing this feat of strength using more might than I knew her to possess, and concerning power, I was well aware of our queen bee's endowments. With explosiveness and violence, my swollen penis received an unceremonious eviction. Leila tossed me such that, for a moment, I experienced the sensation of being airborne before landing with one foot on the floor, a knee on the mattress, arms flailing about to stabilize my equilibrium. Then, with the agility of a cat, Leila sprang upward and was kneeling on the bed; her blonde locks, which were still damp and fragrant from her shower, were flung forward and framing a face made to appear angry by a rigid jaw, flaring nostrils, and swollen eyes. I was about to launch words of protest—*what the fuck!* would have been fitting—but astonishment paralyzed my tongue.

Next, an open hand came crashing down against the side of my defenseless face. From my current juxtaposition to Leila atop the bed, I was unaware I was within striking distance and ignorant that mindfulness was required. Had I not been so flabbergasted and thus more conscious of what transpired and why, I might have been more mindful of Leila's reach. Did I see stars? Jesus Christ, I saw stars! Thousands of them! Millions of them! A whole galaxy of supernovas exploded in my head. I had never been struck so hard, not by anyone or for any reason, though what remained of my cognitive capacity assumed it was karma for the countless occasions I deserved a good swat.

My mouth fell open, and, for some inexplicable reason, my eyes found the photograph of the older woman on Leila's nightstand. I stared at that woman, dumbly perhaps, while up and down, Leila berated me. And while pelted by an unexpected torrent of heated verbiage, I managed to intuit that if the woman in the photo, whoever she was, were present in the room, she could supply some insight as to why Leila would lose her mind, ostensibly, over a kiss.

"Goddamn you, Addison; why'd you have to go and fuck everything up?" Leila was crazed; her anger seemed irrational. It disarmed me; I had no words resting on my lips capable of thwarting what was shaping up as a violent tirade; the scenario was akin to a fire hose aimed at a child playing with matches. Not only did I *feel* helpless, I *was* helpless, and to add to my impotence, I went numb.

"I'm not your goddamn girlfriend, Addison!" The harangue continued. "We're not a couple a kids makin' out in some schoolyard; you got that? Graduation day came and went a long time ago; at least, it did for me. We're here for three reasons: to work, drink, and screw. If yer aim was to fall in love this summer, you shoulda stayed in Philly."

From helplessness to numbness to dejection, I had run the gamut of how one is likely to feel after being rebuffed, forcefully struck, and berated. But it had been a long day, and the hour was late; only so much vigor could one commit to what surged beyond a tyrannical rebuking. As predicted, it began to wane. While what proved an impressive invective neared its end, and with my ear continuing to ring from an unexpected broadsiding, Leila's shoulders sagged—this overinflated never-before-seen version of the gal from Woodsfield shrank before my eyes—no longer did she resemble a jungle cat poised to make a meal of me. She scooted over to the edge of the bed opposite where I stood or was making an effort to remain upright. I interpreted Leila altering her position as a signal that it was also permissible for me to move. I reached for my pants and began dressing. I did not bother with my underwear, not because I found wearing them a nuisance, but for fear that finagling my way into them given the room's climate would cause me to appear awkward and pitiful, and I was not looking to piggyback any additional conditions onto the helplessness, numbness, and dejection presently plaguing me. I left my pants unbuttoned, and with a quick swipe, I gathered my remaining garments, which I had carelessly strewn on the floor earlier. I had no way of knowing whether I had jeopardized, for everyone, what remained of the summer or whether kissing Leila would stand only as a one-night debacle. Whichever, tonight hardly seemed the appropriate time to broach the matter.

I was about to say goodnight when I noticed Leila had altered her position again, having settled in the chair with the Aztec-style afghan draped over it. She had her arms folded to her chest, legs gracelessly parted, toes curled under and pushing into the carpet such that they made her feet resemble fists. She appeared utterly defiant, and this pose of child-like defiance lent her a girlish charm that put me at ease and revived my desire. I went and knelt beside her. Was I expecting to pick up where we left off? One would have to be a cock-eyed optimist; my only goal was to depart on civil terms.

"Sorry," I said. "But there came a moment when I looked down at you, you looked angelic, and all I could think to do was kiss you. I never imagined it would end up the crime of the century."

I hoped a regretful tone would restore the loveliness that came over Leila when I was deep inside her—when, for a fleeting moment, I experienced the sensation we were lovers.

"And so, you got it into your little head that you're the only guy in all my twenty-eight years to make me feel grateful I'm a woman?" Leila's tenor was caustic but not loud. "You feel special, do you, Addison? Entitled? A real crusader for romance, are ya?"

The condescension ringing in her tone caused me to hang my head as one might when schooled and chastised for proving themselves too naïve. Finally, I humbly admitted, "I'm not exactly sitting on a mountain of experience."

With the humility of my words, Leila's defiance seeped forth from her tightly wound form: her eyes softened, her arms unfolded, the gap between her legs narrowed, and her toes uncurled and spread prettily upon the carpet. When she leaned forward, gone were all traces of hostility. "Sorry, Addison," she said. "I forgot your age and that it's yours truly who's playing with fire. Still, we can't be '*a thing*,' you and me. We can't get all wrapped up in a summer romance and play Lord and Lady of the Manor while Cillian and Joey do all the work. I can't imagine a worse thing than three best friends ending up enemies over a woman."

Possibly it was my imagination, but Leila's words seemed to ring with an admission that something exceeding an empty-headed fuck had transpired, and the reality rattled her enough to react fiercely. Then a possibility occurred to me, though I did not dare ask: I reminded Leila of someone—someone she loved long ago, who had stolen her heart as far back as when the woman in the photograph, whoever she was, had an active role in Leila's life. That was the prevailing thought that accompanied me in my bed; it was the only thought that crept between me and exhaustion. Leila Bennett had a story, and I wanted to get to the bottom of it.

The night had reached a juncture when I thought it best to take my leave. It was not my wish to depart without salvaging a night that ended in wreckage; it was more a case of my assuming it was what Leila preferred. Moreover, if the prospect of salvaging a wreck seemed bleak, another bite at the apple was far out of reach. I had to reconcile tonight as a total loss. Yessiree, I would humbly crawl to the back of the line and take my rightful spot in the rotation: Seaver, Koosman, and Matlack. I thought of myself as the ace of the staff. A: because of Joey's diminutive size; B: though the notion was too absurd to consider soberly, Cillian was, despite the stretch, a relation. But tonight, the ace got lit up in the early innings and merited the boos of a disappointed crowd cascading down upon him from the bleachers as he walked back to the dugout. *Hit the showers, kid; you didn't have it tonight.*

Then, the unexpected happened. And why shouldn't the unexpected occur: much of what has transpired thus far in the summer of '77 has been, in a word, unpredictable. As I uncoiled my legs to a standing position, Leila also uncoiled one of hers and extended it such that it drove a foot between my legs at a most unforgiving point. It was not an assault, nor did I perceive it as one; Leila was employing her foot as one might a hook. Her objective? My first guess was to prevent me from leaving, but only a fool would assume anything at this point.

"Why, my dear Mr. Caldwell," she emoted. Despite being an Ohioan, her words possessed all the genteelness of a Southern Belle. "If I'm not mistaken, and rarely I am, you and I have some unfinished business that requires tending to, do we not?" Her antebellum cadence settled in my ear like a favorite song. "You weren't actually thinking of leaving here without having fulfilled Mama, were you?" Following her playfully pretentious tone came the batting of her eyes.

This act traveled far beyond what even the most hardhearted men could resist, and no one could accuse ol' Addison Caldwell of owning an ossified heart.

"I guess not," came my reply, which sprang forth with more wavering and meekness than I wished it had. Then, an impish look flashed in Leila's eyes as she glided the instep of her foot over my denim-clad nuts. Motionless and obediently, I stood as she amused herself—as she played. Supremely confident was Leila that I would not attempt to free myself from the play of her delicate, well-formed foot. And why should I not subjugate myself to a siren at play, especially when I saw little upside in demonstrating the will to leave, thus missing out on where this episode, which thus far featured soaring crescendos and rousing plummets, was leading? Unfortunately, the surge of confidence that emerged in Leila through her playfulness caused her to giggle; it was a girlish giggle, childlike in nature, and it made me feel diminished and toyed with. Indeed, unlike Leila the Southern Belle, which stirred me, her chortling did not settle in my ears with any measure of satisfaction. I wanted to disappear. But how could I? I was a young man standing before a woman whose nakedness was tantamount to a deity descending Mount Olympus, if not the Devil incarnate; I had not the discipline to overpower my curiosity.

Next, with toes surprisingly dexterous, she managed to unzip my already unbuttoned pants and shimmy them down to the floor. It was a helluva trick her slender toes had performed, and it was a performance they delivered with titillating deliberateness. Upon completion, I stood fully erect, naked, with my pants mashed around my ankles. It was a humiliating position for one to find oneself: standing upright as might a child prepared for a whipping for having committed a whip-worthy infraction. Yet, despite being afflicted with what for me, and likely anyone, was the rarest of mixtures: shame, delirium, and lust—and unclear as to which condition, if any, reigned dominant—I managed, deftly, to hop out of my pants and kicked them aside. I performed this nimble soccer maneuver to show I was unfazed by Leila's gamesmanship. But, my agility and abruptness notwithstanding, what followed was the resurgence of Leila, the jungle cat: an alert, fierce, potent, and hungry feline. Before I could react, I found myself planted on the mattress and climbed on; her hands pushed down on my chest and matched pelvic thrusts wildly vigorous, savage-like, far more unconstrained than the thrusts I had delivered earlier. Leila was the captain, her command undisputed. I was the ship, an object without a say, steered over the roughest waters imaginable.

****

"What in the hell were you doing all this time, playing strip poker? Polishing her nails?" Initially, I could not see Cillian's face well enough to determine whether he was curious or annoyed. He might have been a little of each. I couldn't blame him; these nightly interludes with Leila had three speeds: brief, briefer, and briefest, and now here I was, stumbling outside after what must have seemed to Cillian and Joey a bonafide marathon—a genuine romantic interlude.

Joey's shrug and twisted expression revealed similar displeasure.

I considered acting like a prick by haughtily breaking the news that Leila favors my penis, but no sooner than the thought occurred to me, I took a keen interest in why Cillian and Joey were still sitting on the fence.

"We were dialing through the stations, and what luck," said Joey, "we found an Indians/Twins game. The game is in Minnesota, but we're getting the Cleveland feed, naturally. The game's in the bottom of the seventh; they're in the middle of a pitching change."

"Goddamn American League games take forever." Cillian was not complaining so much as he was stating a fact. Then he said, "It's that goddamn designated hitter rule." Okay, *that* was a complaint: Cillian—like many fans whose home team hails from the National League—was a purist. "Well?" he finally asked.

"I fucked up," I admitted, then explained what transpired tonight between Leila and me. "It was all my fault. But don't worry; by the time I left, everything was back to normal, if you can call what we're doing this summer normal." I paused to reflect on the portion of the summer that has now passed. "I know it was a dumbass move on my part, but just once, I wanted it to mean something." Next, I felt two empathetic arms around me. It did not come as a surprise.

"I'm gonna miss this," said Joey, "the way it smells at night, the lightness of the air." Joey inhaled as if it were possible to draw into his nostrils and savor in his lungs the entire farm. The features of a city, especially one the size of Philly, are glaring; they tend to blare and jar one's senses with how they announce their arrivals.

Often, these aggressive broadcasts come in waves, offering rude slaps, kicks, and shouts. Not the country. Its features, or what passes for features, are subtler and, over time, require a developed sensibility to appreciate: the scent of the night air, the sounds of entities not human, the distance sound is capable of traveling, and these features occur under a more expansive and star-studded sky. So yes, it was fair to say when the time comes, we will miss our summer retreat, our universe, Leila Bennett notwithstanding.

The Indians were victorious over the Twins 5—4. The final score did not rank as a matter of concern. What *did* matter, or loaned to our sense of being an added measure of delight, were the dwindling outs of a ballgame broadcasting from afar. Despite the time of night and location combining to make us feel we occupied a domain that some call the middle of nowhere, those dwindling outs assured us that we were still well-anchored in a vast and ever-madding world. Indeed, a fading game that has kept much of a nation in its thrall since Three Finger Brown pitched for the Cubs was as comforting to us as the milelong freight train passing in the night.

The following day, beginning with the dining room—the least used room in the house, thus the least upsetting—we started transforming dingy eggshell white walls that appeared as though they had not seen a coat of paint in decades into a bright, clean canary yellow.

"So, whudda y'all think?" Leila repeatedly asked us as room after room underwent a striking transformation. We met each entreaty by praising her choice of canary yellow walls, accented with sky-blue surbases and the brightest white she could find for the ceilings. The whole house was shaping up to look like a toddler's playroom. If Leila sought the lightheartedness and spontaneity of youth, then every room frothed with inspiration.

"I want every room to remind me of a June sunrise with a million birds singin' in the trees," she crooned. The former prostitute pirouetted like an aspiring ballerina, and her words rang buoyantly.

With all its nooks and crannies and the tedium such irregularity requires, we saved the kitchen for last. It was midday when Leila came bursting through the front door, her hands full with takeout food and a newspaper.

"They caught him!" she bellowed. "They finally caught him!" Typically, Leila, with all her sinuousness and length, sauntered about the house elegantly; her footfalls were stealthy like a cat burglar's. Moreover, the manner in which her feet met and arched off the floor, propelling her splendid form gracefully, was a vision that never failed to enthrall. But today, she came bursting through the door in mimic of a raucous herd of wildebeests chased by ravenous lions.

"Caught *who*? And who are *they*?" There was more mockery in Cillian's tone than curiosity.

Still stampeding her way through the house to the kitchen, Leila gushed, "The .44-caliber killer. They caught him! They actually caught him!" When Leila reached the kitchen, she unburdened the hand that toted the bag of takeout by depositing it with little finesse onto the kitchen table. Next to the bag, with flair, she slammed down the newspaper, making sure that the front page, with its most apparent headline, was in plain view: SUSPECT IN "SON OF SAM" MURDERS ARRESTED IN YONKERS; .44-CALIBER WEAPON IS RECOVERED —

We rested our paintbrushes. Thoughtfully and quietly, we converged around the table. Cillian tugged at the newspaper and read: *A 24-year-old postal employee said by the police to be the "Son of Sam," the .44-caliber killer who took the lives of six young people and wounded seven others in a year-long reign of terror in New York City, was taken into custody late last night in Yonkers, just north of the city.* Pointing down a paragraph, I read: *The suspect was identified as David Berkowitz of 35 Pine Street in Yonkers.* Then Joey, whose eyes had traveled further into the article, read: *When seized, according to the police, Mr. Berkowitz was advised of his rights by arresting officers and responded: "Well, you've got me."* Leila, who, while still in town, had already combed through most of the article before speeding home in her behemoth Ford, read: *Mayor Beame, during a 1:40 a.m. news conference at Police Headquarters in Lower Manhattan, declared: "I am very pleased to announce that the people of the City of New York can rest easy tonight because police have captured a man they believe to be the "Son of Sam."*

Earlier in the spring, as what would pass for dinner got placed on the table, Darrin Caldwell, using his typical *what is this world coming to* note of incredulity, shrieked, "The Son of Sam? A killer who gets his instructions from a dog? A goddamn canine?" Brimming with exasperation, he added, "It's no longer satisfactory to be a typical maniac or serial killer—that's too passé, too routine—nowadays, one must display creativity? Is that the case? And don't think for one minute the media isn't eating it up; if there's one thing they appreciate as much as war, it's a killer on the loose. I'm telling you, it's all this crap they're showing on TV and in the movies; it's putting ideas in people's heads, and people, today, are too damn impressionable."

"*Children*," Claire Caldwell began. Addressing Casey and me as "children" using her best June Cleaver cadence meant Claire was about to mock Darrin. "If neither of you is already a lunatic, television and the movies cannot make you into one. In other words, *little darlings*, if you grow up and discover an irresistible urge to shoot, slash, or bludgeon numerous people over a given span, particularly women, it is best you do not look for anyone else to blame but yourselves." Then she added, somewhat whimsically, "Tsk-tsk-tsk; we mustn't fault Richard Fleischer or Tobe Hooper." They were the respective directors of *The Boston Strangler* and *The Texas Chainsaw Massacre*. Claire was a real horror movie enthusiast.

You've got to love ol' Claire Caldwell, don't you? Instances like her mockery of Darrin's "Son of Sam" rant made her Indian getups, grass toking, and gyrating like Mick Jagger not only forgivable but appreciated.

"Who the hell's the 'Son of Sam?'" Casey wondered aloud. My inquisitive kid sister prompted Darrin and Claire to shout her name in a unified protest over her bold language. Then Claire, condescendingly, *and* unfortunately—unfortunately, because her words served to dull the luster of what only seconds ago marked a brief but amusing monologue—added, "The Son of Sam is a sorta boogieman who murders young girls who curse in front of their parents." Casey made a face. Before Claire could respond with a look of her own, Darrin, who had nothing pertinent to offer but nevertheless felt the urge to speak, said, "Well, Addison, at least you'll be away from Philly, where there's bound to be a copycat lunatic trying to top the 'Son of Sam.' But that's all right; we'll just have to muddle through on our own. Meanwhile, you go ahead and enjoy a nice, wholesome summer in Western Pennsylvania."

A nice, wholesome summer? My eyes were on Leila when I remembered my father's words; it nearly caused me to burst into a fit of laughter. Poor Darrin; he was long on pointing out humanity's flaws but not so hot on solutions. Then my eyes met Cillian's and Joey's. They were looking back at me, seemingly intimating: *are you not thinking what we're thinking?* Then, just like that, my thoughts aligned with theirs due to that synergetic best-friend connectedness that bonds us. All three of us sagged. Why? For nearly four and a half months, the Phils, our boys of summer, hand over fist, pulled and tugged, scraped and clawed, fought tooth and nail, and finally reached the summit—it being the usurping of those notorious faders, the Cubs—but on the very night the world's most current lunatic was apprehended. Indeed, there seemed a twisted sense of irony at play: in the middle of August, a month otherwise known to baseball fans as "the dog days," the Phils took over the lead of the National League's Eastern Division the same night that a man who, of all matters, obeys a dog at long last was taken into police custody. Unlike my God-fearing friends, I am a cynical atheist. But, unfortunately, atheism does not make one immune to superstition and karma or believing that stars were aligning somewhere in the universe, and based on this alignment, a unique brand of cosmic justice explicitly meant to tamper with the destiny of our ballclub was afoot. Yessiree, for the next several days, we adhered to the theory that the fate of the Phils was linked to David Berkowitz, the infamous "Son of Sam."

Despite her past and orchestrating a summer of biblical decadence, Leila—a woman who every Sunday radiates with love for the baby Jesus, wilts with inexhaustible passion for the crucified adult Jesus while offering up her unworthy soul to a loving God who, through faulty interpretations of ecclesiastic mortals, managed to slip in all sorts of silly conditions by which humankind must abide—dismissed the notion of the Phils' fate tied to David Berkowitz as, "Simpleminded claptrap." Typically, people with blind faith are open to far-flung concepts and fall prey to matters that tend to run contrary to logic. Leila surprised me. Her openness to such notions was not "one size fits all." In all likelihood, though, she was right and made no bones, citing we should celebrate a city eradicated of a deranged killer instead of grasping for convoluted ways the Phils, by way of the cosmos, were linked to "The Son of Sam."

Six days later, I got off the phone with my pitiful father: it was the *Elvis Pressley The King is Dead* conversation I alluded to earlier. I had just set down the receiver when Leila—she rumbled down the driveway on her Harley and did not take the time to garage it—came stumbling through the door, half hollering and half sobbing, "Elvis is gone! The King is dead!"

That night, four of us sat on the fence, passing back and forth a bottle of Jack Daniels. An American icon left the stage following a final and unceremonious performance. Thus, there was no feeling that the affected party among us had crashed a party or punctured a universe. *Our* universe, however meager, could well accommodate a fourth presence. As the sun dipped below the horizon, Leila, whose swigs were longer than ours, began to hum a verse of *Love Me Tender*—a somber tribute to America's first pop culture icon, a rock star who sang God knows how many women out of their pants. Next, her quaking voice sang: *Love me tender, love me true, all my dreams fulfilled; for my darlin', I love you, and I always will.* Her quivering crooning hit nary a note, yet there resonated a stirring beauty to what marked an unapologetically pitiable effort—Leila's attempt at singing reached an emotional depth a trained vocalist might not have. Cillian, who could carry a tune, joined Leila: *Love me tender, love me long, take me to your heart; for it's there that I belong, and we'll never part.* Leila broke down. Unable to continue, her cries turned to bitter sobs.

"'Cause I had been a good girl with helpin' out on the farm; Mama bought me that record for my birthday," Leila managed through her sobs. "I didn't have many records—unlike most kids, I couldn't afford to collect 'em—but that was one I wanted more than anything. But Daddy, he was drinkin' more than ever in them days. They had a tough season in '60; the pressure was gettin' to Daddy, Mama too. But Mama always had a way a makin' things bright just when they looked their bleakest. She said, 'Baby girl, how 'bout cha go and put that nice record on I gotcha for your birthday.' I jumped up like I was sittin' on a spring. But then Daddy came home. He was all drunk and demanding to know what garbage was that Mama had fixed for dinner. I hollered, 'Daddy, Mama's doin' the best she can!' It was the first time I raised my voice to Daddy. I'll never forget the look he got in his eye. 'Is that so,' he says. Then, glarin' a hole right through me, he took his plate and emptied it in the garbage. He was a mean drunk, the kind that puts everyone around them on edge. But he was just gettin' warmed up; he went into my room, ripped the record off the turntable, and broke it over his knee. 'Since you seem to know so damn much, girly, why don't you show 'er how it's done.' I didn't say another word. I couldn't if I wanted to. Typical of a young girl, I ran onto the porch and bawled my eyes out. God, how I loved that record."

CHAPTER FIFTEEN
SAYING GOODBYE TO THE SUMMER OF '77

If July flew by, then August was a blur. It could be said that Cillian, Joey, and I each had Leila twenty times. But claiming as much would qualify as a gymnastic sense of reality; the plainer truth was that Leila corralled us for sixty sessions, or fifty-nine sessions and one kerfuffle. Toward the end of the month, we got to perform some genuine farm work. But with the farmers being as they were, renters, there was no room in the budget for three extra hands to draw a salary, so whatever farm work we did was for the sake of gaining experience; there was no compensation involved.

As the days of summer dwindled, we sensed that Leila—save for the evenings, after ten o'clock and before midnight—was distancing herself and used "tavern business" as a handy excuse. It was perfectly justifiable. After all—the breadth of what constitutes moral dilemmas notwithstanding—we had spent several weeks surpassing, by light years, anyone's interpretation of a "normal" summer; thus, how a season of epic turpitude winds its way to a conclusion was a dilemma in and of itself. That being the case, it made sense that Leila distance herself; aloofness was essential if "goodbye" was to prove an easy affair. In other words, we had a beginning, followed by a journey. A conclusion lingered, one that weighed on the minds of all four of us. And why would it not? You do not lie with someone twenty times, and she with you and your two closest friends sixty times, and not develop fondness and affection, however instructional and emotionally detached the sex was meant to have been. Despite Leila's hard line of "working, drinking, and screwing," we got under her skin as significantly as she had burrowed under ours. If truth be told, the affection and fondness I developed for Leila were not attributable to anything that transpired between ten and midnight on Monday and Thursday nights—the nights that Tom Seaver toed the rubber. My feelings

blossomed from watching a Woodsfield hick and former prostitute—
who, if born into different circumstances, might have represented
Ohio in the Miss America Pageant—ride a Harley Davidson Shovelhead Chopper, handle a John Deere right down to getting underneath
the damn contraption and sharpening the blades, and sticking her head
in an engine and pulling apart and fixing a distributor cap. The sweat
on Leila's brow that formed while bent over a hot engine; the long
arms that flexed with each turn of a tractor; the magnificent mane that
waved behind her when she, on her Harley, sliced through the wind:
that was the Leila Bennett I would miss, and savor. That was the Leila
Bennett that would travel to my loins when the king of masturbation
was back in the city.

 "Hey," said Cillian, "it turns out that our last night here will
be a Wednesday. That's perfect."

 "Why would Wednesday equal perfection?" Joey wondered.

 "Because we'll have completed the rotation, that's why. No one
gets cheated—Seaver, Koosman, and Matlack—all three will have had
an equal number of chances to pitch." Cillian seemed delighted to have
enlightened us on this matter. Joey greeted it with a dismissive shrug—
it was a gesture indicating that had our time in Western Pennsylvania
ended with him one screw shy of Cillian and me, it would not have
rated as a point of emphasis. My thinking was aligned with Joey's. Despite being first in the rotation, thus having no chance of getting
cheated a turn, by August 31, I will have experienced more than
enough of Leila Bennett to savor. That being said, aside from the obvious, the ten o'clock hour may have meant something different to
each of us. For Cillian, quite possibly, it was the one part of the day
that his mind was wholly free from the sort of matters that had compelled him to walk a trestle blindfolded, enter a dark tunnel through
which ran a train, and dive into a pool with an undetermined depth
from a dizzying and dangerous height. Quite possibly, Cillian's Tuesdays and Fridays were more affecting than my Mondays and Thursdays
or Joey's Wednesdays and Saturdays.

 "Then again," Cillian chirped, "we could have an all-inclusive
grand finale." He winced no sooner than the words flew from his lips
and had a moment to sink in. So did Joey, as did I. Our social contract, which often required us to have skin so thick you could not
gash it with a utility knife, did not extend to the three of us, all at

once, naked on the same bed, sharing the same woman. In no way did we consider this a shortcoming.

****

August the 31st: Our final night as masters of our Western Pennsylvania universe; our last night sitting on the fence passing back and forth a bottle of Jack Daniels; our final night looking out over acre upon acre of farmland; our final night experiencing the fragrance of country air under a rural night sky. The days were noticeably shorter than at the beginning of summer; we were losing our sun by 7:40 or the completion of the first inning. It did not appear that it would be necessary to return to our former school to give Mrs. Hargrove a piece of our minds, as those notorious faders, the Cubs, had long since sunk like a stone and currently occupied third place, facing a 9 1/2 game deficit. Meanwhile, the Bucs were still hanging tough and within five games, but the Phils appeared poised to charge through September to a second straight division title. When the game ended, John Matlack headed inside for his summer finale. Cillian and I switched to the Indians/Red Sox game; we joined the broadcast in the seventh inning. We remained on the fence, savoring every breath, every country sound to which our ears had grown accustomed. We developed a whole new sensibility, and because of it, we were experiencing some reluctance toward leaving. Tomorrow was the big day; by the late afternoon, we would be back in the city. Joey returned to his spot on the fence for the ninth inning. Those goddamn American League games take forever.

At breakfast, there hovered a sense that the wildest summer anyone could imagine had ascended to its climax, and its participants were better off for having shared the experience. There was plenty of chatter over food and coffee—mainly, we talked about the immediate future and what it might hold in store for three city rats and one Woodsfield hick—but there was no mention of next summer. No one wanted to spoil the afterglow by looking ahead to the possibility of repeating what should remain a once-in-a-lifetime affair. The summer of '77 was not a time that *can* nor *should* see a duplication; it ranked as an experience that does not require an encore or reprise unless you are Hugh Hefner. But just who was Leila Bennett? And how does such a woman come to enter into the lives of three city boys from Philly? Perhaps Leila had pondered the inverse and, like me, lost sleep considering life and its infinite possibilities.

216

So why did fate choose me for this coming-of-age American odyssey? Consummate skeptic that I am, I will simply attribute the summer of '77 to the randomness of a random world sparking a chain of events that, like a vortex, drew me into its core. Aunt Phyllis croaks. Uncle Dave marries his prostitute and follows the absurdity with the act of suicide. The result? I am no longer a virgin ... times twenty! In other words, when the stars align, they don't fool around.

Joey went off into the field to offer his farewells to the farmers. He had not realized farming was so sophisticated, and over the past several days, he developed a fascination for the equipment and technique and asked a million questions. Joey was that kind of guy; he scavenged for every morsel, sponging up all the meticulous details that put most people to sleep. I left Cillian and Leila alone in the kitchen. Standing just outside the kitchen door, I heard her intimate to him, "No matter the demons that drove Uncle Dave to do what he did, he was a good father and had a big enough heart to be a fine husband to two women. The world was a better place 'cause of your Uncle Dave; don't ever forget that."

I went and stood by the fence (our universe) and waited for Joey. I had my chin in my hands, elbows resting on the upper plank, gazing out at the farm; the late summer sun was warm on my face. At once, what gushed over me was a moment of reflection on the summer, eagerness for the city, and life going forward. I guess that's what's called "being in a good place" or "satisfied." I nearly lapsed into a reverie when I felt a presence beside me. Leila mimicked my stance: chin in her clasped hands, elbows on the wood. Our arms and shoulders touched. Funny, but for me, the simple touching of our arms and shoulders felt more intimate than anything that had transpired between us for a summer's worth of Mondays and Thursdays.

"She was a dear friend of my grandmother's," I heard her mutter.

Although my head jerked in Leila's direction, I avoided disturbing our intimacy. I knew, intuitively, that she was referring to the woman in the photo on her nightstand, but it took me by surprise that the subject was finally up for discussion minutes before departing.

"She always seemed to be there, Aunt Pearl, whenever I visited Granny," Leila continued. "She wasn't my real aunt but was better than any aunt a girl could wish for. Granny, God bless her—she truly was a good soul—passed when I was seven, but I never lost touch with Aunt Pearl. It's funny, but even when you're young and don't know a whole bunch, you have a good sense of when someone truly loves you. Some folks'll claim to love you, but they're so screwed up in the head that how they love you don't make no sense—least of all to you—and before long, they churn like poison in your gut.

"When I first left the farm, I hadn't a dream to fulfill or any big ideas whirling 'round my head: food, a roof to settle under, and livin' in peace were all I could think of; I couldn't see past those things and didn't have to think too hard where my best chance was to get 'em. So I went straight to Aunt Pearl's, and without making a fuss, she took me in. I walked miles through the night to get to her place, and I can tell ya, as sure as we're leanin' on this fence, it wasn't the warmest night of the year. Come the morning, Aunt Pearl found me; I was like a lost pup, all curled up and shivering on her doorstep. I didn't mince words; I told her straight up why I left the farm, and she said, 'It ain't no matter, sweet child, you live with me now; no one, from here on, is gonna lay a hand on you.' Years passed, and Aunt Pearl took sick. I cared for her right up 'til the end and was holdin' her hand when she drew her last breath. I tried my hardest to be as good to her as she was to me; I like to think I *was* so good and *am* a good person. With Aunt Pearl gone, I had two choices lookin' me square in the eye: go home or just go. I went. And yeah, Heaven knows I made my share of crappy choices, but I never lost faith that somehow the good Lord, no matter how far I had fallen, was guiding me. Dave Bennett loved me tender. So not only do I feel it in my heart that the good Lord guides me, but I have proof He does."

Leila omitted all the sordid details that drove her from the family farm. Still, lingering was a keen sense there was a lot more to the story of Leila Bennett's tender years than her old man's drinking, that it was more a case of the dark, malevolent places an alcohol-drenched brain can steer a family. Concerning that matter, I did not need Leila to elaborate; I took the allotted space to presume and, with it, drew what I alleged were easy conclusions.

Leila was not looking to elicit sympathy. Not really. I believe her primary aim was to satisfy a curiosity I was sitting on for weeks and give me a piece of her soul upon my departure. I received a few pages of her story—a nice, tidy chapter—but if I cared to read between the

lines, which I did, there was enough meat on the bone for an epic journey sure to traverse a road unfit for the faint of heart. And whether or
not there would be another summer like '77, I could not hazard a guess,
yet there lingered a keen sense that Leila, were the stars to align, would
prefer that we remain in her orbit. Some wishes, though, are too fan-
ciful and beyond the capacity of what stars can deliver. We did, however, help a widow survive a summer that might otherwise have proved
unbearable. It is also fair to say that a widow brought three young men
from Philly even closer together. In sharing Leila, in a way, we were
sharing one another, and if Cillian, Joey, and I were not already irrev-
ocably linked entering the summer, we would be in the future.

Next, Leila blurted out the unfamiliar name, "Billy Allison."
Then, with a gleam in her eye, she touched my face. It was unnecessary
to utter aloud that Billy Allison was the boy of whom I put Leila in
mind.

"What happened," I asked, thinking a story of unrequited love
was to follow. Leila smiled. It was not her country gal beam but an
ironical smile. What followed was an inaudible chortle that puffed
through her nostrils. Next came the measured and decisive words:
"The worst kinda woman is one who takes up so much space in a man's
life, he's got no room to grow." She added with a tenor of regret, "I
didn't wanna be that kinda woman." Then she told me, "Think about
me, Addison. But not *too* much."

Joey emerged from the fields and Cillian from the kitchen. We
tossed our bags in the bed of Leila's behemoth pickup, and off we
drove. Skipping the bus ride, we headed straight for Pittsburgh and the
train station, blasting rockabilly music with the windows rolled down
and enjoying our final time of what Leila called "hellraisin'." As the
train chugged west to east through Pennsylvania, I repeatedly asked
myself: Who was Leila Bennett? Could she have been just a girl, any
girl? Was Leila as common as any one of a million buttercups clustered
in an open field and just as forgettable, or was she a four-leaf clover, a
rare specimen who, over and over, would compel me to search for her
in every crowd every*where*? Was she a young girl in a grown-up girl's
body or a grown-up girl as lost as any child would be when set to wan-
der the vastness of the universe? Air and space: they can prove fickle
entities. Not enough of each can kill you, and too much can kill you
even faster. But whether we blossom in a vast field or cottage garden,

in a way, we all want the same thing: the opportunity to strive for independence while enjoying the strength and comfort of unity. Leila had experienced that aspect of human desire for a time with Aunt Pearl, then later on, for a much briefer spell, with Uncle Dave. I hope, sooner than later, she finds just the right amount of air and space that allows her to bask in the beauty of youth while flourishing as a woman.

I glanced across the aisle at Joey; he had his nose buried in the sports page, his mathematical brain devouring every statistic. Cillian was seated behind him, a newspaper section held loosely in his hands, his head bobbing as he futilely tried to fight off the sleep that would ultimately prevail. As for yours truly? The motion of a train helped me further immerse myself in my thoughts. Striving toward independence and gaining it through the strength of unity: If I had a prevailing theme in my head, that was the one, and it stayed with me for many miles. Then, my blank stare noticed the altering landscape; we were nearing the city. Cillian stirred.

"Back to reality, Addie," he said. Then he shrugged as if to say: *God only knows what I'll find.*

Reality. It represented something different for each of us: clinical depression, amputation as a result of combat, a grass-toking hippie who battled conservatism wherever it flowered. Should they wish to thrive, every man, woman, and child must learn to circumnavigate their way around the influences a harassing world sets before them. Mastering this skill has remained a persistent and unwavering theme since humans first organized themselves into constructs called societies. But if we are lucky, there is always a good friend or two to lighten the burden.

And now I'm back in the city. I did not remember so much brick, concrete, glass, and steel. Christ, it was everywhere! Everything looked so hard, with many corners and sharp edges. Signs, poles, wires, and lights were pervasive, and dozens of nameless, faceless people were clustered in every direction I gazed. Where was my fence, farm, my bottle of Jack Daniels, and transistor radio? Was the bus always this noisy? I felt trapped in a room with a million wind-up toys. Joey was the first one off the bus, then Cillian. I rode the rest of the way with folks whose faces I recognized but whose names I never knew. Then it was my turn. I stepped off the bus and onto an intersection that shrunk sometime during my ten-week absence, and the structures dotting the crossing and beyond seemed to close in on me. I lingered for a while or long enough to acquire a sense of equilibrium in a place that, for fifteen years, I had called home. How fitting that the first *notable* vision I should see walking from the bus stop to my house was Theresa Delvecchio sporting short-shorts and a halter top, and on her face sparkled a smile that intimated someone had missed me. It is positively criminal, I thought, that those tits should spend the next nine months wallowing in anonymity behind an awful ensemble of material known as the dreaded Catholic School uniform. Religion is evil or, at the very least, totalitarian. Back in biblical times, in the land of Canaan—and I'm sure in many other places as well—at our current ages, if I wanted, I could own Theresa, and it would only cost me a couple of my best goats. Now, that's what I call a transaction! *Hey, Mr. D., I come baring goats; go and get the girl.* Where did civilization go wrong? Blame it on education and Western modernity. No sooner than folks get a taste of enlightenment, your goats are worthless, and if you look at a girl cross-eyed, she has got your nuts on a stick. I could not resist sharing this amusing anecdote with Terry Dell; she laughed like the good sport she had always shown herself to be. Doubtless, she found it humorous that her beauty could inspire entertaining quips. Anyway, it was nice to see an old friend.

I turned onto good old Buttonwood Street, and the first image my eyes captured was a vision of Maryellen. It felt strange but also comforting that after all this time, with me experiencing a season for the ages, she was right where I had left her. Well, not precisely. That fine June morning, Maryellen was standing on the landing, putting on airs, dressed to inspire, including prettily polished toenails with which I became ridiculously acquainted. Today, she was seated, a ponytail enslaved her fiery mane, on her head was a sun visor shading a galaxy of freckles, and she appeared the picture of concentration with her nose, not in a newspaper that she was pretending to read but in a book. Doubtless, in typical Maryellen fashion, Maryellen discovered what the upcoming curriculum entailed and decided to leap ahead into the new school year. I wavered between tiptoeing past her and slipping inside—saving our reunion for when she was not so engrossed—and surprising her with a friendly kiss. I did neither, for my presence cast a shadow on her words, thus shattering her concentration. Then, turning her gaze upward, she said with a note of surprise, "Addison?"

Her cadence was pleasant, even lilting. Either I had never heard it resonate like that before or never paid close enough attention to her various modulations. The latter was too unlikely, so the answer must be the former, and it heightened my desire to hear more words fly from her lips. However, Maryellen seemed struck by something unseen—an invisible force holding her to a single expression of incredulity, which happened to be my name. Strange, but the glimmer that flashed in her eyes was not something I recognized; she had turned her gaze upon me in a manner reminiscent of how one might a handsome stranger new in town with whom an impromptu meeting was secretly desired. Had I changed that much in one season? Did I appear to Maryellen as someone who only reminded her of Addison Caldwell?

"It's me," I said, hoping to ease Maryellen from her apparent stupor. I followed with, "How was your summer?" Before she managed a reply, I reached for the novel that had her engrossed before the appearance of my interrupting shadow. In a manner that seemed anomalously and eerily cooperative, she handed it over without bothering to mark her page. *To Kill a Mockingbird*. Claire had been nagging me to read Harper Lee's classic, it seemed, since I was able to breathe air and think thoughts— "Atticus Finch will be your new hero," she had often purported—but, like Darrin, I was more an Aldous Huxley kinda guy.

"It's a good read," Maryellen replied shyly, with slightly downcast eyes.

In the past, Maryellen would make a point of reading novels with substrates offering a strong moral compass, then assert they were beyond my grasp because I was a no-good sonofabitch. Today, her brief reply was, dare I say… humble?

A summer that thus proved nothing less than remarkable was not through doling out its gifts. What came upon me, in a burst, was a sense I had unwittingly stepped through a portal and, as a result, slipped into a parallel universe with foundations predicated on desires, not actualities. It was clear that while I was cooped up all summer on a Western Pennsylvania farm, the rest of the world went and rearranged itself—it was different. *Or*, maybe my suspicions of the world were faulty, and it was *me* who was different? The latter must be the case. The summer must have changed me, for my mere presence was enough to transform the Maryellen I once knew into a bashful schoolgirl—a delightfully shy lass featuring eyes that screamed she was too long on the periphery and longed for experiences.

I handed her back *To Kill a Mockingbird* and asked: "For school, or is this Claire's influence?"

Demurely, she shrugged, then replied, "A little of each."

I was bursting with confidence, my posture authoritative, when I asked Maryellen, "You didn't miss me *too* much this summer, did you?" Her response came in the form of a giggle. It was a little girl's giggle, one that led me to entertain the possibility that the eastbound train derailed, crashed, and exploded, and I was in Heaven with the Maryellen of whom I had always dreamed. I was, however, aware that I was not dead; thus, my first order of business would be to call Leila and thank her for turning me into a man. Finally, Maryellen asserted herself, if you could call bashfully peeping out the words, "How was *your* summer, Addison?" assertive. I lifted her visor to where I could plant an affectionate kiss on her cheek, then told her, "It's good to be home, Maryellen. It's really good to be home."

To be continued...

ABOUT THE AUTHOR

      Michael DeStefano runs a hairstyling salon, where he has spent the past four decades beautifying the super people of Philadelphia. His past titles include the historical family saga *The Gunslinger's Companion*, the comedy/tragedy *Waiting for Grandfather*, and *The Bohemian*. You can find these novels and other writings such as his love essays and perspective pieces at his blog site: Michael's Corner http://michaelscorner.blog.

www.ingramcontent.com/pod-product-compliance
Lightning Source LLC
Chambersburg PA
CBHW030114260626
47156CB00008B/2651